D0909323

Night Whispers

Night Whispers

A STORY OF EVIL

Emmett Clifford

CUMBERLAND HOUSE
NASHVILLE, TENNESSEE

Published by Cumberland House Publishing, Inc., 431 Harding Industrial Park Drive, Nashville, TN 37211-3160.

Cover Design by Gore Studios, Inc.

Library of Congress Cataloging-in-Publication Data

Clifford, Emmett, 1937–
      Night Whispers: a story of evil / Emmett Clifford.
         p. cm.
      ISBN 1-888952-81-4 (alk. paper)
      I. Title.
    PS3553.L4373N54   1998
    813'.54—dc21   98-6928
                                                      CIP

Printed in the United States of America
1 2 3 4 5 6 7—04 03 02 01 00 99 98

In memory of
Sheriff's Lieutenant Emmett E. Clifford Sr.

To the real Cody Rainwalker and Jolinda Risingwaters.
When I walk in the forest, I feel your spirits.

One

You don't get locked up for being crazy;
they lock you up for acting crazy.

SCANNER

Only one predator holds to a steady gait in the forest.

Man.

Beasts of prey farther down the food chain weave and sniff, pause to investigate a scent, circle a tree, examine a rock. Even the magnificent Siberian tiger will linger to stare into the great mystery of the taiga.

Not the human animal. A destination is envisioned and the stride set to arrive at a given time. The focus is straight ahead.

So it was tonight with a human predator who called himself Scanner. He stepped with one foot precisely in front of the other to glide through the dense forest of the East Tennessee mountainside. By placing his weight first on the outside of his foot and allowing it to roll to the inside, he slid through the heavy undergrowth with a minimum of sound. The way was rocky and uneven, but Scanner was on familiar ground. He'd practiced his approach many times in daylight and in darkness.

No more dry runs. Tonight was the real thing.

Although a bright full moon hung in an almost cloudless sky, the thick overhead canopy of hemlock and tulip trees cast the lower level of the forest into inky gloom. Passing through a narrow ray of light that had found a path to the ground, Scanner lifted his wrist to check the time.

Seventeen minutes before midnight.

The scrape of twigs and leaves on his thighs and elbows gave him a sense of where he was going and kept him on the path. He ignored the sting of an occasional thin limb whipping against his cheek. His mind was already a hundred feet ahead of his body.

Scanner mounted a steep rise, slipped out of the bushes and stalked to the rear of the cabin. The racket the horde of tree frogs

7

made was deafening, covering the sound of his steps onto the cramped back porch. Still he crouched and kept his tread light as he crept to the kitchen window and peered inside. He moved his head from one side of the pane to the other, scoping out the kitchen and, beyond it, the living room.

Justine stood naked in the middle of the front room. The bitch always liked to leave a light on. She and Sanford had let the couch out into a bed where Sanford now sprawled looking all worn out. Justine walked over and sat on the edge of the mattress, then leaned over the man's inert form. Scanner shook his head and smiled. Justine never could get enough attention.

It wouldn't matter to either of them later. Tonight they'd both know who held their destiny, who handed out the true rewards. To them, in their diminished awareness, he was just another player of the game; only he realized he was the master who designed the set, put the actors into motion. Sanford and Justine only had bit parts.

Using the same quiet caution as before, Scanner moved away from the window and stepped back into the yard. Then he made his way to the front of the house, where he would wait.

He'd picked a spot six feet above the road's edge, where the limbs of a mountain laurel hung over the drop-off and created deep shadows. They'd never see him there.

There was no driveway, so Sanford and Justine always parked at the pull-off beyond where he would be. The best part: They'd pass right under him.

The chorus of tree frogs went suddenly silent as Scanner sneaked past their roosts. Hyped as he was on uppers, he imagined them hanging on to the damp bark of the hemlocks with tiny suction-cup toes, their bulging little eyes tracking him like radar. A thousand witnesses that would not testify. They'd continue with their chirping as soon as he settled down.

A quick mental checklist assured him he had everything he needed cached at the hiding spot; he'd packed in what he needed the day before, secured it under a tarp, and camouflaged it with fallen branches and leaves. Satisfied with his cerebral inventory, he lowered himself to the ground, then lay down and propped up on his elbow. It wouldn't be long now.

* * *

Inside the cabin, Justine slipped one pendulous breast then the other into her 42-DDD brassiere, a harsh look of annoyance on her face. The trip to the cabin had been for nothing. Sanford had proved to be a disappointment, more interested in getting high than getting it on. Why couldn't she learn? She'd locked herself into a definite pattern, a continuous emotional whirlwind of moving from one man to another, from one level of disappointment to a worse one. Each time she expected the adventure to be different. But it never was. What a waste of time, the long, drawn-out effort of fruitlessly trying to coach Sanford's flaccid penis into anything resembling a sustained erection after his first hurried performance, which had left her unfulfilled.

Always bragging about how educated he was, how good a lawyer. Thought it cute to be fucking his client's wife, but he wasn't any good at it. She'd just as soon take on an unschooled farm hand or auto mechanic with dirt under his nails. At least they wouldn't waste her time trying to explain all the ways they could screw somebody over by using the law.

Justine slipped into her skirt and blouse, then her hard-soled sandals. She'd wake Sanford to escort her to the car. It scared her to be outside in the mountains after dark. No telling what kind of animal was waiting to run out and attack a lone female. She could intellectualize that her fears were unfounded—that they had been passed to her as a very young girl by a hysterical mother who was terrified of everything from darkness to strangers, from lightning to imaginary beasts of prey waiting outside her doors— but the programming held.

The radio was clipped to Scanner's belt—his eavesdropper's special. He removed the earpiece from his jacket pocket, slipped the plastic-covered wire loop over his ear, and snugged it into place. The frequency was already set to that of the bug he'd planted in the cabin. He kept the volume low; didn't want it blasting his ear.

From past listening experiences, a twenty-second-long rumbling sound was someone walking across the wooden floor and scraping furniture. The bug was so sensitive that loud sounds near it were distorted and sometimes tinny.

"Aren't you gonna get up? Walk me out to the car?" Scanner grinned at the surrounding gloom as he recognized Justine's whine.

"Do what?" Sanford said.

"Oh, you sorry asshole. You're so stoned you don't understand a word I'm saying. C'mon, get dressed, walk me to the car. It's dark out there and I'm scared."

"Of what?" Sanford slurred his words. "Nothing out there to grab you."

"All those dark woods—bears and wild hogs. You don't care, do you? You've smoked so much pot . . ." A rattling sound. "Cold air'll wake you up. You even know where you are?"

"I'm home, goddammit! Thass where you better get, is home, before Barry gets back. That open window's freezing my ass."

"You deserve it. You're not a man. You can't keep it up anymore. And I won't be back!"

Scanner heard a clump of footsteps and the door opening and slamming. Justine was right on the money: She'd never be back. Her coming out of the cabin alone just now was an unexpected bonus. Heart racing, Scanner put one of his weapons aside. He breathed faster as his body readied for action. Then he started shaking.

To relax, he pictured himself as one of the big cats, stalking its victim, ready to pounce. His muscles felt tight as banjo strings. He could drop down on her like a leopard plunging from a tree.

No. That wasn't the way he'd planned it. And it wouldn't be fair. A reward shouldn't come falling out of the night, a surprise that would last only for moments. The honorable way was face to face.

Justine stepped off the porch into the brilliant wash of moonlight and hurried down the gravel path. She shivered once so violently she almost stumbled. Fear, not cold, caused her shudder. Damn Sanford. He'd told her himself about hearing the noise on the porch one night, looking out the door to see a young bear sniffing around the rockers. It'd run off once he yelled at it, but what if a full-grown male was prowling?

Thoroughly spooked, Justine focused her attention on getting to her car and escaping the dread. The road was bordered on both sides by the night-blackened forest growing only inches from the edge. Her car looked a mile away. Night sounds—the wingbeats of birds, the rustling in dry leaves of a small animal—hurried her along the hard surface.

Always disorganized, Justine waited until she reached her locked car before she began her search for the key. A good habit, she thought, locking the car. She locked it even in the safety of her own driveway. She fished in the oversized handbag, sweated despite the coolness. Moisture glistened on her thin mustache, popped out on her forehead. In her bag, combs, a compact, and her daily-reminder cartridge of birth-control pills clicked and rattled as she searched.

Scanner dropped to the road, held a crouched position for a moment, then began his approach. He stayed in the shadows at the edge of the road. His soft-soled black running shoes made no sound. The dark strip of road with its thick, overhanging branches and moist, blackened tree trunks formed a tunnel that aimed unswervingly at his quarry.

Keys finally in hand, Justine tried to locate the one for the Camry by feel. Her quivering fingers were almost useless. Holding the keys up before the brilliance of the moon, she tried to identify them by shape. In her haste she dropped them. They fell to the road with a loud jingle, landed a few inches from her toes. Frantic, she stooped and picked them up, held them aloft again.

There it is! Her relief drained tension from taut muscles—until she saw the ghostly streak at her feet.

"Yahhh!" she screamed.

Eyes glowing an eerie bright yellow in the moonlight, a possum scuttled from under her car, shuffling off at top speed. Leering back at her with its death's-head grin, it hissed an evil jeer, then disappeared into the forest's blackness.

God! What if it had run up her leg? She almost collapsed, then sighed with relief. She reached the key to the door, scraped around the lock as she tried for the keyhole.

Something's wrong! Justine thought. The damn key won't go in the lock.

Scanner stopped, gulped a great swallow of air to keep from laughing out loud. After a few seconds he regained control and resumed his slow-motion advance. It would ruin the surprise if she turned and saw him. Sneaking along like this felt like a high school prank: Jump from a dark hiding place, shout boo, and scare the girls.

The dark shadow of a cloud passed over the moon. A bird called hoarsely. Justine tried to force the key, then pulled at the door handle in frustration. Beating her fists against the glass, she thought of the trek back to the cabin to awaken Sanford. Who else would help her and keep quiet about it? Reverend Todd would, she knew. She could call him, or Luther, or better yet, she'd call . . .

Then she remembered. Her cellular phone was locked in the car.

* * *

Scanner stopped once more, smiled a loving smile, and savored the woman's fear. He felt so connected, so involved with Justine. Too bad he wouldn't be able to tie her up, take her somewhere, and keep her captive. What happened tonight had to be enough. Now only he controlled her fate. Was he falling in love? He moved closer, froze in place, moved again, then took a final step. Standing close, mere inches away, he waited for a slow count, reached out, and with light fingertips touched the back of Justine's neck ever so softly.

"Hello, my love," Scanner murmured.

"Yaahh!" Justine screamed and whirled. Clinching her hands, she brought them to her face, dug her fingernails into her fleshy cheeks.

Looking up, she saw Scanner towering over her chubby frame. "Oh—it's you," she said, gasping relief. One palm went to her mouth. "God! You scared the lizard shit outa me. I was thinking about you, about calling you. What're you doing out here?"

"Funny you should ask," Scanner said. "I've done a lot of thinking. You're one of the few people in town who really knows about me. And you know about the park. You can't help it; you're a walking mouth. You'll talk. You've already told Sanford."

"I didn't tell him. Carl did. You know he can't keep anything from Sanford. Even before that, Sanford picked up hints from Barry. But he promised me he'd keep it quiet."

"And Carl promised me," Scanner said. "So much for promises."

"What's so all-fired important about the park? Barry is in charge of all that, so forget it. I sure don't care anything about it," Justine said. "You seem all uptight tonight. Help me get my car unlocked. I'll sit on the edge of the front seat and relax you."

Scanner thought it over. No. Never again. He raised his hand.

Justine looked skyward, her instinct warning her of a creeping evil. She couldn't identify the dully glinting object Scanner held above her. "God—what are you doing?"

"You're wrong about Barry being in charge. I'm in charge!" Scanner's hand swept down in a powerful arc, slashing razor-sharp steel into Justine's face.

Slammed backward by the force of the blow, Justine screamed as a heart-sinking agony sliced into the nerves of her cheek. Her blood splattered to the pavement, showered the side of her car as though a mad painter had slung a gory brush.

Scanner raised his arm once again.

Shrieking, Justine pivoted and fled. She pressed her hand to the shredded skin of her face to staunch the spray of blood.

Scanner had spotted the flow, so mercurial in the light of the moon, and was pumped with a wave of exhilaration. Pausing for a moment, he savored his high. Then, brought back to awareness by another scream from Justine, he pursued his prey with the implacable patience of the insane.

He ran with a greater efficiency than the short woman, seized her at the edge of the forest where she tried to plunge into the hidden safety of the wilderness. A resilient tangle of mountain laurel threw her back.

When Scanner grabbed her hair and spun her, Justine found herself looking into a killer's wild eyes. She would die now, she knew, if she didn't run or fight. But she was frozen, big-eyed as a fawn locked into that terrible, wrenching moment before the wolf or tiger takes it down. Then her mind went away, left her body there alone to deal with the horror of this final instant.

A new and simpler weapon was in Scanner's hand: a foot-long piece of slender steel he had honed to the shape of an ice pick. His gripful of her hair held Justine at arm's length. "You want to know why?" he asked, his voice an icy chill. Death talk.

Justine was paralyzed, shut down, staring blindly ahead. She had stopped crying.

"It's for your own good. You've got a miserable life. You have done some good deeds though. So I'm presenting you with your reward." His fist came in low, a powerful underhanded strike at the middle of her chest.

Justine gurgled and fell to the road like a collapsed balloon.

Scanner bent with her as she fell, knew he had punctured her heart. He withdrew the weapon. Keeping a firm grip on the dead woman's hair, he dragged her off the road and into the bushes. Now to hurry and prepare for his good friend Sanford. Surely he'd be along. If not, Scanner would go to the cabin and pay him a visit.

Two

Forty-four seconds before midnight.

The piercing scream ripped through the open window like the startled screech of a night bird. Sanford fought his consciousness up from the fathomless pit of drugged sleep. Yanked from oblivion into the confusion of the here and now, he struggled to sort reality, twisting his neck from side to side to blink at the murky room. Dozing nude on the couch bed, skin absorbing the refreshing wash of mountain air, he was sprawled directly under the open window overlooking his front porch.

Another shriek—a cry of terror or of excruciating pain. Sanford lurched to his feet, clapped a hand to his throbbing forehead.

At the window, he bent to peer out, felt the cool smoothness of the pine against his palms as he used the sill to steady himself. The white gravel walkway was a narrow, bright ribbon curling around the hillside to the dark road below. All else was in the deep shadows cast by the giant oaks and hemlocks towering in his yard.

No one in sight.

Had it been Justine? How long had she been gone? Shit. That last joint had made him groggy.

Fumbling with the lamp on the nightstand, Sanford clicked the switch to its low-watt setting. In the bulb's jaundiced glow he could make out the clock on the mantel.

Midnight. She'd been gone five minutes. Had he fallen asleep that fast? Did he remember the door slamming, or was that part of a dream? Luther had provided some powerful weed.

Another scream. The hills returned a multitude of echoes, a reverberation: "Oh, God, please! Somebody help me!"

15

It was Justine. Had she seen a bear or a snake? Not a snake. Too cool for snakes. She was scared to death of both, though. Should he go out there and rescue her? Wait. He'd call the sheriff's office. No, that wouldn't work. The whole damn town would know.

The flashlight stood by the clock on the stone slab mantel. His shotgun, an always loaded, double-barreled twelve-gauge, hung over it on a rack of antlers.

Then he noticed. The screams had stopped.

Slipping into jeans and low-cut running shoes without socks, Sanford stepped over and extinguished the lamp so he wouldn't silhouette himself in the doorway. Retrieving the gun and flashlight by feel, he moved to the door with slow caution, cracked it just enough to slip outside to the porch.

The moonlight caught and illuminated his figure. He was tall and rangy with straight, light brown hair. His nose was large with a downward hook, and his big, bulging eyes topped a thin, almost hatchet, face. His profession kept him indoors, so his skin was pasty-white and his body not strong, at least not compared to standards in a community where most men worked outdoors logging and quarrying or handling heavy air-hammers, hauling feed to livestock, or lifting pig-metal in the local foundry.

Not that strength alone would matter. Tonight he needed stealth and cunning of the primordial kind—a subject not taught at the university he'd attended.

Standing in the gloom of the covered porch, Sanford looked into the moonlit front yard. Nothing there. But the screams had not come from this close to the house. She must be down by her car.

Stepping from the porch to the gravel path, he clicked on the flashlight and splashed the beam around the yard. The batteries were fresh, the beam was bright, but there was nothing out of the ordinary. He continued down the path to the road. "Justine? You okay?" he called in a soft voice, fearing both an answer and the lack of one.

A choir of tree frogs answered. Gravel crunched faintly beneath his feet. The lonesome call of an owl sounded from the forest. Keeping the shotgun pointed at the ground, he moved ahead in a slow rhythm, swiveling his head to scan first one side of the path then the other.

At the road he had a moment of dizziness, a few seconds when he couldn't remember how he'd gotten there, like he'd reached another level of awareness. After a quick shake of his head, he glanced up the road and spotted Justine's car still parked to the rear of his pickup. He walked to it quickly, if a little unsteadily, shined his light in the front seat, and took in the splotches and streaks of blood on the door and pavement. A long rivulet of red glistened on the glass; scarlet specks marred the side mirror. The hair on the back of his neck stood on end, his heart beginning to race and pound against the inside of his rib cage. Sanford forgot about his headache.

The shotgun cradled under one arm, he circled the car, swept the light around, then stepped a slow circle around his truck. From far away came the call of a whippoorwill, and barely audible from miles overhead he heard the faint, humming drone of a jet as it painted twin brush-strokes of vapor across the moon.

Justine must be hurt bad. But where was she? And something was out there. Or somebody.

The middle of the road seemed safer, so he moved there rather than stand near the trees where anything in the shadows could be on him without warning. Still puzzled, he checked the steep grade that continued up the mountain, aiming the flashlight to one side of the road then the other. Nothing.

He took it step by step as he tried to overcome his fear. Turn to face downhill. Shine light. What's that? Bright, red spots on the road. Follow their trail.

There. What is it?

Almost hidden from view by a tangle of rhododendron, a dark bulky shape lay in the ditch beyond his pickup. Approaching with caution, Sanford brought the shotgun level and placed his finger on the trigger. The safety lever felt sharp against his knuckle as he clicked it off.

Justine's purse! She was hurt bad and must've run down the road.

When he stooped to retrieve the bag, his light flashed across a shadowy outline on the ground, ten feet off the road under a screening of mountain laurel and scrawny pine saplings.

Justine! He dropped the bag to the ground. Crouching to his hands and knees, flashlight in one hand, dragging the shotgun in the other, he crawled across a soft carpet of hemlock needles to where she lay.

Her long, dark hair, full of twigs and dried grass, showed up clearly in the beam of the flashlight. Her back was to him. "Justine," he called in a low voice. "You okay?"

She didn't move or answer. He was afraid he knew why.

Leveraging himself to a sitting position, Sanford moved closer, shook her shoulder. "Justine."

When she still didn't respond, he grasped her shoulder and rolled her over, his light falling full on her face. "Oh, jezzus! Oh, God." His stomach cramped, muscles contracting. Retching, he leaned forward and vomited onto the ground. Overhead a frightened bird fluttered in the branches. Sanford ducked to the ground, then quickly recovered as he identified the sound.

Her face was ripped to ribbons. Loose, mangled flesh was all that was left of her nose and lips. Where the moonlight managed to filter through the evergreens, blood glistened a flowing silver in the gouges on her cheeks. Her eyes stared past him to an eternity beyond caring.

What had cut her up like that? A bear? A wild boar? Whatever, it was out there, waiting! And he was caught. Everyone would know she'd been to his cabin. Especially Barry. His mouth went cotton dry.

From across the road the sound of a police radio broke the silence. "Mountain County S.O. to unit five," the voice of the female dispatcher said in a clear voice.

A cruiser from the sheriff's office? God, he hoped so. Back on hands and knees, he scooted under the low-hanging boughs to the roadside, then stood and looked around expectantly.

The moon was straight overhead now, illuminating the road to an almost daytime brightness. Peering into the trees on both sides of the road, staring up the road then down, he saw no one. He wanted to turn and run back to his cabin, but he dreaded turning his back on whatever was out there no matter how fast he ran. Also, could someone have heard the screams and called the sheriff? Of course. Why else would a cruiser be there? But where?

"Wanda June, I'm ten-eight at the Cozy Living Trailer Park," said a male voice on the radio.

"Hello? I'm over here!" he called, then instantly realized his mistake. If it was Barry, he could've come looking for Justine. And him. He'd be telling a jealous husband where he was. Real bright move. Barry had a police-band radio in his pickup. Had he flown into a jealous rage? Gone berserk and killed his wife?

"Hello, Sanford," Barry's voice called from behind him.

Sanford whirled and aimed the shotgun into the night. Realizing he was at the edge of a wide swath of moonlight, he moved into darkness. "That you, Barry?" His heart leaped in his chest. Adrenaline surged through his system. Was Barry gonna kill him?

No answer.

"What's up Barry? You didn't kill Justine, did you? Come on out here in the light and let's talk it over."

"Hello, Sanford." Barry's voice was directly in front of him. Sanford swept the light back and forth in two quick motions. Nobody. Where the fuck was he?

There was a slight sound on the road behind him, like a pebble rolling across the asphalt. He spun again.

"Hello, Sanford," the voice said from behind him again. He half turned and pointed the light. Nothing.

* * *

Across the way, Scanner raised his clenched fist and waited, sending a silent message for Sanford to come closer.

* * *

Sanford considered running into the forest, hiding until daylight. He was baffled by the sound of the police radio on one side and Barry calling him from the other. And by the absence of a sheriff's cruiser when he kept hearing one. God! Barry was out there in the dark somewhere, waiting for him. Stalking him. Sanford shook inside, then all over. A rapid vibration rattled his breath, a delayed reaction from seeing the devastation of Justine's face and the realization that it could happen to him.

A slight movement across the road caught his eye. Sanford advanced another step onto the road. "That you, Luther? Bubba! Sheriff Rainwalker! Who's there?" He started to bring up the flashlight.

Steel flickered soundlessly in the moonlight, a speeding glint in the flashlight's beam.

"Oh, shit!" Sanford grunted as the sledgehammer blow slammed into his chest. There was a white-hot, penetrating pain, then a quick, spreading numbness.

Sanford somehow remained standing, but he was dying on his feet.

Scanner stepped to the road and walked toward the crumpling man, noting with satisfaction that recognition of his smiling face was Sanford's last conscious thought.

"Don't think too badly of me," he said. "There was really no choice." He spoke in a bell-clear voice. "You know I'm not a bad person. But really, that's the whole problem, isn't it. Not only do you know me, you know of me. Or is it the other way around? I'll have to think on it some other time. Now, if you'll excuse me, it's downright eerie standing on a dark country road talking to a dead lawyer."

Pausing for a moment, he allowed himself a moment of victory. His drug-swamped mind soared and expanded to the edge of the universe. Then a whippoorwill called, a fox barked, and the spell was broken. Rewards had been given silently, Scanner thought, satisfied with the night's work. Standing. Face to face.

A radio crackled. "Mountain County S.O. This is unit five."

"Go 'head, unit five."

"Somebody was over here snooping around one'a the trailers, Wanda June. Musta seen me coming up the road and run inna woods. I'll pretend to leave, drive back by later, keep an eye on the place. May wanta send another unit around Cataloochie Road, see if they parked back there."

"Ten-four."

Scanner zipped up his jacket pocket to ensure his wireless remote control stayed inside snug and secure. A few steps into the forest to pick up the battery-operated tape recorders, then hustle to his vehicle. He still had a good night's work ahead.

* * *

Later, Scanner drove down the mountain towing Justine's Camry. The excitement had run its course. A sense of calmness had settled in. Popping two Serax had helped. The downers made him drowsy, at peace—for a while. Control. He couldn't allow himself to get too low. There were still many things left undone.

"Mountain County Dispatch to all units."

Scanner recognized the voice on the sheriff's frequency. Wanda June was still on duty.

"Mountain County Dispatch. A bad weather front's moving into the mountains. Weather service advises high surface winds and heavy rain. Flash flooding is likely. Be alert for severe electrical activity. K-I-A eleven-forty-five. Zero-two-twenty-two."

Good, thought Scanner. Heavy showers would wash away all traces of blood. Minutes later, splatters of rain thudded against his hood and windshield.

Just as suddenly, the strobing blue lights of a sheriff's cruiser appeared behind him, flashed its headlights three times, then once again. Scanner turned his lights off, then on, and drove another mile before pulling to the side of the road. The police car pulled up behind him and a deputy walked up the road in the rain toward him as Scanner got out of his own vehicle. The two of them stood hunched against the weather.

"Ever'thing go okay?" the deputy asked.

The only sound was the hissing white noise of the downpour along with the occasional metallic plunk of a big drop hitting the roof of a car. "Like a dream," Scanner said.

* * *

21

One week later. East Tennessee mountainside. Sunrise.

"Yeehaa! Listen to them coon dogs sing," Kennie Calhoun yelled to the mountains. He hoped his own blue heeler, Lucky, was leading the pack. Last time out the hound had gotten lost in the mountains for four days and was half starved when a ranger finally picked him up limping along the highway.

Kennie and the other eleven men in the group with him now were all members of the Mountain County Coon Hunt Club.

"Over here," one of the men hollered. "Let's take the fire road." The road was really a twin dirt track overgrown with weeds, a double slash through the hemlocks. That was all right with Kennie; it was better than fighting his way up the steep slope holding on to saplings and getting ripped to shreds by briars.

The racket from the dogs raised to an hysterical pitch.

"Bet there's more'n one coon," Kennie yelled over the noise.

"One up a tree and one in a creek. Hankering for a fight," a hulking blond mountaineer with greasy hair down to his shoulders said, his eyes alive with excitement. He broke into as much of a run as he could muster up the steep incline. Breathing hard from the exertion, the other club members were close behind.

Stampeding into a clearing, they stopped and stared, slack-jawed at all the confusion. Dogs were running in every direction, snapping and growling at each other, pissing on trees, spinning in circles.

"Where's the fuckin' coons?" Kennie yelled. The men huddled together and looked around. Kennie's blue heeler sat down, pointed his snout skyward, and began to howl. The others joined in.

"What's happening?" one of the men said, covering his ears.

"Look over there!"

"Where?"

"Edge of the woods. Look!"

As one they moved across the clearing in a clump of shuffles. "Oh shit. Dead bodies. Two naked, dead bodies," Kennie Calhoun said. He moved closer, his shoulders hunched from fear, to get a closer look. "Well I'll be dipped in shit. It's Justine Willingham and that lawyer. They didn't run off together after all."

Sanford Sharpless's body was arched upward at a grotesque angle. The shaft of an arrow with bright yellow feathers protruded from his chest.

One of the men moved past Kennie. "Woman's face is all tore up. You sure it's Justine?"

"Recognize that hair and ass anywhere," Kennie said. Realizing what he had said, he began backpedaling. "I mean, you know that long black hair. And she's heavy. You all know what I mean." Kennie didn't want Barry Willingham coming along with his wild hog hunting bow to stretch him out flat out here under the trees and let the foxes and critters have his balls for a midnight snack. He grimaced. Maybe that's what happened to Justine's face—wild hog got ahold of it.

"Let's move back," the club president said. "We're tromping around destroying evidence. I'll call in on channel 9."

At six that frosty October morning, Deputy Sheriff Samantha Goodlocke was the first law officer to arrive on the scene. Other deputies were on the way, but she'd been close by on a complaint that Eddie Edward's cows were out in the middle of the road again. On her preliminary walk-through of the area, she gazed at the two bodies lying side by side, their milked-over eyes staring at the canopy of tulip trees seventy feet overhead.

Sanford's head lay flopped back. Taut skin on his neck held his mouth agape for the entry and exit of whatever insect or mouse happened along. Both bodies were adorned with long, shiny blue ribbons tagged to their genitals with some kind of clip.

One of the hunters appeared at her shoulder. "Don't know what they been up to," he said, "but it looks like they done took first prize."

Samantha wheeled on him. "Get your ass back to the fire road." A comedian in every crowd. Let a coupla young kids lose it on a highway, there'd be some idiot staring at the mangled car, making jokes.

She knew the locals watching the county's first and only female deputy would like to see her faint or puke from the sight of two bodies that had lain so long at the cruel mercy of wild animals and the elements. She waved the men farther away from the area then forced herself to take a slow, painstaking appraisal of the cadavers and the immediate area. She memorized as best she could her first impression of the site. After two years of excellent performance on the job, she knew she must still prove herself on every trouble call to the denizens of the rural county.

Back at the fire road, the club members were more interested in how tight Deputy Goodlocke's uniform pants fit than how she was reacting to the gore. She wore her curly, chestnut-brown hair short to go under the uniform hat, a Smoky Bear style worn by all the county's deputies. The brim slanted down over her forehead and met the mirrored sunglasses, cast her high cheekbones and sharp chin in shadows. She wore a touch of lipstick; her face was dark brown from the outdoor life she led.

The coon hunters snickered and mumbled among themselves that Sheriff Rainwalker oughta bend the dress-code rules and allow her to wear a tight sweater or a tight, white T-shirt. No bra. Hell, they'd prefer topless.

The big 9-millimeter automatic she wore in a black, webbed-nylon holster high over her right hip, though, caused the men some concern and assured better behavior from the group than if she had not been armed. They were all locals and knew she was proficient with the pistol.

She was as tall as most of them, close to six feet. When she walked, her arm swung away from her body to clear the butt of the pistol. This and her length of stride gave her an air of aggressiveness few of the men were apt to challenge.

Samantha fast-walked to the Jeep and called in. Her isolated location on the far side of the mountain from Highwater Town was out of range for her high-frequency walkie, so she used the lower-frequency radio under the dash. "Bubba, get Sheriff Rainwalker headed this way, ten and three-tenths miles off'a Cloudy Cove Road on Fire Road 810. Them boys in cruisers'll have to park and hike it; location's not in the national forest, so it's all ours. Best get a deputy to the firehouse, tell Barry we found his wife. Take a preacher along."

"Ten-four, unit six. Sheriff's not at the S.O. yet. I'll call him at his station R."

Kennie swaggered toward the Jeep. Samantha's back was to

him, and he eyed her panty line, lust in his eyes. Woman like that going to waste. Nobody gettin' any of it since Randy gave her the walking papers. Damn shame too. She could comfort a man on a long, cold, lonely, mountain night. "Looks like ol' Barry done put a end to his ol' lady's carousing ways. And Sharpless—coon hounds found his ass out."

Little weasel, Samantha thought. Pervert's probably thinking how it'd be fun to wear me out with his stubby prick then brag about it to his dumb-assed buddies. She swung around and impaled him with one of her most intimidating stares, a tactic learned at the feet of the master, Sheriff Rainwalker. "You already been called to sit on the goddamn jury, Kennie Calhoun?"

Calhoun ducked his head and backed off two steps. "No'sum."

"Then keep your yap to yourself. I've a mind to cuff your scrawny ass and take you in for destroying a crime scene. Sheriff's sure to talk to you for a while. May go over to the Sack 'n' Tote, talk to your daddy about selling beer on Sunday and selling singles to high school kids."

"Just making a observation," Calhoun mumbled to the ground and scampered back to his cronies. He knew Samantha worked out with weights, power-lifted as much as most men, and handled herself well in the rough-and-tumble occupation she had chosen. He'd seen her club bigger men than him to the rough gravel of the parking lot at the HillTop Tavern.

Samantha watched Kennie slink back to his buddies. He could be right, she thought. Barry was a churchgoer, even if he did drive all the way out of the county to attend that uppity church. He was fire chief, father of a teenage son and daughter, highly thought of by the folks of Highwater Town. Who else would have a motive though, if what looked like happened actually happened? No matter how righteous a man was, to find his wife buck-ass naked in the woods with a man could drive him over the edge. And like a lot of men in the county, Barry hunted deer and wild boar in season—probably sometimes out of season—and he could draw a heavy bow.

Three

Nashville, Tennessee.

Cody Rainwalker eyed the P7 automatic in his partner's hand and wished he'd settle down. Ray's jerky movements made him nervous.

"Why're we after this mutt?" Ray Blizzard said. Leaning forward in the van's front passenger seat, he slid his weapon into the elastic holster he wore over his spine. He had checked the thirteen-shot ammo load three times in the last half hour.

Cody reached an open hand to wipe away the fog from the inside of the windshield, peering through the rainy night at the shabby frame house. It had been years since a paint brush had touched its rough, warped boards, and he bet the rain was leaking through the weather-beaten roof by the bucketful. Hedges ran amuck in the neglected front yard. A dim glow came from a side window. "Asshole's a mid-level drug dealer on the slide from Memphis. Was running some kinda drug house there and this elderly couple across the street threatened to call the cops. He puts 'em both in the hospital; the old guy'll never walk again."

"Whattabout his bud?"

"He keeps out of the way—nothing. He invites himself in— I'll have to put him down."

It was time to take the two men. Cody'd given them enough time to get comfortable after arriving home an hour earlier. Rushing things, though, could get you hurt. He'd have to deal with them both. No way around it. Expecting the other man to stand back and watch his partner being led away by two strangers who weren't even the law wouldn't set well.

Maybe he'd said what he said to Ray to salve his conscience

in case he was forced to kill the wanted man's sidekick. He continued. "His bud, as you call him, is a tagalong. Gofer and a small-time dealer, in and out of the house of many doors." Cody suspected Ray was getting the heebie-jeebies, otherwise he'd be wisecracking.

"What kinda bail this shithead jump?" Ray asked. He was sweating despite the night's coolness.

"Hundred thousand," Cody said. "His druggie friends sprung him through a bail bondsman."

"So what're you getting total to bring him in? Before expenses."

"Five."

"So my share's better'n I can make selling used cars, and I don't have to lie half as much."

That made it four for Cody after he gave Ray his thousand. A risky way to make a living and one he wouldn't take on every day, but the opportunity had presented itself. He was still building his agency and had chosen the high-rent district hoping to rope walk-ins with fat wallets. All he had to do was live through the next five or ten minutes.

"Time to go." Cody opened the door and stepped out into the cold rain, followed by Ray. Neither man spoke. They had worked together since their army intelligence days in Europe, and each knew what to expect from the other. Each knew the other wouldn't desert him if the action turned nasty. Compared to some of the ops they'd been on together, this one should be a walk.

As he edged around the rear of the van, Cody noticed Ray clutching his prop—a bottle of Stoli vodka—by the neck. Quickening his pace, he left the smaller man behind as he turned at the weeded-over driveway and made his way to the end of the porch. There he jumped up to sit on the rotting wood, then stood quietly, pulled his pistol, and backed against the wall. The drumming of the rain on the roof masked what little noise he made.

Cody watched Ray's more conventional approach as he angled from the edge of the road into the walkway. Ray looked up, wiped rain from his forehead with his free hand, glanced up and down the silent street, then mounted the three concrete steps. Cody knew he wouldn't hesitate and he didn't.

Bottle in hand, Ray marched to the door and banged loudly four times; forceful enough to rattle a loose windowpane near Cody's ear. He uncapped the bottle of vodka and took a swig, twisted the top back on and waited, arms dangling at his side, his posture suddenly gone slack.

Cody hugged the wall and moved closer.

The door opened in fifteen seconds or less, but to Cody it seemed forever. Whoever answered stayed inside, out of sight. Ray slouched in the middle of the porch.

"Whatta you want?" a rough male voice said from the doorway.

"Tell Orville I wanta buy some pills," Ray said in a loud, demanding voice. Orville was the code they'd decided to use if the fugitive's partner, not the wanted man himself, answered the door.

"Orville?" the voice said. "The fuck is Orville? You got the wrong house, dickweed."

A deeper voice sounded from inside the house. "Who is it?"

"Scrawny asswipe looking for Orville."

Ray stood his ground, plucked the cap from the bottle and took another swallow. He wiped his mouth with the back of his hand and said, "You retarded freak. Quit standing there picking your butt and get Orville. Otherwise I'll kick your fat, sloppy ass all over the porch."

The man charged out the door with a roar.

Moving instantly, Cody slammed the butt of his automatic behind the rushing man's ear and watched Ray jerk aside as his would-be attacker fell facedown, slid over the edge, and crashed to the ground with a limp thud. Then Cody was pounding into the house behind his cocked pistol. "On the floor, asshole! You know the drill. On the floor!" He heard Ray right behind him.

The outlaw's eyes were wide with fear. He folded toward the floor, all the time looking down the barrel of Cody's automatic. "Who're you fucking guys?" he said.

"Bounty hunters," Cody answered. "Seems you missed an important occasion in Memphis. Consider me your new social secretary. Put the cuffs on him, Ray, and don't forget that great-looking designer chain we brought along for his ankles."

"Doing this different the next time," Ray said as he advanced toward the prone man. He had discarded the bottle somewhere along the way and had a set of cuffs in his hand.

"How's that?" Cody said. He didn't take his eyes off the prisoner.

"Gonna use Jack Daniels instead of vodka. That last jolt liked to knocked me on my ass."

Eleven hours later. Downtown Nashville, Tennessee.

Cody Rainwalker's office was on the second floor of one of the restored warehouses that lined both sides of Nashville's historic Second Avenue. He had rented the space long before it was fashionable, before the discovery of the area by the early entrepreneurs who bombed with their vegetarian restaurants, odds-and-ends and antiquarian book shops, and overpriced houseplant stores. Long gone now, their sole contribution was adding an artsy flavor to the district that still remained.

Like so many ventures in Nashville, it took real money to promote an idea whose time had come. So in had come the big music money, with ties to politicians for rezoning and the clout to build a controversial convention center, a sports arena, a Planet Hollywood, and finally, a pro-football stadium nearby.

Competition with the town of Branson, Missouri, provided the impetus for the development in the district. Folks might not drive to Nashville for the country music anymore without additional entertainment, and something needed to be done.

The Opry House got renovated. A Hard Rock Cafe opened on the corner of Second and Broadway. Mulligan's Pub had been around for a while but was now an even bigger success. And a few doors down the street, the Wildhorse Saloon premiered with what must be one of the South's largest dance floors.

Upscale and hip, the Jack of Eagles Club with its glamorous dancers, singers, hostesses, and waitresses attracted the movers and shakers, the sharks, strivers, arrivers, cons, coke dealers, snorters, let's-pretenders and wannabes. And if eyeball muscles weren't overstrained from that experience, there was always Hooters down the street a ways.

Cody felt like a true pioneer. For a while, so did the bums and the homeless that inhabited the area. But Cody paid rent and was allowed to remain while the homeless were told to find a new place to live.

The downtown district was transformed. Streets once deserted after six or seven when state office buildings, banks, law offices, and insurance companies let go their staff now bustled to all hours, just like the good old days of the fifties and early sixties, when everything was illegal and the tourists enjoyed the hell out of it. Riverboat tours were now packed to the gunwales, and every other ground-floor storefront was a crammed-to-the-walls restaurant.

Moving back to the downtown area from the suburbs became the "in" thing to do. Cody hoped this trend would supply an endless stream of clients. And he knew the music biz folks were just getting started.

He loved his old second-story loft with its brick interior walls. The building had served as a cotton warehouse back in the real riverboat heydays, and the ceilings were high enough for rain clouds to form. Floorboards twelve and fourteen inches wide and two inches thick had been rip-sawed out of the virgin timber that had been plentiful in the area when the settlers arrived. They looked as strong and straight now as the day they were nailed into place, just a little worn from the thousands of feet that had trod them to a smooth shine. The timbers in the building's super-structure were massive as well, and could never be replaced; oaks that size no longer existed.

From his front window, which had once provided a private view of shaggy forms sleeping in doorways, Cody could now people-watch an almost endless stream of humanity. Very few tourists bothered to look up to see "Diving Hawk Investigations" painted on the window over the logo of a red-tailed hawk with talons bared.

Standing now in his office, Cody raised his hand to shield his eyes and squinted into the steady orange blaze of the setting sun. Half blinded by the glare, he stomped over to the window to lower the blinds, then stood for half a minute while his eyes grew accustomed to the dimness before making his way back to the heavy, gray-metal, used-car salesman's desk that served as filing cabinet, gun safe, and catchall for tossed reports.

"Thanks," said Ray.

Cody turned and peered at Ray sitting at a desk that was the twin of his own. Facing the same direction, it stood behind Cody's since the P.I. didn't like people looking at him while he worked. He didn't like anyone behind him, either, but sanctioned Ray's position as a lesser evil.

Ray was rubbing his eyes with the tips of his fingers. The combination of his ever-present grin, straight blond hair, and eyes the frosty blue of juniper berries gave him a happy-go-lucky appearance.

"Yeah, thanks," Noel Saylor said from across the room. "Glare off Ray's scalp was giving me a headache."

Noel was Cody's landlord. A well-known computer software consultant, his office was on the third floor above Cody's, and he and his ever-present Greek sailor's cap were consistent afternoon visitors.

Ray put on an offended face and wiped a hand across his receding hairline. "That's the thanks I get for teaching you what I know about private detecting?" Ray asked.

"If you taught me all you know, how come I feel so dumb?"

"You've felt that way all your life."

Cody loaded high-speed film into a Canon Eos-Rebel whose attached 300 mm variable-zoom lens was larger than the camera's body. He ignored the two men as they went at each other—he had long ago figured out it was strictly for entertainment—and snapped the camera shut. After waiting for the whine of the motor to advance the film, he placed the camera in the bottom right-hand drawer of his desk and snapped a heavy-duty lock over a clasp welded to the metal leg.

Ray grinned. He was inured to Cody's silent ways. His employer's dark, sometimes brooding, face discouraged most conversation. Ray knew that behind Cody's black and penetrating eyes, which seemed to look into the far distance even in a small room, there was no anger directed toward him. The thousand-yard stare, Ray called it.

"What about it, Cody?" Noel said. "When're you going to hire me on as a part-timer? I'm ready to go down and take the test. Be a P.I. and impress all the women." Noel was forever wanting to be an investigator, and would likely forgo pay, the perceived excitement of the job tantalized him so.

Cody grunted. "Your Mercedes'll look real elegant parked in front of a cardboard-box condo, if you take up detecting for a living."

"Almost be worth it to sit on surveillance, chase crooks, get to testify against the bad guys."

"Tell him again, Ray."

Ray enjoyed these afternoon hassles. The arguing provided a means of relaxing before going to stake out his assignment for the night—usually someone an insurance company had sicced the agency on. The companies were forever demanding feature-length videos of seriously injured claimants out for their evening jog. "Don't do any good. You just heard him say how dumb he is. You gotta be dumb to wanna give up a high-paying job to go sit and wait for some insurance cheat to go roller-blading."

Noel wouldn't be put off. "Times are changing. Cyberspace beckons. The information superhighway is upon us. Computer knowledge is going to be a requirement for the knowledgeable P.I. of the future. I'm sure even you yokels have heard of computer forensics."

"That what the coroner does if somebody shoots your computer?" Cody asked.

Ray slammed both feet to the floor, stood, and stretched with his arms out to his sides, back arched. "I feel like road-kill on the information superhighway. What say we go over to the soda shop, get some ribs, turnip greens, pole beans, and corn bread? Continue our worldly discussion over a plate of titillating vittles? North Alabama boys think and talk better after partaking of gourmet food."

Despite Ray's affected speech, Cody wasn't fooled—in addition to southern-country English, Ray spoke German, Hungarian, and a smattering of Russian. His good ol' boy routine was an act he carried off expertly through continuous practice; he lived the part. But he'd been stationed with Cody in the same army intelligence unit for a number of years and felt at home in a half dozen European capitals.

Noel was nodding agreement, but whatever he'd planned on saying was interrupted by the ringing of the phone. Cody reached out and snagged the receiver. "Diving Hawk Investigations. This is Cody." He was mildly surprised to hear the voice of an old hometown friend, Michelle Willingham. Her mountain voice was high-pitched and fast and she spoke without preamble.

"Your daddy's arrested my brother," she said. "Barry's wife Justine's been missing. They found her body along with Barry's attorney, Sanford Sharpless. Everyone in the county thought they'd run off together. Me, I didn't think Sharpless had that poor'a taste."

"Hi, Michelle. Sorry to hear it," Cody said. "You folks helped Daddy get elected sheriff, so he'd need a good reason to arrest Barry."

"Justine's car was found over in Coffee County. It was stripped, and blood was found on the driver's door. Sheriff kept that a secret until today. Barry's bow was found in the trunk, and the lawyer was killed with an arrow through his chest. Justine was killed with some kind of knife, cut up real bad. The bodies were found up in the mountains near the national forest. There's other evidence. I'm sure your father will let you read the report."

"Me?" Cody said. "I'm not an experienced murder investigator."

"Samantha says you're an electronic surveillance expert. Sheriff's investigators found eavesdropping devices on the lawyer's telephone and on Barry's telephone."

"That's interesting," Cody said.

"Family offered a ten-thousand-dollar reward for information on Justine's whereabouts. Barry refused to believe she just ran off and left her children to the ridicule of the county. And this trouble couldn't have happened at a worse time. We're in the middle of some important business negotiations." She launched into some background information.

For the next few minutes Ray and Noel waited with ill-disguised impatience. They'd heard the word murder and wanted to know the scoop. Noel finally edged closer in an attempt to somehow hear both sides of the telephone conversation. When Cody threw a hard glance at him, he jerked back and feigned disinterest by examining his watch.

"Look, Michelle," Cody finally broke in, "murder investigations are not my forte; I'm mostly a finder and follower. But I'll drop by the jail and see Barry sometime tomorrow, then get in touch with you later. I'll drive over tonight, in an hour or so." Good-byes said, Cody hung up the phone.

Ray, anxious to take revenge on Noel for the going-bald jokes and knowing Noel was wild to find out what was up, winked at Cody. "Boss, now you've taken care of business, how's about we run over to the soda shop. My belly thinks my throat's been cut."

"Don't think I'm gonna have time, Ray." Cody thought he had a better scheme. "Gotta pack. I'll get something on the road. You may want to go home and eat dinner, get some rest; you'll be on your own tomorrow."

"Huh? Okay. You say so."

Noel was fidgeting with the bill of his cap and didn't want to ask. Maybe pro P.I.s didn't get all shook up over a murder.

Cody retrieved his 9-mm pistol from the locked desk, placed it in a gun shoe, then crammed it into a small overnight bag. He favored the eight-shot weapon, a Heckler & Koch P7-M8, because of its squeeze-cocker and easy carry. He scratched through the papers on the top of his desk to see what he needed to take along. Then he went to the closet and took out a black leather catalog case in which he stored his electronic snooping and antisnooping gear.

"Taking along your main squeeze?" Ray said, indicating the H&K pistol.

"Never leave home without it."

With a wave, Ray headed for the door.

Noel could stand it no longer. "Wait a minute you all," he said. "Tell you what. I'll buy us all burgers and fries."

Ray stopped, held the door open, waiting for Cody's lead.

"Don't think so, Noel," Cody said. "Had a burger for lunch. I need to get moving."

"Okay goddammit, I'll pop for dinner and beer, the barbecue buffet at the Wildhorse Saloon." He looked pleadingly at Cody, who finally looked at Ray and shrugged.

"Let's do it," Cody and Ray said in harmony.

Four

After talking to Cody, Michelle hung up the phone, picked up her drink from the coffee table, and returned to her snuggled position with Staros on the oversized leather couch. "Now where were we?" she murmured.

"Let's see. Were we here? Or was it right here?" He moved his strong hands intimately over her body, rubbing, then massaging.

"Oh, Rick." She writhed with delight, wiggled her hips to get into a more pleasurable position. Her body was big-boned with heavy breasts and hips. She fought a constant battle against going to seed—Stairmaster, running, and a diet that kept her constantly hungry. But so far she was winning.

The vacation cabin they sat in overlooked the noisy rapids of the Bald River. Through the glass of the wide French doors opening onto the hemlock deck, the river's gigantic gray stones, polished smooth over the eons by floods from thaws and downpours in the mountains above them, were still visible in the gathering twilight. Across the river a five-hundred-foot precipice hung over the narrow road that hooked into a sharp curve and ran parallel to the river. Pines and hemlocks screened a portion of the gorge face, clinging to the limestone and granite with a precarious persistence.

Rick Staros was twelve years Michelle's senior, tall, dark-complected, hair black with streaks of a silvery gray, fit and distinguished. Always a careful dresser, tonight he wore expensive designer jeans and a wine-colored velour shirt. His shoes were brown buckskins.

They had met in Las Vegas the year before when Michelle attended a medical convention. She had been intrigued by the mysterious aura surrounding him, an ambiance that carried with it a faint hint of danger. She was also aroused by his cosmopoli-

---

tan savoir-faire. After a brief fling they remained friends. Impressed with his knowledge of business and investments, when her recent stupendous real estate opportunity presented itself, she thought of him immediately. Staros had been awed by the scope of the project. Thought it the insider's deal of the century.

When Staros had first met Michelle he'd wondered at his choice of an afternoon companion. Just idle conversation in a bar. Then he'd discovered she was a doctor. His thought at the time was that he'd never had sex with a doctor. He plotted his course and two nights later seduced her in his hotel room.

After he'd overcome her first clumsiness, he'd discovered she was wild, a ripe peach waiting to be plucked. Most of the women he knew had the hard glaze of Vegas or New York, so her provincialism had been refreshing. For a while; then he missed the familiarity of what he'd been weaned on, what Michelle referred to as well-practiced, Yankee sluts.

Ten months later, when she called to ask for financial advice on what seemed to be the mother of all real estate deals, Staros saw two opportunities.

After a conference with his partners, he'd driven to Tennessee, leased the riverside vacation cabin in the nearby town of Tellico Plains, and resumed the affair with Michelle more or less for convenience and as leverage to gain more insider knowledge of what she and her brothers were up to. She understood there was no long-term, romantic commitment. At least he hoped she did.

"Is the hick-town detective taking the job?" Staros asked.

"The hick-town definition is back. Why is it you think anyone who's not L.A., or Vegas, or New York, is provincially incompetent? That big-city chauvinism just doesn't become you and could cause you to delude yourself about the capabilities of others who are quite competent," Michelle said.

"I stand chastised. But what can a private investigator accomplish? Most spend their time peeping through keyholes, tracking wayward spouses and insurance cheats. Forensics and scientific methods—that's the way murderers are caught." If he could gain some advantage by leaving Barry in the lockup, Rick would leave him there until he rotted. He couldn't figure how Barry staying in jail would give him a larger cut. He'd think on it some more.

"If Cody can find who planted the bugs and why, Barry'll be cleared," Michelle said. "Cody was born in Mountain County. He can talk mountain talk to the mountain people; not easy for an outsider. Cody left home right after high school and joined the army. Got out, married a local girl, and moved to Los Angeles. Before his divorce, he was in the L.A. police department. Then he went private. It's not like he got a private detective's badge out of a cereal box."

"Okay. I'm convinced," Staros said. "Your Cody's a veritable Sherlock. Let's hope he's not sharp enough to uncover our little project. One whisper of what we're really up to and we're out of business and millions in the hole. Deal's too big to let that happen."

"After watching the news today I'm more excited than ever," Michelle said. "The Olympic kayaking competition was held on the Ocoee River. You realize that's only thirty miles from here? The best part is . . . it's in the Cherokee National Forest."

"The publicity's tremendous—it'll make the property that much more valuable. And the quicker we move the better," Staros said.

Michelle pulled his head down and kissed him on the lips. "Cody has a cabin on one of the mountains. On a hundred acres. A few months ago the property was worthless. Now it's right in the middle of the planned takeover. Prime and scenic."

"You're very clever my dear. Hiring him is a stroke of pure genius. Of course you'll make him a generous offer—before the word leaks out."

"You're teasing. Barry or I will make an offer. You can count on it."

He remained quiet for a few minutes, his thoughts racing from one possible scenario to another. How could he maximize his position with the men in Vegas? On the surface they cared for his welfare, his earnings, his long-term survival. But he'd observed the senior partners, as he referred to them. When there was money with lots of zeros at stake, their eyes would glaze over, their stares become reptilian. He imagined them squatting in their oversized, plush offices like overgrown, fat toads, thinking, scheming. Their demeanor gave him the uneasy feeling of being secretly watched from a distance, like a small bug crawling exposed across a large, flat rock. At any time a rough tongue could come zipping out of nowhere and snap him up.

He was covering where he could. Justine and Sanford—too bad about them. He must be careful and not let their murders screw up the works. He'd remain anonymous. The farther he stayed from the investigation the better.

"Thoughts?" Michelle said.

"Just thinking about the two dearly departed, my love," Staros said.

"Are you being sarcastic? I didn't think you were impressed by either of them."

Staros smiled down at her, ran his hands over her breasts and down over her stomach to her thighs. "When I met Justine, I thought she was a great drag on Barry, that he should dump her. I kept my thoughts to myself. Sanford? A nonentity. He's no great loss."

"Justine was impressed by you. She would jiggle all over when you walked into the room. You were polite to her, gentlemanly. That turned her on."

"Why don't we change the subject," Staros said. "Dead people depress me." Inwardly he sighed—the entire populace was a pack of hayseeds. And Carl Taggart, so twisted that a few moments spent around him made your skin crawl. How had Carl tumbled to the deal? There was a leak somewhere.

After Michelle left to make the drive home to Highwater Town, Staros went over to his laptop computer and flipped it open, powered it on, and waited for it to boot up. He'd already typed his report. At the Windows display, he clicked on Trumpet Windsock and entered his password. The computer fast-dialed and connected to the service provider. Staros clicked on his e-mail icon, attached a file, and zipped the already encrypted message to his masters in Vegas.

In the bedroom, he opened the drawer of his bedside table.

He'd placed the scanner out of sight under a file folder. He turned it on and placed it on the table. After taking his shoes off he lay back with his head on the pillow and listened to the chatter on the Mountain County sheriff's frequency. Keeping track of any progress in the murder investigation was a part of his ongoing strategy. Cody Rainwalker was an unknown element he hadn't considered. He'd need to find out as much about the detective as possible. Wait and learn, don't make any premature moves.

He toyed with the idea of doing a line of cocaine, but he put that thought aside. He would need discipline and focus for the time being. Recreation would come later, after the business at hand.

Michelle had proven to be a good source for the downers he needed these days to fall asleep. She could provide other drugs if he needed them, he had also discovered. She was so eager to please. Just like Justine had been eager to please.

Justine. It had been a big mistake letting her in the front door that day. She'd arrived under the pretext that she wanted to discuss the business of the park. Once inside, she was all over him. He'd pushed her away and accidentally placed his palm on one of her breasts. She'd gone ape shit, unzipped his pants, and plunged him deep into her mouth, moaning and stroking him to climax.

She was good at what she craved, he'd give her that. And she'd kept coming back for more. But there'd be no more lapses of discipline now. In his business a lack of discipline could get you killed. Quick.

* * *

Cody made the two-hundred-thirty-mile trip from Nashville to his hometown of Highwater Town, Tennessee, late that night. The air conditioner in his dirty red Ford 4x4 was on the fritz, but it didn't matter; the cool night air through the open window provided a welcome change from driving in city traffic, windows down, inhaling the noxious fumes of trucks and buses.

Crossing the line into Mountain County, he smiled as his

radar detector warbled. He spotted the cruiser in his rear-view mirror, the white sedan ghosting from its dirt-road hiding place and dropping in behind him. The deputy had apparently taken note of his Davidson County license plate. Xenophobia was as instilled in the law as it was in the rest of the populace.

He knew the feeling well, had had to overcome it when as a teenager he'd enlisted in the army. The deputy would be wondering what some big city dude was up to this late at night. Besides, the county derived much of its revenue from the speed of out-of-towners.

The cruiser stayed on him, radar lit. To prevent the fuzz-buster's tone from aggravating him, Cody thumbed it to city-driving mode, then when it continued to rattle his nerves, turned it off altogether.

He took it slow, kept his lights on bright; didn't want a deer or a bear ricocheting off his hood and joining him to ride shot-gun. If he had to make a choice, he'd choose the bear. A deer would cut you to ribbons with its sharp hooves. He'd seen it happen.

Twenty minutes later he pulled into the dirt and gravel parking lot of the Riverside Motel, got out of his pickup, and headed for the motel office. He felt the bitterness returning, building slowly from the subtle hints of familiarity. Happened every time he came back home, he thought.

The cruiser had followed him into the motel lot, catching him in high beams. Cody resented anyone spotlighting him. He considered kicking the cruiser's headlights out.

The cruiser approached Cody and pulled to a stop beside him. Cody watched the deputy lower his window. "Oh, it's you, Cody. Didn't recognize your truck. How you doing?"

"Okay, Luther. See you're up to your old tricks, harassing tourists."

"That what you are now? Your daddy know you're in town?"

"Reckon he'll know now, soon's you call in and tell him."

"Hear about the excitement? Made the national news. We got Barry Willingham over in the lockup. Done killed his wife and his lawyer. Caught 'em fucking in the woods. He done a good deed, putting that lawyer outa business."

41

"I heard."

With a wave, Cody headed for the motel door. He rang the night bell five long rings before the office light came on and Elton Crabtree, motel owner and night-desk clerk, opened the office door.

"Want a room?" Elton asked. Looked at head-on, the runty, middle-aged man appeared thin. Seen from the side, his potbelly overhung his low-slung pants, made him swayback, caused his dirty white shirt to pull up in back and creep out of his waistband. His eyes were red and rheumy, his lips and mouth a constant pucker around the ever-present cigarette forever on the threshold of dropping a long gray ash on his protruding gut.

"Naw, Elton. I'm a goddamn door-to-door salesman."

Surprised, Elton looked into the piercing black eyes of the man glowering down at him. A shiver of fear went through him. He recognized the caller. His fear deepened.

"Oh—it's you, Cody. Sheriff know you're in town?" Elton fled inside, scooted behind the desk. He felt safer with a barrier between himself and the menacing man he knew only by reputation. In years past fear had kept him from approaching even a teenage Cody Rainwalker. Elton's older brother, Elwood, feared Cody even more, had spent years expecting the part-Cherokee to materialize out of the darkness one spooky night and put his cowardly ass in the cold, cold ground. Elton, ever vengeful over both real and imagined indignities committed by his brother, often stimulated Elwood's fear with false reports of Cody sightings—a vindictive specter lurking in the woods near Elwood's home. The accounts never failed to send Elwood, now Mountain County Hospital's administrator, into shaking fits of anxiety, a condition Elton secretly relished.

Cody followed Elton inside, leaned on the registration desk with both elbows. "Yeah. It's me, and my daddy knows I'm in town."

"Hear talk you're a private detective up in Nashville."

"You hear right."

"Well, what you want?"

"You tell me, Elton. What do folks want that ring your bell late at night? You still selling whiskey after hours? Maybe some whacky smokes? Seems I remember hearing talk . . ."

"You want a room?" Elton was so nervous he shifted from foot to foot. Cody may have decided to take reprisal on the entire Crabtree clan, beginning with him, right now. After all, it was a time-honored mountain tradition to strike out at any member of an offending family. The real enemy could be reached and taken care of at any time after he was worn out with funerals.

"Right, Elton. I want a room."

"Got a credit card?"

Cody reached across the counter, gave the cigarette in Elton's mouth a backhanded slap before grabbing the sweating man by his shirt collar and dragging him onto the desk. Their faces almost touched. "Elton, you either hand me a registration card, or I'm gonna get pissed, take your bony, decrepit ass back to the river rapids, and use it for a kayak."

When released, Elton almost fell to his knees. Hand shaking, he produced the document. "All you had to do was ask."

Later, flopped on the lumpy cotton mattress in his dingy, mildewed room, Cody reviewed the episode. Welcome to Mountain County. The place he loved to hate. Lot of folks like Elton in town. Genetic disorder. He thought of Elton's brother, Elwood, and how one day he'd settle that score. But not now. Business first.

Oh, well. At least he'd get to spend a few days and nights at his cabin. Get over the big-town jitters.

Deputy Luther Hamby drove his cruiser back to the S.O. and hung around for over an hour gossiping with the dispatcher, the jailer, and some other deputies engaged in shift turnover. After gleaning what information he could, he went back out to his cruiser to use his cellular phone.

"Hello," Bobby Joe Jennerton answered on the first ring.

"Hey, Bobby Joe. This here's Luther. Saw a friend'a yours a little while ago."

"Yeah? Who's that?" Bobby Joe's voice was gruff, almost hoarse.

"Why, Mister Cody Rainwalker, just as big as life over to the

Riverside Motel. Done come to town to catch the big, bad killer."

"So? I'm the fucking radio station?"

"Now, I thought you and Cody was good friends," Luther said. "Especially since he gave you that permanent hair-part with a gear-shift handle. I remember right, it came offa logging truck. Course you're probably in no rush to see Cody."

"Yeah? I'll stomp a mud hole in Cody's ass and walk it dry."

"I'll believe it when I see it," Luther said. "Anyways, I hear he's meeting Samantha at the Riverside Cafe tomorrow morning."

"That Justine done made the headlines. Wouldn't surprise me none if ol' Lonnie didn't do her."

Luther smiled into the cell phone. "What makes you say something like that?"

"One time Justine and Lonnie was together, and she'd got hold of some of those anal beads. Justine got to whuffing and hollering and yanked on those beads like she's starting a weed-eater. Lonnie hobbled around for a week before he went to the clinic down in Ooltewah."

* * *

Parked at a pull-off on Cove Road, Scanner rolled Luther and Bobby Joe's telephone conversation over in his mind. The trailer park across the street was dark and silent at this time of night; he stared at the dim outline of mobile homes that filled what once had been a pasture full of Holsteins and fragrant hay. So Cody was in town. The man was unpredictable, and dangerous, if all the county's legends about him were true. He might not be as easily fooled as the local deputies.

He opened the driver's door and stepped out onto the gravel, crunched up the steep rise of Barry's driveway and into the front yard. Deep in thought, kicking at the wet grass, Scanner strolled over to the sweetgum tree on the opposite side of the front yard. The dogs either heard or saw him coming and rose up to sniff his legs, white-tipped tails wagging in the moonlight. The portable he carried in his hand was still tuned to the cellular phone channels. Scanner heard the rattle of a phone ringing, a man's deep voice answering, "Hello?"

"How you doing," a female voice said. She was whispering so low Scanner had to bring the set to his ear.

"Just driving home," the male voice said. "Hasn't been thirty minutes since I saw you."

"I know—but you gave it to me so good I can't get over it," the disembodied voice whispered. Even though the voice was barely audible, Scanner detected excitement there, and yearning.

"Where are you?" the man said.

"I came right home," came the whisper.

"You sure your husband can't hear you?"

"Just a minute—I'll check." There was the quiet thunk of the phone being placed on a hard object. In a moment the whispers returned. "He's watching TV. I told you, didn't I? All he ever does is eat, sleep, watch TV, and fish for bluegill. He ain't ever give it to me good like you just did."

"Lotta law driving around in the county. I don't want to get stopped over there."

"It's the crazy killer," the whisperer said. "Must be some nut-case, some sicko. They got the wrong man in jail."

"You sure about that?" the man asked.

"It's what folks are saying." The voice was a hiss in Scanner's ear. His anger rose.

The whisperer barely paused for a breath. "I bet when they find out who it is, it'll be some pathetic jerk that nobody likes. Some weirdo."

"I'm pulling into my driveway," the bass voice said. "Gotta go." The callers clicked off.

Scanner brought the portable around in front of his face and stared at it like he held a poisonous snake. "You fucking bitch," he said to the radio. "Whispering about me behind my back. I'll find out who you are, and you'll see how pathetic I am. Nobody gets away with whispering behind my back."

He shuddered. Control. He had to bring himself under control. Couldn't be freaking out in Barry's yard. Or anywhere else, for that matter. He began to take deep breaths, gulped the fresh night air.

A minute later he clicked the membrane switch on the portable and listened to chattering intermittent calls to and from sheriff's deputies. He'd set the volume low to keep from waking Barry's children, but he could still make out the voice of the male dispatcher. "Unit six. Disturbance call at the HillTop Tavern. Caller says there's five or six men fighting in the parking lot."

"Ten-four." The deputy's answer was a slow, relaxed drawl.

Scanner's eyes narrowed. The tavern was a magnet for all the troublemakers. The dump needed to be closed up for good. An eyesore like that created a bad image, and in the near future, Highwater Town would need all the good publicity it could get if things were to go right, like he'd planned.

Looking up through the scattered clouds, Scanner watched stars twinkle in the clear mountain air. Which one was he from? Hadn't scientists just discovered that the universe was much larger than they'd expected? This increased his possibilities by several billion. Smiling at the void, he remembered his boyhood fantasies that he was so different from the other kids he had to be from another planet, likely even another galaxy or solar system, dropped off here by alien craft to observe and report on the earthlings. Did growing up with parents that were so antagonistic toward one another, so caught up in their own battles that they ignored their offspring—would that cause such thoughts in a child? Or had he just forgotten where to report? And to whom?

He strolled up the walkway and lowered himself to the bottom porch step, leaned back on the one above it, relaxed there, and thought what a fine house Barry had. All that land he owned and the one-hundred-unit trailer park across the road. Barry was in jail so Scanner would act as Barry's alter ego. Time someone took over his thinking for him. Actually, he'd done Barry a favor, ridding him of his treacherous old lady. Wasn't she the object of a standing joke around town: that a toll-free hotline had been set up for men to call in on that hadn't fucked her yet? She was sort of like that slut he'd just heard on the radio—"give it to me good" bullshit.

Another thing. The time was ripe to hand out other rewards. Really, there were many long overdue.

"Mountain County—unit five," the radio cracked.

"Go ahead," the dispatcher answered.

Five

After a hard night of tossing on the cheap cotton mattress, Cody was up bright and early. He walked down the road to the food mart and bought a large cup of yogurt, a banana, and a peach. On the balcony outside his room he ate breakfast and listened to the rush of the river, one of the best trout streams in the state. Highwater River plummeted out of the mountains to the east of town and dropped over two thousand feet in twenty miles. After its plunge from the mountains, the Highwater River followed the Highwater Valley, winding its way through the rugged, heavily forested mountains of the lower Appalachian chain. They loomed over the town, closed it in, like they closed in the minds of the inhabitants. He'd heard reports that kayakers cluttered the stream at higher elevations, enraging the trout fishermen.

Against the slight chill, Cody wore a dark blue rugby pullover, jeans, and black running shoes. Wearing a suit in Highwater Town would attract unfavorable attention—not that he wouldn't attract enough just being here.

A major aggravation in returning to his hometown was how easy it was to fall into the speech patterns of the mountain people. He'd practiced for years to learn what he considered passable proper English. Ten minutes talking to a good ol' boy, though, and it was all down the tubes.

After checking his watch, Cody dropped his food scraps into a wastebasket and walked over to the Riverside Motel's restaurant like a condemned man walking the last mile. He dreaded enmeshing himself into the tiresome, ongoing feuds and insipid politics of the county. Not that he would bother to get involved; just that it would take him back to memories he'd rather not drag into the here and now. He'd left most of his failures lying around here, and in a churchyard not too far away his mother and brother and grandmother lay buried, departed long before their time. One day that debt would be paid.

As always, after the relative flatness of Nashville and the middle-Tennessee area, he first noticed the mountains, caught himself eyeing the bluffs that ran along the ridges and the misted-over, verdant escarpments that lay before them. They drew his gaze and tugged on his soul like a magnet. It would be days before he took them for granted.

Wolf's Head Mountain, where he'd built his small cabin after returning home from the army, was, at six thousand feet, the highest elevation in the area. The rock bluffs forming the head were jagged Thunderhead sandstone, now glowing a coppery red in the early morning sun. Two huge quartz intrusions formed the wolf's eyes. Young people in the area had taken to calling the formation Castle Rock. He longed to be up there instead of where he was headed.

The Riverside Motel, like the name said, was built along the river. A dirty brown in color, it was constructed of stucco, a one-story, flattened-out U with the office and restaurant in the middle. The two wings had twelve rooms each. Individual entrances were protected from the elements by a flat-roofed porch that followed the lines of the building.

Cody noticed the cruiser parked near the motel's front entrance, with at least twenty cars and pickups keeping it company. Samantha was already there. He'd met her once since she came to work for the department. She sure spruced up the office. A welcome change from all the hairy ankles. 'Course she'd worn her uniform trousers, so her ankles might be just as hairy. . . . Nah. She was a good looker and took care of herself.

Sound battered him when he opened the restaurant door. He smelled old grease. Dishes clattered, men yelled across the room to one another, an oversized TV on a wooden shelf was tuned to a Chattanooga station and blared in competition to the raucous crowd. Then silence—all but the TV. Heads turned his way. He recognized a few; a few reciprocated. A beat of silence, then the racket started again, like he'd suddenly become invisible. A silent chorus of, "Oh. Heard you's in town."

Samantha sat at a table by the window.

Cody weaved through tables, chairs, and sprawled legs that were scattered in no discernible pattern.

Elbows nudged sides. Mouths stopped chewing. Forks paused in midair. Cody sat. The world turned. Fucking place was already driving him nuts.

Darryl Hankins had looked up when Cody came in the front door. He was one of the silent gawkers at the P.I.'s entrance. Hankins's eighteen-year-old son, Gordon, had turned in his chair at the sudden silence.

"Who's that?" Gordon said.

Hankins followed Cody's progress through the crowd, a worried expression on his face. "Cody Rainwalker, sheriff's son." Cody brought to Hankins's mind a book on the American frontier he'd picked up in Chattanooga for his son. One of the old pictures showed a well-built Indian dressed up in city finery. The photographer's flash powder had brought out a fierceness in the man's eyes, gave him a feral appearance. The clothes were only a temporary covering, a disguise to be cast off once the true self was ready to appear, a wild being of the forest or plains.

That was Cody in his dark, long-sleeved pullover. Cody's chest and shoulders were heavy but his face was gaunt, his cheek bones protruded from his face like bumpers under his dark eyes. Hankins had boxed during his stint in the navy and knew the kind of physical conditioning needed for a man Cody's size to have such stark facial features.

Samantha was eating breakfast: two eggs up, country ham, biscuits slathered in butter and honey. "I'll have coffee," Cody told the waitress.

Elton, at his post in the rear near a rack of chips, crackers, and candy, looked even worse than last night. Pretending not to, he had watched Cody enter, then scurried over with the coffee, rattled cup and saucer to the table, poured, backed off two steps and stood, waiting.

Samantha banged her fork down, glaring at the waiting man. "Elton? You waiting on something special?"

Elton fled.

"Wants to hear what we're saying so he can tell ever'body," she said, extending her hand. "Glad you're here."

Cody shook it. It was warm and dry. "Why's that?"

"Barry can use all the help he can get. How's it feel to be home?"

"I could sell tickets."

"Seems like after being in L.A., ever'thing would seem sane."

"After a while—you forget. Barry still in Slam City?"

"Much to his chagrin. Hope you're charging Michelle a bundle. Rich, horny bitch. Saw her tooling around town with some stranger in a Mercedes with Nevada tags a few days ago."

"My expenses'll be low but my rates are high when I drop everything and work outa town," Cody said. "What I'll do is stay at my uncle's after today. Another night around Elton skulking, I'd be in the cell next to Barry."

"He does irritate. If you don't get him, one day Luther or your daddy will." Samantha switched gears. "About these murders. We found both weapons."

"Tell me—why're you rooting for Barry? You convinced my daddy's locked up the wrong man?"

"Got a feeling. I can't see how Barry would've had all that time to take his wife's car over to Coffee County, ninety miles away. And lots of folks knowed Justine was community pussy. That is, maybe ever'body but Barry."

Barry knew about Justine's messing around. Was his client really innocent?

"New deputy, Bubba Whittlemore, goes along on some of Barry's outings. He says Barry's a knowledgeable spelunker, but sort of a risk-taker," Samantha said.

"What does this Bubba think of Barry's guilt or innocence?"

"Thinks Barry's innocent. That's what ever'body expects him to think though. He's Barry's friend."

Cody sipped his coffee, looked into Samantha's gray eyes. She'd hardened since he last saw her. What being a deputy in this county would do for you. "The murder weapons," he prodded.

"Found 'em in Justine's trunk. Car was abandoned halfway up a mountain road on Highway 50 in Coffee County. There'd been a landslide that took one lane of the road after a heavy rain. The county had come in and made the repairs, had this pull-off where they'd dumped a big pile of gravel. Her car was found in the woods behind it, you couldn't see it from the road. Car'd been partially stripped. A bow, not one of them sissy, yuppie, compound bows, all the pulleys and strings. One of those bows looks like a cupid's bow."

"Recurve? Traditional?"

"That's it. Recurve bow and a tiger claw, not a real tiger claw—one'a them Jap things. Belonged to Barry, like the bow belonged to Barry."

The front door crashed open. Bobby Joe Jennerton swaggered into the room wearing his motorcycle class A uniform: heavy scuffed boots, black leather vest with a Harley-Davidson emblem, wide leather bracelets with heavy metal studs, black jeans that stretched tight over huge thighs. He was big and muscular. And he'd heard black was bad.

He glanced in Cody's direction with an exaggerated sneer.

An old jingle from Dave Gardener, the dead southern humorist, popped into Cody's head, "zippers up his sleeves and zippers up his back and a tattoo on his arm saying Mammy You The Most."

He snapped back to the present. "You mean a Nina tiger claw? Those metal claws used to climb trees? Razor sharp, would cut somebody to pieces."

"Justine was a mess, face all ripped up. Sharpless didn't look too good after the weather and the animals. He wasn't all tore up like Justine. We found a pair of boots in Barry's closet. Blood on them's being checked at the state lab, and there's dirt that seems to come from the area where the bodies were found. Bloody boot print found in Sanford's cabin. There's more. You can read about it in Luther's report."

While she spoke, Samantha eyed Bobby Joe. Dumb-ass would have to make his appearance, she thought. Him and his one-man, outlaw motorcycle gang. The sheriff had told her how, when Cody was a high school freshman, two older, larger sophomores had waylaid him. Bobby Joe Jennerton and Kennie Calhoun had chased Cody into a barn. Both older boys had been found later and carried to the hospital. Cody had parted their hair with a gear-shift handle. Now the two men could live with the shame or get even. Kennie had chosen the easier route. Or so it seemed.

"Looks like Barry's got a hard row to hoe," Cody said.

"Forty miles of bad road. Randy Gateline, you remember him, owns the drugstore and now the Stick and String Archery Shop and the new exercise gym. Randy says two days before Justine went missing, Barry bought ten arrows just like the one that killed Sharpless, bright yellow feathers and all. Forensics can't really narrow time of death. We figure they died the night they disappeared. Damning evidence, but Barry'd have to be real dumb to buy arrows right here in a small town. He coulda bought 'em up in Maryville or Newport if he was really trying to hide something."

Cody followed the progress of a tall, rangy, red-haired young man who had entered the restaurant carrying an official-looking clipboard. His eyes were riveted on the rear of the room where Elton kept tabs on the waitresses and patrons. He wore dark green pants and a shirt to match. A round patch on his left shoulder announced he was with the Highwater Electric Cooperative.

Sensitive to body language and adept at reading intentions in facial expressions from his years on the streets, Cody evaluated the man's gaze as determined, like he was on his way to do something he didn't look forward to doing. He passed out of view but Cody could feel him in the room. Instinctively he hitched forward in his chair.

Samantha noticed Cody's movement and glanced back to where the Co-op man was approaching Elton. "Wilbur Dunbar. Works for the electric company. He—"

"Don't come in here fucking with me, Wilbur, goddammit!" Elton yelled from the rear of the room. "I done told you people I paid that electric. Took the canceled checks down to the office and showed 'em to that goddam goofy clerk and she marked 'em off. Now git your lanky ass outa my place of business."

"You got no call cussin' me, Elton," Wilbur said. "Co-op sent me here to cut the electric off. I coulda just pulled your meter you know. Instead, I come in here first to let you know. So I wouldn't be puttin' all these good folks in the dark."

"Pull my meter! Why you sonofabitch. I'll pull your plug for good."

Elton disappeared into the back room.

Samantha's chair scraped. "Time to go to work," she said, heading for Wilbur, who stood in stunned silence deciding whether or not to stand his ground and maybe go down in Co-op immortality.

Elton came out of the back room with a double-barreled shotgun under one arm. He'd broken it open and was fumbling two shells into the breech.

Samantha stepped into his face. "Elton. Put the shotgun down or I'm slapping you into next week."

The little man skidded to a halt so quick he almost fell over backward. He was so angry and afraid, he began drooling; slobber ran off his chin and dribbled on the front of his nasty shirt. He backed up two steps and with slow deliberation, took a shaking thumb and forefinger and pried the shells from the weapon. Using the same caution, he placed the shotgun on the counter. "Now Samantha. You heard Wilbur," he whined. "Man's got a right to protect his place of business."

"That's what I get paid for. Let's see if we can work this out without anybody dying."

Cody tuned the commotion out. Samantha had a handle on the situation. Confident. Probably made a good deputy.

Scanning the room he noticed the show was most likely over. The rumble of conversation gradually resumed its previous level, with a couple of hard quick laughs at Elton's expense.

Five minutes later, Samantha returned to her chair. "Never figured I'd have to side with Elton. He's right though. Had the canceled checks and a receipt. Damn Co-op must have their heads up their ass. We're having a lot of weird problems like that lately, water company cutting folks off, folks' bank accounts getting messed up. Always say it's a computer problem. People using 'em if you ask me. Mountain folks can get mighty upset when you disconnect their utilities or lose their money."

Cody smiled and shook his head. "We were talking about Randy Gateline. You and Randy still engaged?"

A sad look came over Samantha's face. She stared down at the table for a moment; with a forefinger she drew invisible circles on the wooden tabletop. When she brought her gaze back up, her cheeks were flushed. "You're out of touch. We broke up about two months after I joined the department." Her voice was quiet with a meekness not there a few seconds earlier. Her defenses were down, and for the moment she was a small girl again.

Things changed fast, Cody thought. Last he remembered, Randy was a newly graduated pharmacist all but married to Samantha. Randy the over-achiever. "Reckon I'll head over to the jail, talk to my client," Cody said.

"I'll give you a lift. Driving a regular cruiser today, Jeep's in the shop."

They walked out together. From the corner of his eye, Cody saw Bobby Joe get up and follow. A gaggle of men tagged along. So predictable, he thought. He could write Bobby Joe's script.

"We got company," Samantha said without looking around.

"Bet you thought no one cared. I'm gonna have the tour bus park right out front. There on the edge of the gravel where they can get a close look and still give all the yahoos room to maneuver. This'll be the early morning stop.

"Wanta be my partner? Big city folks'll get a rush outa the place. And I figure the Japs'll eat it up. I can hear their cameras clicking now. Hell—won't even have to stage the gunfights. The townsfolk'll be the actors and they'll work for free, just doing what comes naturally."

Samantha kept quiet. She enjoyed the new slant on the characters in town and what to her were everyday occurrences. Experience had taught her that under certain circumstances the best action to take was no action at all, to relax and let the situation flow, not try for control. So she eyed the crowd gathering behind them and, although alert, waited for what she knew was going to happen next.

The sheriff had told her some of Cody's history. Other townsfolk had added episodes. An interesting and eventful morning was in the works. For her part, she'd bet most mornings, and evenings, spent around Cody Rainwalker would be exciting and eventful. Especially eventful. Didn't seem like too

bad of a prospect either. Better than going home alone and reading paperback love stories and pumping iron. She flushed from
the thought of maybe her and Cody arranging some other form
of exercise. Calm down, Horny, she thought to herself. But it had
been way too long.

They walked across the lot to the cruiser. A chalky white dust
puffed around their shoes with each step. A dry east wind blew
the powder under and around the vehicle.

The crowd was quiet. They expected the performance to start
any minute now. Not every morning in Highwater Town could
you see Elton have an apoplectic fit and somebody get their ass
kicked in the parking lot, all within ten minutes.

"Hey! Rainwalker!" Bobby Joe yelled from the restaurant
door.

Cody didn't answer or bother to turn.

Bobby Joe approached the cruiser with long even strides,
heavy boots making a loud crunch on the gravel with each step.

To Cody the big man sounded like he was goose-stepping.

With non-rhythmic crunches, five hangers-on followed.
Those who chose not to come outside gathered in the restaurant's window.

Cody stood six feet, but Bobby Joe topped him by four
inches. Cody weighed 195. Bobby Joe had him by forty-five
pounds.

Bobby Joe walked closer, hovered around Cody like a chopper looking to land.

Samantha took two steps forward, leaned over to reach
through the open window of the cruiser, picked the mike from its
hook on the dash and brought it near her mouth. "Mountain
County S.O., this is unit six."

"Go ahead, unit six," said Sheriff Rainwalker.

The man was psychic, Samantha thought. Always on the spot
when trouble's going down. Or did he always expect trouble
when his son was in town?

"Sheriff—Bobby Joe Jennerton's here at the Riverside, gonna
start a fight with Cody."

The sheriff's voice was slow and easy, deep and drawling.
"That's ten-four, unit six. I'll get Bobby Joe a ten-forty-seven

headed that way," he said, using the ten-code for an ambulance. "'Bout time too. Bobby Joe's been a pain in the ass ever since he started lifting those weights."

"Ten-four, Sheriff."

"Unit six, let me talk to Bobby Joe."

Samantha waved the big man over and handed him the mike.

"You wanna talk to me, Sheriff?" Bobby Joe asked.

"Bobby Joe. You got any hospitalization insurance?"

"No suh."

"Didn't think so. You think the county's got unlimited resources, can pay to put your ass back together, like you're some kinda idiot Humpty Dumpty?"

"Now, Sheriff, I been working out at Gateline's Gym. You don't worry 'bout me none."

"You hear me, Cody?" the sheriff called out.

Samantha grabbed the mike back. "He's nodding yes, Sheriff."

"Don't go breaking any of his bones, son. You do and he'll have to be hauled up to Maryville or down to Chattanooga to get patched up. And for God's sake, don't kill him. There'll be paperwork like you wouldn't believe."

"He's nodding again, Sheriff," Samantha said. She pitched the mike onto the front seat. Everyone but Cody turned to watch her walk to the rear of the cruiser and open the trunk. Hauling out a heavy-duty, industrial-sized first-aid kit, she toted it around and laid it on the hood. "You can get on with your shit now, Bobby Joe."

The consequences of his actions were closing in on Bobby Joe. But he'd brought his own audience. "Cody's bad with a knife," Bobby Joe said. "You gonna pull a knife?"

Cody shook his head. He didn't want to be here; he needed to get it over with and get on to the jail.

Bobby Joe was broad at the shoulders; his upper arms demonstrated the results of many barbell curls. An over-developed trapezius sloped up to a size-eighteen neck. His head was big, square, and blond. Pale blue Germanic eyes reflected indifference instead of the insuperable ignorance that lay behind them. "I'm gonna whup your ass," he told Cody.

"Bobby Joe, believe it or not, in the real world, grown men do not fight like children in restaurant parking lots," Cody said as he turned to get in the cruiser.

Bobby Joe struck as soon as Cody's back was turned. He took a long stride forward and swung at Cody's head.

Cody raised his shoulder in time to take most of the impact with his deltoid muscle but Bobby Joe's fist still had enough force to knock him against the cruiser. Cody tried to turn but Bobby Joe moved in and slammed him in the middle of the back with both hands.

Cody pushed away from the car and pivoted to face the bigger man. Bobby Joe threw a roundhouse right. Cody blocked it with his forearm, used the same hand to pop his assailant across the bridge of his nose.

Bobby Joe backed up a step as Cody advanced, punching the big man in the sternum with the flat of his hand, throwing him off balance, then striking three times with alternating fists to the larynx, sternum, and bridge of the nose. Blood splattered the gravel as the big man froze, unconscious on his feet, then crashed to the ground.

Samantha had heard of Cody's fast moves from his father and knew Bobby Joe was hurt. How badly was the big question. She reached for the mike. "Sheriff, better hurry that forty-seven."

"Ten-four, unit six."

A siren sounded in the distance. After a moment, another one joined it.

The ambulance arrived a minute later. Fishtailing in the loose gravel, Luther tail-gated it to a halt and jumped out of his cruiser. "Aw, damn," he said, looking down at the big man writhing in the dirt, holding his throat and gasping for breath. "I done missed the show." Leaning over the prostrate figure, he said in a raspy voice, "Bobby Joe, a man can really count on you. You fight like old people fuck."

Six

"Your daddy says you know martial arts," Samantha said to Cody after they got into the cruiser and pulled away from the crowd. "Thought you'd give Bobby Joe one of them fancy kicks. He's got two or three coming."

"Not unless he'd pulled a gun or a knife. Start kicking a man around these parts and the crowd turns on you, says you're not fighting fair. That's the reason I turned my back on Bobby Joe. When he hit me from behind he put the crowd on my side. When I hurt him they say he got what he deserved. Mob psychology."

The sheriff's office was a quarter mile from the motel, a squat, brick, single-story structure built in the early 1800s. Its road frontage was narrow, the building ran longways back from the road. Two tall antennas with slanting guy wires adorned the front of its flat roof, one for the Sheriff's Net, the other a link to the Tennessee Highway Patrol. "Mountain County Sheriff's Office and County Jail," announced a hand-painted, weather-worn wooden sign nailed over the front entrance.

Across from the S.O., and separated from the main drag by a narrow brick sidewalk, stood a row of one-story brick buildings housing Highwater Town Hose and Gasket, Madden's Jewelry, MacDonald's Upholstery Shop, and Cherokee Mountain Auto and Truck Parts. American flags left over from Labor Day flew from each storefront. Traffic was light but steady.

Down the road on the same side as the S.O., a grouping of buildings held the Mountain County Savings and Loan, the Cove Road Cafe & Ice Cream Parlor, and Lucifer's Liquor Store. Straight back from the jail stood the promontory of Wolf's Head Mountain.

Samantha parked the cruiser between its twin and the sheriff's vehicle, a big, black Dodge Ram utility wagon with oversized tires and emergency lights on the roof. She and Cody entered the small lobby, dim after the brightness of the early morning sun. A black vinyl couch and two tattered matching chairs backed up against off-white walls. A plain wooden table held a scramble of ragged hunting, fishing, and gun magazines. In the corner a soft drink machine kept a candy and chips machine company. On a high shelf in the dispatcher's area, a closed-circuit TV flashed from one jailhouse scene to the other, showing a cell block then a hallway lined with steel bars, then the outside of the rear door, repeating the sequence. A sign was posted on the wall with a single nail; hand-written on cardboard with a black marker, it read: "Attention prisoners, this is a jail not a fast food restaurant. we'll have it our way."

"Hi Cody, Samantha," called the dispatcher from her perch on a high stool. A sliding-glass window opened over a counter-like desk, where the woman sat shuffling papers from one stack to another.

"Hi yourself, Wanda June," Cody said. Wanda June looked cute and perky. He remembered her ebullient personality. Bright red hair, tight sweater and jeans, great figure, in her early twenties. He walked closer and saw the gold wedding band twinkle on her finger.

She smiled back, arched one brow and gave him a sexy, low-lidded, direct look in appreciation of his obvious appraisal. "Your daddy's in his office, wants to see you." She buzzed him in through the security door.

"You sure do liven up the county," Sheriff Rainwalker said a minute later. "We can go for a year or two around here without a broad-open-daylight fistfight. Your first morning in town breaks that chain." He leaned back in his chair behind a tan, wood desk in the small windowless room; a dark, dusky man, he was not quite as stocky as his son, but almost. His waist had widened some in the last few years. His eyes and hair were dark brown, his features stern, his brows heavy, bushy, flecked with gray. The overall effect was one of sadness, a man who had seen too much, more than enough for one lifetime. On a high shelf above his head, a twin of the closed-circuit TV monitor in the lobby displayed the same jailhouse panorama.

"Just heard on the radio," the sheriff continued, "paramedics thought they's gonna have to give Bobby Joe a emergency tracheotomy. About midnight—fifteen, twenty minutes after you hit town—Elton shows at the E.R. Blood pressure's 3,000 over 450, and he's pegging the needles on the cardiograph machine. Wanted a CAT-scan only the hospital don't have one. E.R. doctor had to give him nitro pills and tranquilizers."

"Didn't want to rent me a room," Cody interjected.

"He's been highly pissed since I threatened to close him for a number of offenses, several involving some of our more adventurous teenage girls. On a scale of one to ten, he's a fifteen on the lowlife scale, leaves a trail of slime when he walks. So how you been, son?"

"Fair to middling. Things here started up right where they left off." Cody had sworn an oath prior to leaving Nashville; he'd at least be civil to his father. He couldn't be a son any longer. The shaking out of events in his youth had seen to that.

"They's never a dull moment when you come to town."

"Ever'where else I go, things are peaceful and quiet."

"Maybe you oughta start acting the same way here you do ever'where's else."

Cody decided to change the conversation from personal to business. "Justine's car been brought in yet?"

"Platform wrecker's picking it up from the Coffee County S.O. Course, we went over and dusted it, photographed it, vacuumed it, checked it real close, you know the drill. Tires and wheels were missing, so were a lot of the engine parts. Somebody had it up on cinder blocks and had ripped out the transmission and rear-end. Stereo was gone, of course, and the rear and side-door speakers. Justine supposedly had a cellular phone. It hasn't been found but there's been no calls made on it so as we can tell."

"Keys left in the car?"

"Under the front seat, passenger side. Key chain with house and car keys. Purse was in the trunk, not much left in it—lipstick, tissues, there's an inventory in the report. You can read it now or later. Windows were all rolled down on the car, white Toyota Camry, what's left of it. We found dried blood on the outside of the driver's door. None inside."

Grabbing a chair, Cody spun it and straddled the wooden seat, propped both elbows on the high back. "Any leads on the bodies, clues, anything to go on?"

"State handles the forensics, we sent the bodies up to Nashville. They got a full plate, always running way behind. On a prelim, the medical examiner believes both victims were killed on their feet. The wounds on Justine's face, would've been awkward for someone to cut her like that while she was lying down. Angle of entry in Sanford Sharpless, a slight downward trajectory. Whoever shot the arrow into him was a mite taller or standing higher. Seventy-five-pound pull on the bow rules out all the county's little ol' ladies."

Cody wished for a window; then he could get up, look out, and think. He felt claustrophobic in the tiny room. "Were they killed where they were found?"

The sheriff nodded his head, then he paused, looked up at the ceiling before answering, considering what to say. "Luther says they were caught there screwing on the ground, made to stand up, killed on the spot. I don't know whether he's got it nailed down that tight or not. More like a intellectual leap using a vaulting pole if you ask me. Sometimes the M.E. can tell if the body's been moved by the settling of blood in the extremities. Pooling they call it, or lividity. The condition of these bodies prevented that sort of determination. Their clothes haven't been found. Justine's or Sanford's. Not a thread."

Does Daddy put any faith in Luther's investigative skills? Cody wondered. "Of course the ground was gone over good where you found them. Find anything there?"

"Just old blood. We figure they'd been lying there almost a week, counting from the time Justine was reported missing. Coon hunting set who found 'em strode around for a while before they reported it. Don't think they'd pick up anything, put it in their pockets. They'd know their ass is grass and I'm a wide-cut ride mower."

"I'll want their names. Gotta talk to all of them or Michelle won't think she's getting her money's worth. What do you think? Did Barry kill his wife and his lawyer?"

The sheriff laughed. "Using interrogation techniques against your daddy, switching the subject like that. Oughta be ashamed. No. I don't think Barry did it. But I might be wrong. Too bad about them two. Sometimes, fact most times, folks create their own problems. Justine was at home like she shoulda been, she'd be alive today, so would Sharpless.

"His wife left him two years ago, couldn't stand his ways. He moved into a mobile home until somebody put a rifle bullet through it late one night. Him being a lawyer, there's plenty folks with a good motive to kill him."

"You're blaming the victim? I thought the defense attorney would use that strategy," Cody said.

"Ever'body don't blame somebody else. Had a fella in here one night. From Florida I think he was, picked him up drunk, driving a stolen truck, pulling a stolen horse trailer, hauling two stolen horses, stolen gas credit cards in his billfold, you talk about the saying of being in a heap a trouble.

"Well this fella, he didn't blame the law, or the way his mama brought him up, or society. Said if anybody else had done to him what he'd done to himself, he'd kill 'em. You could use the same philosophy with Bobby Joe, him being his own worst enemy. Is that feud ended?"

Cody gave his head a negative shake. "Bobby Joe's gonna bring it along to where he's gonna make me kill him. He'll put me in a place where I'll have no other choice."

Sheriff Rainwalker remained silent for a long time. When he finally spoke, his voice was serious. "Don't let any Mountain County folks hear you say that. They's still talk around how old man Coleman happened to set himself on fire in his own house after he got on your teenage shit-list."

Cody felt his anger rising, refused to be baited. "You know I was in the army when that happened. Now, can I see the prisoner? My client, the accused, whatever. So I can hurry all this up, take the next rocket-ship back to earth."

His dad stood up, stepped to his office door, opened it, and gestured with his palm up. "You know the way. Oh, and Jolinda's been calling here ever' fifteen minutes, wants to know when you'll be home."

Cody nodded understanding and passed through the security room where deputies deposited their weapons prior to entering the lockup area with a prisoner. A concrete-block wall had been constructed inside the room and imbedded with pigeon holes. These were covered with heavy metal doors where weapons could be locked out of the eager grasp of a wannabe jail-breaker. Off to one side in the booking room, a young deputy was inking a roller, preparing to take prints from a bedraggled male prisoner.

Barry lounged in the "day room," the area deputies used for a break area. Drinking a soda, eating a pack of peanut-butter crackers, he watched a soap on the color TV mounted high on the wall with heavy metal brackets. Ten years older than Cody, five-ten, powerfully built with heavy shoulders and chest, Barry kept in shape for his rescue work with the fire department. He had straight brown hair, a plain, flat face, and sad brown eyes.

"What. They can't keep you in a cell?" Cody said.

"No TV in there. Over at the fire hall I've always got the TV going. Your daddy knows I'm not going anywhere, gonna be bailed out this afternoon I hope, if Monk O'Malley pulls it off. They got the drunks and serious offenders in the back cells."

Cody took a chair next to the prisoner. "Guess your sister told you she's hired me."

"I didn't do it, Cody. I was coming back from Marion County, over above Whitwell. You may remember I'm a spelunker. Figure I was crawling around in a cave when somebody killed my wife, got five witnesses."

"Then how come you're here?"

"'Cause the law can't say for sure when she was killed. Luther would have folks believe I coulda done it a lotta different ways. Truth is, I got home around twelve-thirty, twelve forty-five in the morning, it was starting to thunder and lightning—it rained later on, real bad storm. I found she wasn't there. She's usually always home that time of night at least; my kids were worried sick. We waited around for a hour and a half or so, then called the sheriff's office. Luther says I could've followed them out to the woods, killed 'em, moved the bodies, drove the car over to

Coffee County and hitched back or had somebody help me, like drive me back home. Hell, that'd be impossible. Besides—I didn't do it. If he'd asked the right questions, I wouldn't be here."

Cody allowed the possibility of his client's guilt to crawl through the backwoods of his mind. Could Barry have done it yet another way? Say killed them and hid the car and the bodies, then later placed the bodies out in the open and driven the car over to Coffee County on a different night altogether. What other possibilities were there? "Did you have a suspicion your wife was messing around with your lawyer?"

"She was going to that crazy church where he went. And she'd been acting funny, plus she was always complaining when I went outa town. I'd go over to Savage Gulf, rappelling down the bluffs, practicing for the county rescue squad. You know how many cars we get in winter running offa roads and down into ravines? Drunks'r doing it year round, rolling their pickups, shotguns and dogs flying ever'where. She didn't want me doing nothing." Barry stood up, walked over to a wastebasket, and dropped his soda can in it. "That bow the deputies recovered, Osage orange wood—hand-made—cost me over a thousand dollars new. No way I'd leave it anywhere."

If Barry wasn't telling the truth, he was putting on a good show. For some reason, though, he'd dodged the question. "Tell me more about this church. Weird you say. In what way?"

"It's more like a cult than a church. Like no religion I ever heard of. She gave in and joined the Episcopal church when we got married. Then about a year ago she started complaining that folks at church were stuck up and all they cared about was how big their house was and how they dressed and how much money they had and who's family arrived in the area first. And she said she didn't like having to drive all the way to Monroe County ever' Sunday."

"What's this church called?"

"The Mountain Church of Jesus. Sonny Todd, he's around fifty-five, I guess, got this great-looking young gal living with him out there in the woods in a double-wide. He's been outa the county for years. Last I heard, he was working down at Sequoyah

65

Nuclear Plant. Some kind of electronics job, designing controls or something. He gets riffed on the job—big layoff they're having—goes down to Kennedy Space Center for a while and a repeat of the reduction in force.

"Then he shows up here and a month later buys an old run-down house up on the mountain and starts his own church. Guess he couldn't find a real job. When he preaches he wears this white robe and carries a big shepherd's crook. Crook. That's what he is. Reverend Todd, Justine called him. He's no more a reverend than I am."

Two men began yelling obscenities at one another in the cell block. Cody waited while a jailor restored calm. "This Todd. He have a big turnout?"

"That's the crazy part. Place's packed to the walls. Pickups parked all in the woods and along the road where you can't get by. Drive by and there's all this singing and hollering like ever'-body's having the time of their life. They got pianos and guitars and fiddles and banjos and I hear they get up and buck dance in the aisle if the spirit moves 'em, which it does mighty often. I think what really moves 'em is the grass they're smoking."

"Sounds a lot different from when I went to church," Cody said, remembering his austere Catholic upbringing. "What I'll do is prowl around some, read the investigator's report, go out and take a look at the eavesdropping devices they found, make a gen-uine nuisance of myself around town. Maybe I'll piss somebody off bad enough, they'll confess. Also I'll talk to Monk, see what I can come up with."

"Another thing, Cody. If I was gonna pick a time to kill my wife, it sure as hell wouldn't be now. I'm involved in an impor-tant business deal, and I need every minute."

"What kind of business?"

"Very hush-hush. Got nothing to do with what happened to Justine."

"So what," Cody said. "You think you can tell a jury you were just too damn busy to kill your wife?"

"You know what I mean. My mind was just on other things. And anyhow, that woman was getting fatter and uglier every year. Maybe that's why she was out there, she felt so bad about herself, the way she looked. She'd sit and read these diet books, all these no-fat fad diets, and at the same time, she'd be stuffing food in her face.

"The week she was missing, I wondered where she was, and the kids were just out of it the whole time. Me—I was glad she was gone. I hoped she'd run off with Sharpless and they wouldn't ever come back. I didn't love her anymore, didn't even like her. She was always whining about one thing or other. It was too hot or it was too cold or the goddam house looked like a funeral home. Hell, my ancestors built that house.

"Still I treated her good. Ever' once in a while I'd make these oink sounds to make her stop eating. Didn't work."

"Did Sharpless know about this hush-hush business?"

"He had to know some, not everything. He was going to handle closings if I bought some properties. But all this has nothing to do with any murders. Some crazy killed my wife and my lawyer."

"Hopefully I'll prove that. You write down the names of all your witnesses, and where they live. I'll ask the right questions."

Seven

The sheriff was waiting in the jailhouse lobby with two men when Cody came out. "This here's Albert Feltus and Johnny Knight. They're the investigators that've been helping Luther. Along with the rest of the deputies, of course, but their job descrips are 'investigator.' Neither is state-certified homicide yet, but they know what questions to ask. Albert moved here from Knoxville P.D. and Johnny is from down Polk County."

Cody shook hands with the two men as he sized them up. Both were in plainclothes. Feltus, the bigger of the two, wore a brown leather jacket, a white shirt, a blue and red tie, and shiny black shoes. He was beefy and red-faced. His posture was erect like he stood at attention; Cody guessed at a military background. The way he pushed his face forward and shot his hand out, made the detective stamp him as aggressive.

"Good to meet you," Feltus said.

Knight was thinner and sleepy-looking, with serious gray eyes. He wore a tweed coat, a blue shirt with no tie that exposed a sun-browned neck, and scruffy shoes. His Adam's apple bobbed when he talked. His hand was hard and horny with calluses. He didn't say anything, just nodded his head.

"Way we'll work it," the sheriff said, "you need any info or wanta pass something along, you come to me."

"That'll work," Cody said.

"What do you think?" asked Samantha. She had waited outside in her cruiser.

"Too early to tell," Cody said, getting in the front seat beside her, cramping his knees to avoid all the electronic equipment installed below the dash. To see Samantha, he had to look over

68

the big Kustom HR12 radar gun mounted in the middle of the vehicle. "Would you take me to Sanford Sharpless's cabin?"

"You want to go there first? Not to Barry's?"

"Barry'll be home by the time we get back if Monk's sober enough to spring him. He can show me around, see if anything's been taken, being he's saying somebody's been walking around in his boots."

"I saw Albert and Johnny on their way into the S.O.," Samantha said. "You meet them?"

"Yeah. Daddy says they're helping Luther with the investigation."

Samantha backed the cruiser out and headed in a direction opposite from the Riverside Motel. "They work pretty good together. Albert's a little overbearing at times. Before all the excitement they were working a rash of daytime burglaries. Of course this case gets top priority."

Cody watched the buildings go by. Town looked the same. Wasn't like Nashville where the city was constantly being rebuilt. "Barry was telling me about this church his wife belonged to," Cody said. "Mountain Church of Jesus, he called it. You know anything about it?"

"I go to church there myself," Samantha said, looking over at him with a wide grin on her face. "Bet Barry had some nice things to say about it, him being an Episcopalian. To hear him tell it, the place oughta be fire-bombed."

"He mentioned a Sonny Todd. Said he was something of a cult leader."

"Sonny is a great old teddy bear. He loves these mountains and the people. He was a Baptist minister years ago, went to seminary in Nashville, I think. Then he sorta lost his faith and went back to school and wound up working with computers. It's a long story but he finally came back home. Brandy's his girlfriend and he makes no secret they're living together."

Sounded like swingers, Cody thought. "What's Brandy like?"

"Outspoken and beautiful. She intimidates most of the mountain women at first. After they see where her heart's at, they come around."

Now he'd heard from the opposite end of the spectrum.

Cody decided to pay the church a visit and make up his own mind.

The cabin Cody and Samamtha approached stood in a clearing protected on three sides by ancient hemlocks and oaks. The logs appeared new, without that aged, gray, weather-seasoned look. Fifty yards back the land was open, then took a sharp slope upward to a distant stand of towering tulip trees. The front porch ran the full width of the dwelling and was supported by six knotty cedar posts. A single upstairs window looked out over the wood shingle porch roof.

Even at midday, the air was cool. Cody luxuriated in the moistness of it, allowed it to revitalize his skin. "How high are we?"

"I guess thirty-five hundred feet," Samantha said. "Trees should be turning soon; sycamore and cottonwood leaves are ready to drop. Higher up, you can tell fall's on the way— dogwoods and maples are tingeing red, acorns are all over the ground. Deer and wild hog bow seasons open this month; squirrel season too."

"Little cool for a man and a woman to be running around in the woods at night buck-ass naked, wouldn't you say?" Cody asked as Samantha lifted the crime-scene tape, unlocked the front door and held it open for him.

"Even in the throes of passion?" she said as she followed him inside.

"Where'd you all find the transmitter?" Cody took a quick look around the living room. A narrow flight of stairs ran along one wall, led up to a loft that overlooked the living room and stone fireplace. A small dining area sat under the loft. A door led from there to a mini-kitchen and a bathroom off to one side. He could see the tulip trees through the back window.

"I asked Luther to leave it in place. He wasn't happy, but the sheriff ordered it."

"Who found it?"

"Here. Let me show you." Samantha walked to a square wooden telephone table at the foot of the stairs, pulled it away from the wall, then kneeled on the floor behind it. "I shined my flashlight around, looking for anything, saw this little square thingamajig by the phone jack. It was hidden by the table leg until I moved it and got down on my hands and knees."

Cody took the light from Samantha, bent down close to her. Their legs touched in the confined space behind the table. He felt her heat through the double layer of material.

"In-line phone tap," he said. "No batteries. Gets power from the phone line. This one has a condenser mike piggybacked so it'll pick up conversations in the cabin when the phone's on the hook. Mike has a built-in FET pre-amp, so it'd pick up a whisper from anywhere in the house. Low-powered, though; whoever's listening couldn't be more'n two hundred yards away. Strictly amateur."

Samantha stood, gave him a curious look. "Amateur?"

"Yeah. Unless there's a room mike upstairs in the loft or bedroom, the higher up the better, or a radio-type relay. What a knowledgeable snoop would do is put a receiver somewhere near, have it feed a more powerful transmitter to rebroadcast what's being picked up in the cabin. Putting the bug near the floor limits the range unless you do that. The bug itself is mail order, cost maybe sixty, seventy dollars; I could build one like it for fifteen or twenty, buy parts at Radio Shack.

"If I'd planted it, I'd put it inside the wall. Then it'd take a debugging crew to find it. From the antenna length I'd say it's in the VHF band, right below the FM broadcast band. Crystal-controlled so there's no frequency drift."

Arching her eyebrows in respect, Samantha said, "You can tell all that by looking?"

Cody nodded. "With my gear, I can nail the frequency. Should be a manufacturer's name on it somewhere, maybe we can find out who ordered the damn thing."

"I wrote down the name, it's back at the S.O. in my notes. And it looks the same as the one I found at Barry's."

Now Cody returned the look of respect. "Maybe whoever bought them got a volume discount, we'll find 'em all over the county. But you found it? Not Luther? Luther being the county investigator, a three striper bucking for chief deputy. Ain't he being mighty lackadaisical letting a relative rookie find all the evidence?"

"He didn't like it one bit."

Cody noted her change of expression and mood. "You and Luther not getting along?"

"Nothing I can't handle."

He decided he'd take a long, slow look at Luther, see if he had anything to gain if the victims were dead. "Leave the bug; I'll come back, wander around, see if I can find where the listening post was. Whoever was listening wouldn't park along the road. That'd be too obvious."

Cody prowled the downstairs of the cabin, then upstairs, checked drawers and closets, under beds, chairs and couches, in the refrigerator, under the microwave, inside the washer and dryer, came up with zilch. Back in the living room he walked to the fireplace and lifted the shotgun from the deer-antler hooks, broke it open and sighted down both barrels, ran a finger inside, then sniffed for powder residue.

"It was loaded, number three shot," Samantha said, walking up to stand beside him. "I put the shells in the desk drawer."

"Sanford must've felt safe or he would have had the gun with him. When you checked it, was the safety on or off?"

"Now I'm angry at myself. I can't remember."

"Find anything else important?"

"You'll find it on the inventory page in the case file. Found empty Fleet enema bottles by the couch over there and full ones upstairs in a closet. K-Y Jelly and various sizes of dildos and a seven-horsepower vibrator—fired it up and it sounded like a chain saw. Place was well stocked with all the latest in sexual paraphernalia."

"Condoms?"

"Colors of the rainbow and some glow-in-the-dark novelties; one had a rubber kangaroo on it. Here lately this lady from Cookeville has been having these weird parties. They are women only and supposedly they're to sell lingerie. After the party progresses some she digs in her suitcase and starts coming out with all sorts of sexual toys. Could be where all of these got bought. Techs took all sorts of fingerprints; it'll take forever to sort them all out. Lotta folks in town may be nervous if they ever visited here for a night of ecstasy."

Samantha's radio interrupted with a squawk. Barry had been released on bond. He'd wait for them at his house.

Barry's house sprawled on a low hill. The front yard overlooked a trailer park packed to the edges with an assortment of double-wides, single-wides, and a few camper trailers. Television antennas sprouted like river cane, some yards grew satellite dishes.

To the rear of the house, a stand of burley tobacco stubble was all that was left of the year's crop. A twenty-acre hillside field of corn had also been harvested. Brown, bone-dry stalks stood silhouetted against the blue sky. Hovering over the scene, a high mountain ridge with white limestone bluffs sheltered the farm's western edge.

"Cozy Living Trailer Park," announced the sign a few hundred feet before the turn-in to Barry's driveway. "When'd all this happen?" Cody said.

Samantha aimed the cruiser into the bare-dirt drive, guided it up the rock-strewn hill. A metal sign by the drive informed them the house was on the Historic Register and had been built in 1814. "Trailer park? Vinyl siding plant opened last year. Barry and his sister owned this empty land, pastured cattle here, then built a trailer park and are making another fortune."

Beyond the fields, a twisting, rutted dirt road meandered through stands of hickory and oak, then led to two well-maintained tenement houses. Each was surrounded by a white picket fence topped by two strands of barbed wire.

From their shady spot under a sweet gum, two lazy black-and-tan hounds hauled themselves up with what appeared to be great effort and dutifully bayed at the approaching cruiser, wagging their metronomic tails in a rapid tick-tock and wailing at the sky.

The house had been built in the federal style, with a three-bay facade and a central passage running from front door to back. High chimneys stood on each side of the house above the roof like matched bookends. One for the kitchen, one for the living and sleeping area, had been the thinking in pioneer times. The brick work was a Flemish bond and had weathered well for the one hundred eighty years since it was laid.

The driveway changed from dirt and rock to an out-of-place aggregate. It made a wide circle past a parking area big enough for four or five cars. Samantha stopped in front of the sidewalk that led to a high front porch.

A well-built young man in his mid-twenties wearing a deputy's uniform walked toward where the hounds stood under the tree. The dogs bounded to meet him halfway. The man scratched each of them behind the ears.

"That's Bubba Whittlemore," Samantha said.

Barry walked out to greet them, hands in his pockets, wearing a green suede jacket and tan cord pants. "We can talk out in the fresh air. I been inside long enough," he said to Cody. "Howdy, Samantha. Good to see you when you ain't hauling me to jail. We can sit here on the front porch, if you like."

Samantha and Cody each took a wicker chair. Cody, facing the trailer park, wondered if Barry liked to sit up here evenings and look down on the commoners and watch his money grow. Deputy Whittlemore stayed in the front yard, gave them the privacy they needed to talk.

"Thought of anything else you'd like to tell me?" Cody asked Barry. What Cody wanted really—why he was here in the first place—was to get a look at the bug. That and to read Barry's facial expressions and observe his actions when not locked away in jail. Funny how being in jail could cause the most innocent man to look guilty.

"Just remembered here lately we were getting a lot of hang-up telephone calls. Don't know if that means anything or not." Barry's hangdog look screamed out he'd been wronged.

"Find anything else missing?"

"Looks like somebody's been rummaging in my hunting stuff but that could've been the law. Way I'd know if anything's missing would be to some day go look for something particular and it not be there. That tiger claw was one of a pair; its mate is gone."

Cody looked Barry in the eyes. "You know anything about electronics or telephones?"

"Know how to turn a radio on and off and talk on a phone. You talking about the bugs they found?"

"Way a prosecutor would handle it would be to convince the jury you've been listening to your wife and her lover on the phone making plans and whispering all these endearments. You followed them around and when you found the right opportunity—the arrow and the claw. What we need is to find out who bought the transmitters in the first place. Shouldn't be too hard to do; companies like that probably don't get a lot of business from Mountain County."

"What then?"

"You know anyone dislikes you enough to frame you for murder? Or anyone who'd want to kill your wife?" Cody said.

"I've racked my brain, can't think of a soul. Of course Sanford was a lawyer. Lotta people out there with a grudge against him. She coulda been killed for being in the wrong place at the wrong time."

"The mutilation of her body means to me the murder was premeditated and that she was one of the targets. It's interesting that she was maimed and the lawyer wasn't. If you're telling the truth, which I believe you are, you need to know there's somebody means you some serious harm."

The interior of the house had the original flooring, which had been bleached and rubbed to a high luster. Cody squatted and examined the miniature transmitter. Like its twin, the bug had been placed near the baseboard, this time behind a long sofa. He managed to get a name from the inch-square circuit board: DREKO.

With a short, pocket-sized screwdriver he disconnected the bug, held it by its wire antenna, being careful not to touch the body of the instrument. Samantha held out an evidence bag and he dropped it in. Then he moved the couch back against the wall and looked around the room. It had been converted into an office with a large oak desk, a black leather chair on rollers, and a computer stand with a desktop computer and laser printer. "You use the computer?" he asked Barry.

"Had to learn, keeping track of business and the farm and taxes. Don't know how I lived without it, that and my fax machine. My daughter taught me how to use the computer."

Samantha and Cody were on their way out when they heard

the transmission from the sheriff's office on her hand-held, "Four-twenty-seven, you wanta run by the Sack 'n' Tote Market? Lonnie Calhoun called, says there's a buncha kids over there throwing firecrackers on his porch."

"'At's ten-four, Wanda June."

"You got a police radio?" Cody said.

"Got a hand-held. And a mobile in the pickup. Fire calls come in to the sheriff's office and the dispatcher pages. I monitor the radio all the time—it's a habit."

Cody watched Barry in the rear-view mirror as Samantha guided the cruiser down the rough driveway. Barry walked over to Bubba Whittlemore, placed a hand on the younger man's shoulder. Together the two men turned and headed toward the dirt road behind the house. The three hounds scouted out front, their noses close to the ground, coursing for rabbits.

Eight

After Samantha dropped him at the motel, Cody drove his pickup back up the mountain road to Sharpless's cabin. Alone, he could better diagnose the listening device. He also wanted to prowl around on his own, far from the provoking proximity of Samantha's warm flesh crouching next to him.

In the cabin, after determining the frequency of the bug by using a spectrum analyzer and a frequency counter, he brought out his favorite instruments for locating other eavesdropping devices: an old fashioned wind-up clock and a detuned FM portable.

He wound the clock, then placed it near the bug. He would use its ticking as a constant sound source. He tuned the radio to 80 megahertz, the frequency of the bug. Keeping the volume low to prevent feedback, he brought the small speaker to his ear and listened for the ticking. It came in loud and clear. Now he would perform the distance test.

Outside, he turned up the volume and headed away from the house. He made his way down to the road then up the hill until he lost the sound. After coming back within range, he began a wide circle of the cabin.

He'd almost gone full circle when he discovered the listening post, a spot in the trees where the vegetation had been trampled, fern fronds bent, a thin rhododendron limb twisted, almost broken. He could make out a faint impression of where someone had hidden to hear the conversations in the cabin. He moved around the spot with care, looked for a discarded cigarette butt, a candy wrapper, anything. It took a lot of patience to hang around and listen for something that might never happen.

After a five-minute search, he gave up. Whoever the eavesdropper was, he'd either cleaned up after himself or had been careful not to leave anything behind.

He'd turned to start through the trees toward the cabin when he heard the police radio. "Mountain County, this is seven-twenty-nine. Put me ten-eight at the S.O." The voice was apparently that of a male deputy.

"Ten-four, seven-twenty-nine, you're ten-eight," the dispatcher answered.

The sound came from above him. He hadn't realized there was a road up there.

Reversing directions, he moved through the trees toward the steep incline. There was no more radio traffic. Just the stillness of the forest, a wind high in the hemlocks, blue jays squabbling in a distant hollow. He stopped to listen.

Nothing moved but nature.

After waiting another minute, he reached the incline and quietly began his climb. Every couple of minutes, he would stop and listen. When he got higher he smelled cigarette smoke. In the woods you could smell a smoker for a mile.

Making sure he stepped on the soft carpet of hemlock needles, he made a quiet, cautious circle, facing away from the wind. Then he climbed, wanting to come out above whoever was there.

Clambering over a rocky outcropping, he peered down and spotted a man in a deputy's uniform. Undergrowth partially blocked his view, so Cody waited, knowing most people were unable to remain still for any length of time. He was rewarded when the man finally moved into the open, took a lethal-looking drag on his cigarette, and instantly broke into a fit of coughing and gagging.

"You okay, Luther?" Cody said after the hacking spell passed.

Startled, the deputy whirled. Recognition crossed his face. "Your daddy says you move real quiet in the woods."

"Indian blood," Cody said. "Coulda scalped you while you were taking a smoke break. You got the cabin staked out? Didn't see your car."

"Pulled it down a fire trail and walked up. Wondered just who'd come sneaking around." Luther Hamby was tall, slightly hunch-backed, narrow through the shoulders. His stomach protruded over his holster belt and betraying hand-held. He was bald down the middle of his head. The narrow fringe of hair left on either side was going from black to gray. The skin exposed to the elements was weathered nut brown. A yellowish brown stain marked two fingers of his left hand and all his teeth.

Cody thought the man was covering up, and wondered why. The cabin wasn't visible through the trees and heavy undergrowth. "Anybody besides me come around?"

"Not a soul. Wild-goose chase. Wanta walk down?" Luther said.

"After you."

Cody climbed down from his rock and let Luther lead the way back down the incline. He waited until the slope was not so difficult to walk on before he spoke. "So what you think of all this?"

Luther glanced over his shoulder, then looked straight ahead, grabbed a sapling to help himself over a rough spot. "I think you're wasting time up here. I had the killer in jail. I'll find more evidence and put him back. Barry's using you for window dressing, hiring a private detective to look for the real killer; thinks it'll throw suspicion offa him. I think maybe he had a helper—Barry killed 'em, had somebody else drive the car over to Coffee County. Real reason I was up there, I was thinking Barry might be sneaking around, picking something up he hid in the woods."

They reached the road. Cody ducked under a limb and waited on the hardtop for Luther to brush leaves and twigs from his uniform pants. Then he looked the deputy in the eye. "Why leave junk around everybody knows is his, like the bow and that metal claw, put himself in jeopardy? If he did all that to confuse the law, the man's a big gambler."

"Figgers with all his money, he can hire lawyers and get away with it."

"Take some kind of a fool to stack the deck against himself," Cody said.

Cody waited for Luther to leave before continuing his search. It proved futile. There were no other listening devices.

He walked down to his truck and was prepared to get in when he noticed the spots on the road. Blood, he thought, bending down for a closer look. It looked weeks old, and the weather had taken its toll; the spots were a brownish color. But he'd seen blood on the streets of Los Angeles. Of course, it would take a chemical analysis to prove it.

It was fortunate he'd come back. With Samantha along, he'd been too distracted.

There was another washed-out splotch in the middle of the road, plus another on the far edge. He hadn't heard anything about an investigation around the cabin, just where the victims were found. Luther was the assigned investigator, the county's only certified murder investigator other than the sheriff himself. After a careful search along the roadside, he came to a mark on the ground where something had been dragged along, making an indentation in the soft dirt.

On hands and knees, he clambered to a spot under a clump of saplings. There was blood on the ground covering the light sprinkle of hemlock and pine straw. Looked like more evidence— and sloppy investigative work.

"You sure about this, son?" his father said on the phone.

"Plain as day."

"And Luther was hanging above the cabin?"

"Hanging or hiding."

"I'm taking a ride out there. First though, I want to get my camera and some evidence bags, get some scrapings and samples. From what you describe, at least one'a them was killed at the cabin. I'll have a TBI tech come out soon as we can get one headed this way."

Monk O'Malley held court in Fuzzy's Place. A small group of men surrounded him at the bar, offered to buy drinks, prodded for information. "You fine gentlemen know I cannot discuss this case. Besides being inappropriate, it would violate my client's confidentiality, and just might be downright criminal, could land my wretched ass in the house of many doors."

Old beer signs with pictures of boats and horses hung on the walls of the dim room. Brass spittoons stood at either end of the bar. Red plastic bowls of boiled peanuts were assigned to every table. Cigarette smoke and a stale beer smell hung heavy in the air. In a recessed corner, four roughly dressed men hovered over an equal number of video-poker machines, fed the digital thieves quarters earned at the rock quarry, foundry, or feed mill. Focused on their addiction, they ignored the ruckus around the short, stocky lawyer.

Two men played shuffleboard close by the front door, scooted the puck along between intermittent pulls on long-neck bottles of beer and single dollar bets. Two frizzle-haired women in shorts and halters popped their gum and looked on with twitching impatience.

The door opened and bright sunlight flooded the room. Cody stepped in and allowed the door to swing shut behind him.

The room stopped and stared, settled back, waited for night vision to return. Another poker game began at the drop of a quarter.

A huge man edged through the crowd toward Cody. Taller than Bobby Joe by three inches, he outweighed him by forty pounds. "I'm Big 'Un," he said.

"You ain't said shit." Cody looked up at a moon face, distorted into a lopsided grin. Fleshy, tennis-ball-sized red cheeks squeezed Big 'Un's pale eyes to a piggy squint.

"I mean my name's Big 'Un, least that's what ever'body in Mountain County calls me. We don't want no trouble in here."

"See you don't start none."

"What happened was, the sheriff done called over here, said you's coming over, told Fuzzy, anybody give you any trouble, he's gonna close the place down. I'm the bouncer."

"Good to meet you, Big 'Un. I'll be talking to that short, stubby lawyer; when you look at his pants, looks like he's got an advanced case of the gone-ass. He gives any problems, you got my permission to stomp him into the floorboards."

Cody left Big 'Un standing with a dazed expression on his face and walked to a table at the opposite end of the room from the poker machines. He jerked his head at Monk O'Malley as he passed the crowd at the bar.

Monk almost fell when he climbed down from his stool. Wobbling across the floor on short legs, he approached Cody's table. "Permission to take a seat, sir," he said, looking at Cody over the rims of his half-moon glasses, lifting his drink in a mock toast.

"Permission granted." Cody nodded to a chair next to his; better to talk to Monk without being overheard in the bleachers.

Taking the proffered chair, Monk placed his glass on the table, leaned close to Cody, and gave him a whiff of hundred-proof breath. "Well, young Cody, hope you have come with glad tidings, to apprise me my client no longer needs my services. You have unearthed the true, hidden perpetrator of the loathsome deed and your stalwart father, honest and forthright protector of our fair county, has the fiend in custody."

"Not exactly."

The attorney recoiled in feigned anguish. "Then you must be bitterly distressed to be the bearer of such disappointing news. Will you join me in a taste?"

"Thanks, Monk, a little early for me. I did discover some evidence the law overlooked in their haste to proceed with the case."

"We measure cyclical time by the rotation of this great earth we inhabit. Surely the sun must be over some unnamed yardarm far to our east. But enough scientific babble. What did you discover?"

Cody told him of the bloodstains found around the remote cabin. "Sheriff will bring in a state forensics team now, sweep the entire area since it can be assumed that's where the killings really took place."

"Slipshod investigative work. Perhaps I can use this newly found evidence to get my client off the hook altogether, released from his bail obligation, cleansed of the tar flung on him by a distrustful community."

"Or perhaps our persevering sheriff's department can use the newly found clues to nail Barry's already somewhat imperiled ass even more snugly to the cross," Cody said.

"Then tell me, brave Cody, seeker of truth, what is your estimate of the situation?"

"I'll be straight with you, Monk," Cody said. "It don't look good for Barry. Nailing the time of death might clear him or it might convict."

"You are aware, of course, the evidence is all circumstantial, there are no eyewitnesses, no direct evidence Barry was involved. The bloody boot can be explained to a jury as someone trying to place Barry at the scene."

Cody stood and looked over the crowd, turned back to the lawyer. "I'll let you handle the jury, Counselor. I'm off to my uncle's place to get settled in my old camper trailer. Establish my base of operations."

"Well said," cheered Monk, raising his now empty glass in salute. "Ah yes, I forgot—fair Jolinda Risingwaters has been calling, inquiring of your presence."

Without answering, Cody moved to the door and walked out into the light. Behind him, he heard Monk call in his cultured voice, "Bartender."

* * *

Scanner listened on the hand-held. He was trying to pick up some info on the investigation, see what the townspeople were talking about.

"You coming to town again tonight?" whispered a female voice. "That idiot who's killing people hasn't been caught yet." A voice on the edge of Scanner's recognition. Who was it? He just couldn't place it. Calling him names, whispering behind his back.

"Gotta work," a male voice answered.

"You sure give it to me good last night. I don't think you ever give it to me that good before. I want you to give it to me like that again tonight."

"Gotta work."

"You drive home this morning, give it to your wife?"

"Whatta you think I am? Some kinda machine? Where's your husband? You sure he can't hear you talking?"

"I'll check," the whisperer said.

To Scanner her hissing voice oozed with a conspiratorial excitement. If the radio had not been constructed of durable plastic, it would have been crushed in his powerful grip. To calm down during the silence, the eavesdropper drummed on the heavy plastic with spastic fingers.

"He's watching the TV, just like always," whispered the voice after what seemed to Scanner like an hour. "All he ever does is eat, sleep, watch TV, and fish for bluegill. Never gives it to me like you do. You sure you can't come back to the county?"

"Gotta go. Page me tomorrow." The man sounded bored, disconnected. The scanner automatically searched for another voice.

Scanner smoldered, then losing control, exploded. "Slut! Whore! I hope your husband catches you and rips your fucking throat out."

Nine

No one was home when Cody arrived at Ogden Two Bears's farm. More than likely his uncle was still at work and Jolinda Risingwaters was with one of her school chums. He let himself into the neat house to get a spare phone for his camper trailer. He'd lived in the camper after his divorce, right after returning home from L.A. Except for intermittent stays in his mountain cabin, these cramped quarters had been his home for a few years.

His uncle had helped him dig a septic tank, run a pipe from the mountain spring for water, hook into the electric and run a phone line from the main house. Three hundred yards away, partially hidden under a clump of pines, it provided the privacy he desired, and shade from the overhanging conifers allowed him to live without an air conditioner on the hottest summer day.

He expected to be greeted by musty air plus a year's accumulation of dust. Instead he found the interior clean, the air fresh. Jolinda had cleaned the place. He should have known she would.

He thought of the two telephone bugs when he plugged the phone into the jack low on the trailer wall. Had Luther planted them?

He plugged the phone's base into an outlet to let the batteries charge. Sanford Sharpless's phone was a cordless, and so was the phone at Barry's.

Going back to his truck, he brought in his bag and his electronic equipment. He had to get to the store soon, get a few groceries laid in. Not many. He wouldn't be here that long.

Light was beginning to go. Cody lay down on the small sofa in the camper's cramped living room–dining room combination and instantly dropped off to sleep.

* * *

Concealed by weeds and tall grass, Scanner lay near a split-rail fence, watched the man through the window, waited for the internal message to signal the time for the reward. The 10x50 binoculars weren't necessary only a hundred feet from the window but Scanner required a close study of the face, wanted to minutely observe the fleeting moments of finality. When death approached in this manner was there an unconscious knowing? Did a cosmic messenger deliver a scrambled note not completely deciphered by the brain of the intended? Did a combination of cells release a yet-to-be-discovered chemical trigger? Or was the signal more spiritual in nature, a supernatural harmonic of the message received by the presenter of the reward? Tweaking the focus lever on the powerful glasses, Scanner brought the face closer.

Scanner felt a cresting surge of excitement, and his breathing became quicker, deeper, his heart beat more rapidly. Reaching to the ground, Scanner fingered the length of rope. It took an effort of will not to carry the reward forward at once, to feel the longed-for release that had steadily intensified since he'd sent Sanford and Justine on their way.

Patience would make the event more satisfying. More complete. And of course more proper. There was, after all, a procedure to be followed.

* * *

Getting dressed up excited Carl Taggart. He was saddened that Sanford wasn't around to watch but Carl needed the distraction. Things had been so sad since Justine and Sanford were killed. So boring.

Of course he'd been forced to wait until his wife made one of those unscheduled visits to her mother down in Athens. She would call and her mother would invite her and the two children for a visit, offer to take them all to Chattanooga, shopping at one of the malls, break the boredom of living in a small town with no movies and no shopping. Satellite TV and renting videos was the only entertainment for most, unless like Carl, when your wife was out of town, you got dressed up and provided your own entertainment.

Standing nude in front of the full-length mirror, he turned and looked at himself from every angle. He had a head full of dark thick hair. He held his head at a slight angle and examined himself from head to toe. His chest, arms, and legs were relatively clean of hair. He kept a small patch of pubic hair trimmed for his bikini panties. He was tall, sallow, slightly stooped, his chest was sunken, but he would make up for that with the padded bra. His arms were spindly from lack of exercise and fit well into a feminine blouse.

He went to the bedroom dresser, picked up a pack of cigarettes, shook one out, lit it from the butt in the ashtray. Taking a deep drag, he whirled around, raised on his toes, and watched himself in the mirror as he held the cigarette out, elbow bent, palm up.

In the bedroom closet he bent to open a shoebox and retrieved a new pair of taupe pantyhose. Back in front of the mirror, he slipped them on, rotated his hips, cigarette clinched in his teeth, nostrils flared, a grimace of pleasure on his face. Leaning closer to the mirror he applied his lipstick.

It was always the same lately, he thought: He'd be all dressed up with no one around to appreciate him. He was really alone with Sanford gone. At least he'd be dressed sharp. He could sit around the house and watch TV, smoke all he wanted without that bitch complaining. Back in the closet, he brought out a wig and a bra. Skipping to the mirror, Carl went through his often repeated ritual of becoming Carlene.

Once, on a business trip to Huntsville, Alabama, disaster had almost struck. He'd been dressed in a miniskirt, a halter, net stockings, two-inch heels, and a blonde wig. Looking through the window of an apartment, he'd been watching a young, well-built stud work out with weights. Focused on the man and enthusiastically loping his mule, he had not noticed the woman peering down at him from an upstairs apartment window.

The offended woman had called the police and a wild foot chase ensued, with Carlene jumping over hedges, climbing into back yards, and finally discarding the outfit and wig to become a barefoot male jogger. Carl had then directed the baffled cops down the street, telling them a woman had jumped into a red convertible and zoomed off in the opposite direction. No, he didn't get the license number.

Why couldn't his wife leave for the entire weekend, Carl thought. He'd wear his nice clothes and go to Knoxville, see his friends. The red skirt with his new matching shoes and purse would knock 'em dead.

Carl ran the heating-oil distributorship owned by his father, could not take time off during the week to go on these jaunts. When his compulsions struck, he was at their mercy, and at times would hurriedly drive into the national forest, hide in the trees, put on his clothes. Tonight's privacy would relieve the pressure.

Cody was wakened by someone opening the camper door. He felt the slight pressure change from inside to outside air.

He lay still, waited.

A soft step inside, the door closed quietly. A few seconds' pause, a slow intake of breath, a release barely heard as the intruder moved toward the couch.

A glint of moonlight penetrated the tiny windows, enough to see the shadow approach. He watched an arm move toward his face. When the hand almost touched him, he grabbed it and jerked hard.

The intruder was on him, screaming, squealing. Cody felt a soft breast, caught a whiff of perfume.

"Goddammit, Jolinda. One day you're gonna make me hurt you."

Jolinda grabbed his face in both hands, kissed him hard on the lips, stuck her tongue in his mouth, moaned loudly.

Cody jerked away. "Come on, Jo. Get off me so I can turn on the light." He dumped her on the floor with a thud that shook the camper. Finding the wall switch, he flipped it on, blinked at the brightness.

"You're an old killjoy," Jolinda said, still on the floor, her lips pouted, head hung in disappointment.

Cody stared down at her, thought she was prettier than a frosty autumn morning.

Jolinda Risingwaters wore tight blue-jean shorts and a white halter, brilliant against her dark skin. Her thick, raven-black hair hung past her shoulders. High cheekbones were those of a model, as were the dark eyes and short, straight nose. "And you're not very romantic, either," she added with a tinge of anger.

"When're you gonna get it though your pretty, thick skull? You're only seventeen. I could romanticize myself into the local lockup in a heartbeat."

"Just your excuse. Half the girls in the county are married by the time they're my age."

Cody reached a hand down to help her up. "Come on, Jolinda. Quit acting silly and sit up here on the couch. Thanks for cleaning the camper."

She took his hand, came to her feet. "Don't know why I bother. You don't appreciate me."

"Sure I do, honey," Cody gave her a one-arm hug, careful she didn't try to lock up with him again.

"Uncle Ogden knows I come over here. He don't care."

"What'd Ogden say to you before you come over?"

"Made me promise I wouldn't sneak over and crawl in bed with you."

"You've started back to school. You're what—a junior?"

"You know better'n. I'm a senior and in a few months I'll be eighteen."

Cody looked in the mini refrigerator, found she'd stocked it for him, got himself a cold beer, and brought Jolinda a diet soda. "Let's sit here on the couch, you tell me what you been up to."

Sitting there listening to her bringing him up to date, Cody remembered the first time he looked into her obsidian eyes and saw those perfect cupid's bow lips. He'd been twelve years old and a few months earlier had buried his mother after her shotgun suicide. He'd moved in with the Two Bears and was just getting adjusted to living down in the valley on Ogden's farm.

That Christmas morning Ogden and his wife gave Cody a thick red mackinaw then loaded him into the pickup with a box full of gifts and drove to the cabin on Rattlesnake Creek. The stream had recently flooded and they had almost drowned the old

Ford's engine when they crossed the submerged bridge. Cody took off his shoes and coat, jumped into the water and towed the thick cable to the opposite bank where he made a turn around a giant tulip tree. After winching the truck to safety they bucked and slid down the muddy road to their destination.

Ogden's brother-in-law, a hulking young man with light brown hair, was waiting for them on the front porch. His nose was red from the cold, and his boots, which he removed from cold feet before entering the cabin, were muddy from hauling firewood.

Cody was shivering. A grand fire roared in the giant stone fireplace. He stood near the flames to dry his jeans as he stared at the cedar Christmas tree in the corner covered with tinsel. Then Ogden called him into the bedroom.

The room was decorated with brightly patterned quilts, lace curtains, and an embroidered bedspread. He could almost remember the pattern, the memory was so clear. The bed, an oversized four-poster, was fortified with gigantic pillows. A feathered dream catcher hung from the ceiling on a long piece of string. The setting instantly reminded him of his mother's bedroom in their old homestead on the mountain. The window beside the bed looked over the raging creek.

"This is my baby sister," Ogden said, smiling at a pretty dark-haired girl who stood folding clothes and placing them in the top drawer of a chest. She looked wan and exhausted, like she'd just recovered from a long illness. The beaded headband on her forehead made her complexion seem lighter.

She motioned Cody to the bed. "And here is my brand-new daughter," she said. "Born early this morning. The water was rising so fast we couldn't get to the hospital. My husband delivered her."

Cody went awkwardly to the bed. When the mother removed the covering from the baby's head it woke her. She blinked, then focused on Cody with a startled expression that included a slight jump. And she smiled.

It was Cody's first look at a newborn, and he became lost in the baby girl's eyes. He was hypnotized. "What's her name?" Cody asked.

"I haven't decided on a first name yet," the mother said. "But her Indian name will be Risingwaters."

"So how long are you staying?" Jolinda asked.

"Huh?" Cody jerked back to the present.

"You haven't heard a word I said." Jolinda put on a hurt face. "How long are you gonna be home?"

"Until I can catch me a killer," Cody said, thinking: In two and a half months that memory will be eighteen years old.

"Good," Jolinda said. "That means you'll be here a while."

Carl considered his blue blouse, held it up in front of him while he stood in front of the mirror, pushed one hip out, then the other. He eventually chose the white one. It would show up his necklace much better. He was slipping it on when the phone rang.

He grabbed the cordless from its charger, prissed back to the mirror. "Hello," he said, evaluating the skill he'd used to apply his eye shadow.

"Hi, Carl," his wife said.

"Becky. You're not on the way home are you?"

"I said I'd be spending the night. Just wondering if you're okay."

"I'm great."

"You sound better. I was getting worried. You've been so down the last several days."

* * *

Alerted when Carl picked up the phone, Scanner activated his hand-held receiver, listened to the conversation between the man and wife. Carl had purchased one of the new 900 megahertz cordless phones for privacy. It made for good eavesdropping, the voices were super clear. Primed by the voice of the intended, Scanner rose from his hiding place and crept to the rear porch.

Carl replaced the portable in the charger, continued to button his blouse, then tucked it into his skirt. The necklace in place, he adjusted it under the collar of his blouse, then snapped on a dainty gold bracelet. Back at the mirror, he touched up his makeup. Satisfied, he walked into the living room. Being careful not to trip on the carpet with the two-inch heels he wore, he lowered himself to the sofa, crossed his legs, exposing the lace of his slip, and reached for the remote.

Scanner found the back door unlocked. Using a cloth so as not to leave prints, the killer entered the house and eased the door closed, then moved slowly across the darkened kitchen and down the hall toward the living room. Sounds of applause, then laughter came from the TV. Scanner almost gagged from the pall of smoke that engulfed the front rooms of the house.

Carl sensed a movement behind him and jerked around in frightened reaction. Seeing Scanner's calm demeanor, though, his fear quickly dissipated. This might not be such a boring evening after all, he thought. He stood up and smiled at his guest. "What a surprise. What're you doing here?"

Scanner brought the rope into view. "Why my love," he murmured softly, "I'm here with your reward."

Carl had never been so scared in his life. "Why'd you bring me up here?" The ropes bit into his wrists so hard his hands tingled.

"Look out there," Scanner said, gesturing toward the town. "All the lights in the tiny houses. Inside them are tiny people with tiny minds. Sanford and Justine had tiny minds."

They were almost to the top of the mountain, just outside the boundary of the national forest. Carl had never been up here before. His high heels sank into the soft dirt of the fire road, and to take a step he had to pull the heels out one at a time. He was cold, too, wearing only the light skirt and blouse. "You killed them, it was you. Why . . ."

"Shut up!" Scanner said. "Soon I'll own all Barry's land. His house. Everything. I'll have it all. You want to know why? Because I deserve it. That's how it started but now I realize I was just greedy. It's gone beyond that now. When I took their pitiful lives, I was released. You can't understand that can you? Released. Their deaths washed away my inner turmoil. I feel so clean."

Carl was realizing now that Scanner was insane. He knew he had to go along with him if he was going to live. "Sure you do, and I'll help you," Carl whined. "Barry had me kicked off the fire department. He's always been against me. I hate him too."

"I don't hate Barry. Barry's a good man. He just doesn't deserve what he has because he didn't suffer for it. Like you haven't suffered for anything you have."

"Can we stop this now?" Carl said. "You're scaring me. Can I go back home?"

Scanner turned from looking over the town and walked over to Carl. "So you want to go home?"

"Please take me home."

"Sorry," Scanner said. He walked to the back of the truck, reached into the bed and came out with a coil of rope. "I'm in charge of how far you can go and can't go. It's my decision. I can only take you part of the way."

Ten

Titus Cornstubble was the only moonshiner left in Mountain County. The making of the potent brew was an art form from the past. He wanted to give the occupation up altogether. Given a choice, he'd pick a more profitable career, which was why he was here. No money in white whiskey anymore. Not even enough to keep a roof over a man's family.

The plot of weed he had on the mountain was ready for harvest. That was where the money was. He'd been on the way to chop it and hang it to dry when he ran headlong into Luther Hamby. The deputy ran him back home, chopped down his crop. Now he had to find a new site, start over. He was out early, scouting for a screened area that would allow the sun in from overhead, enough light to nurture the crop, not enough clearing to be spotted by the state marijuana-control chopper.

Cornstubble was descended from the breed of men who had scared the hell out of the Yankees during the War for Southern Independence. Slat thin, wiry and strong, he could head out cross-country, scamper along mountain trails, wade fast-running creeks, scoot through blackberry brambles that would tear the flesh from a flatlander, live on a handful of food. He walked the fire trail with a shuffling mountaineer's gait, a mile-eating pace he could maintain all day. From his jacket he took a brown twist of tobacco, bit off a chaw, pocketed the rest. Chewing the dried tobacco, he began to moisten it with his saliva. Pale, watery blue eyes scanned both sides of the overgrown path.

He spotted the body as he navigated a muddy switchback.

Stepping closer, he slowed, then stopped. He had the wariness of a wild animal, a wolf or coyote prepared to leap back and flee at the slightest threat. He leaned forward.

"Jezzus, gawd almighty. Somebody done tore this woman all to hell."

Cornstubble pivoted and sprinted down the trail.

Samantha got the call.

"Mountain County—unit six."

"Go ahead."

"Samantha, Titus Cornstubble stopped at Ellie Mae Stover's house to use the phone. Says there's a woman's body up on fire trail one-oh-seven."

"Most likely he's been sampling some'a his own stuff. He still at Ellie Mae's?"

"Ten-four."

"I'll run by—ride him up the mountain."

"Ten-four. K-I-A eleven-forty-five, zero-seven-oh-five."

"It's right up here, Deputy Goodlocke. I ain't making it up. I swear." Cornstubble sat in the rear seat, giving directions. He was nervous. He seldom rode in a car.

The cruiser couldn't make the steep curve, its rear tires slid around, almost slammed the tail-end into an embankment. They got out and walked. Samantha spotted the red skirt and dirty white blouse. "Stay here," she told Cornstubble. She didn't want this crime scene disturbed. The sheriff had gone ballistic over the last one and the clues missed by both deputies.

She approached the body with caution, checking the surface of the road as she moved, staying in the middle of the path. She halted six feet away. Was this a real woman? Or had somebody thrown a department store mannequin on the trail? Looked like a part of it got broke off.

Moving forward a step at a time, she looked around for tracks in the soft dirt. Then she saw the hands. They were tied together in front. A red purse strap hung on one arm. The hands were the only part of the body visible to her with any flesh left on it.

She headed for the cruiser to call it in.

The phone jarred Cody awake. For a moment he didn't know where he was, looked around. The phone rang again.

"Yeah."

"We got another one," the sheriff said.

"Another one?"

"Another body, another murder. Woman's body found on the fire trail running offa Rocky Face Road, way up. Samantha just called it in. Thought I'd let you know."

"Thanks," Cody said, coming fully awake. "I'm on my way."

An hour later, Cody parked behind the line of cruisers and the Mountain County EMS ambulance. He had to walk up the trail for a hundred yards. The first two people he saw were Luther and Cornstubble.

"Luther, you know I ain't never kilt no woman," Cornstubble was saying in a pleading voice.

"Then what you doing up here? I say you killed her."

"Woman's tore all up. You keep talkin' like that, you gonna make me sick to my stomach."

Cody passed by. Luther was beginning to bore him. He knew it best not to tarry near the man when he was in that frame of mind.

At the scene, his daddy and Samantha were taking pictures. They had used a can of white spray paint for an outline in the dirt around the body. Deputy Bubba Whittlemore held a tape measure in his hand. Albert Feltus scanned the scene with a slow-panning camcorder. Johnny Knight knelt by the body and made notes in his casebook. Bubba knelt to take measurements, then entered them on a pad he carried. Samantha looked a little green around the gills.

"Mornin' folks," Cody said to announce his presence.

"Mornin', son," the sheriff said, looking around. "Our killer struck again," he said to answer Cody's unspoken question.

"Why's Luther hassling Titus?"

"Luther keeps his shit up, he'll be giving me the ass like a show dog. I'm wondering if he's working for the county, or he's got his own agenda."

"So what's happened here?"

"Come on," his father said. "Walk on up the mountain with me. Let's see what went on up there. We got enough folks investigating the dump site."

The drag marks led straight up the fire road. The sun had been up for hours but the air was still frosty. In the distance, Cody could hear water running, cascading down the mountain to eventually join up with the Highwater River flowing into the Hiwassee. The fire trail was steep. At this altitude, the ground foliage consisted mainly of rhododendron, some of it growing twenty to thirty feet high. The trees were mostly tulip trees and hemlock that formed a high canopy. The two men walked up the trail for almost a mile, to where the narrow furrow started.

The sheriff stopped and turned. Holding his walkie in his hand, he looked down on the scene below. "We got us a sick one, son."

"A sick one?"

"Yeah. What every lawman dreads. A psycho on the loose. Look there at the shoulder of the fire road, right along the edge, leading up the incline."

Cody bent down, looked closely. "Looks like someone's punched holes on the side of the path with a sharp pole."

"High heels. I suspect they'll go up a ways."

"You sure?"

"Running high heels. I heard of a killing like this maybe a year ago over in Marion County, around Monteagle Mountain and the Fiery Gizzard Trail. Old mountain custom. Tie somebody to your pickup, make 'em run along until they can't run no more, then drag 'em behind 'til there ain't no meat left on their bones."

Cody noticed the more upset his dad allowed himself to get, the more pronounced his mountain drawl became.

"Might as well walk on up to see where it all started," the sheriff said.

Samantha's voice came over the hand-held. "Sheriff Rainwalker. We were moving the body, hair fell off, it's a man."

"Ten-four, unit six. Signal sixteen." The sheriff broadcast the code to cease radio traffic.

"'At's ten-four," Samantha answered in a slow drawl.

"Half the county knows about the wig now. They listen on their police-band radios, folks at the drive-ins, the beauty parlors, the wrecker crews. Police bands are the new party line. Whole county will know in fifteen minutes. We can check the top of the trail, see where the victim was put out of the truck. Had to be a four-wheeler. Later I'll go down and see if there's another blue ribbon."

There was.

Fuzzy's was in an uproar, with everyone yapping about the murder. Cody and Monk sat at their corner table and took in the chaos. Monk had his usual water glass of Jack Black. Cody sipped a beer.

"Little early for you?" Monk said, looking at his watch. The thick hair on his wrist almost obscured the instrument's face. He peered over the glasses, a knowing grin on his simian face.

"You see what I just seen, you'd be drinking too," Cody said, ignoring the glass of whiskey in the lawyer's paw.

Across the room someone sounded off to overcome the din, "Way I see it, ol' Carl woulda made it all way down the mountain if she hadn'ta throwed a high heel." There was a chorus of laughter.

"Naw," chimed in another voice. "She'd a made it barefoot if it weren't for that tight skirt. You go pickup truckin' you need a billowy skirt." Louder laughter.

"Got some real comedians," Cody said with a grim expression.

"You fellers know how to tell if Carl was a wearing her pantyhose?" a big lanky mill worker asked. His long, greasy black hair hung to his shoulders, and a twisted pistolero mustache drooped to beyond his chin.

"How's that Chester?"

"When she farted, her ankles swelled up."

There was an uproar of laughter.

"Dark humor," Monk said. "That's how they handle the fear, knowing something just as ghastly could happen to them."

"Tell me, Mister Attorney Man, your client and mine—does he have a good alibi?"

"I'm afraid not, Cody. He sent his son, Edmund, to stay with his parents, his daughter went to Michelle's. He was at home all night, alone."

"No one from the fire hall stopped over."

"Yes. Earlier. The time element of this crime has been narrowed. Becky spoke to her husband at nine-thirty last night. We know he was alive then. Randy Gateline visited Barry at seven-thirty, thereabouts, stayed for ten minutes, then left. Bubba Whittlemore came by at a quarter after eight and stayed fifteen minutes."

"They don't think Barry done it, do they?"

Monk gestured to the crowd around the bar, then at the smaller crowd talking around the shuffleboard. "Look around at these men. At this moment, to them, Barry Willingham is a folk hero. They perceive reality as being: Barry caught his wife and Sanford en flagrante, gave them a good dose of mountain justice, then did away with a weirdo who violated his code of behavior. Later. Perhaps tonight, in the silence of their rooms, when anxiety rules the night and fear of the unknown comes to haunt them, the paradigm will shift. They will began to wonder if, in the distant past, they have somehow angered Barry."

"Then they'll turn against their hero and demand he be hung from the highest tree?" Cody said.

"You are quick, brave Cody. However, in their rush to justice, a nearby lamp post will suffice."

Cody took a sip of his beer, his expression thoughtful, "Whatta you know about Luther Hamby?"

"Ah. Do I detect suspicion?"

"Curiosity."

"Yes Luther, ambitious Luther. Our industrious Mr. Hamby would be chief deputy for a while, if that would lead to the high sheriffship. Your father reluctantly inherited Luther when we had the referendum. The voters decided to do away with the city police and fire department and turn everything over to the county."

"Figures," Cody said. "Luther ain't getting any younger—he's losing all his hair and his skin don't look good, got jowls like a bloodhound, dark pouches under his eyes, gives him a two-toned look. Figures he won't be up to scrabbling in the gravel with a drunken redneck, putting him in the cruiser. Also, only thing went out on the radio was the wig. All the pantyhose, high-heeled, tight-skirt info had to come from someone at the scene."

"Age can do funny things to a man—they reach that climacteric stage, become cognizant of their irrelevance. I have traveled the state defending men in their fifties who have lived honorable lives, never at odds with their fellow man, who get laid off at work, go to the closet for the shotgun, back to the shed for the stump-removing dynamite and the court will disallow any mention of nostology. It's a sign of our times. Plus the layoffs. Our industries are trashing a generation in exchange for low-paid youth."

Cody expected the lawyer to ramble; he relaxed, waited for him to finish his diatribe. "I'm lucky I still got a library card, all the vocabulary you're throwing around. Luther and Barry? They get along?"

"Do I perceive a private line of investigation?"

"They get along?"

"Not at all. Luther realizes Barry might also covet the sheriff's office. Unlike Luther, Barry has the personal wherewithal to run for the office."

"The Willingham family always backed Daddy come election time," Cody said.

"Tides and loyalties change. Barry is also ambitious. Unlike Luther, he has a likable streak, knows how to get along, has read a book, perhaps even two."

"They have any hassles?"

"Their enmity is buried deep in their psyches, they greet one another amicably. On a visceral level, they loath with full reciprocity."

"You think Luther would try to frame our client?" Cody asked.

"Luther is an ambitious man."

"Monk. Telephone." Fuzzy's gravelly voice boomed out over the din.

"Duty calls. I shall return," Monk said, rising from his chair. He weaved through the crowd to the wall phone by a poker machine.

Alone at the table, Cody's thoughts stayed on Luther. A deputy could get around easily enough at night, he thought.

That's what he was getting paid to do. Also, he'd know what was going on in the community, who was seeing who, and when, have access to eavesdropping equipment. He would know where to purchase the bugs found in Sanford's and Barry's houses.

Cody wanted to find out if Luther was on duty last night, when Carl was murdered. And on the night Justine and Sanford were reported missing.

Cody's train of thought was interrupted by the sight of Monk hurrying back to the table. His expression was one of concern.

"My client has panicked, fears imminent incarceration."

What a client he'd found for himself, Cody thought. "Any proof he done the deed?"

"Our ambitious Deputy Hamby has found incriminating photographs in Barry's truck. Also a rope similar to the one used to tie Taggart's hands. It matches rock-climbing rope found in Barry's basement. Last but not least, the rope used to pull Taggart along, same rope, a length of it, worn down, was found tied under Barry's truck."

"You going to the jail, or to Barry's house?" Cody said.

"House. Want to accompany me?"

"You bet. Either Barry is the stupidest killer to come down the pike, or he's being set up."

"You drive," the lawyer said. "I can't have our ambitious Luther giving a DUI to my client's attorney."

Eleven

"Big turnout," Cody said, eyeing the five cruisers strewn like cast yarrow straws in Barry's front yard.

"I venture Barry would be grateful for solitude—and I don't mean as in solitary confinement," Monk said from the passenger seat. He looked out of place in his upscale, lawyer's gray pinstripe.

The black-and-tan hounds, having a full day of it, set up their baying, announcing another arrival.

Luther, Samantha, and Bubba Whittlemore swarmed Barry's black 4x4 pickup like sweat bees buzzing a garbage can. White splotches of fingerprint powder adorned the areas around the door handles and the front of the hood. Cody looked around for his dad, then Barry, spotted neither. "Guess they're inside."

The two men headed for the front door, where the sheriff let them in. Barry sprawled on the living room couch, his entire body broadcasting dejection. Even his country gentleman threads couldn't give him the air of assurance an accused man would want to project.

Deputies Johnny Knight and Albert Feltus stood to one side of the room scribbling in their notebooks. Cody guessed they'd been asking Barry some uncomfortable and hard to answer questions. Feltus looked pleased with himself; Knight wore the same bored, half-asleep expression as when Cody first met him.

Monk joined his client, patted him on the back in a gesture of support and waved him into another room.

Hands thrust in his pockets, Cody shuffled by the door, then followed his dad outside. "What's the scoop?" he asked.

"Luther found some pictures in Barry's truck."

"Monk told me," Cody said.

102

"Shows Justine in bed with Sanford Sharpless and Carl Taggart. Justine and Sanford are nude. Carl is wearing a stunning string bikini. Ugliest sight you ever did see. Turned my stomach. Justine and Sanford don't look good either."

"Where in the truck?"

"Under the driver's seat, but sticking out some. Plain view, you know. Something else. We were checking tire tracks at the murder scene, tried to make a mold but the ground's sort of crumbly. We got one good tread mark. But Barry happened to put a new set of tires on his truck this morning, old ones he says he threw in the county Dumpster. We can't find them. And we got there before the pickup."

"I hear Luther found the pictures. Anyone with him when he made the discovery?" Cody said.

"What're you saying?"

"Ain't saying, asking."

"Deputy Whittlemore was with him. New deputy by six months."

"You already ask?"

"In a roundabout way," the sheriff said.

"Whittlemore and Luther real close?"

"Not so's you'd notice. Why?"

"Just checking," Cody said.

"You know something I oughta know?"

"Monk apprised me of the political situation."

Cody's attention was caught by the hounds getting out of the shade again and going silently to greet another 4x4 pickup pulling close to Barry's. The CB antenna on its rear bumper oscillated for a few rebounds, then was dampened to a halfhearted, quivering vibration by the tennis ball it penetrated to half its length.

"Randy Gateline," the sheriff said.

"Don't look like he's aged a day since the last time I saw him," Cody said. "That's been a number of years."

"When he was twenty-five, he looked seventeen or eighteen. He's twenty-nine, thereabouts, looks like twenty to me."

Cody watched Samantha's posture and expression change when Randy passed where she stood by the truck, saw her come to point as she reacted to an emotion she likely thought she had laid to rest. She smiled, straightened. "Hello, Randy," she said.

Cody could hear the yearning in her voice.

"Hi," Randy said as he swept by.

Walked by like she's a fucking fence post, Cody thought.

Samantha followed Randy's progress with a melancholy gaze as he made his way to Cody and the sheriff.

"Hello, Cody." Randy reached out and took Cody's extended hand and shook it. "Been a while. Oughta come home more often. You wanted to see me, Sheriff?"

To Cody, Randy resembled a male model one would find in a men's fashion magazine. He had a full head of thick, curly hair, tossed with what appeared to be a planned unruliness. His lashes were long, girlish, his eyebrows heavy. He had a squared-off, dimpled chin and high cheekbones, all tapering down symmetrically from a flat, wide forehead. His muscular frame filled out the plaid shirt he wore along with tight jeans over his slender hips. The pants narrowed to fit snugly over a dusty but obviously expensive pair of black cowboy boots.

To Cody an accurate description of Randy's appearance would be: pretty. He bet Randy made all the young girls tingle. Especially Samantha. He paused for a moment of self-analysis; was he getting interested in Samantha? Ray would get a real kick out of his boss having an affair with a deputy.

"Barry says you were over last night," the sheriff said.

"That's right, Sheriff. Came by to say hello, give Barry some moral support. God knows he needs it."

"What time?"

"Seven-twenty, seven-thirty, thereabouts. Stayed fifteen or twenty minutes."

"How was Barry acting?"

"Tired, he said; wanted to watch a little TV, go to bed. He was real sad, not excited. Barry is just not capable of killing anybody. He's a life-saver, not a life-taker."

"Where'd you go after you left here?"

Randy grinned an aw-shucks grin and kicked at the dirt; he seemed embarrassed at the question, or semi-accusation. "Went back to my gym, watched folks work out for a while, did some book work, then went to bed. Luther's already checked me out. Am I on your suspect list, Sheriff?"

"I wanta know where ever'body in the county was last night. Did you sell Barry that pair of metal claws?"

"He bought them over in Sweetwater, one of them flea market things where you can rent booths," Randy said.

After getting permission from the sheriff, Randy went inside to join Monk and Barry.

Cody and the sheriff walked over to Barry's truck. "Midnight lightning," a professionally painted red logo announced on the rear side of the bed.

Deputy Whittlemore had the hood open and was looking at the engine compartment.

"Checking out the engine or did you find something?" the sheriff asked.

"All the four-wheels I ever owned, hardest place to clean the mud off was over the brush-guard that protects the bottom of the radiator and the front-drive housing," Whittlemore said, looking around as they passed him. "When you're horsing it, mud gets all up in the wheel wells and on the manifold. I got some dirt samples offa there."

"Anything else?" the sheriff asked Luther.

"Naw. Gone through the glove compartment, with Barry's permission of course, looked inside door liners. Just the pictures —and the rope."

Cody kept an eye on Luther while Whittlemore talked. He could discern no evasiveness.

Luther noticed the attention. "Something?"

"Can I see one of those pictures?" Cody said.

Luther gave the sheriff a look before passing one over. "You seen one, you seen 'em all. Not very professional or creative."

The shot was taken at Sanford's cabin. Cody recognized the mantel with its overhanging shotgun in the dim background. The smile on Justine's face looked forced, her expression was glazed. Smoking grass? From her position on the floor, her thatch of pubic hair, dark, heavy, was the center of the picture. Her breasts were the size of cantaloupes, her big belly with its imbedded navel arched toward the camera. What did they call this kind of snap? Beaver shot?

The two men were on either side.

Sanford, nude, had his legs slightly crossed, was leaning back with a blank expression on his face. He seemed dull, drowsy, his eyes were half closed.

On the other side, Carl, in his day-glo, pink bikini, was up on stage, posed. One hand was held behind his head like he was modeling, the other reached behind Justine, could have been touching Sanford surreptitiously. The meager hair on his fish-white belly and skinny legs sent a shiver of repulsion through Cody.

Samantha had moved in closer while Cody inspected the photo. "Luther, didn't you catch Carl once over at the Riverside Motel exposing himself to an outtatown businessman?"

The deputy gave Samantha an angry look. "Yeah. Thought maybe he was drunk. Told him to get his ass back home."

Sheriff Rainwalker gave Luther an accusing stare. "You never said anything about it."

"Wasn't worth mentioning."

"Goddammit, Luther, I decide what's important."

Luther's expression became dark. Rage smoldered behind his eyes.

"One thing's missing," Cody said, the picture still in his hand.

"What's that?" Luther asked quickly.

"Person who took the shots."

"You taking Barry in?" Cody asked later.

The sheriff shook his head. "Not on evidence so obviously planted. 'Course the county prosecutor may have other ideas. Luther's going to split a gut, wants Barry locked up, may try to cause some trouble. Albert agrees with him, thinks Barry's the one. He's just not as hot to jail him, thinks we should gather more evidence. Him and Johnny Knight were still out asking questions on the other murders. Interviewing friends and enemies of both victims."

Cody told his dad Carl being found dead in drag was common knowledge around town.

"That's what Deputy Whittlemore's been telling me," the sheriff said. "I got eyes and ears out there, son. Eyes and ears."

"What about Randy Gateline?" Cody said. "Looks like he has easy access to Barry's house."

"Luther checked his alibi for when Justine and Sanford were killed. Three witnesses corroborated it. He checked him out again today for last night. Checks out. Randy is Barry's biggest supporter and a friend of the family."

Even though it was late afternoon, it was still cool on the mountainside. Cody walked by the spray-painted outline of the body. It seemed a ghostly clue there on the loose, black soil, a grim reminder of what had taken place on the spot. He continued upward, taking his time, looking for something overlooked by the investigators. What, he didn't know. Twice he stopped, bent to check the soil by the side of the trail, hoping to dredge up some knowledge hidden there.

How did the killer get Carl to come along with him? Were they friends? Lovers, even? Or was Carl compelled to come along at gunpoint? Could it be a combination? Lured, then when he figured out what was really going to happen, forced?

Two miles past where the body had come to rest, the trail leveled out. An old landslide had sent trees and rocks tumbling down the mountain for a thousand feet. Cody stared at the piles of brush and dirt, thought no one would risk climbing down that tangle of undergrowth.

This is where the downhill run started, he thought, as he looked about. A vehicle had turned around here. What happened on the spot? Did Carl plead for his life? Was he too scared to talk? What did the killer say? Other than the body itself, there were no real clues on the trail.

He turned to look back down the road from where he had climbed when he caught a movement to his left, in the trees up the steep incline. Not turning to look, he feigned interest in the landslide.

There it was again. Barely in his peripheral vision, a quick motion.

When he turned he spotted a man disappearing behind the

107

trunk of a huge tulip tree. Giving it a slow count of ten, Cody followed.

Keeping the quarry in sight, Cody moved like the experienced woodsman he was. The moist ground cover of the forest floor aided his stealth. Hopefully the man he pursued did not know he was being trailed. Leaning forward against the incline, Cody kept up a swift pace. He exercised regularly, ran, did the Stairmaster-thing, but this was something else. The altitude made a significant difference. He broke into a sweat but kept pushing it.

Half an hour later the terrain leveled off. Cody wondered why the man had struck out cross-country, had not cut back to the fire trail. The going would be much easier. Finally on level ground, he increased his pace to a quick jog.

A hundred yards in front, the man saw him and began to run flat out.

Damn, Cody thought fifteen minutes later. Running on a track or a city street was one thing. Running through the woods, dodging trees, sliding under limbs, made a man want to stay home in his easy chair. His breath was coming in ragged gasps. He'd gained some, not much. He set his jaw and increased the pace, arms and legs pumping. His legs were starting to burn. To take his mind off the agony, his thoughts went back to private detective stories he'd read or seen in movies.

The hero would smoke three packs a day, drink a quart of booze, chase the bad guy for miles without breaking a sweat, jump over fences, across gaping chasms between buildings, run headlong down freeways and through city traffic, and their hair wouldn't even get mussed. Start drinking before noon and still have muscles described as being sharp as honed knives. Better men than him.

He unbuttoned his shirt as he ran to let the chilly air hit his chest. He was coming out on a bald, a slick the mountain folk called it, and he could see a greater distance, saw he'd gained a few more yards.

Ten minutes later, the ground sloped sharply downward. Cody ran recklessly, headlong, ignoring the danger of not being able to stop and hitting a tree head-on or breaking a leg in a rut.

Finally he recognized who he pursued.

"Titus!" he managed to call out breathlessly. "Titus Cornstubble! It's me. Cody."

The man didn't slow.

"Come on Titus! I need to talk to you. We can't run all day. Least I can't."

Cornstubble veered, looked over his shoulder, didn't slow. "What you want, boy?"

"Wanta talk," was all Cody could manage.

"Talk about what?"

"Goddammit, Titus. Let's either run or talk. I can't do both." Cody estimated he'd run at least five miles. His ankles throbbed. Pain shot up his legs.

Cornstubble stumbled to a halt, walked to the shell-like hulk of a once gigantic chestnut tree and braced himself with a hand, gasping for breath. "I wont an old man, you'd never caught up to me. And I been sick some lately."

"Thank God for small favors," Cody said. This was where the pop culture P.I. would have a glib rejoinder. Cody flopped on the ground, drew in great draughts of air.

Cornstubble slid to the ground, rested his back against the tree.

"What you wanta talk about, Cody?"

"What you doing here?" Cody panted back.

"Public land up this high, national forest land."

Cody sat up. "Come on, Titus. I'm not saying you shouldn't be here. There was a murder up here. I just want to know some things."

"I remember you, boy. I'd see you and that big dog a'yours running these woods day 'n' night. I knowed your grandmama and your mama. Good people. Indian folks. Sometime they got treated the same as me. You the law now, boy, like your daddy?"

"I'm a private investigator. Barry's sister hired me to help prove her brother didn't kill anybody."

Cornstubble pulled a twist of tobacco from his coat, gestured with it, offering Cody a chaw.

Cody managed a negative shake.

"Barry never kilt nobody. You ask me, Luther's the devil's son, always giving folks trouble."

"Luther's the law, Titus. Law's supposed to be bad news."

"I'm talking Luther's law."

"Why he's giving you a hard time, when I saw you earlier?"

"You go back and tell Luther what I'm telling you? You do, he'll come some night to burn my shack."

"I report to my client, Michelle Willingham."

"Rich folks ain't never done nothing good for me. But Barry's not a bad sort, don't give trouble for the fun of it. What I'm doing is looking for a new spot to start my crop. Too late to get one going but I can start on the land."

"You mean marijuana."

"What else can a man grow out'n the woods? I had a good crop and Luther come chopped it down."

"Burned it did he?"

"Not that devil. Loaded it in a truck, hauled it off under a tarp, said I told anybody, I'd go to jail for life. He thinks I got a still up here somewheres. Wants some'a that, or all of it. Pushed me around when I told him I couldn't afford to make whiskey anymore, way he charges Elton for selling it at the motel now. Says he's gonna be sheriff and he'll run me outa the county if I don't do what he says."

So that's the story, Cody thought. Looked like Luther had his hand in every pie.

"You see anybody on the mountain last night?"

"Won't up here. I's over in Hangin' Dog visiting my daddy and looking for a spot, came back over Chinquapin Ridge then headed up to Indian Boundary."

Hanging Dog's in Graham County, North Carolina, Cody thought, twenty miles away. Many times you couldn't tell what state you were in. He was sure Cornstubble couldn't care less, considered himself to be outside of society and not concerned with imaginary lines.

"Reverend Todd, you ever sell any weed to him?"

"That new preacher man? No, I haven't."

"You ever see Carl up here?"

"Boy's strange. Seen him in women's clothes. One time he

110

set the woods on fire, laughin', jumpin' up and down an' squeal-ing like a little girl. I told Luther just to get him to leave me alone. Don't like folks that burn the woods."

Cody had caught his breath well enough to stand and decided to head back to his truck and leave Titus alone on the mountain.

"I've heard the howler up here. Mostly at night. Sometimes I hear him in the daytime."

"Howler?" Cody said, baffled by the news. "You mean like a wolf?"

"No animal making that noise. Sounds like a lost soul scream-ing to be let outa hell. When I'm up here at night by myself it scares me down to my gizzard."

Twelve

Cody rose early to walk in the milky mists of a Mountain County morning. Then he jogged in place and did a series of deep knee bends to work the kinks out of his legs. After a quick breakfast cooked on the tiny camper stove, he waited in the driveway for Samantha to stop by. When she arrived, they drove to the Taggart house together to search for hidden eavesdropping devices. He was sore from the long chase after Cornstubble and had hobbled to the cruiser like he'd sprained both ankles.

The Taggart house was the first dwelling they came to after turning onto a narrow, gravel road. Two wagon wheels, painted stark white, marked either side of a wide concrete drive. The house sat back from the road; a small shed with a tin roof stood a hundred feet behind it. A split-rail fence marked the property's right-hand boundary, a row of loblolly pines marked the left.

The sides of the house were painted a pale green, with shutters in a contrasting dark lime green. White, high-backed rockers alternated with a few metal gliders on the deep front porch. On one end of the porch, children's toys hid out under a wooden swing. Two large, cone-shaped holly bushes guarded each corner of the porch and flat-topped Irish yews stood on either side of the front steps. The planting area along the front of the house had been recently mulched and the azaleas and rhododendron, devoid of blooms this late in the season, were lush and healthy.

The overall impression was one of neatness, a proud family, possibly on the way up, careful of how they presented themselves to their neighbors. Until now.

"Carl done okay for himself," Cody said as he followed along the walkway a short distance behind Samantha.

"In-laws," she said, glancing back at him. Her grim smile

112

barely lifted each end of her lips. "Without them and his daddy, he'd have squat. He was lazy, thought the world was a big hand-out."

"Do I detect malice?"

"Well-earned malice. Becky, his wife, widow, is a friend of mine. We went to school together. Carl came up from Dalton, Georgia, to open the heating-oil distributorship for his dad. Otherwise he'd have never had the job. Left to his own he'd be eating outa garbage cans, or shacked up as a live-in queen."

"Anybody home?" Cody asked. Samantha was really down on the guy. Talk about speaking ill of the dead.

"Becky's at the funeral home, kids are with her mama. The body will be at the medical examiner's in Nashville for a while. She still has to make the arrangements. Door's unlocked," Samantha said as she mounted the porch steps.

Cody carried a heavy black leather catalog case packed with his electronic gear.

Samantha held the door and let him into a spacious living room. Cody smelled the stench of cigarette smoke that hung on drapes and the pale green carpet. A ceiling fan on low speed stirred the stale air.

Opening his bag of tricks, he removed a field-strength meter and walked around the room. "Built this myself," he said. "Standard field-strength meter with two stages of RF amplification. I come anywhere near a bug, it'll peg the meter and start whistling."

"If you say so," Samantha said. Her eyes seemed to glaze.

Cody circled the room, swept the stiff antenna of the FSM under tables, got on his knees, wiped it under the couch. "Nada."

Samantha lounged on the couch while he went through all three bedrooms, the kitchen, and the dining room. He found nothing. Returning to the catalog case he dropped in the FSM and took out a device he called a whistler. "This uses regenerative feedback, like a mike you hear squeal on a stage sometimes; get near the bug, it'll squeal."

Samantha's answer was a bewildered stare.

Repeating the tour of the house with the whistler, he came up with zilch.

"We checked the phones real good, you know, after Barry and Sharpless had bugs on theirs," she said. "Didn't find anything."

"If you don't mind, I'll check 'em myself." He found the outlets, loosened each from the walls, inspected them using a small flashlight.

"Now for the phone."

"Got two," she said. "Regular phone in the kitchen and a portable in the master bedroom."

He took the kitchen phone apart, stared at it, turned it over, stared at it some more, found nothing, reassembled it.

The bedroom was large, the Chippendale furniture in a North Carolina black mountain cherry with rococo ornamentation. Its cost would make a good down payment on a house, he thought. The bed was a king-size with nightstands on either side. There were a chest of drawers, a triple-mirrored vanity, and a gigantic armoire. The portable phone was on the vanity, cream-colored against the reddish black. Turning it upside down, he removed the screws, slipped off the cover, examined it closely, found nothing that didn't seem to belong, then did the same with the handset.

Leaving the bedroom, he stopped at the door. Stared back at the phone. Something was nagging at him.

"You ever hear of Luther, or anybody else at the S.O. moonlighting as a P.I., doing a little divorce work on the side?" Cody said when he'd returned to the living room.

"Not a whisper," Samantha said.

"Did Becky ever say she wanted a divorce?"

"That was one of our frictions. Becky found out too late that Carl was some kind of pervert. But she had what she wanted: a husband, no matter how flawed, two children, and a house. Her high school dream."

"Now she's twenty-five percent light."

"And a hundred percent ahead, if you ask me. Just like Barry's ahead without Justine."

Cody was mildly surprised at Samantha's attitude. He remained silent for a while wondering if he should check for physical evidence that either Luther or Samantha and the other deputies had missed at the scene. He knew his father had done a follow-up this time but could've missed something. But the techs had spent a whole day here.

Driving back toward Ogden's farm, Samantha was uncomfortable with the silence. "I talked to the sheriff last night," she said as she turned on to Stecoah Road. "Justine's and Sanford's credit cards were missing. Nothing has been charged on any of them."

"Of course robbery wasn't the motive," Cody said. "Still, some killers would have dropped the cards in an area where they would be found and possibly used. It's a good tactic to spread confusion."

Samantha cut her eyes toward Cody. Did he really know what he was doing or was he trying to show off with all the techno-babble? He had said himself that he was no murder investigator, but he had spent the time with law enforcement in California and his dad had told her about the intelligence schools he'd attended in the military. Surely something had rubbed off.

He had been to the places she dreamed of visiting one day, out of Mountain County. Out of the whole damn state. She loved where she lived but didn't want to be tied there all her life. She wanted to live and experience new things.

That was why she had been so attracted to Randy Gateline, and so devastated when he dropped her.

Could Cody take his place? "Sheriff says you're on your own after today. No more rides at county expense," Samantha said. She wished it could have lasted a little longer.

But she had better be careful of him. Cody could be trouble. He was dangerous—and exciting.

Cody rode in silence for the rest of the trip. These murders had something in common. Something besides the victims being tagged with a blue ribbon and being part of a sex club or what-ever it was they were a part of. When he found out what linked them together, he'd have the answer.

Jolinda was waiting in the trailer when he got back. "Why's that oversexed bitch chauffeuring you all over the county?"

Cody wasn't surprised by her aggression. He went to the refrigerator to get a soda before answering. "I think she's got a real case of the hots for me; she comes sniffing around here all the time."

"She's got the hots for Randy Gateline. The big hots. He dumped her, and she's going around with that long sad face."

"Why'd he dump her?"

"Nobody knows but Randy. I don't think even Samantha knows. He just switched her out of his life one day, like she was a lightbulb."

"I thought school was in session. You playing hooky?"

"Ho ho. Mister Funny Man. Teacher's meeting. Some people are going to a memorial for Sanford Sharpless."

"You going?"

Jolinda plopped down by Cody on the couch, scooted close to him, her leg touching his. "No. I never did like him. He was weird."

"Weird?" Cody put his arm around her shoulder but didn't move any closer.

"Yeah. Tried to get me to come to work for him part-time. He looked at me funny a lot. I could feel his eyes on me. My girlfriend, Robin Kingsly—you remember Robin—she says he did her the same way. Asked her to come over to his place one time. She only has eyes for that new deputy, Bubba Whittlemore, and he's sweet on her too."

"Sharpless ever ask you to stop over?"

"Yeah. I told him I was engaged."

"Engaged?" Cody placed his soda can on the coffee table, turned to stare at Jolinda. "Who're you engaged to?"

"To you, silly."

"Oh. I forgot."

"You better not forget. I remember when I was twelve, or thirteen. I told you we were engaged."

"Okay, but you're still going to college before you marry anybody."

"You're trying to trick me, think I'll forget. It won't work."

"Any girls from school ever go out to the Sharpless cabin?"

"I heard one or two did," Jolinda said.

"Could one of them been Barry's daughter?"

"Biba? She could have gone out there once or twice. There's

talk at school she's given some of the football players hand-jobs."

"I thought her name was Polly," Cody said.

"It is, but all the kids at school call her Biba. It's a pet name her grandma calls her. Why're you asking about Biba? You think that's the reason Barry killed the lawyer?"

"Don't be so smart, little Miss Detective. I don't think Barry killed anybody."

"Who did?"

"That's what I'm gettin' paid to find out."

"Then when are you gonna start earning your money, Mister Detective?"

"Right now as a matter of fact," Cody said. He stood and headed for the door.

"Where you going?"

"To church."

The outside of the chapel needed a good coat of paint. Cody opened the door and stepped inside. The lights were off but enough illumination came through the tops of the Palladian windows and the stained glass to let him see that the carpet in the aisle leading up to the altar looked new. So did the polished wooden benches. It smelled like most churches he had entered in his life: musty, of prayer and song books with a floral undercurrent from past funerals.

Despite what Barry had said, the place looked legitimate. Nothing indicated worship that was strange or far out. In fact the decor was conservative, down-home.

He'd noticed five vehicles parked in the church lot. But he didn't see anyone around. The arrow on the sign out front pointed out the church office to the rear. Not seeing a way through behind the altar, he went back out the front door and around to the office. It was unlocked, but the lights were out and there was no one in the small room.

He backed out of the office and walked to the long white building at the back of the church. When he came close enough to the door he read the lettering on a new brass plaque, "Mable Perkins Activity Center."

Opening the door, he found three women sitting at a long

table drinking coffee and eating a snack of what looked and smelled like homemade fried peach pies. A group of small children were gathered at the far end of the building, engaged in a noisy game led by a slightly older, brown-haired girl. The room looked fresh and new. The floor was a shiny parquet and across the room a massive oak table with elaborate carved legs backed up to a wall of white-curtained windows. Near the door, on a line of bronze hooks, hung Boy Scout, Cub Scout, and Girl Scout uniforms looking fresh from the laundry. A showcase window exhibited ribbons from different Scout Camporees.

"Hello," Cody said to the women, who had looked up expectantly when he entered. "Reverend Todd around?"

"You mean Sonny?" one woman said. "He's back up the path in the trailer, likely working on his computers this time of day. Aren't you Cody?" She was slender with gray hair and eyes. Her face had the toughened look many mountain women get hoeing and chopping in all weather, taking the cold and heat and hard times without complaint, forging ahead with a determined, straight-ahead stare. His mother and grandmother'd had that look.

"Yes ma'am, I'm Cody."

"I'm Constance Merriweather. You probably don't remember me. Your mama and me were friends. We went to school together. Last I saw of you was at her funeral. I hear you're working for Doctor Willingham, trying to clear her brother."

"Nice to see you again, ma'am. And that's right; I am working for Doctor Willingham. Either of you ladies have any information you'd like to volunteer? Sure need all the help I can get. I understand Justine attended church here."

The two younger women each gave him an embarrassed negative shake of their head.

"Hardly ever missed a Sunday," Constance said. "She'd come to the outside activities, too, like the dances and the potluck dinners. Barry never came with her, he's always out doing his man things. We've talked amongst ourselves about the killings and all. I can't think of anybody wanting to kill her unless it was Barry. I wouldn't want to go into his reasoning."

"I'd appreciate it, if you hear anything, you'll get in touch with me at my uncle's. Or call the sheriff's office. They'll know how to reach me."

Cody set off up the steep path to the big double-wide trailer, where he knocked on the door. A young woman with long dark hair answered; she looked nervous, strung-out, a little shaky. "Yes?" she said.

"I'm Cody Rainwalker. Is Reverend Todd here?"

"Come on in," she said. "I'm Brandy. Brandy Brusseau. I'll tell him you're here."

Cody observed that she was tall and strong-looking. She wore a tight, white, short-sleeved sweater that emphasized her upper torso, which tapered down to a flat-tummied waist, flared hips, and long slender legs. Her sinewy arms looked accustomed to heavy work. She waited while he appraised her, gave him a flat, level, patient gaze. "You through inspecting me now?" she asked in a quiet voice.

"For the time being," he said. Looked like the reverend had him a tiger by the tail. Or by wherever it was he had her by. There were several enticing choices. He watched her hips move as she swayed across the room and down the hall, wondered if she was exaggerating her walk for his benefit.

Half a minute later Sonny Todd strode up the hall. Sonny was a tall, sandy-haired man with a pleasant smile. His blue eyes flashed with goodwill, his handshake felt firm as he placed his other hand over the grasped one in a bonding camaraderie. Sonny's actions and presence broadcast to Cody that him dropping by was the best thing that could have possibly happened to Sonny all day. The man obviously had the rare gift of meeting others and making them feel glad they were there at that time and in that place. All the good con artists had that gift. Cody felt the friendly warmth but also felt his hand was entrapped, that Sonny had entered his space. A preacher's handshake. And it emanated total sincerity, like Sonny was in the presence of the most interesting person he had met all year.

"Sonny Todd. Pleased to make your acquaintance. I've heard of you, of course. Brandy left you standing. Come on and sit on the sofa. We'll get you some coffee."

"Coffee'd be nice. Black." Cody took a seat on the sofa,

Sonny Todd took a chair facing him.

"Brandy will bring us coffee," he said. "How goes the investigation?"

"Haven't made much headway so far, Reverend. Justine was a member of your church, I hear. You have any idea who'd want her dead?"

"Call me Sonny," he said. "I can't think of anybody that disliked her that much. Of course you know by now that Justine's morals were a little loose. Some of the church ladies thought it inappropriate for her to attend services. But who needs it more? The sinner or the saint? Their loathings were likely motivated by the fear their husbands would get caught up in her indiscretions."

"From what I hear, indiscretions is a mild description," Cody said.

"May be true, but I'm not here to judge. Merely to bring what I honestly believe to be the true teachings of our Savior."

Brandy came in carrying two cups of coffee. She gave one to Cody and kept the other for herself. She then took a seat on the far end of the couch, crossed her legs, and took a sip, giving Cody a challenging stare.

"Why don't you join us, my dear," Sonny said pleasantly.

"Why, thank you, Sonny. Think I will," she answered just as nicely. She held herself erect, brought the saucer up under her cup as she took another sip.

"We're talking about Justine's indiscretions," Cody said.

"What else," she said. "Justine had very little to be discreet about. A husband that didn't love her. Called her a fat pig. Never took her anywhere; preferred his semiliterate friends to her company; he used her as a maid and a baby-sitting service. And oh, yeah. Maybe he fucked her twice a year, New Year's and Christmas."

Cody flashed a look at Sonny. The preacher maintained the same bland expression with just the slightest hint of a smile. "Brandy's a free spirit," he said. "At times though she's a little hesitant about expressing herself."

"From what I'm told, New Year's and Christmas may have been the only open slot," Cody said, then cringed at the unintended double-entendre.

If Brandy picked up on the phrase she chose to ignore it. "I felt so sorry for her. She was abused—not physically but emotionally. The stress made her easy pickings, caused her to seek out the company of men who were just as abusive but did at least pay her some attention as long as she was satisfying their needs. A lot of the men in town picked up on the fact that if they gave her the slightest compliment she'd go to bed with them. If they were really nice, maybe told her she had pretty hair, which she did, she'd give them head 'til the cows came home."

"She's trying to shock you," Sonny said.

Brandy leaned forward and placed her cup and saucer on the glass top of the coffee table. "Goddammit, Sonny! I don't need a running commentary."

"Barry blames your church for Justine's downfall," Cody said. "Says it's a cult. What are you anyhow—Baptist? Methodist? I saw the sign. Mountain Church of Jesus."

Sonny leaned forward to speak but Brandy cut him off. "So we're the Mountain Church of Jesus. Know why Church of Christ members won't fuck standing up? They're afraid somebody will think they're dancing."

Sonny made a quieting motion with his hand. "Down girl. Down. Heel. It's not every humble mountain preacher that has his own attack broad. Seriously. I think Cody is here to find answers, not to attack the church."

She couldn't be controlled so easily. "Barry is an arrogant asshole. He thinks he can do no wrong because his family owns half the county. Maybe your dad is going to take him down. It'd serve him right."

Cody thought if he made her angry enough, she might let something slip. Something she wouldn't want to reveal. "Barry led me to believe you were a pack of backwoods snake-handlers, up here buck-dancing, smoking grass, playing your fiddles, and foaming at the mouth with a kind of holy-roller fervor. After talking to him, I thought the Jehovah's Witnesses were mainstream."

She came out of her chair ready to fight. Sonny gave her a warning look and a negative shake of his head. "Settle down, Brandy. Why don't you go log on to the 'Net and get some work done. Help me pay a few bills somewhere down the road."

She stomped across the room, stopped and looked over her shoulder. There was fire in her eyes. "Okay. But only if you promise to talk about me behind my back."

"I promise," Sonny said.

Brandy disappeared down the hall. They could hear her slamming around for a minute or two.

Sonny sat patiently until she had quieted down. "Brandy's high spirited."

Cody thought of Jolinda, thought her and Brandy were similar. "As I was saying—Barry thinks your church is a front for some sort of sex-drug ring."

Sonny didn't rise to the bait but answered in a calm, reasonable tone. "What you have with most religions—Baptist, Church of Christ, Presbyterian, Methodist, whatever—is what we have in our government. Not only our government but all governments. Bureaucracy. And what does a bureaucracy ever accomplish? Nothing. The proof of that statement is as close as our nearest public school system.

"My church is not organized; don't have a home office to report to. There are no big printing presses that belch Sunday School books so we're not looking to increase our members and our cash flow. There's just this one church, sitting all alone on a mountainside, not trying to change the world but to live in it. I think it's the way we should be. Of course, a person used to being dipped in a large church organization will find us strange."

"I'm not here to find the true way," Cody said. "I'm looking for a motive for murder. If you're running some kind of flaked-out fringe group, we could have the killer hiding in your midst."

Sonny kept his voice calm. "Killers have been known to go to Mass every Sunday. They don't limit their worship to churches like ours. Really the only difference in my beliefs and say, Catholicism, is that I ask where Jesus was from the time he was twelve until he showed up on the scene again at thirty. I believe the keepers of the Dead Sea Scrolls, the Israelis, are keeping the truth from the world out of fear of a mass exodus to Christianity. Other than that, I'm a conformist. You couldn't tell me from a Methodist."

"Who knows what the Izzies are up to. And what you're saying sounds like an interesting theory and one the scholars can debate till hell freezes over," Cody said. "So. I'll bite. Where was he?"

"It's my belief our Savior traveled the world during his lost years—lost to us, not him. He went to India where Buddhism was in full flourish at the time. While there he studied the philosophy of Buddha."

"Doesn't sound too far out to me," Cody said. "If I ever have a year or two to spare, I'll listen to you argue your theory with a Jesuit scholar. Right now I'm looking for a killer. You have any ideas at all? Anybody in your flock fit the pattern of a sicko?"

"Not in my presence. You realize of course folks are on their best behavior when they attend church. That's as it should be. It's much easier to act yourself into thinking than it is to think yourself into acting. Don't you agree?"

"I'll have to think that one over," Cody said. "Carl Taggart was a member of your flock, wasn't he?"

"Carl and Becky and the kids came every Sunday unless Becky took the kids down to visit her mother over a weekend. For some reason Carl would never attend services alone."

"Did you get any hints from your flock Carl might be dancing on the wrong side of the ballroom?"

"Brandy says there was some snickering among the kids, and the men never had anything to say to him unless they were absolutely forced to. I would imagine the image was rough on the Taggart children, with the other children teasing them, as children will."

After a few more pleasantries, Sonny walked Cody to his truck. He explained he was only a part-time preacher, that he programmed computers for a living, mainly for a large consulting firm. By logging on to their mainframes and servers via the Internet, he could work and live in the mountains, a situation he found highly desirable.

He'd met Brandy in Cocoa Beach, Florida, he said, where they both worked on a government contract for NASA. When the contract ended they'd stayed together. She'd also had it with the rat race of living in town.

"I don't want to be a part of what's going on in our society," Sonny said. "The dumbing-down, heavy metal, rap, drive-by

123

shootings, crack smoking, what's-in-it-for-me attitudes all seem to have replaced decency for a man who's lived in better times."

Cody thought it over as he drove back down Mountain Chapel Road. He couldn't decide if he'd uncovered anything or if he'd been intentionally rough on Sonny Todd. He'd have to process what little information he'd picked up, compare that to what he'd gleaned from other sources. That's the way these things usually worked. He did notice Sonny did not deny the church was a front for a sex-drug club.

Samantha made the traffic stop early that morning. She'd spotted the old Dodge 4x4 pickup from a block away as it turned down an alley in the mainly residential neighborhood. She didn't recognize the truck as being one from Mountain County. Somebody might be cruising the rear of the houses looking for one ripe for breaking into.

She called it in, followed the vehicle down the alley and flipped on her emergency lights. She gave the siren a short burst then got out of the cruiser when the pickup halted. "Stay in the truck please," she said when the man opened the driver's door. She kept close to the side of the truck as she'd been taught and loosened the strap over her automatic. "You want to hand me your driver's license?"

The driver didn't match the truck. It was old and green and battered. The man behind the wheel wore an expensive-looking leather coat. His hair was mostly gray. When he spoke she knew he was from out of state. "What's the trouble, Officer?" he asked as he handed his license out the window.

"No trouble. This vehicle matches the description of one used in a robbery a few days ago." It was the law enforcement lie. A cause to stop. "You wanta remain in your vehicle." She walked back to the cruiser to call in the Nevada D.L. number and the Tennessee tag on the truck. The D.L. came back clean. Richard Staros, she read on the license. Guy looked familiar. Then she remembered. He was the same man she'd seen driving Michelle around town in the Mercedes.

She walked back to the truck and returned the license. "Any particular reason you're driving down alleys?"

Staros eyed the deputy and compared her to Michelle. His eyes came to rest on the bulge of her uniform blouse. Why couldn't she come over to Tellico and keep him company? It would be a much better treat than Michelle. He was tiring of her. "Well, my dear, I am unfamiliar with the street layout. I made a wrong turn and came down the alley instead of driving all the way around the block."

"You can address me as Deputy or Officer Goodlocke. Any particular house you're looking for?"

"Just those with for-sale signs in the yard."

"There's been a string of murders in town. The sheriff's office is being very cautious. That's not your truck your driving. It's got Monroe County tags and comes back with the owner being Roger Townsley."

"Roger owns the motel I'm staying in," Staros said. "My car's not up to some of the roads here in your fair county. Roger was kind enough to rent me his 4x4 for an exorbitant fee. You can check it out."

"We already are," Samantha said. "Dispatcher is giving him a call now." Samantha got the all clear over her walkie, then waved Staros on his way.

"What's your first name, Deputy Goodlocke?" he called back to her.

"Samantha," she said over her shoulder.

Samantha, he thought as he drove away. He checked her out in the rear-view mirror, liked what he saw. He'd trade five Michelles for her. Make it ten. But Michelle came with a built-in, million-dollar opportunity. Maybe he could have both. He thought again of discipline and of his partners in Vegas. They wouldn't understand his dalliance with a hillbilly girl. Still, he might just arrange to see Samantha again.

He stopped at the entrance to Owl Hollow Cemetery. Five minutes later the cruiser pulled in behind him. Staros watched in the side mirror as Luther walked up to the truck. "Hello Luther," he said when the deputy reached him. "Hard to drive around this burg without getting pulled over."

"Yeah. I heard it on my radio. We're stopping ever'thing that moves."

"You said on the telephone it was important," Staros said.

"Cody Rainwalker, he's snooping into ever'body's business, says he's after the killer. For some reason he's eyeballing me. I'm afraid he may stumble onto the business about the park. He does, then his dad will know and it'll be all over town," Luther said.

"I thought you were going to see to it Cody got discouraged."

"I already tried," Luther said. "Sent this big ol' boy after him to kick his ass."

"I hear your big ol' boy was the one who received the ass kicking," Staros said. "You said I could depend on you. You're not going to get sloppy and kill Cody are you? That would bring more pressure than we can stand."

"He won't be killed. Just scared off."

"Couldn't we have discussed this on the phone?"

"Sure. Only then you couldn't give me the money you promised," Luther said.

Staros reached in his pocket and pulled out three one-hundred-dollar bills. "I want your assurance Cody doesn't come across anything that will send him to me. If he does, I want you to see that he leaves town—hurt, if necessary, but not dead."

"Yes, sir, Mister Staros. You just leave it to me. And when all this works out and you make sure I'm elected sheriff . . . then we'll make some real money."

Thirteen

The Tellicafe stood back from Old Highway 68 in Tellico Plains, Tennessee. The community center was on one side and a vacant lot on the other. In the background, peaks of distant mountains loomed into a dying, reddish sunset that ignited the late-afternoon haze. The one-story wooden building looked newer than other businesses in the area. The dining area was enclosed in glass and Cody could see a full complement of customers through the windows.

Next door in the vacant field, a crowd of teenagers had gathered and were evaluating 4x4 vehicles: Jeeps, jacked-up trucks, and ordinary farm trucks with four-wheel drives. When the heavy snows came to the mountains, nothing would stand in the way of the four-wheelers and their thrill-seeking on the steep mountain roads.

Cody pulled into the graveled lot, spotted a long, gray Mercedes four-door he guessed belonged to Dr. Michelle Willingham, and pulled in next to it. There were at least twenty other cars in the lot, mostly late-model vans, pickups, sedans, and two expensive-looking Harley motorcycles. The eatery obviously had a decent dinner trade.

The brunette hostess looked harried. Eight couples crowded the entrance waiting for tables to clear. The dining room was packed. The crowd was country and well to do. A faint odor of garlic rode bareback on the smoky aroma of seared beef cooking over an open fire. In a decorator's corner to his right, a maple-colored piano stood with its back to the tables. A violin surrounded by purple flowers substituted for a candelabra. Burlap Brazilian coffee sacks stamped with Portuguese writing had been recycled to form the ceiling.

Michelle rose from a cramped corner table across from the piano.

Cody remembered her as being awkward-looking, sort of big and raw-boned for a high school girl, freckled, with heavy glasses, but always with a manner of self-assuredness he now realized came from being a have in a community of have-nots.

He recalled that ugly-duckling tales from the youth or late teen years were legion—the kind of stories movies were made of, magazine articles were full of. The awkward, buck-toothed teenager matures into a ravishing beauty.

Sadly, it hadn't happened for Michelle. Money couldn't buy everything after all. She looked basically the same, only older. She smiled and waved him over.

Another P.I. myth shot to hell: dashing detective is hired by the beautiful, horny client. Noel would be disappointed. At least she had done something about her teeth and her glasses, which had been traded in for blue-tinted contacts. She wore a brown, light wool suit. The elaborately tied scarf at her neck was the orangy tint of autumn.

Cody sat in the chair across from her, took the hand she offered across the table, felt her warm, firm grip. "I saw you park and took the liberty of ordering you a blackened prime rib. It's their special tonight and always delicious. New Orleans style. I specified medium, you can change it. Comes with steamed veggies and a baked sweet potato with cinnamon butter."

"Medium's fine and I can use the beta carotene." Cody noticed a squashed cigarette butt in the ashtray. On the table-cloth near to his elbow, a wet ring of moisture remained from a glass no longer there.

"When you called and said a place out of Mountain County, I thought of here," Michelle said.

Cody looked around at the other diners. The tables were so close. He kept his voice low. "If we were to meet in Highwater Town, word would be all over the county with fourteen versions of what was said. And none of them would be right."

"I'm not complaining. Do you have anything to tell me?" Michelle looked hopeful.

He hated to disappoint her. "Nothing to prove Barry innocent. At this point everything's confused, especially me."

"An honest answer. How refreshing. I knew I'd picked the right person."

"Barry ever say anything to you about Polly going out to the Sharpless cabin?" Cody said.

"Oh, God. Not Biba too. What an evil man."

"If I know, the prosecutor will eventually know, if it ever comes to trial," Cody said. "Barry ever have any run-ins with Carl Taggart?"

Michelle remained silent, sipping iced water from a crystal goblet.

The waitress arrived with a bottle of red wine and two thin-stemmed glasses, poured them a half glass each, removed the ashtray, and pressed a towel to the wet ring.

Cody waited. From the look on Michelle's face, he knew he'd hit another clay pigeon with the Carl Taggart question.

"When Carl first moved to Highwater Town," she said after the waitress moved away, "he joined the volunteer fire department and was highly enthusiastic. Every month or so he would report a fire. He tried to be the first on the scene. At first he was making a real hero's name for himself."

"Then Barry got suspicious," Cody finished it for her.

"How'd you know?"

"A little mountain bird whispered it in my ear. Seriously, I'd rather not reveal my sources."

"Barry never proved anything," Michelle said, "but the suspicions forced Carl to resign. The county fire marshall and the state fire marshall interviewed him. Prior to that, for about a year, it was difficult to get fire insurance in Mountain County, so many mysterious fires were taking place."

"Strike two," Cody said. "Please don't be offended. I'm playing the devil's advocate. I'm sure this is what the county prosecutor's office will be thinking."

"I understand. You're proposing that whoever is trying to frame my brother knows all these things, knows they can be used against him."

He took a sip of wine. It was chilled and too sweet for his taste. "Right at this moment, I can only think of one person who would have a motive. Unfortunately, I don't think Luther has the brains to concoct such an elaborate scheme without help."

"Heavens! A conspiracy?" Michelle said. She compressed her lips, took a slug of wine, and leaned back in her chair.

"Maybe," Cody said. "Barry could have done it himself. Planted the clues I mean. He might think no one would believe he would be so stupid as to leave all that clutter around."

A sad smile changed her look from one of distress to that of the eternal sufferer. "Please, Cody. Don't give poor Barry that much credit either. He's such a clod, the prototypical country bumpkin. And his ambition? Can you believe he eventually wants to rise to the exalted station of mayor of Highwater Town?"

Wasn't much of an accomplishment for a doctor. "Didn't Barry go to college?"

"At my parents' insistence. The same as me. My parents programmed me as the youngest for the caretaker's role, should they become ill and need nursing. I understand that now. Barry is fated to be the hero, all unconsciously of course."

"What about your oldest brother, Victor?"

"A surrogate parent to take over in case my parents died young, which they have not. The courses Barry took in college—a sham, a Bachelor of Nothingness. In a large city he would be qualified to manage a fast-food restaurant. Here he bathes in the glowing admiration of a pack of rednecks who cloak themselves with invincible ignorance."

Sweet or not, Cody took another sip of wine. "I would think that invincible ignorance is the most enjoyable part of being a redneck. That and a pickup load of beagle hounds barking at all the civilians. Barry says he's into an important business deal."

She looked flustered, attempting to cover it by taking a sip of wine and staring down into the liquid. "Damn Barry can't keep his cards out of sight. Dammit! He married that tiresome little slut, she ruined his name and the family name being tied to all those evil perversions. Barry was so busy running all over the county rescuing strangers, he allowed his own family to flounder."

Looking across the table at his client, Cody became aware of her looking at him strangely, realized he'd simply gone away for a few moments. "I'm back," he said.

"Glad to hear it," she said with a teasing smile. "I've hired a thinker as well as an honest man."

"I think it was William James who said that a lot of people who believe they're thinking are simply rearranging their prejudices."

"And a scholar, all for the same low price," she teased. "That would have been some family to be raised in, the James family. Not Jesse and Frank. Can you imagine?"

"I would have hid in the woods to avoid the competition. Jesse and Frank I could've handled. We'd a had a lot in common. You have any psychiatric training?"

"About as much as your average taxi driver."

"Speaking of hiding in the woods brings up another weird happening, of which Mountain County seems more blessed than most. What would you say about the mental health of someone who went into the mountains, say at night, and howled like they had lost their soul, as my little mountain bird describes it."

Michelle leaned forward, placed both hands flat on the table. "I'll give you a telephone number and you can check with a psychiatrist colleague of mine in Nashville, a Doctor Sharon Bronson. For my part, I'd say this person is disturbed."

"I agree. My daddy thinks it's a psycho doing the killings. I'll ask this Doctor Bronson for some sort of profile, describe to her what was done to the victims."

"Okay. I'll let her know to expect your call."

"Did Barry carry a large life insurance policy on Justine?"

"A minimal amount, I believe. Fifty thousand. With my brother's holdings and income, that's not much money."

Maybe not to her, Cody thought. To a jury it would be a convincing motive.

"At last," Michelle said. "Here comes our food."

Michelle was right on the money, Cody thought later. The prime rib hit the spot. "Surprisingly good food and service for a small town," he said as he watched a young, strawberry-blonde girl, in black jeans, a pullover shirt, and expensive running shoes, bus a table across from them.

"Their lunch is great too."

The waitress offered a list of desserts, which they both declined.

"How long do you think it's going to take—your investigation I mean?" Michelle said.

Cody took a slow drink of water, stalling, wanting to put it just right. "I'm sorry, but it'll take as long as it takes. Only way I know to say it. If I try to rush along I may miss something important. Something that may save your brother's life, or his freedom. Let me assure you I'm devoting all my professional time to this case. It's not on a time-share basis."

"I believe you. It's just—I'm having trouble sleeping nights. I lay awake wondering what terrible thing is going to happen next. Is the killing over, I ask myself." Tears came to her eyes as she reached for a napkin.

"I'm in it for the long haul," Cody said, "if that's what it takes. Or until you say quit."

In the restaurant parking lot, Cody and Michelle paused and savored the cool mountain air. It was dark now and looking up, away from city lights, Cody saw the Milky Way for the first time in months. He stopped at the rear of a Mercedes to continue the conversation. "A common thread in the killings is that all three victims seem to have been linked to some sort of sex club." The sheriff's department was withholding the fact that Carl had also been tagged on the penis with a plain blue ribbon.

"Oh, I hope you're not serious. The scandal is terrible enough already. Our family will be the laughing stock of the county." Michelle stared at the lustrous, expensive sedan. She looked uneasy. "Always wanted one of these. The way I work, visiting kids on mountain dirt roads, I'd destroy it. Oh, and Cody—please don't mention anything about Barry's business deal."

"Everything you say to me is confidential," Cody said. "Anyway, Barry didn't give me any details."

Crunching on past Cody's 4x4, Michelle climbed into a

beat-up Chevy K-5 Blazer with Colorado Wide Boss tires and backed out of the parking spot.

Cody followed the progress of the powerful vehicle as it headed toward Tellico on Old 68, then checked out the Mercedes a little closer. It had Nevada plates. Now wasn't he a hell of a detective?

As Cody drove from the lot, Rick Staros exited the restaurant and watched him drive straight across Old Highway 68 into a lit-up gas station and drive-in market combination. Staros lit a cigarette, exhaled slowly, then crunched through the gravel to his Mercedes.

Cody pulled into the busy gas station, filled his pickup with gas, and bought a few items. The place was loaded with locals and tourists stocking up on beer, ice, fried chicken, and camping supplies. There were numerous campgrounds in the area and not that many stores.

* * *

Ten minutes later and a mile away, Scanner was ready as he waited along the road for Cody to pass. Pulled into the parking lot of an abandoned tavern, Scanner's vehicle was partially hidden behind a dilapidated yellow portable sign.

Cody sped by in his pickup. Scanner waited.

You've come to challenge me, Scanner thought. You'll be a worthy opponent, not like the others, who were so weak, so unaware.

Waiting until the taillights were almost out of sight, Scanner tracked the tracker.

"Unit four—Mountain County," came the call on the sheriff's frequency.

"Go ahead, unit four."

"Mountain County, I'm ten-eighty-one with an eighty-eight white Mustang in front of the HillTop Tavern. Tennessee license, Mary-Oscar-Victor-Charlie—zero-three-one-three." It was a deputy stopping a vehicle for a traffic violation.

"Ten-four, unit four."

Driving slowly on the winding, mountain road, Scanner held back. He didn't need to rush; the road led to only one possible destination—Highwater Town.

Fourteen

Ogden Two Bears rocked in a high-back wooden rocker on his front porch. "Nice night," he said, meaning, How you been, Cody; come sit a spell and we'll talk.

Cody heard what Ogden didn't say, pulled up another rocker a few feet away. It was dark on the porch. No lights were on in the house. In the dimness, he couldn't see Ogden, but in his mind's eye he brought up the man's face to talk to—dark, broad with a long, slightly flattened nose, skin weathered from the farming he'd done for years, crow's feet around the eyes from the sun and from the blazing hot furnaces he'd stared into at the foundry. "Nice and cool. 'Bout forty, I'd say."

"'Bout right," Ogden said. "You making any headway?"

"Not much. Went and saw Michelle over in Tellico, made my report."

"Michelle was out here about three months back. Sit out here on the porch and made me a offer for the farm. Good offer, little over what it's worth."

Cody thought it over a minute before he replied, "You selling?"

"You know better."

"All the land they own. What's she want with more?"

"Says they need land to run cows. They lost pasture when the trailer park was built. She's the driving force in that family; always has been since she graduated medical school. Your daddy likes to stay on her right side. She can swing a lot of weight come election time."

Did Michelle's visit have anything to do with the business the Willinghams were keeping so hush-hush? "That why he put her brother in jail?"

"Put him in jail cause he had to, you know that."

"Yeah. I noticed he didn't put him in jail again."

It was Ogden's turn to stay silent for a while. When he spoke there was conviction in his voice. "If he had good evidence he'd put him in jail, lose an election or not. He's a fair man and he sets high standards for himself."

"You say so. Jolinda still staying here?"

"Gone to bed. Stayed awake for you a while then gave it up."

Both men looked up as the headlights of a vehicle pulling into the quarter-mile entrance to the farm's driveway swept a distant line of trees. The lights wiped the trees again in the opposite direction.

"Somebody just turning around in the driveway," Ogden said.

In a nearby pasture one of Ogden's cows bawled, another answered, then both sang a short duet. Cody sniffed the country smells; the sweet smell of hay was heady, almost overpowering. There was also the scent of hemlock wood lumber, a contrast of pungent astringency. "She fighting with her stepmama again?"

"That's a war that'll never end," Ogden said. "Jolinda's made up her mind this time. She'll stay here until she graduates from school. And it's safer here for her with this nut out there. You think this killer's going to strike again?"

"The killer is going to kill until he's stopped. He's a real nut-case, a sicko."

"You say he. You know it's a man?"

"Really hadn't thought of a woman. Women usually don't kill like that."

Ogden rocked silently. Cody visualized him thinking.

"Your daddy comes out at night sometimes, sits and rocks and talks."

"That right?"

"Talks about you, about your mama, about Betty Jean, all way up in Canada, about Tiffany down in Mexico. He's a lonesome man. He wishes he had all his family around him."

Cody rocked, looked into the night and thought about the family he'd lost. Tiffany was his daughter, spirited away to Acapulco by his ex-wife, a nurse who'd left him for the security of marriage to her employer, a doctor twenty-five years her senior. Betty Jean, his older sister by a year, had lived in British Columbia for ten years now.

"Jolinda's good company to me," Ogden continued. "So were you before you left. I know just how your daddy feels."

Cody maintained his silence, leaned his head back and closed his eyes and remembered coming home after school that long ago winter's day to find his mother leaning against her bedroom wall, bleeding from a self-inflicted gunshot wound. She died two days later. The day after her funeral, Cody moved into Ogden's hayloft and lived there for almost a week before he was discovered and brought into the house and adopted as a nephew into Ogden Two Bears's family. "Family's full of sadness," Cody said finally.

"And anger," Ogden said. "Don't forget the anger."

"I'm 'bout ready to turn in. With all this shit going on, you wanta keep a close look after Jolinda."

Ogden walked with Cody to the bottom of the porch steps. "'Night, son," he said. He understood Cody wasn't in the mood to talk about family.

"Goodnight, Uncle Ogden." Cody knew Ogden was headed for the family plot to say goodnight to Evvie, the young wife he'd lost so many years ago. She'd been a passenger in the fatal car crash with Jolinda's mother and was killed along with her unborn daughter. "Lot of sadness," Cody muttered, tears in his eyes, as he turned toward his trailer. Beyond the trailer where the forest began he heard the short, yapping bark of a fox.

Half a mile down the country road from Ogden's farmhouse, breath fogging the windshield, Scanner sat in the darkened vehicle, wiped the glass with a rag, watched and waited until the lights came on in Cody's trailer. Twenty minutes later the lights went off. Satisfied the detective was settling in for the night, the prowler left on his nightly rounds of the county.

At the Cozy Living Trailer Park, in the third trailer from the entrance—a brown double-wide with white painted underpinning and an add-on front porch—Donna Sue Vandergriff lay back on the bed and talked on the phone in a sleepy voice. Chasing after her young son all day had worn her to a frazzle, she was telling her husband, wishing he was home to comfort her and to watch the boy's crawling explorations. She wore a thin, short nightgown, and her long, beautiful legs were gathered under her. She tossed her thick blonde hair away from the receiver at her ear. Her nine-month-old son was pushed up close to her on the king-size bed, sound asleep. She talked softly so as not to waken him.

"I sure wish you was home, Harlan," she said to her husband.

"I do, too, honey, only you know I can't get off this boat." Harlan Vandergriff worked as a deckhand on the *Lucy Walker,* one of the many tugs that towed and pushed gigantic barges up and down the Tennessee River. Every night, when near a town on the river, Harlan called his young wife on his cellular phone.

"Where are you now?" asked Donna Sue.

"Just went through the locks on Nickajack and Guntersville Lakes. We're headed toward Huntsville and Muscle Shoals. I sure wish I was home, in bed with you."

"I do too. I'm scared with all these killings in town."

"The door locked?"

"Of course. But you know the locks and the doors on these trailers are so flimsy."

"I get home, I'm gonna teach you how to shoot the pistol."

"The dog wasn't a good idea," Donna Sue said.

"Yeah. A dog that won't bark. Like a pistol without bullets."

"Hope they catch ever who's doing all this," Donna Sue said.

"Here comes Captain Vann. Gotta go. I'll call back a little later. Love you. Kiss the baby."

"Love you, too, Harlan."

Donna Sue placed the phone on the bedside table, reached over her head and turned off the night light. Harlan Junior had been tiring today, rampaging into everything, under the counter shelves, trying to get out the front door, went everywhere he shouldn't have. She dropped off to sleep immediately.

Cody lay flat on his back in the darkened camper. Are they going to find this killer? Was he? It wasn't really his job. He'd been hired to clear Barry, not find the murderer. Only way he knew to clear him, though, was to track down the real killer. Then was it his job to find the real killer if he wanted to clear his client? Was he splitting hairs? It was his job to find him—or her. No. Not a her.

Tomorrow he would start all over, go through all the moves again, see if he had overlooked something.

He had the small windows cranked open to let in the cool air. Night sounds came to him, yet familiar when recalled. Not like his miniature apartment on Elliston Place in Nashville with the constant traffic, no matter what time of night, the drunks calling to each other as they scrounged the neighborhood trash, the sirens of ambulances on the way to the numerous hospitals in the area, the police cars responding to emergencies. Those had been his night sounds for years now, what he was attuned to.

What was the old saying? When you can hear the silence, everything else is wild.

The last thing he remembered before falling asleep was the hawing of one of Ogden's mules.

At the Cozy Living Trailer Park, all was quiet.

A shadow moved from the road to a clump of forsythia that grew near the line of trailers, then kneeled close to the ground and waited, prepared to flee if any alarms were raised. After a five-minute wait, the skulker lay flat on the ground, belly-crawled to the porch of the Vandergriff's double-wide. Waited once more.

Dressed all in black—cotton pullover, running shoes, athletic pants—the prowler was almost invisible. Slowly the figure rose and crept to the door. Stooping low, reaching in a pocket for the key, he unlocked the door and entered the living room.

In her bedroom, Donna Sue, sound asleep, was disturbed by the subtle air-pressure change, but did not wake. She squirmed under the sheet and pulled it up around her shoulders. Harlan Junior whimpered in his sleep.

One hundred and fifty miles to the west, Donna Sue's husband was thinking of his family as he stood under a bright floodlight and automatically dressed a mooring rope around a tie-off point. He paused a moment to watch the ghostly shape of a dark heron sail silently over the barge in front of him. The stealthy flight of the big waterbird created an uneasy feeling, an omen. He wished, as he often did, for a job closer to home.

Back at Donna Sue's trailer, the intruder moved as if knowledgeable of the room's layout, did not bump into walls or furniture in the darkness. On silent feet, one slow step at a time, the prowler headed for the bedroom door, opened it quietly, moved to stand at the foot of the bed, then looked down at the dark forms of the sleeping woman and child, barely making out the shapes. He brought a length of rope from under his shirt, moved to Donna Sue's side, and bent over her.

Donna Sue, sensing something different, came wide awake. Seeing the shadow looming over her, she screamed.

"Shut up, bitch," said a man's coarse voice.

Donna Sue smelled the strong odor of cigarette smoke on the man's clothes. "Who are you?" she yelled.

"Goddammit, I said shut up or I'll choke you." The man reached for her, caught her defending hand, and pulled her from the bed.

She resisted, pushed the man away with both of her hands against his chest, and ran around the foot of the bed to get to the other bedroom.

The attacker followed, grabbed at her, ripped the flimsy nightgown from her body. As he chased her, he heard a strange scratching sound nearby, but couldn't place it. "Come back here, you fucking bitch."

Donna Sue reached for the table, snatched up the phone, and slammed it into the attacker's face. "Get away from me, you sonofabitch!"

Struck sharply across the bridge of the nose, the man fell back two steps, recovered his balance, shook his head to clear it, then came at her again.

Donna Sue was already lunging for the door to the connecting bedroom. Hands grabbed her now-naked hips from behind.

From beyond the door, a terrible clamor began. Fast scratching sounds tore at the wood.

With a frantic sob Donna Sue yanked the door open.

A black shape roared past her—a predatory, snarling, bone-crunching horror.

"Kill him, Go-rilla!" Donna Sue screamed. "Kill the mother-fucker!"

The one-hundred-ten-pound rottweiler was already on the attacker. Locking onto the man's bristly face with its powerful jaws, the beast went berserk with rage, using the strength of an immense, muscular neck to shake the man like a captured rat. The dog's sharp front and back claws tore through clothes and into the intruder's bared flesh, exposing the bones of his chest and ribs.

Donna Sue found the lights and flicked them on, grabbed a howling young Harlan from the covers, and fled. On her way out the door she paused long enough to yell, "Kill the sonofabitch, Go-rilla! Kill 'im!"

Prodded by the command, Go-rilla gave a high-pitched growl through tightly clenched teeth that scraped, then shattered, the hard bones of the man's face. He shook his head violently, paused, shook it again.

The prowler tried to yell for help but his jaws were locked down with teeth that could crack a steer's leg. Before he lost consciousness, the most the man could manage was a keening moan.

Flashing blue and red emergency lights illuminated the roadway leading to the trailer park. Cody counted six sheriff's department vehicles, two highway patrol cruisers, an ambulance, a fire truck, and a 4x4 Dodge from the Tennessee Fish and Game.

Wildlife services? What'n the hell was going on?

Wanda June had wakened Cody, calling him on the sheriff's instructions. "Killer broke into a trailer at the Cozy Living. He's in custody," was all she told him.

Looked like the whole town had turned out. Cody parked behind a pickup he thought was Randy Gateline's and walked the hundred yards to the trailer park entrance. On the way, he passed Michelle Willingham's Blazer. On its roof a red emergency light beat a steady tempo. Cody heard the voice of the county radio dispatcher through the rolled-down passenger's window.

At the driveway, bare-headed and in a yellow fireman's coat, Barry Willingham hung on to the open driver's door of the fire truck; its red light splashed his face with a steady, strobing pulse

141

and gave his features a carnival look. Shoulders hunched against the night's chill, Randy Gateline stood a few feet away, his hands in his jeans pockets.

"Why the fire engine?" Cody asked. "Killer torch the place?"

"Wanda June hit the fucking panic button," Barry said. "Had the goddamn air-raid siren on top the courthouse going off. Didn't know if we was being invaded or a tornado hit town."

"Looks like both," Cody said, nodding at the still-gathering crowd.

"Looks like your job's over with," Barry said. "I can start getting my life back together now."

Randy smiled and stepped closer, brought his hands out of his pockets and rubbed his arms. "Yeah, Cody. It's not like we're not glad to have you here. I'm glad it's over too. Town's been crazy since all this started."

Cody looked from one man to the other. "So both of you're convinced the killer's been caught."

Randy stared at Barry for a second, then shrugged and gave Cody an exasperated look. "What else? How many killers you think Highwater Town can have at any given time?"

"Hope you gentlemen are right. Don't want to see anybody else killed."

Leaving Barry and Randy at the fire truck, Cody approached his dad and the deputies grouped around giving their reports. There was Samantha, three deputies he didn't know. The two investigators, Albert Feltus and Johnny Knight, were standing with their notebooks in a group of what Cody took to be witnesses. Where's Luther? Cody thought. At the trailer next door to the victim's, Cody spotted Michelle holding a small baby in her arms. She was talking to a young blonde woman wrapped in a quilt.

He watched Samantha take her hat off and wipe her forehead with the back of her hand as she left the group and walked unsteadily to the rear of the ambulance to speak urgently to a paramedic. He brought out a portable oxygen bottle and placed a mask over her face. She held it with one hand, inhaled a few deep gasps, then removed it with a gesture of thanks.

"Zoo in town?" Cody asked his dad.

"I don't need none of your smart-ass at three in the morning."

Cody had decided years previously to never be intimidated by anyone. "So what's going on?" he persisted.

"Got a yahoo, I.D. as yet unknown, broke into a trailer on a young wife and her baby, husband is away. Made one mistake. There is the meanest, snarlingest, slaveringest dog I ever laid eyes on in there. Had to get the wildlife folks to dart him before we could get to the body."

"The body?"

"Killed the intruder—tore half his head off. No real need for you to go in there and see that mess."

"Seen enough in my time. You don't recognize him? He a local?"

"Don't know. Hasn't got a face to recognize."

Samantha returned to the group. "Hello, Cody," she said, smiling at him weakly as she put her hat back on.

"You go in there?" he said, nodding at the trailer.

"Wish I hadn't. There's blood on the walls and on the ceiling. Furniture all turned over and broke. Neighbors say the trailer was doing the rock-and-roll."

Deputy Whittlemore came down the metal steps of the double-wide's add-on porch carrying a video camera and walked to the group of officers. His face was sweaty despite the chill. "There's blood, hair, and shit all over the room," he said quietly, a stunned expression on his face. He began to gag.

"Over there's where I puked," Sheriff Rainwalker said, tapping the deputy lightly on the shoulder, pointing to the far end of the trailer.

Whittlemore ran for the spot, one hand over his mouth, camera dangling in the other.

Cody turned his back at the sound of retching, spotted a young, slender highway patrolman approaching the group. His hat was off. He wore his blond hair in a crew cut. He tapped a small notebook on the palm of his hand. Anxious to relay his information, the patrolman began talking before he got to the group. "Ran the plates on the truck. Comes back on a Thomas G. Yount, male, white, forty-six, address this city. Know him?"

"I do," Samantha offered. "Tommy Yount. Works for Vic

Willingham's Mobile Home Sales. Handyman, part-time drunk and a full-time lowlife. Kicked out of the marines a few years back on a dishonorable."

Sheriff Rainwalker nodded. "Had him locked up on D & D a number of times. Regular at the HillTop Tavern."

The Game and Fish ranger joined the group, a large red-headed, red-faced man. "Sheriff, drug's wearing off. Gave him a load I would've a large bear cub. Owner's got a chain on him."

"Hope it's a strong one," Samantha said.

"Small towing chain. When I first got here, that animal was prowling from one end of the trailer to the other, all bristled up and growling deep down in his throat. Walked up to the body—hiked his leg and pissed five good shots right in the dead guy's ear. Woman owns it couldn't get it calmed down. Go-rilla, she calls him. Sumbitch sure is named right."

Jolinda Risingwaters was coming out the front door as Cody mounted the porch steps. Her black hair hung in two long braids, each adorned with a small, bright feather. Ready for school, she carried two books and a notepad in one hand.

"Morning, Jolinda," Cody said sleepily.

Moving in fast, she popped him in the lower abdomen with her fist. When he bent forward in reaction, she brought her forearm down hard on the back of his neck.

He stumbled and fell to his knees. "Goddammit, Jolinda! I didn't teach you to use that shit on me."

"Asshole! You didn't wake me up and take me with you last night when they caught the murderer!"

Ogden had watched through the living-room window. He stepped onto the porch as Jolinda stormed off to drive herself to class. "Little girl's getting all grown up," he said.

"Let's hope she mellows out before college," Cody said as he rose to his feet.

"Be glad she didn't use the little ball-bat she carries behind the seat of her pickup. Heard on the radio they caught the killer. That right?"

Cody told his uncle what had transpired.

"Tom Yount? Seen him around. Worked at the foundry for a

month or so, but he was too weak to really lift anything, or too lazy. Walked all hunched over like he had lung problems. Consumptive. Your grandfather had black lung; he walked like that right before he died, but he was over sixty."

"They say they've caught the killer, so what I'm gonna do is go up to the cabin for two, three days—before it snows and I can't make it without an ATV."

Fifteen

Near the summit of Wolf's Head Mountain later that afternoon, Cody carried a load of groceries into his cabin and placed them on the homemade kitchen table. It took two more trips to tote his ice chest and a chain saw he'd borrowed from Ogden. Although groggy from lack of sleep, he made the rounds of the cabin, checked for weather damage or vandalism, moved the table back and pried up the floor. The trap door led to a concrete cellar he had dug himself.

Large wooden shelves against the basement's rear wall hid the entrance to a cave. The cave was his air conditioner on the rare days when the temperature rose to eighty or better. No need to open it up today. He kept it hidden, knowing that with all the radical spelunkers in the area, the news of an unexplored cave would bring them on the run, and his cabin would be destroyed in the process. Other than himself, only Jolinda and Ogden knew of its existence.

He'd discovered it as a young boy, hiking the mountain with his dog. Actually Wolf had been fascinated with the smell of the place and had clambered down in the shallow sinkhole looking for a rabbit or a varmint. Cody and the dog went inside a few feet but weak flashlight batteries and fear drove them back. Strange, he thought. He'd never had the urge to explore the cave further.

On the shelves against the walls of the cellar lay some of his put-aside possessions, once considered treasures. The stone-tipped lance he'd made, using a flint point he had found. The point was over a foot long and as sharp as honed steel. He had envisioned a primitive ancestor, a flint knapper, shaping the hunting tool. On the shelf lay a steel hatchet, actually a tomahawk, designed for throwing. He recalled that at one time he'd been proficient at hitting a designated spot on an ancient oak, time after time. No time for games anymore. It sure was hell to grow up. If that's what he'd done.

Later, Cody walked the boundaries of his one hundred wooded acres. He loved the mountaintop property left to him and his sister by his mother. It was the only thing she'd had to leave them. The only thing the lawyer, Coleman, hadn't managed to steal. No wonder folks thought he'd killed him. Sonofabitch deserved what he got.

From the high peak towering over the property flowed the mountain spring that eventually became the Highwater River. Two hundred yards downslope from the cabin, it cascaded noisily through his holdings. The Cherokee National Forest Fish Hatchery kept it stocked with rainbow trout, and there were still native brook trout to be found in some pools. Specs, the mountain folks called them. They were actually char. What more could a man want? One day, Cody thought, I'll be able to live up here full time.

Yeah. Dream away.

Once again he familiarized himself with the red spruce and Canada hemlock flourishing at the altitude, the floras of the area that were found more commonly in the far north. He'd arrived too late for the white rhododendron that bloomed in mid-July. The dogwoods were showing a red tinge, a forecaster of fall. Stepping over to the bluffs overlooking the Highwater Valley, he scanned the thick foliage of moosewood and mountain ash directly below the sandstone formation. Peering through the screen he identified the hulking silhouette of Walking Crow Mountain in the far distance. Everything a man could want and then some.

It was cold too. The way he liked it. He didn't like hot weather, really never wanted to feel hot weather again. He remembered the last summer in Nashville, how dreadful it had been in the snarled traffic and on steaming streets and sidewalks. Did he really have any choice? He had to earn a living.

Once back in the one-room cabin, he made a bed with the thick quilts he'd brought along, then ate a sandwich from his ice chest. He'd been humiliated by the chase after Titus Cornstubble and was determined to rise early the next morning and get acclimated again to exercising at high altitude. With that in mind he went to bed early, read a few pages of the latest G. M. Ford P.I. mystery by the light of an old kerosene lantern, then dropped off to sleep thinking about street people, Pacific fishing schooners, and Seattle.

Samantha, Deputy Whittlemore, and the sheriff were in conference, sitting around the sheriff's desk. Albert Feltus and Johnny Knight leaned against the wall. Each deputy had a notepad, read over the entries they had made. Luther was absent, having rotated the day before on two days off. The sheriff was winding it down, speaking in a tired drawl, "Okay folks, key found in Yount's pocket fit the front door of the Vandergriffs's house trailer. They bought the trailer at Vic's, where Yount was employed. Yount liked what he saw in Donna Sue, got a duplicate key, then waited until her husband was out of town. Ever'body agree?"

The deputies nodded.

"Bubba," he said to Whittlemore. "You talked to his fellow employees. What you got?"

"Two of 'em say Yount talked about how he'd like to get some of Donna Sue, told 'em she'd been flirting with him. Also say he'd been dipping into Justine Willingham, and they'd seen him riding in Carl Taggart's truck from time to time."

"Samantha?"

"Talked to Donna Sue. She didn't know Tom Yount existed, even though he helped set up their mobile home when they first bought it. Neighbors say she's a straight arrow, crazy in love with her husband."

The sheriff sighed. His eyes looked weak, tired. "What you all think? Albert? Johnny? Think we oughta make an announcement we have the killer that has been terrorizing our fair community?" he said in a sarcastic, out-of-character tone.

Bubba shrugged his shoulders.

"We have a tie-in with two victims," Samantha said.

"What say we sleep on it?" Johnny Knight said.

"I agree with Johnny," Albert Feltus said.

* * *

Later that night, the whisperer was back on the phone. "You sure you can't come to the county tonight, give it to me good?" she whispered.

Don't murmur! Speak! Scanner desperately wanted the owner of the voice.

"Gotta stay home once I get there," said the male voice on the cellular.

"You gonna give it to your wife real good?"

"I'll meet you tomorrow, same time, same place."

"I need it right now."

"You sure your husband can't hear you?"

"Just a minute, I'll check." There was a clunk as the phone was laid on the table.

In the vehicle, straining for an unspoken clue on the attached speaker, Scanner waited, every second a torment. Who was she? Who was this whisperer?

After what seemed to Scanner like a lifetime, she was back on the phone. "He's watching the TV. I done told you. All he ever does is eat, sleep, watch TV, and fish for bluegill. He never gives it to me like you do."

"I'm pulling into my driveway. Gotta go."

The callers disconnected.

"Aaarggh!" Scanner's fury was uncontrollable. "Bitch! Whore! I'll find you. I'll kill you!"

* * *

Monk O'Malley was the center of attention at Fuzzy's.

Behind the bar, sweat beading on his slick, bald head, Fuzzy watched the attorney closely, knew he was near his limit. He watched for the familiar signs. Like the death grip the lawyer now maintained on the edge of the bar. Those surrounding him were not in much better straits, but this was a special night. The cash register played Fuzzy's favorite tune. The men had just drunk yet another round to Go-rilla, the wonder dog.

"I agree with you, my fellow citizens," announced Monk in

his orator's voice. "That splendid canine has saved the county the cost of trying the fiend and the state the cost of the electricity to fry him. We'll award the splendid pooch a hero's medal—a gold medallion emblazoned with *Cave Canem*. Monk teetered as he gesticulated with his hands and body.

Fuzzy nodded to Big 'Un. The bouncer approached, plowing through the crowd like a redneck icebreaker. Standing by Monk's barstool, he placed his hand lightly on the attorney's shoulder. "Time to go, Mister Monk. Mister Fuzzy's rule is: You start talking them furrin languages, you're out the door."

"Ah. Young Anteaus," slurred Monk, his bleary eyes peering over the trick glasses. "Is that you glowing in the reflection of yon exit light or has the full moon risen tonight bearing the goofiest of grins?"

"See there, Mister Monk. You don't even know who I am."

Big 'Un drove Monk to the rear entrance of his office on Court House Square. The big man never hurried anywhere, so he was patient as he helped the inebriated attorney mount the stairs leading up to his bachelor digs. Monk never locked his apartment door, Big 'Un knew. He helped the diminutive man to the couch. "Have a good night, Mister Monk."

"Farewell, Titan," called Monk from the couch.

Big 'Un closed the door behind him and descended the stairs. "Don't even know who I am," he grumbled, shaking his head.

* * *

With his thoughts flip-flopping crazily from the whereabouts of the missing Cody Rainwalker to the identity of the horny whisperer, Scanner parked under an ancient sweet gum in front of the Town Square Feed and Hardware Store and followed Big 'Un's progress with growing impatience.

Move, don't amble, you oversized clod. Scanner's mind was speeding, zipping around in the enclosure of his skull.

The huge bouncer apparently didn't pick up the suggestion, continuing to move with his slow-motion, Clem Kadiddlehopper walk. After fumbling for his ignition keys a coon's age, he climbed into his pickup, backed around, and headed back to work.

Upstairs, Monk had passed out on his couch.

Now they would know he existed, Scanner thought. Know no one could imitate the quality of his work. The man had been a fool to try. Imagine the gall.

Eventually Cody Rainwalker would come for him.

Then a killer would meet a killer.

Scanner exited the truck, paused, and checked the immediate area. No one around. Slipping on dark cotton gloves to prevent leaving fingerprints, he moved swiftly to the stairway leading to Monk's apartment.

Sixteen

Cody was awake but didn't want to get out from under the warm quilts. Damn it was cold, he thought. He shoulda built a fire. He lay there for a few more minutes, then, dressed in only his underwear, forced himself to bounce up and throw three logs into the fireplace. Splashing kerosene over them, he threw in a lit wooden match and jumped back in bed. Fifteen minutes later the room was warm enough for him to get up and dress.

After a light breakfast of fruit and yogurt, he took the chain saw outside and went scouting for fallen trees. He knew that during the winter, heavy winds and snow surged over the western brow of the mountains and loaded the shallow-rooted conifers with snow, causing many to fall under the double load. There was never a need to cut a live, standing tree. Nature handled that chore. He would clean up by sawing fallen logs into lengths he could burn in the fireplace, then splitting them with a heavy wood-splitting maul and wide chisel.

By ten o'clock, he'd had all the chain-sawing he could stand for one day. His forearms and shoulders ached from the unaccustomed exertion. Placing the saw on a stack of wood and picking up his denim jacket, he stretched, decided to hike to the mountain's summit and give his upper body a rest.

As he followed the rutted fire road that ran by his cabin, he forced a fast pace up the steep incline for three miles until he came to the marker announcing the North Carolina state line, and that he was entering the Nantahala National Forest. At this point he was only a few miles directly south of Smoky Mountain National Park.

He rested out of the cold wind, in the lee of a tangled laurel slick as the mountain folk called the heavy growths of Catawba rhododendron. In the midst of a patch of ladyferns, he thought of where he had been, and where he might be going, and if he could manage to live long enough to get there.

He remembered what his father had to say about "if." "Son, if a bullfrog had a hip pocket, he'd carry a pistol to shoot snakes with."

Flopping back on the ground, he stared at a faultless blue sky. A pair of ravens circled into view. Spirit birds, his grandmother had called them. She had told him they'd bring warnings if you respected them. A member of the crow family, their wingspans could reach four feet. He'd read they were rated as the largest of songbirds. Only songs he'd heard them sing sounded like they had a sore throat. The pair spun above him then whirled off the edge of the earth, or so it appeared as they dropped below the ridge. He raised up to watch them swoop back, then glide to the upper branches of a dead Fraser fir to roost and squabble. The deceased giant was almost a hundred feet high. The southern Appalachian variety grew much taller than its cousins to the north.

The Fraser fir was becoming endangered and that angered him. Insects were destroying the majestic trees that grew mainly above six thousand feet, sometimes intermixed with red spruce at slightly lower altitudes. The introduction of the insects was a repeat of the human introduction of the fungus that had killed off all the chestnut trees.

The wild boar of the area were not native and had also been introduced by man. They proved themselves pests by destroying needed watershed. The boar were being slowly eradicated by hunters and the newly reintroduced wolves and the few remaining mountain lions in the area. Why didn't the fuckers leave his mountain alone?

From inside his blue jeans pant leg, Cody withdrew the Buck hunting knife he'd carried since his days as an undercover cop on the streets of Los Angeles. He had fashioned the velcro holster himself, wore the knife handle pointed down for quick and easy access. Choosing a dry stick from the natural debris around him, he began to whittle and to think about the killer everyone thought they'd caught. He didn't believe it for a minute. When he got back to town, he needed to talk to Monk first thing.

The afternoon Cody left for his cabin, Jolinda came home from school worried she'd gone too far by punching him. Changing into rough workclothes, she took care of her daily chores until Uncle Ogden came home from work, then joined him at the kitchen table with the supper she'd prepared.

"Before he went up on the mountain, Cody had a call from some woman doctor in Nashville," Ogden said. "Said she was a psychiatrist."

Jolinda didn't respond, sat there with a worried expression.

"What you so down in the mouth about?" Ogden asked after he'd eaten a forkful of turnip greens seasoned with the dried cayenne peppers he had grown himself and a full slice of griddle-fried corn bread. He chewed and swallowed some more while he waited for an answer.

"Was Cody mad when he went up the mountain?"

"You feed and water the mules?"

"I always feed and water the mules. Was he mad?"

"Mad? Wasn't mad. Fact, he said you'd learned what he taught you just right, good timing and all."

"He did?" Jolinda smiled her pleasure. "I sure took him by surprise."

"Maybe. Maybe not. You can never tell about Cody. He's a strange one. Has been all his life. His mama and grandmama made him strange, especially his grandmama, teaching all that Cherokee witch-doctor nonsense, like my mama, your grand-mama wanted to teach me. Living out in la-la land didn't unstrange him any either. Same old stuff, meditation and martial arts. I'm surprised he's got as much sense as he has left."

Ogden watched Jolinda cock her head to one side and look at him half cross-eyed, the way she always did when she was being mischievous. "The deputy-bitch stopped me and asked where he was. She's hornier'n a three-balled tomcat after Randy Gateline dumped her."

"You tell her?" He knew the answer, had asked automatically to carry his end of the conversation. He also knew better than to chide her about manners. She was that much like Cody. They were a pair.

"Didn't tell anybody anything," Jolinda said.

Ogden nodded as he gnawed a pork chop bone. "Cody gets itchy after he's been in a big city a while. One day he'll realize he belongs on the mountain."

"Tell me again about when he first laid eyes on me."

Ogden placed the stripped bone in his plate and took a sip of cold spring water to wash away the smoked, salty taste. "It was a cold winter night, 'cause you chose to be born in December, Christmas day, so I guess Santy Claus brought you. It'd been even colder early on, had snowed a heap, about three feet or better up in the mountains. Then it turned warm. The thaw brought the Highwater River out of its banks and Rattlesnake Creek where y'all lived back then became a raging river. Then it got cold again. It was your mama's time, and yours. Your daddy couldn't get you all to the hospital so you were born at home. For some reason your mama decided to call you Risingwaters instead'a Rudolf or Rattlesnake."

"Wonder why?" Jolinda said, ducking her head bashfully.

"Waters went down a week later. I brought Cody by to see you. He'd just come to live with me, wouldn't live with his daddy; his mama had killed herself just a few months earlier. I remember I'd just bought him a red mackinaw. He didn't have a decent coat back then. Wouldn't wear a hat."

Jolinda's face was radiant. She loved the tale. "Did he think I was an ugly baby?"

"I don't know what he thought. Your mama pulled the little pink blanket back from your face. You'd been sleeping. Your eyes popped open at the light. You looked up at Cody and smiled like you recognized him, like you'd known him from somewhere before, only I knew that was impossible. You haven't stopped smiling at him since."

"But what did Cody think?" She knew Ogden was drawing it out to increase her enjoyment.

"Looked at you like you were some kind of angel. Worshipped you from the first time he saw you. Beats anything I ever saw. Your mama said so too."

"You miss my mama like I do?"

"I loved my baby sister. When she died, a little of me died, like when my Evvie died. Now I got you and Cody to love."

"Why's all the people in the county afraid of Cody?"

"You afraid of him?" Ogden asked.

"No."

"I ain't either. We live in the county. So ever'body's not afraid of him."

Jolinda dug into her baked sweet potato with a fork, pulled out a steaming chunk, waved it in the air to cool it. "I knew you'd clam up about things like that."

"No clamming up to it. Folks leave Cody alone, he leaves them alone. Known him all his life an' he's never picked a fight—never."

She started giggling in spite of the seriousness of the subject. "He's sure finished a bunch."

Ogden Two Bears grunted, rolled a spoonful of raw, chopped-up onions onto a square of butter-slathered corn bread and took a magnificent bite.

"Now that's a fact," he said after he was done chewing.

As Cody knelt in his cabin pouring kerosene on his fire logs, down in Highwater Valley, Barry Willingham stood peering through the glass door of Monk O'Malley's office. "Terrance T. O'Malley, Attorney-at-Law," read the hand-painted sign on the glass. The office door was locked.

Barry rapped on the door with a knuckle. He was anxious, wanted to know what repercussions, if any, the capture and death of the burglar/would-be-rapist would have on his predicament. Would he be allowed off bond? When no one responded, he shaded his eyes with both hands pressed to the glass and stared harder into the darkened interior.

Where was that damn Monk? Barry had heard the attorney was always up bright and early no matter what shape he'd gotten himself into the night before. Grabbing the knob, Barry rattled the door loudly, then waited. And waited. There was no response.

He scratched his head, turned to look around the square. It

was early. A few cars droned by. Gerald Hanston, owner of the hardware store, was just arriving to open the place up. Barry walked down the sidewalk to meet him as the middle-aged man climbed from his pickup.

"Mornin', Gerald. Seen Monk?"

"Howdy, Barry. No, I haven't. I ate breakfast at the Riverside earlier. There's some reporters in town covering the murders. Big doings for Mountain County. I heard Monk got run off at Fuzzy's again last night. Folks said he was speaking some kind of foreign language."

"Foreign language?" Barry said. "He likes to quote Latin. Thinks it impresses folks. What it does over at Fuzzy's is confuse 'em."

"Yeah, and that Fuzzy, he don't want nobody saying anything he can't charge for. Fucker's so tight, ever' time he blinks his eyes, he skins his dick back."

"Heard that right." Barry stuck his hands in his pockets, turned to look around the square again. "Ain't like Monk, though, not coming to work. I'm gonna go 'round the back to his apartment and wake him up."

"See you around, Barry."

After the bright sunlight of the alley, the stairway to Monk's apartment was dark. Barry held on to the handrail to keep from stumbling. At the apartment door he knocked lightly, then called out, "Monk? You up yet?"

He put his ear to the door, didn't hear a sound. Rapped harder, louder. The sound echoed down the stairwell. "Monk? You awake?"

Silence.

He turned the knob and stepped into more darkness. Down on the street, a heavy truck roared by. Raking a hand along the wall by the door, Barry searched for the light switch. Found it. Flipped it on.

The bare overhead bulb was a weak forty-watter. In its dim light he saw Monk sprawled on the couch, one arm dangled to the floor. Walking across the room he looked down at the attorney, "What the fuck?" he said in amazement. "Oh, shit—Monk? You okay, Monk?"

There was no answer. He grabbed the attorney's shoulder, shook it roughly. "Monk. Say something, goddammit!"

"Huh?" Monk grunted. "Whozzat?"

"Lay still, Monk! Don't try to move. Where's your phone? I gotta call the sheriff."

"Do what? Am I hurt? Am I dead or something?"

"Just don't move." Barry spotted the phone, called the sheriff's office. "Wanda June? This is Barry, get the sheriff. I'm at Monk O'Malley's apartment and the killer's been here." Less than a minute later he heard the sound of sirens. Another minute and someone pounded up the stairs and slammed through the door.

"I was right around the corner. What's happened?" Bubba Whittlemore was breathing hard from the fast climb.

Barry waved him over. "Look at this! Lay back down, Monk. Be still."

"Have I been shot?"

"Well, I'll be dipped in shit!" the excited deputy said.

"What?" Monk was beginning to panic. "Am I gonna live?"

"Be still, Monk!" Bubba said. "I'm going downstairs for my camera." He ran for the door.

"Camera?" Monk hollered. "I don't need a camera. I need a goddamn doctor!"

"Hush up," Barry said. "Lie still!"

"Call an ambulance!" Monk started to raise up.

Barry stepped over and pushed him back down by placing a flat palm on his forehead. "Be still, Monk, goddammit. Bubba's gonna take a picture of you." Outside, other sirens were closer now. Tires screeched. Doors slammed. Men yelled.

"You heartless motherfucker. I'm dying and all you want is a picture."

"You ain't dying. Now lie still."

There was a louder pounding up the stairs; Bubba and Luther lunged across the threshold. More footsteps could be heard running up the stairs. Bubba stepped up, aimed his camera, and shot.

Monk blinked from the flash. "You people are crazy!"

"One more shot," Bubba said. The flash fired again.

Luther reached for Monk's chest. "Who hung this around your neck?" He flipped the cardboard sign everyone had been staring at. Monk could read the large cut-out letters without his cheaters.

"I killed the three sinners," it read. "I seek revenge."

Underneath the cutouts was a short phrase composed of different-sized letters. "I am Scanner."

"Say, Luther," Bubba said as the sheriff and Samantha entered the room. "Don't think you should've handled the evidence."

"Evidence, shit. Barry come up here and hung the sign around Monk's neck then called it in. He knowed Monk'd be hung over."

Barry grabbed Luther by the front of his shirt with both hands and threw him to the floor halfway across the room, then stomped after him.

Bubba blocked Barry's path. "Whoa. Ease off now."

Luther jumped up and reached for his night stick.

"Luther!" the sheriff stepped in front of the enraged deputy.

His face red with fury, Luther attempted to move around the sheriff.

The sheriff slid sideways to intervene.

"I'm gonna club him to the floor," Luther said.

"You are suspended. Give me your badge and your weapon. I've had enough of your shit."

"Suspended! You sonofabitch!" Luther charged Sheriff Rainwalker.

The sheriff's fist caught him square on the jaw.

Luther hit the floor again, rolled to one side to reach for his sidearm.

"Leave it, Luther!" Samantha yelled. Her voice was angry and threatening.

Luther glanced up to look down the barrel of her 9 mm. He started to reach again.

"You'll never make it," Samantha said. She held the pistol in a two-handed shooter's position. Her face was grim, determined.

Luther sat back, placed both hands flat on his thighs.

The sheriff was in a rage. "You ever call me a sonofabitch again, I'll take my fist and break ever' goddamn bone in your fucking face. Bubba, take his weapon. Luther, you tell anybody about the sign, I'll lock you away for impeding an investigation in progress."

With a sneer, Luther left the room. Reporters were waiting in the apartment's stairwell. After the death of Tom Yount the night before, additional reporters had been sent from Nashville, Knoxville, and Chattanooga. The reporters wanted a head start. They knew the big city media was on the way. Like a pack of hounds in full cry they smelled a sensational story that would be in the news for days. Careers would be built on the headlines.

"Has someone else been killed?" A pretty brunette reporter stuck a microphone in Luther's face. She noticed a trickle of blood on his mouth.

Behind her a cameraman jockeyed for position in the still-gathering crowd. The logo on his video camera indicated he was from a Knoxville station. A relay truck was being set up across the square for satellite transmission. Heavy drama for tiny Highwater Town. Excitement rippled through the crowd.

Luther made his decision. This was his big chance to under-mine the sheriff, poison the well to enhance his own position come next election. "The sheriff's got the killer in custody, caught him red-handed. Only thing—he's a big campaign con-tributor. When I tried to arrest him, the sheriff suspended me—took my gun and my badge and hit me in the face. He'll let the killer go."

The TV reporter was surprised. "Let him go? What happened in there?"

Luther slowed down. "The killer sneaked in there and hung a sign around his lawyer's neck while he was asleep, then called the sheriff's office like he'd just found him."

"What does the sign say?" the reporter wanted to know.

"Sheriff said if I told anybody, he'd lock me up. Can you believe that?" Luther hung his head, shook it, then looked up into the camera, the image of a deputy who had been sorely wronged.

"Who did you try to arrest?"

Luther paused for effect. "Barry Willingham!" he yelled more to the crowd than to the reporter. "I tried to arrest Barry

Willingham, just like before, for murder. And the sheriff stopped me."

"Barry Willingham," voices in the crowd passed it back to those in the rear. "Says he tried to arrest Barry Willingham."

With a last vindictive look, Luther left for the hospital to have the cut in his mouth looked at.

The crowd of reporters and lookers-on milled around and grew as they waited for something new. They fell back slightly when the sheriff finally stepped out of the stairwell. Behind Sheriff Rainwalker, Barry and Monk, both looking somber, glanced around at their frenzied neighbors. Bubba Whittlemore and Samantha Goodlocke brought up the rear.

"Sheriff Rainwalker," the brunette reporter called loudly to be heard over the crowd. Standing close behind her, a male reporter poked a microphone over her shoulder.

"No comment," the sheriff said. His face was a sullen mask.

"Do you think Barry Willingham is the killer?"

"No comment. All right! Clear a way here. Bubba, Samantha. Clear us a path." The sheriff's voice was a whip that drove the front lines of the throng back. However, they were prevented from giving way more than a few steps because of the crush of bodies and the narrowness of the alley. Also, reporters at the rear were aggressively shoving those in front of them in an effort to move even closer to the action.

The sheriff noticed and lifted the walkie from his belt. "Wanda June, get some more deputies over to the alley behind Monk's office, help get this crowd to moving."

"Ten-four, Sheriff."

Seventeen

Following an extended journey from the Gulf of Mexico or sometimes an end run from the Atlantic, across South Carolina and northward around the mountains of north Georgia, moisture-laden clouds are driven up and over the western escarpment of the southern Appalachians. At higher altitudes and on westerly ridges, a mini taiga formed by spruce, fir, and hemlocks combs the clouds for moisture. Droplets of water form on the needles, branches, and trunks of the conifers, until, heavy with their harvest, they give up moisture to the highly acidic soil, thus influencing the water and aquatic life downstream.

Here begins the first supply of an abundance of water for the lower slopes, for the cove hardwoods, for the numerous species of plant and animal life that make their home in the verdant hills. To this purloined treasure, nature adds eighty-plus inches of rainfall a year, bringing the area to almost rain forest levels of precipitation.

Cody relaxed and whittled away in this luxuriant environment while five thousand feet below and twenty miles distant, all hell was breaking loose in Highwater Town. Unaware of new developments, he checked off in his mind the things he must do when he returned to civilization, if the community could be described as civilized. He'd been driven by events since he arrived, had been continuously reacting instead of acting. His methods had to change if he was going to make headway.

First thing was to get in touch with the company that supplied the telephone bugs. There were ways of getting the desired information without a court order. Whoever ordered them, if not the actual killer, might be able to shed light on the true motives behind the murders. Tapping a telephone was a serious offense that violated both state and federal laws. The fear of doing some serious prison time could open a dialogue.

If Luther had performed the search of Justine Willingham's car, then he wanted a shot at it himself. Was Luther involved in something besides apparent smalltime rip-offs of some of the criminal elements in town? Was Titus Cornstubble telling the truth? Had Luther found something that could clear Barry and simply destroyed it? Or kept it back to make a deal? Lots of possibilities there. And what was Luther doing sneaking around on the mountainside above Sanford Sharpless's cabin?

Was a psycho doing the killings? He had a hard time buying the serial-killer scenario. Didn't serial killers usually have some sort of ritual? Blue ribbons didn't seem substantial enough. Shouldn't there be special cuts on the neck or genitals? From all the evidence and from what the forensic science center in Nashville said, the killer of Justine and Sanford stood in front of them to kill them. Carl was killed by being dragged to death. Or was he? With all the damage to the body, he could have been killed, then dragged along behind the vehicle just to confuse things. Have to wait for the medical examiner's report.

It would be interesting to know what Michelle Willingham's psychiatrist-friend from Nashville had to say about the way the murders were accomplished, plus any thoughts on the brutality of the killer.

Back to Luther. He was really an unknown. There had to be a way to check out his background, maybe get in touch with Noel, have him perform some of his computer magic.

Tom Yount, the guy eaten by the dog, was irrelevant to the case, Cody felt—a nonentity. Idiot was going to break in and rape the girl, maybe even kill her and let the blame fall on the town's serial killer. What an opportunity. Asshole probably thought he'd skate on it.

Was Barry the killer? He could have accidently come across his wife and Sanford, thought it would be a good time to dump a big liability. If he did have political ambitions, however small, a wife with the tag of community pussy wouldn't be the ticket to the mayor's office. That and the fact he thought her to be double ugly could be an excellent motive for murder.

163

Samantha had hung the tag on her. And Samantha thought Carl's death was good news for her friend Becky. Could Samantha and Barry have been getting it on after Randy Gateline dumped her? And why had Randy dumped her in the first place? Also, she looked strong enough to draw a seventy-five-pound pull bow.

There were several young girls who worked out at his Nashville health club that were in phenomenal condition, could bench-press twice their body weight, ride the life cycle for an hour as a warm-up for their ninety-minute aerobics class. And hadn't he read somewhere that a female ballet dancer could maintain a better strength-to-body-weight ratio than a pro-football player? Samantha hadn't seemed too sad that any of the victims had met an untimely demise.

Neither had his dad. He thought they'd brought their problems on themselves. Say you go out at midnight to get a pizza and you get whacked; are you at fault because you shoulda stayed home in bed?

Tapes of the nights of the murders. Tapes of all radio and telephone calls made to and from the sheriff's office. The tapes were required by law and insurance companies and could contain a clue or an alibi.

Cody dropped his whittling stick, placed his knife back in the leg scabbard, stood up and stretched, bringing his hands above his head and arching his back. He saw the ravens were back, cruising the mountaintop. They veered away as he made his way down the trail toward his cabin. He watched them head for their dead-spruce roost, then veer off again as if surprised. They beat their wings powerfully, fighting for altitude. One let out a hoarse squawk as a warning to its partner. Something's scared them off, Cody thought. Something or some one.

He left the trail and made his way silently through the woods, aiming for the dead tree.

The ground was marshy here, smelled strongly of a characteristic earthy odor. A depression caught the run-off from the slopes and held the moisture. Mosses and lichens thrived in the shade provided by the thick canopy a hundred feet overhead. Fallen limbs provided the decaying fodder so necessary for fungi, saprophytes, and the mushrooms that were so numerous in the area, especially in the fall. Cody had read that over two thousand species of fungi made their home in these mountains.

Wet ground sucked at his shoes, tried to pull them from his feet. Seemed to be nobody around.

At the base of the dead sentinel, he scoured the ground for signs of footprints. Nothing.

Beyond the tree a thick growth of blackberry bushes occupied a small clearing. He made his way to their now almost bare branches, stark against the background of undergrowth. The growth was thick. He knew better than to try to force his way through the whip-like shoots with their tiny barbs. He'd wind up with scratches all over him. He knew bears and other animals congregated here when the berries were ripe. Could a bear be scouring the area? More than likely the normally shy animals would be harvesting the acorns and beechnuts at this time of year. It was an exceptionally good mast year. A good sign for all the wild critters. Meant it would be a cold winter according to the mountain folklore.

Nothing. Maybe the ravens spotted a hawk or an eagle, or maybe his spirit birds were faking him out. Baffled, he headed back to his cabin.

The media converged on Highwater Town. At the Riverside Motel, Elton gloated over all the rooms being rented, over the throng of money-spending customers in the restaurant. Lot better than the farmers who'd show up in their bib overalls, sit around drinking coffee all day, flapping their jaws and hardly spending a dollar, using the place for entertainment. These newspaper folks were hungry after driving the narrow and sometimes treacherous roads it took to cross Mountain County, what with the yokels pulling out in the road with their tractors and combines, not looking left or right or sometimes even straight ahead.

Elton's brother Elwood was over from the hospital, having a late lunch. They sat in the back booth, watched the riotous crowd haul out their billfolds. Elton could hear the paper rattle as they counted out the tens and twenties. He'd called in two extra waitresses. Too bad he hadn't had a warning, he could have had another menu printed, raised prices to what city folks were used to paying. Oh well. The new menus would be ready tomorrow; he'd run the job over to the printers this morning.

Elwood ate with one hand and smoked with the other, alternating a bite with a long, drawn-out drag on the unfiltered cigarette. His mouth was wizened where nicotine had dried the glands around it. The rest of his face was following the same path, with deep wrinkles in his cheeks and around his eyes. He was gaunt almost to the point of emaciation even though his appetite was voracious and he ate mightily. The gray hair poking out in tufts from his ears matched the color of the straight hair he oiled and combed back on his head. His eyebrows were bushy and black with streaks of gray. His eyes watered from continuous streams of smoke that poured from his mouth and nose. "What you think of all this?" he said.

Elton spoke without removing the cigarette from his mouth. "Think I gotta make hay while the sun shines. These news folks ain't gonna be here forever. When they leave it'll be business as usual, which is slow and cheap."

Elwood resented his brother's success at the hotel, wondered how he could increase his own income at the hospital. Had to be careful with the drugs, a few Valium here, a Percodan there. Once in a while he could sneak a few tablets of Xanax or Halcion. The kids lately were into exotic fun, like the nitrous oxide he could sneak out in balloons. Then he had to cut greedy Elton in on it for a room where the kids would get together and sniff the gas. None of it was making him rich, not enough so he could leave his job behind and move to Florida, which was his dream. "I mean, what do you think of all the murders in town?" Elwood clarified.

"For a while there, I was getting scared, thought some crazy was running loose. If what Luther says is so, that it's Barry, hell I ain't never done nothing to rile Barry. Least I don't think I have." Elton looked thoughtful.

"Don't tell me you believe Luther. Sonofabitch has made you pay through the nose. Got his cut on the whiskey, on the smokes, on the young hookers. He's spreading stories to better his position come election next year. Let him be sheriff, he'll charge a fucking toll to walk down the street," Elwood said.

"Well, who you think's doing the killing, Mr. Smart Ass?" The two brothers had grown up rivals, fought as youngsters over the nonexistent affections of their parents, struggled for the rare attaboys an illiterate and emotionally distant, alcoholic father had intermittently thrown their way.

"Who'd best be able to get away with it?" Elwood asked. "I think the sheriff's killing folks, laying off on Barry 'cause he may run against him."

"You're outa your rabbit-assed mind. Sheriff'd be crazy to do something like that. He ain't the type of man who'd kill folks for profit. Make him mad, and that'd be another story. He sure knocked shit outa Luther."

Elwood's mind was made up. "Killing runs in families, just like drinking. Cody's a stone killer; you can see it in his eyes. If he hadn't been outa town, I'd say he done the killings—if he was really outa town, wasn't sneaking around like when he's a kid."

"You saying that because of talk about old man Coleman?"

"And other things. Know how he watched me after his brother died. Nine years old, but he didn't forget. Still hasn't."

Elton smiled inwardly. This was a good chance to scare the dog shit out of Elwood. "Yeah. Always wondered when Cody's gonna get around to you. Waited eight years to kill Coleman. Thought he'd invited you to a private barbecue by now."

"Don't talk that trash." Elwood's hand shook so hard he almost missed his mouth with the cigarette. "Weren't my fault his mama didn't have no money to pay his baby brother's hospital bill."

"You're maybe right. But I bet Cody don't see it that way. Just in case, I been thinking about taking out a large accident policy on your ass. Maybe your wife oughta do the same."

Elwood jumped up from the table, bumping it with his knee, turning his coffee over. The remains of his hamburger and fries slid to the floor. "You start shit with me, maybe I'll tell him how you tried to get his sister to come to work screwing out-a-town salesmen when she's only fifteen."

"You better not! I'll tell the sheriff about . . ." Elton remembered there was nothing he could tell the sheriff without incriminating himself. "I's joking about the insurance."

"I gotta get back to work," Elwood said, still angry. Tomorrow he'd eat at the Lunch Box, he decided. He stomped out of the restaurant, almost ran into two more reporters coming through the door, thought about telling them they'd get food poisoning if they ate here. Instead he flipped the cardboard sign on the glass door to read, "closed."

Elwood scooted back to the hospital, hoped he wouldn't accidently meet Cody Rainwalker on the way. He recalled it had been a severely cold winter when Cody's brother, Simon, was sick with pneumonia. Snow had stayed around for months, with the temperature well below freezing and below zero even for days at a time.

Cody's mother, Susanna Dawn, and her mother, that spooky old Indian bitch, had lived where the recreation area was now. Their old run-down house was up on the hill near where the entrance to the old coal mine had been. Sheriff Rainwalker was in the army, long before he was the law. That wasn't his fault, Elwood thought.

He was the hospital administrator. People have to have money or insurance to come to the hospital. Least they did back then before all the crazy laws were passed. Now he'd go to jail for what he'd done, making Susanna take Simon out of the hospital so that she and her mother had had to nurse him. He'd died. There had been insurance after all, but the paperwork was a long time coming. Hell, the kid could've died if he'd stayed.

Now there was a stone killer after him. Cody was biding his time, and Elwood was scared to death. The half-Cherokee was letting him suffer, twist in the wind. One night he'd step out the door to the hospital, on the way home, and Cody'd be waiting— and he'd be under the dirt, just like Cody's brother and mama.

He had some vacation time coming. Maybe him and the old lady best ease on down to Destin, Florida, 'til all this blew over and Cody went back to Nashville.

* * *

Scanner watched Elwood cross the road and head up the hill toward the hospital. He'd heard the town gossip. He bet that little weasel Elwood was sweating bullets since Cody come to town. It'd serve him right if Cody decided to drop him off the end of the earth somewhere, like down a sinkhole where he'd never be found or take him out and feed him to somebody's hogs.

A female voice came over his hand-held. "I'd be a lot better off if I could stay over in Sweetwater, or at least in Madisonville, only safe place to get a drink in town is a dump called Fuzzy's. They got a bouncer in there looks like Hulk Hogan with a thyroid problem," said the voice. She was talking on a cellular phone from somewhere in town, Scanner knew.

"How far's Sweetwater from Highwater Town?" a male voice wanted to know. The voice carried a tone of authority.

"I think about forty miles. Perhaps fifty."

"You listen to me, Wilma, goddammit. You got all the people from the TV stations staying in town. If you're fifty miles away and that asshole kills somebody else, you're left sucking hind tit. You understand me."

"I understand Lou. But this Riverside Hotel is a real shithole. They're having a roach festival."

"So go to the store and buy some bug spray—and quit whining. You're on expenses and you bring back a story, nobody's going to check the paperwork real close. Know what I mean?"

"Gotcha, Lou. Talk to you tonight?"

"Yeah. Check in. Call me at home."

Scanner wished the handset was a two-way, could be spoken into to tell Lou to get fucked. With a thumbnail, Scanner flicked the advance button to check on another phone conversation. In a large city it would be useless to use a monitor to listen in on cellular telephone conversations. In Highwater Town, high-tech was in the future. There were so few mobile telephones, most of the subscriber's voices could be recognized—until the influx of all the media people. But there were ways of identifying users if, as they did so many times, they identified themselves and broadcast where they were staying, just as poor Wilma had.

He had to get back, make some phone calls. Tonight the airways would be full of the voices of the innocent—and the damned.

"Ten-fourteen, Mountain County," the dispatcher's voice sounded over the speaker.

"Ten-fourteen," a deputy responded.

"Gotta call from Louise at the Dixie Freeze. Says there's five or six men fistfighting in the parking lot at the HillTop Tavern. Respond code one. I'll get you a back headed that way."

"Ten-four."

Eighteen

Sheriff Rainwalker prepared himself mentally for the chore. He was a man who appreciated his peace and quiet. His almost obsessive desire for order in his life had led him, first to become a deputy, then years later to seek the rat race of running for the office of Mountain County sheriff every four years. From this height above the commonfolk he could control at least some of the disorder in the community. Order in their lives was the payoff of his obsession. Those citizens who created disorder found that he did his best to see that the Tennessee state prison system eliminated their disruptive behavior.

He was a compassionate man, did his best to reason out why some folks could not abide by the rules necessary for a community of people to exist. He would not tolerate arrogance or brutality from his deputies. He even agreed, unlike many in the law enforcement community, that events from childhood, events beyond the control of the individual, could send them spiraling down into the hellish existence of living a life opposed to the law. Abuse as a child, alcoholism, fetal alcohol syndrome, dementia, lack of education, even bad luck or bad timing—all of these contributed to the misery of those locked away.

Sometimes alone in his office or at home, he mused on the misfortune of those he so often came in contact with. He tried to give a break to some who broke the law. Others he saw as animals, fit only to be locked away, or executed since he considered life in a prison cell much more cruel than a few moments in a crude electrified wooden chair.

The killer he now sought, he placed in a separate category. Sane or insane, the killer should be executed as an example to those who would emulate him. These crimes could not be tolerated in a civilized society. Especially not in his county. He considered this type of crime a Yankee crime—a crime of the North, of slums, of the neighborhoods of liberal politicians, a crime that had migrated south along with the credo of professional whiners.

Years ago such a crime would have been unheard of in the South. Sheriff Rainwalker resented the North, wrote it in lowercase when necessary to mention it, considered it an alien place where children ate leaded paint, breathed leaded air, played in filthy, rat-infested streets, and grew up to be that greatly untolerated, backward-brained individual who came South to instruct the natives on how to foul up their communities just like the ones they had left behind.

Imagine someone coming from New York or Detroit or Washington, D.C., to instruct on southern law enforcement or crime prevention. The scenario was ludicrous.

He knew better than to express his feelings. Such thoughts were best kept to oneself. He'd have mobs of the politically correct howling at his heels; the thought police whose obsession with conformity to their way of thinking was so driven—so addictive and overwhelming—that their pursuit of him in the press would be relentless.

Lately, the mountains around Highwater Town were becoming a refuge, a haven for families who thought the same as he, who wanted to escape lifestyles mandated by politicians and the out-of-control, liberal press. These were the computer types, the high-tech workers who could log on to mainframes a hundred or a thousand miles away at a plant or office building surrounded by blight, yet live in God's clean air. He believed these immigrants shared many of his views.

The sheriff also resented the press sticking their noses into his investigation. Now he not only had to contend with the day-and-night investigation that sucked up all his available manpower, he was going to have to spoon-feed the media a morsel a day to keep them from going off the rails.

He'd thought about it long and hard, the best way to handle the media. One way would be to clam up. Then they'd be digging on their own, worrying the families of the victims, which they were doing anyhow. Complaints were already coming in from the Willinghams about the two children, Biba and Edmund, being followed and photographed by TV and print reporters. The media could be persistent when their jobs depended on how brazen and aggressive they were.

Popularity with the media was a heady feeling, though. He could call the reporters in, a few selected personalities from the big stations, show them confidential charts or evidence, get them on his side. He'd be known nationally overnight. Then all the attention would be focused on him, and maybe for a while away from the victim's families.

Best way would be a balance. Open up a little at a time, a scrap here, a tidbit there. No disinformation to throw the killer off, which could backfire, make the killer kill again. Probably would kill again anyhow, but he didn't want lives on his conscience, innocent or not.

His mind made up, Sheriff Rainwalker stepped out the front door of his office and into the late afternoon sunshine. The sun was in his eyes, as he had expected, which was why he wore the mirrored sunglasses. Not his fault if the press viewed their presence as a sign of his cold professionalism. His attire added to this impression: a black, western-cut suit, black cowboy boots, and a big, cream-colored Stetson he'd bought at Shepler's in Nashville.

Some members of the press corps were camped outside the office. Others were scrambling around town with their electronic shovels, digging up what dirt they could find. His appearance would send a message: The info was here where the investigation was centered, not out in the quaint frame houses shaded by ancient maples, oaks, and sweet gums. Not in the clean neighborhoods of this town hundreds of miles from the urban blight from whence the reporters had been launched, but here in the solidly built brick jailhouse, where the perpetrator would soon reside.

The mob came to attention, yelling a few questions.

The sheriff waited, held up his hands for quiet. "Okay, ladies and gentlemen. I have this afternoon's press release. We do not employ a press agent here, so the release will be a verbal one.

"Evidence found at the scene of last night's break-in, during which the perpetrator was killed by a watchdog, and additional evidence uncovered by department investigators, leads us to believe Tom Yount was a simple burglar and would-be rapist. He was not the killer of Justine Willingham, Sanford Sharpless, or Carl Taggart. I regret to say their killer is still loose in our midst, and we are continuing our investigation of these murders. Thank you." The sheriff retreated back into the building.

The reporters shouted their questions at the closed jailhouse door.

High on Wolf's Head Mountain the chill arrived with the night. From the cabin's narrow front porch, Cody stared at the sky. The brilliance of the stars amazed him and made him feel vulnerable, alone. Imagine all the cold, empty space out there for billions and billions of miles. Bright lights blocking out the night sky allowed city dwellers to forget how alone they were in the universe. Closed in by buildings you could allow yourself some false sense of security. On the mountain, you really were alone. You came to realize, everyone was at the mercy of the universe.

He hadn't checked lately but was sure his puny cabin was the only structure on the mountain. The hundred acres from his mother's side of the family had been a land grant and was now totally enclosed by the Cherokee and Nantahala National Forests. There was some private land owned by a lumber company but the location was so remote, economics prevented logging.

He felt sort of nasty after all the chainsawing. He went in the cabin and picked up soap and towel, then headed down the dark, brush-tangled slope toward the loud turbulence of the rivers. There was no moon, so he was forced to feel his way along the overgrown path. He took off his shirt as he walked.

When he came near the stream, the phosphorescence of the water and the gurgle and rumble it made guided him. He'd bathed in the shallow pool here many times. Sitting on the bank he removed his shoes and pants, then stripped off his socks and underwear.

He stepped into the freezing water, forced himself to stay and not jump out immediately. The chilling shock of it took his breath away. He had to fight his need to wrap his arms around himself and jump back onto the bank. Sitting on the stoney bottom, he ducked his head under the water and rubbed his hands through his hair. He rubbed his body briskly then stood and soaped himself. Once again he plunged under the water to rinse. Unable to stand the chill any longer, he bounded up onto the bank, toweled off, and bundled up his clothes, wrapping the towel around his waist.

He felt refreshed as he walked back through the night. Barefoot, he stepped carefully, cautious of stones on the pathway.

"Mountain County S.O. to unit seven."

The sound of the radio so close by startled Cody, caused a sharp intake of breath. Who'n the fuck's that?

A sweeping flashlight's beam stabbed into the night, caught Cody in its glare.

Cody ducked behind a nearby bush.

"Oh! Holy shit!" a female voice cried out.

"This is unit seven. Go ahead, Mountain County."

"Is that you, Cody?" The voice sounded like Samantha's. "You wearing that white towel, thought I'd seen a ghost."

Before Cody could answer, the radio Samantha held blasted a loud call. "Bubba. We got a ruckus up to the Riverside Motel. Elton called, said the whole place is dog drunk, reporters are tearing up the rooms, and somebody hung a closed sign on the restaurant."

"Ten-four."

"Cody! Come out so I can see you!"

"Samantha?"

"It's me. Where'd you go?" She shined the light around.

"Turn that damn light off. I ain't got any clothes on."

"What you doing naked? Romancing a she bear?"

"Taking a bath in the river. What're you doing up here?"

"Drove my Jeep up the fire road. A big pine fell down a mile or so back and is blocking the way. I had to get out and hike it. I have some news from town. Things are happening fast."

"Come back to the cabin and you can tell me all about it."

On his front porch and dressed, Cody gave up his wooden rocker to Samantha. He sat on the edge of the porch and leaned back on a hemlock post. He'd brought his kerosene lantern out to provide light.

Samantha was out of uniform in jeans, a plaid shirt, and a denim jacket. Leaning forward in the chair, she relayed to Cody the whole scene at Monk's apartment with Barry finding the note hanging around Monk's neck. She also told him of his father's fight with Luther and of the arrival of hordes of big-city media.

"So Daddy punched him?"

"Knocked him flat on his ass. Luther started to go for his weapon, so I drew down on him."

"Why do I get the feeling you would've enjoyed putting a round in him?"

Samantha said nothing.

He had yet another feeling something had happened between her and Luther. Something real heavy.

"How'd you know I was up here?"

"Just guessed. And I remembered your daddy once told me you had a cabin up here. Couple of months ago Michelle and Barry was over at the Riverside Restaurant, just talking, and asked me how much land you had up here. Sure is lonely."

"I like it for a getaway."

"Jolinda wouldn't say where you were. Said you went to shit and the hogs ate you."

Cody smiled, knew Jolinda wouldn't tell anybody anything unless they were family. Even then she'd be close-mouthed. "So Monk was wound up tight about getting signed. You don't think Barry did it to throw suspicion off himself?"

"It'd be a stupid move. With all the evidence already against him, he'd know better. Sure confirms the sheriff's theory it's a psycho doing the killing. Wanting everybody to know it was him that done it—sick."

"Or smart. Law goes looking for a nut and all the time there's somebody out there with a real motive. And you're assuming the killer's a man. Could be a woman, you know."

"Not very likely," Samantha said. "If three people turned up dead from eating ant poison, I'd say, yeah, it's a woman. Women don't like messes, won't dirty up people's clothes or their cars. Killer's a man; you can take it to the bank."

"Calls himself Scanner? Scanner. Confirms a hunch I've had

since I checked out the eavesdropping transmitters at Barry's and Sanford's houses."

"Wanta share it?"

"You don't mind, for right now it's just a hunch. Anything comes of it, you'll be the second to know, after me."

Samantha rocked a bit before she spoke. "You have any ideas who it could be?"

"Not really. Whoever it is, they have to be pretty strong to lift the bodies and move them around, draw a seventy-five-pound bow."

"I can do that, I bet."

"Yeah. I reckon you can. A week before I came over, I got a haircut in Green Hills; it's an area of Nashville. I'm in the barber shop and it's a good, long wait. So I read the magazines and people-watch. The guys coming in—arms like women. No offense; I mean, no muscular shape at all. Chests like Luther, scrawny shoulders, weak legs. These little spoiled kids, most in their twenties, some in their thirties, have had it all given to 'em. Rode to school instead of walked. Never picked up anything unless it's Dad's car keys. Delicate, soft hands. A passel of pansies."

"So what's your point?"

"Here it's different. People work outdoors. Barry's in good shape. Bobby Joe's in good shape. Luther—he was probably in good condition once when he was younger, until the booze and cigarettes took their toll. Bubba Whittlemore and Randy Gateline both look to be in good shape. Sonny Todd and his girlfriend Brandy both seem to be in good shape. I tried to catch up with Titus Cornstubble a couple days ago; he's over sixty and he 'bout run me into the ground. The wimps here would be the machos in Green Hills. So the killer is strong. So—who isn't? See what I mean?"

"So you got no real clues," Samantha said, "and we, the sheriff's department, got no real clues. We're real pros. Sorta gives you a feeling of accomplishment, don't it?"

"I got one thing I'll share," Cody said. "Just a thought."

"So share."

"Something's not right. Serial killers, if that's what we got, go in for ritual. First two victims, Sanford and Justine, were killed from the front—standing up, the medical examiner says. Carl was dragged to death. We got two killers out there?"

"That's a pleasant thought," Samantha said. "But what about the blue ribbons?"

"Copycat or a diversion. Did you say Monk was passed out when the killer, or whoever, hung a note around his neck? Wonder what would have happened if he'd been sober enough to stand."

"Don't ever tell Monk being drunk saved his life. He hears that, he'll never sober up."

"Another thing," Cody said. "I talked to a lady psychiatrist from over in Nashville a few days ago. She's done some profiling of serial killers."

Samantha straightened up and looked Cody in the eye. "She any help?"

"Help? Don't know. She did offer some suggestions. Said the odds are high that our killer is male and under thirty-five."

"Why's that?" Samantha said.

"She says there's two basic types of serial killers: paranoid schizophrenic and the sexual sadist. From the info I gave her, we're blessed with the latter." Cody shifted and wrapped his hands around one knee.

"What else besides our guy being an under-thirty-five male," Samantha said.

"He's clever, stealthy, and strong. He probably has or had a passive, cruel, or estranged father and a seductive, dominant mother. The sexual sadist seeks revenge against past mistreatment."

"Have you come across a suspect that matches the profile? I sure can't think of one," Samantha said.

"Neither can I. And I don't see how I can delve into the past of everyone I'm suspicious of. That takes resources like the FBI has."

Samantha closed her eyes for a few moments then sighed. "The doctor have any other gems of wisdom?"

"She says there's a new theory among those who study serial killers. It's scary. They theorize that some sort of brain damage the killer received as a child, like being shaken real hard or slammed into a wall, may cause the killing urge. What's chilling, if this is so, is that the killer has no more choice over whether or not he kills than you and me breathing."

"If it's a local, then I would know someone with that profile," Samantha said. "Nobody fits."

Both of them were talked out. Cody was tired and it showed. He wiped his hands over his face in an attempt to be more alert.

Samantha stood and walked over to the edge of the porch. Stretching with her hands over her head, she looked up at the sky, held her hands out to either side and arched her back.

Cody checked her out, liked the way she filled out her dark stretch jeans.

She turned quickly and caught him looking. "Like what you see, cowboy?"

"I reckon I do."

She stepped over to Cody and lowered herself next to him. Leaning over, she kissed him lightly on the lips.

Without a thought, Cody pulled her into his arms, turned her head, and kissed her hungrily. Their tongues met.

Samantha moaned. "Oh, God, Cody. It's been so long." Her hands went under his shirt, her nails tracing over him lightly.

Cody shivered from the feel of her hands on his body, felt a stirring in his groin. Reaching under her blouse with one hand, he slipped his fingers under her bra, cupped her firm and ample breast in his hand. He felt her hard nipple on his palm, found it with his fingertips, and massaged it.

Samantha moaned again, shivering in the cold air. She reached down and tentatively searched for his hardness, squeezing him.

Cody impatiently unbuttoned her shirt as she struggled out of her jacket and the blouse, then finally her bra. He gazed at her naked breasts in the lantern light. Both nipples stood erect from the excitement and the cold. He kissed one then the other.

Samantha slowly unzipped his pants. Reaching into his underwear, she massaged him, rolled over to kiss him. They explored each other's bodies.

After a while, Cody shifted Samantha from his lap and hurriedly shucked out of his clothes, watching silently as she stripped off her jeans and panties. Their clothes fell in a pile on the grass in front of the porch.

Naked and shivering, Samantha wrapped herself around him.

Cody rolled her onto the wooden porch, rose over her. He could feel the strength in her arms and legs, felt the firmness in the muscles of her shoulders and back.

Opening her legs, Samantha brought Cody into her. "So long," she whispered. "It's been so long."

Neither Cody nor Samantha noticed the furtive shadow approaching in the darkness.

Nineteen

Scanner stopped thirty feet from the cabin, barely out of the semicircle of flickering light thrown by the lantern. Such passion. How romantic. Should he have brought his camcorder?

A charge of power surged through the killer. He was totally in control of their lives, their very fate rested on his whim. He could take them both so easily now. Almost before they could react. Why not now? Both were here, and eventually both would need to die. Cody was quick, but entwined in the arms of Samantha he wouldn't stand a chance.

Samantha. She was getting a good measure of what she came up the mountain for. But, lovers or not, they were no different from the others. Their deaths must also take place standing and face to face.

Samantha cried out, a half yelp, half moan, and writhed with abandon as she came to climax.

Scanner, his mind as chilling as the night, sent Cody a silent message to hold on tight. Hang on or she might buck him off. That was what he called laying down the law.

Feeling powerful, in control of the flow of the universe, Scanner settled down to wait in the blackness. Later he watched as Cody picked up a limp Samantha from the porch and carried her inside. Cody's strong back and shoulder muscles were so beautiful in the light from the lantern, the killer thought. It would almost be a shame when it came time to waste his flesh.

Scanner crept close to the cabin. Crouching against the outside wall, with an ear pressed against the logs, the stalker could hear murmurs and intermittent sounds but could not make out the words.

Important deeds await me, oh night fuckers. Farewell young

lovers. I'll have my vengeance at a more opportune time. No one can say I do not respect budding romance. And no one can really say I'm not a nice person.

Scanner silently disappeared into the mysterious hush of the mountaintop haze.

Scanner used extra caution driving down the fire road. The way was steep, and it wouldn't do for either Cody or Samantha to find an abandoned 4x4 should it run off the trail and become stuck or, worse yet, go tumbling down a ravine, winding its occupant up like a five-dollar alarm clock. The prowler had considered disabling Samantha's Jeep just for fun, but reconsidered. It would be best if they remained ignorant of any presence on the mountain. One less time span to account for if anyone should ask him where he had been on this night.

The power trip was still there, creating a feeling of calm well-being, of strength, wisdom, and creativity. No one could have planned this as well. He was so cool.

At this altitude, radio reception would be terrific. He was physically and intellectually above all the rabble in that scrawny village down there. Like a god looking down on the lights winking through the trees. If he listened closely he might be able to hear their tiny thoughts. He wished he could tune in on their individual thoughts instead of the few conversations he overheard.

Reaching to the dash, Scanner flipped on the radio, touched the buttons to tune it to the cellular frequencies, the best listening to date, what with all the media people in town.

"Can you come over and give it to me good tonight?" the whisperer said.

"Bitch! You goddamn whispering whore!" Scanner screamed, violently twisting the knob on the radio to turn it off. "I can't take any more of your 'give it to me good' bullshit! It's driving me fucking crazy! How can I work when all you're thinking about is somebody giving it to you good. You're all over the spectrum, give it to me good give it to me good give it to me good, like a fucking broken record. I'll find out who you are one day, I swear it. I swear. One day I'll find you, slut! It'll be different with you, you'll be my captive for a while, then I'll kill you!"

* * *

Cody opened his eyes, sensed he was alone in the cabin, then remembered falling asleep with Samantha in his arms as he dropped off. They had made love two more times, Samantha crushing him to her, holding his head as he kissed her breasts, as he ran his tongue over her body, shivering, moaning, sometimes crying. He'd felt her tears on his face, on his shoulder when she placed her warm cheek against it. "What's wrong?" he'd asked.

"Nothing's wrong. Everything's right. I feel so good, so whole."

He hadn't pressed her about the tears, thought he understood. She had broken up with someone she still cared for. It was painful and would take a time for her to recover.

He reached out, just to make sure. She wasn't there.

"Samantha," he called. No answer.

Cody got out of bed and slipped his pants on. Stepping carefully on the cold floor, he walked to the open door.

Samantha was outside in the rocker. She had on her jeans, a quilt thrown over her shoulders.

"Whatcha doing?" Cody asked.

"Sitting—thinking."

"Thinking?"

"Yeah. Thinking. You know, Cody, I haven't told anyone about this. But I feel I can trust you. Not just because we've been to bed together, although that helps some. I think you're honest, and you're not really from Highwater Town—you don't still live here, is what I mean."

Cody stood beside her, looked out into the night. Heavy fog created a halo where the sun would rise. He felt woozy. He hadn't had much sleep. "You wanta tell me about it?"

"I want to. I really do. I tried to tell Randy, but he wouldn't give me a chance. After all the time we were together, he wouldn't give me the chance. I wanted to tell Becky, but I was afraid she would confide in Carl. That would've been a mistake. It's about Luther."

"Luther?"

Samantha struggled with where to start. "Well, it happened—

It—when I first hired on with the department, your daddy would assign me to ride with different deputies, to learn the ropes. I was the first and so far only female deputy. Ever'body treated me real good. Luther did, too, until that night."

Cody didn't think he was going to like what was coming. His stomach muscles tightened. "What happened?" he asked, his voice a whisper on the early morning breeze.

"It had been a hard night. We had to break up a big fight at the HillTop, which is more or less a nightly occurrence. One of the wild drunks had backhanded the shit outa me, busted my lip. Luther was there and parted his hair with his six-cell flashlight, put him away for the night. Later on we had a terrible wreck where one of the drunks who ran away from the HillTop hit a big oak tree, dead-center. Big mess."

"Can't understand why Daddy don't just close the place."

"Don't think he's far from it. Anyhow—we were going off shift, and I was feeling grateful to Luther for saving my ass and we stopped by his place. He'd always been a gentleman, never came on to me like some of the younger deputies. Well, he asked me to come in for a beer and he'd take a look at the cut on my lip. I did, drank the beer—one beer—and the next thing I know, it's morning and I'm buck naked and in bed with Luther, and the entire room smells like sex."

"What? You can't hold your liquor?"

"Luther put something in my beer."

"Lowlife sonofabitch. You're sure?"

"I'm sure, from the dry, powdery taste I had in my mouth— chemical taste. Maybe spiked it with a Xanax or a Halcion or something like it. I felt like hell, confused all day. Guilty, mad, stupid. That night I went to see Randy at the gym. He treated me like I was a stranger, cold. I wondered if Luther bragged to him we'd been together, but I don't think so.

"Randy and I had dated since he come out of the navy. He moved here from Harrisburg, Pennsylvania. We planned houses, mortgages and furniture and futures and babies. Randy thought it was a good idea, me going to work for the department; said if I played my cards right I could be the state's first lady sheriff. The plans we made. It's destroyed my life."

Cody was so mad his heart pounded in his chest. "I knew you'd been going with Randy a long time. You couldn't tell him about what Luther done?"

"I thought about it, and started to, but changed my mind. Maybe I should have. Randy came to me a short while later, said he couldn't take me being on this job, said he had at first thought he could, but he was wrong. Said he didn't want to worry about me night after night, whether I'd be killed out doing what I do. It hurt so much." Samantha started quietly crying.

Cody put his hand on her shoulder, massaged it through the quilt. "You sure you don't want my daddy to know about Luther?"

"He'd fire Luther, or try to, and there would be a big court fight and ever'body in town would know about it. My effectiveness as a law enforcement officer would be destroyed."

"Luther's an older man and no match for me, but goddammit, it's just not right. Makes me wanta take my fist and break every fucking bone in his face. Rotten bastard! How could he do that to somebody he knew he was going to be working with?"

To Samantha, Cody sounded just like his dad when he was angry. "I don't know. Maybe he don't care."

"When I get through with that sonofabitch, he'll care. He'll care a lot. Randy's some kind of asshole too."

"Please. Don't do anything. Sometimes I think Randy's messed up because of what happened to his family. His father dying and his mother abandoning him and his sister, Regina. She's a year younger than him and sick a lot. He sends her money to help her out and that puts pressure on him. Randy's mother is dead now. Died a few years after the old man. And Luther's out of the department now for a while. Maybe things will work out."

"You're a much better person than either one of those sonofabitches," Cody said.

Later they walked to the river and Cody convinced Samantha to take a cold dip with him. They dried each other off, held hands coming back up the slope to the cabin, and shivered in unison. "I've got to get down the mountain, go to work," she said.

Emmett Clifford

"When you decide to put some clothes on, I'll drive you to your Jeep."

Cody drove Samantha the mile or so to where her vehicle was blocked on the fire road. He let her out of the truck and watched her step over the fallen tree. She'd been quiet, subdued, on the short ride from the cabin. He climbed down and grabbed the chain saw out of the back.

"Looks like somebody turned around here," she said, pointing to the ground behind her Jeep.

He put the chain saw down and vaulted over the log. She was right. The ground was freshly churned up. "You didn't try to go around the log or anything, did you?"

"Too dark and I don't know these woods. I was afraid I'd drive off a bluff. Looks like somebody drove up, saw my Jeep here, turned around, and left."

"Wonder who it was?" He hoped it wasn't Jolinda. She'd be fighting mad.

Samantha climbed into her Jeep. Before she drove off, Cody had a caveat for her. "Luther will be vindictive, you can count on it. Watch out for him."

"Luther comes after me, you can count on me shooting him. I've fantasized on it. First round will go in his nuts. Second one too. And you can take it to the bank."

Thirty minutes later, Cody drove down the mountain, pulled out of the muddy fire road onto Cataloochee Road and headed toward town. He had places to go and people to talk to. He was still mad about the trick Luther had pulled on Samantha. What did he put in her drink? And where did he get it?

He'd driven three miles toward town when he came upon a lone figure running along the road in his direction. When he got closer he saw it was Michelle Willingham.

She recognized his truck, stopped and waved to him. When he stopped in the middle of the road like all the farmers did, she walked over to his window. "Who you running from, Doc?"

She wore a bulky sweatshirt, gray athletic pants with a wide red stripe down each leg, and blue New Balance running shoes.

186

An elastic headband across her eyebrows kept hair and sweat out of her face. She wiped her face with a sleeved forearm. "Thunder thighs and old age. You haven't been around."

"The night the dog ate the idiot, when everyone thought the killer'd been caught, I took some time off."

"You hear about Monk getting scared to death?"

"I heard. How's Barry handling things?"

"Not so good, which is to be expected. He's been the hero for years. Now some of the folks who worshipped him think he's a killer. He's surprised at how fickle and disloyal folks can be."

"You talk to your Nashville shrink friend?" Cody asked.

"Shri—? Oh, you mean Doctor Bronson. Yes, I did. She said you called. Was she helpful?"

"She gave me a profile. It may narrow down the suspects if I ever find any."

"Well I hope your daddy catches him quick," Michelle said. "People are starting to complain about the lack of an arrest in the case."

"Were they complaining when your brother was in jail?"

Her eyes flared with anger. "Hell, no. They don't care who's in jail, just so somebody is so they can sleep at night. And if it's a member of one of the county's leading families, so much the better; shows the law's impartial."

"You don't seem to be scared, out running on a lonely road."

"I live on this road, and I got this." She lifted her sweatshirt to show a portion of naked skin and a .44 Colt Python in a hip holster.

"You shoot 'em with that and it'll smart for sure."

"You bet your ass it will."

"Use your phone?" Cody asked his dad once he'd reached the sheriff's office.

"Help yourself. Have a good rest?"

"Real good," Cody said. "Feel refreshed and raring to go."

"Funny thing. Deputy of mine, you may know her—Samantha Goodlocke. She come in this morning all bright-eyed and bushy tailed, said she was feeling on top of the world. Best spirits I've seen her in in six months or more."

"Must be something going around."

"Must be."

Thinking you never could get away with anything in a small town, Cody dialed toll-free information, asked for Dreko, Incorporated—the logo on the bugging transmitters—and was given a number. He dialed it. He had a hunch.

"Dreko, good morning," said a cheery male voice.

"Hi. My name's Barry Willingham. I've purchased some items from you, and I can't find your latest catalog. Could you send me one? Also tell me what address you have for me, Barry Willingham in Tennessee."

"Of course, sir. Let me enter your name in the computer." Cody heard the clicking of a keyboard. "Here we are. Barry Willingham, 12475 Andrew Jackson Parkway, Suite 402, Madisonville, Tennessee. Is that correct, sir?"

"Yes, it is. And tell me, did you receive prompt payment for my last order?"

"For the in-line telephone transmitter? Yessir, it was charged to your MasterCard."

"Thank you, and please don't forget the catalog."

"Thank you, sir. I'll drop it in the mail today."

Cody hung up the phone. "Well, sonofabitch." He stuck his head into the other office. "Thanks, Daddy. I'm out the door."

On the way through the lobby he spotted Wanda June coming in the front door, arriving for work. Her bright red hair hung over her shoulders. She wore a tight brown sweater and blue jeans he knew she'd had trouble pulling over her hips. "Howdy, Wanda June," he said as he passed her.

She gave him a smile and a provocative look out of soft blue eyes. "Howdy yourself, Cody. You running off right as I get to work, I might think you're unfriendly."

"You're looking so good, I hate to run, but I gotta head over to Madisonville." With a smile, he headed out the door.

Damn, he thought as he drove away from the office. Get laid and it's all I can think about, like some kinda addict. And why am I not surprised the transmitters were ordered in Barry's name?

The address in Madisonville turned out to be a private post office. Suite 402 was the box number. The clerk, who was also the owner, didn't want to cooperate at first. "So you're a private detective. So what." He was skinny, with a protruding Adam's apple and dirty fingernails. Cody had caught him picking his nose when he came through the front door. He smelled in need of fresh water.

"So I'm investigating the possible illegal use of the mail. I'd like to know who rented box 402 and who picks up the mail and how often."

"Private business; take a walk."

"I'll take a walk to the nearest phone, call the Mountain County sheriff's office, have him call the local county sheriff and the FBI and the Treasury Department, and they'll be on your ass like a short overcoat. Add the BATF to the list because I strongly suspect that illegal firearms and explosives are sent through here. Then I'll get a court order and come question you in a fucking federal pen. Which way you want it?"

"Box 402, you said?"

"402," Cody said.

"Young girl rented it about six, seven months ago. Got real long black hair. Young, hard to tell how old. Tall, good-looking. Tits from here to yonder. She picks up packages and letters up from time to time. She must know when they're coming 'cause she don't come any other time. Never have seen anybody else. 'Course the customers have keys. Somebody can come in at night and get the mail."

"She sign any kind of card, give an address? You require any I.D.?"

"Give me a break; you know that's private."

"What's your name?"

"Simcox. Karl Simcox."

"Thanks for what you've given me, Karl. Now listen close. I am going to make a phone call. You're going to have law here like you can't believe. Cooperate. Smile. Be nice, and you may keep out of serious trouble, not have your business closed down. Card the girl signed—don't even touch it. The fingerprint techs will want it clean as possible. Now. Where's your phone?"

Cody hung around until his dad and Bubba Whittlemore arrived. Bubba's cheek was bruised, and he had a swollen lower lip. "What happened?" Cody wanted to know.

"Broke up a fight at the HillTop 'bout midnight."

"I'd close the place," Cody said.

"It's on the list," the sheriff said. "Now, we got print techs from Monroe County Sheriff's Office on the way and a sketch artist coming down from Knoxville."

Karl fidgeted behind the counter, looked like he'd ate something that tasted bad.

The sheriff placed his hand on Cody's shoulder. "Son, you realize this is the first and only real break we've had in this case. I've always thought you needed to come to work for me. You'd be sheriff one day."

Bubba looked uncomfortable, stared at the floor and shuffled his feet.

"Thanks but no thanks. It's not I'm such a great investigator. Luther is a lousy one. He wants Barry to be guilty, so every clue he finds points to him. And the sonofabitch has been shaking down poor old Titus Cornstubble, chopping his crop and hauling it off. Not for evidence, I'm sure, and not burning it in the presence of other officers and making an arrest. Been shaking down Elton at the motel and who knows who else."

The sheriff caught Bubba's eye. The deputy nodded.

"We been keeping an eye on Luther. Was about ready to close in on him, rid ourselves of him for good when all this came up."

"If you knew ever'thing the bastard did, you might kill him; what he deserves. Luther and me may take a ride together and have a long talk."

"Don't go getting yourself in trouble, son. What else should I know?"

"Confidential informant."

The sheriff looked exasperated. "Don't go holding out on me, Cody."

"Ain't holding out, Daddy. I got a feeling somebody's gonna be coming along, filling your ear full about Luther. He may be heisting drugs at the hospital. I can hand you that."

The sheriff caught Bubba's eye again, held it.

Old man was on top'a shit after all, Cody thought.

"Hear Elwood Crabtree's been contemplating a week of marital bliss on the Redneck Riviera," Bubba said with a wry smile. "Elton says he's off to Destin, Florida. Going deep-sea fishing until Cody leaves town."

"That's downright unfriendly," Cody said.

The sheriff looked grim. "Bubba, we get back to Highwater Town, drop by the hospital, and see how that fella's doing who took a swing at you last night. And stop in the admin office and suggest to Elwood he best stay put. Make it a strong suggestion."

"Reporters been giving you a hard time?" Cody said.

"Had a couple try to follow us over here. Monroe County's got 'em in for questioning and will keep 'em occupied for a while answering questions about possible stolen cameras and rental cars that don't have the proper registration. Who knows, one of 'em may be packing some funny smokes."

The fingerprint techs arrived five minutes later. Cody headed for the local Radio Shack.

Twenty

At Radio Shack, Cody bought a Police Call Radio Guide listing all Tennessee emergency and law enforcement frequencies plus the channels used by portable and cellular phones. The female clerk handed him a free copy of emergency frequencies for surrounding counties. He hoped he wasn't wasting time and money.

Additionally he bought an auxiliary speaker to plug into his police scanner, a lighter plug adapter, and a roof-mount antenna for hooking the radio up in his pickup. Then he drove down the street and ate a greasy lunch.

Coming out of the restaurant he noticed it was beginning to cloud up and the temperature had dropped. Good, he thought. He enjoyed cool, rainy weather. It made him feel more alive.

As he raced the rain to Mountain County he spotted his dad's big Dodge pulled into the circular driveway of a nursing home. Wonder what he's doing in there? Cody thought.

In Highwater Town, Cody made the rounds, interviewed some of the men who were with Barry on the night his wife was reported missing. Concentrating on the time element, he convinced himself there was no way Barry could have accomplished all the running around necessary to kill his wife and the lawyer and dispose of the bodies, murder weapons, and car. For Monk O'Malley's sake he took careful notes. After he left each interview, he dictated his thoughts into a mini-cassette recorder while the witness's statement was fresh in his mind. He had to be a pro on this one. Luther had screwed it up big time, or else had deliberately covered up evidence that would clear Barry.

Later that afternoon at the sheriff's office he told his dad what he thought.

"We may have enough evidence to bring charges against Luther for his shenanigans," the sheriff said.

"You find out who rented the postal drop?" Cody said.

"Only prints on the card were from the clerk. Barry's signature was obviously traced. When I left, the sketch artist was still at work trying to come up with something."

"Saw your cruiser at the nursing home when I came by."

Sheriff Rainwalker looked embarrassed. He stared at the floor before answering. "Bubba's mamma has some kind of dementia, like Alzheimer's only different somehow. She comes and goes. Saddest thing you ever did see. It's enough to break your heart."

Cody was silent for a moment, thinking. "I need to take a look at Justine Willingham's Toyota. Keys around?"

"It's locked up in the lot around back. Keys are where Luther found them. Under the seat."

The Toyota had once been white. The rain was falling heavily now. Not hard enough though to remove all the dirt and road grime from the car. Cody looked inside. Someone had obviously taken a knife to the seat covers, split them open and exposed the springs and padding. The headliner had been ripped and hung from the interior of the roof like a torn curtain.

Cody retrieved the keys from under the passenger's seat, tried them in the door. They didn't fit. Around to the driver's side and it was the same. What the hell was going on?

He examined the keys closely, then knelt on the wet macadam and peered into the keyhole. Blocked.

The sheriff was so furious he stomped around in his office slapping at his desk and the walls. "Goddamn Luther missed something that obvious and simple?"

"Looks like it," Cody said. "Either missed it or overlooked it on purpose. Let's say the killer fills the door locks with super glue. Justine comes to get in her car and he has all the time in the world to take her. Maybe Sanford is with her at the time and they're both locked out on a country road."

"So what's your gut feeling on who did the deeds?" the sheriff asked.

"Luther Hamby looks like a good suspect to me. Of course

there's no evidence to prove that theory."

"We'll find out," the sheriff said. Bubba and Samantha are bringing Luther in for questioning. Samantha's doing a lot of grinning."

Before he left, Cody called Michelle at her office. "Got some news."

"Good or bad?"

"Just news."

"I've got patients lined up. Same time, same place?"

"Fine with me," Cody said.

* * *

"Little Percy wants another pair of Nikes?" the man on the cellular phone said. "Shit! I just bought him a pair a month ago."

"They're worthless now," the woman said. "He's been wading creeks in them."

Scanner listened on the hand-held radio.

"Wading creeks in a pair of hundred-dollar shoes?" The man sounded astounded and skeptical.

"And the van needs work and the swimming pool needs a new pump; some kids threw sand on the bottom and clogged it up. Car and house insurance's going up." The wrath in the woman's voice was apparent even over the tiny speaker.

"This alimony is killing me," the man said. "It never cost us that much to live. You're living too high; you're spoiled."

"You'da let that seventeen-year-old pussy alone you'd be living a lot cheaper," the woman said. "Send the money or talk to the judge."

Scanner flipped the membrane button to scan for another call. Events at the sheriff's office were accelerating his timetable. The schedule would have to be moved up a few days. Actually, that would work out better. And he'd feel more productive.

* * *

The rain fell in heavy drops. Lightning flashed in the western sky as a storm cell moved toward the valley. Thunder shook the mountains. Water stood on the roads and formed pools in the low spots. Creeks threatened their banks.

Cody decided to stop by Fuzzy's for a taste. He was at loose ends and wouldn't meet Michelle for a few more hours. Besides, it was the only place he could be sure to find Monk, and he needed to update him.

The bar was a replay of the other night with the regulars talking about the murders. Three men and a woman sitting at the bar looked like outsiders.

Monk was at his power spot.

Cody jerked his head. Monk climbed off the stool and followed him to the corner table.

A weasely looking man Cody recognized as a county resident approached one of the males at the bar, tugged on his coat sleeve. When he had his attention he spoke to him and pointed at Cody.

"Them reporters at the bar?" Cody asked Monk as they took a seat at a clean table.

Monk brought along a glass half full of Jack, no ice. "From various and sundry rags. The lady I think is from Nashville. They've attempted to question me, of course."

"Found where and how the bugging transmitters were ordered, but not the who." Cody told Monk about the postal drop in Madisonville.

"How convoluted. And of course there will be official investigators dropping by this Dreko company."

"Yeah. It's in upstate New York. Local cops there will gather up the records and fax them down."

"You heard of my adventure?" Monk asked. His smile was weak, embarrassed, like he had done something outrageous.

"You live an adventurous and exciting life, Counselor."

"Can we expect any motion from the sheriff's office?" Monk asked.

"They're on their way to pick up ambitious Luther. Hopefully they will ask some embarrassing and hard-to-answer questions."

"Brave Cody—you are a wonder." Monk gave a salute with his glass.

Cody's beer arrived. He took a long pull, then told Monk about the Toyota.

"You're a double-wonder." He saluted Cody again.

"I'm almost afraid to tell you the results from questioning Barry's caving companions about the night in question." But he did.

"Cody Rainwalker! Telephone!" Fuzzy yelled out over the racket.

All eyes in the bar followed Cody as he walked over to the wall phone. "Yeah?"

"Got some more news for you; just heard," the sheriff said.

"Lay it on me."

"You and Samantha had a discussion about the cause of death on Carl Taggart. M.E. called after you left. He found the ten-inch shaft of a rat-tail file rammed into Taggart's heart. Whoever stabbed him must've broke the handle off and poked the shaft on in so the wound would close. You were right on the money. They're gonna take another look at Justine's body. I'm starting a reinvestigation; we're going to cover these murders like they've never been investigated—which they haven't. Also, we're reviewing all the telephone and radio tapes off the logging recorder. This news is confidential."

"You talking on a portable or a cellular phone?" Cody asked.

"Not now, never will be," the sheriff said.

"You got good moves too."

On the way back to his table, Cody decided the old man had his ear to the ground, knowing he was at Fuzzy's and taking the time to talk to Samantha.

As soon as he sat down, a local popped his head in the door, yelled at the top of his voice. "Sheriff's deputies just took Luther Hamby outa his house. Got him in handcuffs."

The reporters at the bar joined the stampede out the door. Along with Cody and Monk, only the players at the poker machine remained in the bar.

"Goddammit!" Fuzzy said, throwing his bar rag across the room.

"Exciting night," Cody said.

"Never a dull moment once you hit town," Monk said.

"I've heard that shit before."

Twenty-one

Cody arrived at the Tellicafe an hour late for his meeting with Michelle. The weather had turned worse. A pickup pulling a bass boat hydroplaned in front of him and hit a car, blocking the road to Tellico Plains for forty minutes.

Michelle, wearing a tan gabardine wool suit and matching low-heel pumps, waited with obvious impatience at a table in the semi-concealed section to the right of the restaurant's entrance. A half bottle of white wine sat on the table in front of her. She poured her empty glass full of the clear liquid as Cody took a chair. "You're late," she slurred.

"You're shit-faced," Cody said, thinking maybe she wore the lower-heeled shoes because of self-consciousness about her height.

"You're still late. I've been sitting here drinking for two hours or more."

"Congratulations," Cody said. I've been sitting behind a wreck on the highway."

"You're a sarcastic sonofabitch. And I pay you well."

"And I deliver the goods."

"Well, deliver, you sarcastic sonofabitch," Michelle said.

Cody told her what he'd discovered. Told her of the time element, of finding the phony mail drop, about the glue in the Toyota's doors, and of Luther's sloppy investigation techniques and the possible motivation behind them. "Last but not least, the sheriff's office picked Luther up about two hours ago. In handcuffs, I'm told."

"You sarcastic sonofabitch. You do deliver. Tell me, Cody— are you getting laid often?"

The waitress had arrived to take his order and was obviously shocked at what she overheard.

"It's all right, my dear. I'm a doctor," Michelle said.

Cody ordered a beer. "I'll look over the menu and let you know," he told the waitress.

Embarrassed and red-faced, she hustled off.

Cody wondered if Michelle had spotted Samantha on Cataloochee Road and had put two and two together. "You gonna eat something, aren't you?"

"Don't worry Cody. I'll put something in my stomach to soak up the alcohol. You didn't answer my question."

"Is it really a medical question?" he chided.

She slapped an open palm on the table. Startled, customers at surrounding tables looked toward Cody and Michelle to see what would happen next. "Most definitely. Not getting laid can distract you and cause a lack of effectiveness at work. I should know. I'm not getting laid regular; not even irregular." Michelle's thoughts were on Rick Staros, who was acting strange lately and had been spending a lot of time on the telephone with his partners in Vegas. He'd told her he may have to fly back for a hastily called sit-down.

Could she get this drunk on that small amount of wine? Cody wondered. Or is she fudging a little? "Come on, Michelle. We're having, or supposed to be having, a professional discussion here."

She looked sad. Cody thought she was going to cry.

But she didn't. She sat up straighter in her chair. "You're right. Thank you for being so diligent, for uncovering what Luther was trying to hide. Do you think he's the killer and he was covering his own tracks?"

"We'll know more tomorrow, after he's been grilled for a while. I know Daddy's in no mood for him."

Cody decided to give Michelle a ride home after they ate. She walked to the parking lot all right, but the weather was turning worse, so why take chances? He would be negligent if he allowed her to nose the Blazer into a ditch.

Forty-five minutes later, he turned off Cataloochee Road into her driveway, a steep, gravel-and-rock path that wound uphill through hemlocks and oaks. Churning wisps of ground fog reflected his headlights and created a spooky, English-movie setting. Cody visualized men in capes and high hats carrying canes, listened for the sound of horses on cobblestones. A good place for the howler. A long, drawn-out wail would make the scene complete.

The house was an exotic-looking, two-story, light blue stucco with halogen security lights aimed at all sides. The roof was steeply pitched for the occasional three- and even four-foot snowfalls that plagued the area in late fall and early spring when excessive moisture moved through. The driveway circled in front and had been widened for parking at the steps that led to a well-lit, wide, glass-and-wood entrance. To its right stood a detached three-car garage constructed of the same drivet material as the dwelling.

To Cody the house was a mansion. "How many square feet do you have here, Michelle?"

"You need to ask Vic or Barry, but I think it's around five thousand."

"Gives you room to stretch," Cody said, still in awe of the house.

"Biba is staying with me right now. And I have upstairs quarters for the maid. I do like the space. I luxuriate in it."

What she's had all her life, Cody thought as he stopped on the walkway to the front steps. "Aren't you afraid staying out here with what's going on in the county?"

"My alarm system will wake the dead. And everyone here knows how to handle a weapon." She fumbled in her purse. "Come in for a minute, I'll show you around."

After deactivating the alarm, Michelle let him in to give him a quick tour. He was impressed. There was a huge brass chandelier hanging just inside the entrance. The floor was of highly polished, wide oak boards.

"The boards were taken from my maternal grandparents' house when it was torn down," Michelle said. "The wood was logged out of the mountains over a hundred years ago."

The living room was gigantic. A pair of tall brass lamps at least seven feet tall guarded each side of a huge stone fireplace. The overhanging mantel was ornately carved with images of owls and eagles. Cody stared at it, impressed.

"It's chestnut," Michelle said. "And older than the flooring. All my kitchen cabinets are chestnut also."

"I love this house."

"Thanks, Cody. I've always wanted it all: money, looks, great sex. I've got money."

"Three hundred ain't a bad batting average."

She backed up to the fireplace. Tiny tongues of flame licked around a single, as yet unconsumed, hickory log. She posed with her elbow on the mantel, drew Cody's attention again to how big and raw-boned she was, a regular lumberjack's daughter. "Oh my, how honest you are. Most men, if I'd bring them here and show them all this expensive elegance, would already be telling me how really classical my nose and chin is. They'd say beauty is in the eyes of the beholder and I was beautiful to them. All the while their minds would be in overdrive thinking of how they could get their hands on the property. The sad thing is, I'd let them lead me back to the bedroom and convince me their motives were pure."

"You do have nice tits and a great ass."

Michelle threw her head back and brayed. "God, Cody—you are one in a million."

The bedroom was nearly as large as the living room. The iron bed was king-sized with a ruffled canopy. The Laura Ashley comforter was pricey, matched the drapes and the wide border that circled the room under the dental molding. Cody could see an enormous bath beyond the extra-wide doors on the far side of the room.

"A house is so much more livable with the master bedroom downstairs, don't you think?" Michelle said, then went on talking without waiting for an answer. "This is where I waste away after slaving at the clinic all day." She hurried ahead, again not waiting for an answer.

"You're on a real mean pity-pot trip tonight. I'll go home to my two-hundred-square-foot camper trailer, lie awake all night worrying about how tough your life is. When I first got to Nashville my address was: back seat, burgundy Plymouth Fury Three."

"Cody, you are an asshole—a one-in-a-million asshole. I'll show you the upstairs if you like."

201

"By all means."

Halfway up the stairs, Michelle stopped and pointed to a large framed print. It was of a piano, sheet music, and brass candle holders. "This is my favorite possession. It's not all that expensive, but it's beautiful. If you look closely you'll find cherubs hidden in the painting."

"I've been mentally comparing your house to Barry's," Cody said. "This one is so different—do I want to say opulent—where his is kind of drab."

"There's not much of a gap in his income and mine. In fact, his may be more. I don't worry about that sort of thing. It's that Justine's taste was in her ass. She was an ignorant slut."

They bypassed the maid's quarters. The niece's room was down the hall. "I always keep a room for Biba. She comes any time she wants."

The room was not as large as the master bedroom but was an oversized one for any home. Laura Ashley ruled here also in the bright print of the comforter, the drapes, and the covers of an overstuffed chair. A boombox stood on a nightstand by the bed. The desktop computer, crouched on the French-country desk across the room, looked out of its era.

Cody walked over to the computer and examined it. It was a Pentium 200Mhz. Computer of the pros, he thought. Or an expensive toy for a spoiled, poor little rich girl. "Your niece into computers?"

"She's a computer nerd. She'll stay up here for hours running programs, doing whatever a computer nerd does. She's already doing work part-time for Mountain County Savings and Loan, and she helps out at the Electric Co-op. You know anything about computers?"

"Some. Not much," Cody said. "If I really need to know something, I have a friend who's been in the business for years. Noel can bring a lively party to a grinding halt with all his megabytes, modems, and baud rates."

A small, ornate silver picture frame was next to the computer. Cody picked it up and let his eyes track over it. Bubba Whittlemore's smiling face stared back at him. With one booted foot propped on a log and the big 30.06 rifle cradled in his arms, he looked outdoorsy and macho in his spanking new deputy's duds. "Love, Bubba" was signed in the lower left-hand corner.

"Biba's got a wild crush on Bubba. He so handsome. Don't you think?"

"Bubba's not exactly my type," Cody said.

Michelle's home office was across the hall. A big desk held the twin of the other computer. "Biba's so technical. She's connected the computers so they can talk to one another. She can sit in her room and work with my computer. And she's got a camera; I don't know exactly how it works, but she can take a picture then put it on her computer somehow."

"Video capture," Cody said. Michelle didn't seem to hear him.

There was a rogue's gallery of pictures hanging on the wall. One showed the sheriff in his uniform, hat held in front of him in one hand, standing with Michelle. Michelle wore a rose-colored pantsuit and a big smile for the camera. From the big ribbon hanging across the doorway of the new-looking, concrete building behind them, Cody guessed they were in front of Michelle's clinic.

"Picture was taken at my grand opening," she confirmed. "Your daddy was very helpful."

Biba walked in the front door as Cody was leaving. She looked excited, flushed, almost breathless. Michelle introduced them. They shook hands. Her tight, green pants matched the pullover sweater and buckskin shoes she wore. She had a firm chin and a straight, narrow nose. Green eyes bored into Cody. Her gaze was steady, impertinent.

She smelled fresh and clean from the outside air. And she was built good, nice-looking with her strawberry-blonde hair—what Michelle would have looked like if she had turned out pretty. Wonder how Bubba and her got together?

"Cody is using high-tech investigating techniques to go after the killer," Michelle said. "He got the latest equipment to detect telephone taps."

"Jolinda's told me all about you," Biba said with a cute little smile. She elevated her nose slightly, turned her head to one side and looked at him out of the corners of her eyes.

"That's nice," Cody said.

After Cody left, Michelle and Biba sat at the kitchen table and talked. "I didn't see your Blazer outside," Biba said.

Michelle explained how she'd gotten a little tipsy and Cody had driven her home.

"Is he going to help out Dad?" Biba said. "I've been so confused lately. Everything is so gloomy, like there's no use going to school, or getting up even."

"That's called depression, dear," Michelle said. "I'm not fussing at you now, but the pills you were taking can cause serious depression. That added on to what happened to your mother."

"That's all over now," Biba lied. She had gotten all shaky just this morning and dipped into her stash. It was the first one in a few days. Bubba had told her she needed to come off of them slow so as not to get cravings. She could go see Sonny Todd. Sonny may be able to help her, if she could get him away from Brandy for a while.

"I'm proud of you, honey, for facing something like this so bravely," Michelle said. "Your mother and I had our differences, but she was still your mom, and there's no one that can replace her."

"I feel so alone," Biba said. She could feel her eyes tearing up, the heat coming to her face. There was a tingling sensation in her arms. "I hope so much Dad didn't kill her."

Michelle went to the refrigerator and brought back two cans of diet soft drinks. She popped the tops on both and passed one to Biba. "Barry didn't kill anybody. Cody will prove that."

"Sometimes I don't trust Cody or Sheriff Rainwalker," Biba said. "Sometimes I don't trust anybody. Especially myself."

"You can always trust me," Michelle said.

"I know that. The kids at school, they all resent me because I get good grades, because we have money and they don't. I'm an outsider in my own hometown."

"Thought you'd be back in Nashville by now," Ray Blizzard said.

Cody had called Ray at home to say the Willingham case was

nowhere near over. "What we have is a very uncooperative perp. If he'd just walk into the S.O. and give up, I could spend another day or two at the cabin, then get back on the insurance scammers' cases."

"You ain't missing much but driving in the rain and having Noel drive you nuts. Hear him tell it, computer crime is the wave of the future. Says he's been studying all the books you lent him, and he can ace the P.I. test. I told him he'd disqualified himself by being dumb enough to want to come to work here in the first place. Also, I spent all day sitting on the Daugherty case. Insurance company wants videos of him climbing a tree with a fucking tractor tire under his arm or something. Guy ain't been outa the house in a week; when he does he walks kinda shaky."

"What adjusters can't accept is sometimes a claimant has a legitimate injury. Anyhow, I'm into something you'd feel at home with," Cody said.

"Blonde or redhead?"

Cody waited while a hay truck with a bad muffler rattled and roared by the drive-in market. He didn't trust the portable phone in his camper. "Radios. I had a hunch the killer was using a police band radio to target his victims. Now he's left a note calling himself Scanner. Could be a hacker handle."

"Hacker? Like in computer hacker?"

"There's all types of hackers: computer hackers, telephone hackers, explosive hackers, radio hackers."

"Explosive hackers?" Ray asked.

"Some creeps get off on explosives, laugh their ass off at a big bang. This guy, Scanner, gets off on radios—and killing."

"You got a lead?"

"Got squat," Cody said. "What I do have is my own portables. I can monitor the portable and cellular telephone bands, see what I come up with."

"Hey. It's worked before." Ray referred to the time he had planted on a particularly high-dollar case. The insurance company was about to pay some big bucks when he'd heard the supposedly severely injured victim planning an Austrian ski vacation after he got the settlement. He couldn't tell the company how he'd come by the info. He'd possibly committed a federal crime himself by intercepting the call. The company had held off paying, and Diving Hawk Investigations came away heroes, with a big bonus.

"Hello, Dave. There's gonna be a wild and crazy party in room seven tonight," the female caller said. "You're invited."

"At the Riverside Motel?" the male voice said.

"Where else in this hick town? Things'll kick off at about eight."

"Sounds great, Susie. What's the program?"

"My newspaper's paying for everything," the female voice answered. "There's gonna be some drinking, some snacks, dancing, a little fooling around, some more drinking and maybe a funny cigarette or two and then some real heavy sex, which will last to the wee hours of the morning."

"Sounds like my kind of party," Dave said. "What should I wear?"

"Don't really matter," Susie said. "It's just gonna be you and me."

Cody chuckled and flicked the membrane switch on his hand-held scanner. It was a two-hundred-channel programmable radio any serious private detective could not do without. He knew narcotics squads in most cities monitored the cellular bands, listened to the druggers planning meets and buys and hits. With it he could continuously scan from one end of the cellular spectrum to the other, over and over, automatically. He'd been at it since arriving back in his camper trailer and his eyes were tired from focusing so long. He kept nodding off. He hit the scan button to monitor the sheriff's office frequency, down in the 154 megahertz range.

"One-oh-seven, Mountain County." A male deputy was calling in.

"Mountain County. Go 'head, one-oh-seven." Cody heard there was a male dispatcher tonight. More than likely one of the deputies rotating jobs, he thought.

"Jason. This Monte Carlo done cut this pole in half. Better get the crew from the Electric Co-op headed this way, got some live wires down in a puddle of water, fire dancing all over the road. Driver is very forty-two, blew a point two-five on the breathalyzer. Send a forty-eight to tow the car and a forty-seven for the driver."

"Ten-four, one-oh-seven. What's your twenty?"

"I'm down a ways from the high school, right in front of the Mane Event Hair place."

"Ten-four," was the last thing Cody heard before he dozed off.

Twenty-two

The rain had stopped; Scanner noticed and flicked off the wipers. Nerve-wracking is what they were with the noisy scrape and thud as they moved from side to side in hypnotic rhythm. Could the drugs make him a more suitable subject for hypnosis? Wouldn't it be wild for a deputy to find him sitting here all zonked out? What would the explanation be?

Why worry? Wasn't he a pillar of the community, a well-thought-of citizen who would do no wrong, follow all the rules? His rules, but they didn't realize it with their minuscule minds, their so-inadequate brains with thoughts of only getting through the day, not growing, not attaining, who are they anyhow, not really human.

He would rise above them all. He knew their thoughts because they told him their thoughts. Their fears, their secrets they blabbed over the airways for anyone to hear, oh they were all so helpless, so innocent and so guilty.

Damn! He realized his mind had almost run away, so powerful it was, so unchained, so creative. Why, then, couldn't he uncover the identity of the whisperer, whose husband ate, slept, and watched TV and fished for bluegill while she cavorted and fucked and whispered behind his back and, he'd wager, screamed out to her lover with her give-it-to-me-good! give-it-to-me-good! over and over, the crazy bitch—and there he went again with his mind running away attaining a speed that he would one day not be able to recapture. Oh, shit! He had to slow down. Stop.

Scanner pulled to the curb on the dark street and waited, breathed deeply, breathe in, breathe out, one—breathe in, breathe out, two—all the way to ten, then start over. After ten minutes, Scanner pulled away from the curb and continued toward his destination and the presentation of yet another reward.

As Scanner neared the corner, a fat yellow cat ran in front of his vehicle. The stalker swerved, almost ran up on the sidewalk. He didn't want a cat's death on his conscience. It was strange how little kitties would always wait until you were right on them, then dash out at the last minute.

The street was dark and deserted, midnight black from the rain. A cold north wind whistled in the cracks of the dried-out weather stripping around the windows, shook the vehicle slightly now and then, whipped branches around. Detached leaves occasionally brushed the windshield, stuck for a moment to the wet glass, then blew away to be replaced by another. Lock your doors, Scanner thought. Hide your sons and daughters in your homes, oh guilty ones. You know who you are, all of you—but relax.

His target was chosen. He was launched as surely as a bullet fired from a marksman's rifle. And it was a great night for it and no one could say he wasn't expert, that he didn't do good work.

He was at the house.

* * *

Samantha was in a happy mood and it felt great for a change. Relaxed, fulfilled—satisfied, is that what it was? Like a huge, painful knot had been cut out of her stomach. When she moved she felt almost weightless, her stride was longer, stronger, she breathed deeper and the air tasted better. The sheriff had looked at her funny. Did he know? Was she so dependent on men she couldn't be a whole person unless she was in a relationship? Was she the sum total of whether the relationship was going well?

Michelle Willingham'd sure given her a hard stare when she'd driven past her out on Cataloochee Road trying to sweat off those big, meaty thighs and that fat, ugly ass. Wonder if Michelle had guessed where she'd been and what she'd been up to? If she had, bet she was wishing she had been in her place. That's the way she had acted with Randy, tried to get him in her bed. She may have succeeded. Damn bitch owned half the county and her brothers owned the other half, and she still wanted what other people had.

Was she so happy because Luther was finally getting his? Or was it Cody? Have a climax or three or four and all's well with the world. More than likely a combination of the two. Luther had been let go at about eight; the reporters were crowded around the jail yelling questions at him as he ducked his head and made a run down the street in the direction of his house. The reporters had started to follow, but the sheriff stepped out on the sidewalk and they crowded around him, asking if Luther was suspected of being the serial killer.

"I don't think there is a serial killer," the sheriff had said. "There's some nut running around loose, and we're going to bring him down. Luther Hamby was brought in for questioning and released. That's it." He had turned and walked back in the door of the jail.

Samantha admired the sheriff, thought of him as a truly honest man. And thoughtful. Concerned for the welfare of his deputies and for the people he was born to protect. He took the job seriously.

She pushed through a set of behind-the-neck barbell presses as she let her mind roam over the events of the day and the preceding night. The rendezvous with Cody had been a planned occurrence, she admitted to herself, and he'd probably figured it out. Bringing the news of what had happened to Monk was really a lame excuse to drive twenty miles of fire roads in four-wheel-low.

She had watched Cody from that first day in the restaurant. Had she subconsciously began plotting to seduce him when he first walked in the door and she saw how sexy he looked? She hadn't really noticed him on his previous infrequent trips to Mountain County, or even before. Randy was all that was on her mind then. Now she thought she could finally get over Randy.

Had Michelle driven up the mountain fire trail last night? Did she suspect Cody was at his cabin? That big Blazer could make it with no problem. Bet she'd been pissed when she saw the Jeep. Goes to show you—money can't buy everything.

Samantha picked up a pair of thirty-pound dumbbells and

began a set of alternating curls, keeping her eyes straight ahead, rocking her body slightly with each move. When her biceps began to burn, she did four more reps with each arm, then bent over and placed the weights lightly on the floor.

"Mountain County to unit eight. Give me a signal six here at the S.O."

"'At's ten-four."

The sound of the radio calls came from her front porch. Was one of the deputies out there?

There was a light knock on the door.

Samantha rolled the dumbbells to the wall with her foot then brushed her hair back out of her eyes. Who was it? She looked at the clock on the wall: 9:35. Making sure her sweatshirt and sweat pants were not hiked up or pulled down anywhere, exposing naked flesh—or the automatic pistol she carried in her waistband—she stepped to the door and opened it.

"Hello. What's the occasion?" she asked her visitor.

"Why, my dear. I'm here with your reward."

Cody jerked awake. He'd fallen asleep on the couch. He looked at his watch. Midnight. He might as well get undressed and go to bed. Still half asleep, he flinched at the radio's blare of a warbling siren sound. "Mountain County, unit seven on the way." The voice was Bubba Whittlemore's.

"Go man, go! Go, goddammit—Samantha's house is the fifth one down after you turn onto Balsam Gap Road. Frame house sets back off the road, got a old stone wall runs along the north side."

"Ten-four, I know it. I'm rolling at over a hundred!" Bubba was breathing hard from excitement, he talked loud to make himself heard over the siren. "You still trying to get her on the phone?"

"No answer. Miss Paysinger says she heard gunshots. She called in right away. I'm rolling a forty-seven."

"Ten-four. You wanta start blocking off roads? Start with the highway then Cataloochee Road—Balsam Gap dead-ends into it."

"Ten-four." The dispatcher began setting up a net around Highwater Town.

"Aw, shit!" Cody said. He grabbed his leather jacket and headed out the door to his pickup. The windshield had iced over. He quickly scraped a circle large enough to see through, jumped in the truck and switched the defroster on high as he threw gravel getting out of the driveway onto the narrow road. Goddammit! What he needed was an emergency light. He barrelled ahead through the light fog.

He made the five miles to Samantha's house in just over five minutes. Flashing red and blue lights guided him the last half mile. Like fucking L.A., he thought, something going down every night. Parking two hundred feet away, he left it in the middle of the road and ran up the street to what was obviously Samantha's house. An ambulance was parked at the curb in front; the attendants cooled their heels at its open rear door, smoking and talking. That didn't look good.

He ran up the front walk.

A young deputy stepped in his way and was knocked aside. Cody didn't look back.

At the doorway his dad tried to stop him. "You don't wanta go in there, son!" The sheriff looked gray, like he'd aged ten years since Cody had last seen him.

Cody smelled the coppery aroma of mayhem as he pushed by his father and stepped in the doorway. The entrance was covered with blood. Bright splotches had showered the inside of the door and the nearby wall. He stopped quickly, then stepped around spots on the floor as best he could. He stepped close along the edge of the green-and-red sofa in front of the living room windows to avoid making tracks on the beige rug.

Luther lay flat on his back in the middle of the room. He wore a pair of brown trousers, brown shoes, and a red-and-black checked shirt. The top of his head was missing. There were two small holes in the middle of his chest.

"Looks like Samantha put four rounds in him," his dad said at his shoulder, placing his hand on Cody's arm and gripping it.

"Two in the heart and two in the head . . ." Cody said.

"Makes the bad guy fall down dead," the sheriff finished the law enforcement jingle.

"Where's Samantha?"

"Right inside the bedroom door," the sheriff said. "Let us take care of it."

Cody stepped around Luther's sprawled corpse and the weight bench that stood next to it with a barbell in the bench-press rack and headed to where Bubba was loading fresh film into his camera. Tears rolled down the deputy's cheeks. He broke into a shuddering sob.

The sheriff stepped over. "Here, Bubba, let me do it, son." He took the camera and patted Bubba on the shoulder. "Fucking Luther. Shoulda put him down when I had a chance."

Cody stepped to the bedroom door and looked inside. "Oh, goddammit!" he screamed.

Samantha was nude. Her service automatic was gripped in a still, pale hand. Her neck was a purple mass of bruises. The flesh on her chest and stomach was shredded in even cuts an inch apart. Most of the blood had drained out of her body. She looked diminished, deflated by the loss of body fluids. Her arms and legs were cut up, ripped to ribbons. Her face was unmarked, eyes closed as if asleep. Cody thought somehow, as weird as it seemed, she looked at peace. What was it the old church choirs would sing? He heard it ringing in his ears: The peace that passeth understanding. Was that what it meant?

Talk about nightmares. He'd see this in his mind forever. His throat constricted with anger; he felt a feverish heat in his face that traveled down his body and arms. He remembered this morning, telling her she was a good person and things would work out for her. Hell of a fucking fortuneteller he was.

A white spread covered the double bed in the middle of the small bedroom. Gray house shoes stood on a blue throw rug by the bed. Over the headboard, on a crocheted framed square with a gold-colored cross, read, "God bless this house." Long, white, knotted tassels dangled from the shade of a crystal lamp, half-way to the top of a nightstand by the bed. Samantha's phone, an ivory, cordless Princess, was in its cradle a few inches away. The room looked neat, feminine, like Samantha, smelled of her perfume, was a continuation of her personality, he thought.

Cody had thought he was through with all the blood and mayhem. Chasing insurance cheats was a mellowed-out existence

213

compared to what his life had been as a cop. Now someone he knew intimately had bought it in a horrible way. "Fuck!" he screamed as he began pounding the wall with his fist.

Standing quietly for a few moments, he brought himself under control. With a face darkened with rage, Cody turned his flinty eyes on his dad. "The missing tiger's claw?" he asked.

Sheriff Rainwalker pointed into the living room at Luther's hand. The bloody metal claw was clutched in a true death grip. "Looks like a few strands of hair caught in his hand. Could be Samantha's. We'll have to wait."

Cody stepped over to get a closer look at Luther, bent down to inspect the wounds. "You sure just four shots?"

The sheriff nodded, "Two and two. Just like she was taught for close-up shooting."

"Send deputies to check the neighbors. See if anybody saw a car drive off after they heard the shots. And don't take down the roadblocks. Do it without using the radio."

"I already gave those orders," the sheriff said. "No way she could've shot Luther after the wounds she received, or he coulda clawed her up with the top of his head blowed off. There's other ways through town for somebody who knows their way around. Can drive through Owl Hollow Cemetery or the schoolyard or down a dirt road through the woods and be gone. You know something?"

"Got a strong suspicion we're seeing what somebody wants us to see. Or they're trying to mind-fuck the law."

"How'd you figure it?" the sheriff asked.

"Samantha told me if she ever had to shoot Luther, she'd put the first round in his nuts."

"Why didn't she come to me when it happened?" the sheriff said sadly. "I've had my suspicions about Luther. I'd a suspended him right off."

Cody had told his dad about Luther drugging Samantha a year earlier. "She could've thought she was somehow at fault. We'll never know now. Unless she said something to Becky Taggart. Don't think she did though. She didn't trust her not to tell Carl." Cody heard yelling outside in the street. He walked to the window and pulled back the curtain. Deputies were holding back an unruly crowd. "The media has arrived in force."

"Just what we need," the sheriff said. "There's a forensics specialist on the way from Chattanooga and a local doctor on the way to pronounce them. Gotta make sure they get through. Preacher's on the way. Sonny Todd. He'll drive down to Etowah later and notify Samantha's folks. God, I don't look forward to seeing them. She was in my care. Then Bubba and I will bag their hands and feet—and send two more bodies to the M.E. in Nashville."

Cody knew his father was rambling, in shock. "I'm going over this house for listening devices. I bet three to one she's been watched and bugged," Cody said. "And if you wanta take the fucking scum that did this to trial, you better find him before I do."

"Don't care if he goes to trial or not. Just so we get him off the street."

The young deputy Cody had almost knocked off his feet stuck his head in the doorway. He was bareheaded, his dark hair tossed by the wind, his high cheeks and long, pointed nose red from the cold. "Young girl down the way, she woke up and looked out her window when she heard the shots. Said a woman ran through her back yard. Family had the back-porch light on and she's sure the runner's female. Said she had long hair down past her shoulders. Minute later she heard a car door slam and a engine start. Then it drove off."

"A woman?" the sheriff said. He glanced over at Cody, who didn't seem at all surprised.

"You go sit with that girl, Robbie," the sheriff said to the deputy. "Keep her inside and don't let any reporters near her. Any try to come in, give a holler on the radio and I'll put their ass in the slammer."

The forensics specialist was through, the bodies bagged and out the door. Cody had gone over the house with his instruments, sat at the kitchen table and made his report to the sheriff who sat across from him. It was six in the morning. Both men were exhausted.

Sheriff Rainwalker removed his hat, started to lay it on the small table, then changed his mind, put it back on his head and adjusted it carefully like he wanted to broach a subject but felt ill at ease with the content. "While you were looking around the house, climbing under furniture and all, the forensics guy did his things, one of which was to comb Samantha's pubic hair, see if they's any in there that's not hers. How you feel about that?"

Cody's elbow was on the table. Weary, he leaned his chin on his palm and looked his dad straight in the eye. "May find one or two of mine. She came up to the cabin. We washed in the river, but who knows. M.E. will be able to determine if she was raped. But if the perp was a woman . . . ?"

"Prints could show up something. We'll look for footprints now that it's light out. There's a scrape on the rock wall that runs by the house, looks like a shoe scuffed it recently. Somehow I can't imagine a woman doing something like this. Shooting Luther—yeah, I can see that. But mutilating somebody with steel claws? I don't know."

Cody's anger melted to sadness. "She never had time to tell me all those little things about herself. How she fell out of a tree when she was little, or got the bike she wanted for Christmas. I didn't get to tell her about my dog or about my time in Europe. We just shared a few hours, didn't get a chance to let each other really know how we came to be in the here and now."

He took a deep breath. "I expected to find bugs, but what I didn't expect was the level of sophistication I found. The devices recovered from the Taggart house and from Barry's and the lawyer's place were strictly amateur. What we have here is a combination of hard-wired microphones and bugging transmitters wired into the electrical system so they don't need batteries. Also I found a room monitor that uses the house electric wires to transmit a signal. Bedroom was the major target, but the bugs can be so sensitive, anybody talking in this size house could be heard." He paused. "You have any reason to suspect Samantha was under investigation by any federal agency?"

The sheriff was puzzled. "Federal agency? Not to my knowledge. I don't think Samantha was up to anything illegal. Why do you ask?"

Cody held a miniature frequency counter in one hand. He used its extended antenna as a pointer, poked a small disk on the kitchen table. "Telephone company always runs a four-wire cable in for your phone. Only use two in most cases; other two are for a second phone. This mike was wired to the yellow and black, the spare wires. When it gets light enough out, I'll take a look, but what I'm betting is that either on a nearby pole or where the phone wire comes into the house, I'll find the amplifier for this little jewel. Also I'll find what's called an infinity transmitter. An eavesdropper can call the phone spare, send a tone down the line, and listen in on what's going on in the house."

"Wouldn't the spare have to be connected to the telephone company switchboard somehow?" the sheriff said.

"Yeah, which gives me the federal agency angle. Phone company is not likely to allow a tap like this without a warrant, and, the cost of it. The federal agency would have to pay to lease the line seven days a week, twenty-four hours a day as long as the tap was on, the only way a phone company will go along with it. That can be expensive. Also the wire, as they call the tap, would have to be manned. If someone not named in the warrant was in the house having an innocent conversation with another party, feds would have to switch it off. Least that's how it's supposed to work. A Title Three, the feds call it."

The sheriff took his hat off and rubbed his fingers through his hair. His eyes were red from lack of sleep. "Could the agency, whoever they might be, have bugged the house, then not found anything and forgot about it?"

"They would've sent their black-bag team in to remove the bugs. That's the way they do things. Other devices I found, somebody could sit in a vehicle a couple blocks away and listen in. Samantha's phone is a portable, so whoever's listening in didn't need to bug it. Just listen in on the 40-megahertz band and scan through the channels. With the ight antenna and radio, they could pick her conversation up from half a mile away or better."

"What's next?" the sheriff asked. "I mean, you're the expert here. Small department like mine can't afford your kind of talent."

"I'll find the amp and transmitter, then you can go down and talk to the local telephone company, being you're the law. It still a small private company?"

The sheriff nodded and reached into his pocket. He took out a badge and held it in his hand. "Raise your right hand."

"Huh?"

"I'm going to deputize you, son. Raise your right hand. This is Samantha's badge."

"Aw, come on, Daddy. This your way of getting me to join the department?"

"Son, we've got over 640 square miles to patrol and we're already spread thin. Now I've lost two deputies and I've got a nut loose in the county. I need your help; you're more experienced than any deputy I have."

Cody still wasn't sure. He'd left one police department behind and he hadn't missed it a single day he could recall. "What about I work undercover at first, only two people that know will be you and me. I don't want to ever wear a uniform."

"Fine with me. Raise your right hand . . ."

The sheriff examined the scrape mark on the top stone of the rock wall. "Looks like shoe leather," he said.

"You're right, Sheriff," Bubba said. "Looks like light tan finished leather, scraped right off."

The ground was bare near the wall. The outline of a footprint was obvious. "Looks like a woman's shoe made it," Bubba said. "Looks like one'a those mini-heel types, maybe half inch or a inch. I got a steel rule, so I'll check for sure."

"Make a cast," the sheriff said. "And bag the leather particles."

Back inside the house, the sheriff found Cody hooking into a phone line with a telephone test-set retrieved from the leather bag in his truck. "Whatcha up to there?"

"Phone phreaking is what the hackers call it. Phone phreaks use their technical knowledge to ride roughshod over the common herd. They think it gives them power. What I'm gonna do here is dial my Skypager, do some rough-riding of my own. When I give you the nod, use a pen or a pencil point to hit the redial button on Samantha's cordless."

Cody dialed his pager's toll-free number; at the beep he entered his access code then signaled his dad when he heard the triple beep. The sheriff hit redial, then hung up the phone and waited.

"Data's in the queue," Cody said.

Thirty seconds later his pager sounded. He snatched it from his belt and showed his dad the number in the liquid crystal display. "Telephone number mean anything to you?"

"I'm not sure. But it looks like the number at the HillTop Tavern."

Cody dialed it to be sure.

There was no answer.

"Place's closed this time'a morning," the sheriff said. "And thanks for the technical lesson. That's one I won't forget."

Twenty-three

Fuzzy's was the place to be, all the out of town, big-city reporters surmised. Besides offering the only safe place for the reporters to unwind, the watering hole was the center of the universe of swirling rumors about the prolific killer stalking the county. Big 'Un's orders were to protect the out-of-town visitors and their expense accounts at any and all costs. News was scarce, thanks to the sheriff keeping all hints and clues to himself. A creative reporter could find local color and indulge in fantasizing with the town folk as to why the killer was doing what he did and where he would strike next. Hopefully an editor, eager to fill space on the front page, would allow the wild speculations to be submitted in the place of hard news.

Monk, bored with the entire ordeal and thankful of being spared death or dismemberment by his close encounter, no longer held forth at his power spot at the bar. Fuzzy was lightening up some too. Earlier in the day Monk had been talking to a reporter from Tampa and had accidently let slip the phrase modus operandi. Instead of having Big 'Un drive him home, the bald tavern owner had merely eyed him suspiciously, then gone back to leering at the crowd and doodling on a piece of paper, doing his best to keep a running total of the gross daily receipts as he kept track of the ringing of the register's bell.

It was eight in the evening, prime time for drinkers, shuffleboarders, and electronic poker sharks, when Rooster Armbrewster, an unemployed painting contractor from the southern section of the county, stuck his head in the door. Rooster had received his nickname due to his self-appointed duties of crowing about all the local happenings. "Cody Rainwalker's up to the HillTop, an' he's snot-slingin' drunk! Got a sawed-off under his arm, and he's drinking vodka straight outa the bottle. He's chasing it with a slug of gasoline outa a big gas can."

Later, Fuzzy would wake in the middle of the night, sweating, and estimate once again his bar had emptied in under ten seconds. He vowed that Rooster would never again darken his door (he was always trying to run a tab anyway). Even Monk and the poker players had deserted him. Big 'Un had wanted to join the stampede but had caught his employer's eye just prior to deserting his post and reconsidered.

Fuzzy, panic-stricken, had called the big bouncer over and offered him fifty dollars to go to the rival establishment and kick Cody Rainwalker's traitorous ass.

Fifty dollars seemed a tremendous sum to Big 'Un. He rolled his eyes and thought it over, remembered the stories he'd heard about Cody. "No, thank you, Mr. Fuzzy. Big 'Un don't fight nobody that drinks gasoline."

"Mountain County Sheriff's Department," Wanda June answered the telephone.

"This here's Baily at the HillTop. Cody Rainwalker's here and he's scared all my customers off. Got a twelve-gauge sawed-off and a five-gallon can'a gas he keeps drinking and spitting all over the place."

"Hello? Mountain County Sheriff's Department."

"Come on, Wanda June. This is important. The sheriff there? Lemme talk to him."

"Hello. Hello? Mountain County S.O. Hello?"

"Now, Wanda June. Ain't got no fire insurance. Least get in touch with Barry Willingham, have him stand by with the firetruck."

"Hello?"

Baily hung up the phone in disgust. He knew he was on his own now. He had a peacekeeping shotgun behind the bar but knew if he went for it Cody would cut him down. Besides the scatter gun Cody carried, Baily had spied the evil-looking automatic in the shoulder holster under Cody's black leather jacket.

He decided to plead his case with the man in front of him.

"Now, Cody. I ain't never done nothing to you. Why you gonna burn my place?"

Cody had swallowed a lot of vodka. He'd slept fitfully during the day but kept waking up after dreaming of Samantha being cut to ribbons by a nightmare-created, automated meat saw. Flesh and blood flew all over the room until only her bones stood stark against a black background until they collapsed in a tangled heap at his feet. "Now, Buds," Cody slurred. He needed to keep his cool. He didn't want to go berserk and kill the tavern owner. "You're getting excited over nothing here. Just come in for a taste."

Baily looked beyond Cody to where the customer lay who had taken umbrage when the P.I. had first walked into the tavern. Cody had given the irate man a backhand set of knuckles across the bridge of his nose, then knocked him unconscious with a short elbow jab to the temple. The bouncer—a heavy, hairy bruiser of a man—lay beyond the customer, his leg bent at an awkward, impossible angle. Baily considered the possibility the man was dead. After having his leg broken by a side-kick delivered by Cody almost without breaking his stride, the man had made the mistake of reaching under his shirt for a .38 caliber revolver. Cody had back-kicked him in the face, breaking his nose and removing a good number of teeth, some of which now lay scattered on the dirty floor.

"Come over here, Buds." Cody wiggled his finger. "That your name? Buds?"

"Name's Baily. Wanna call me Buds, name's Buds." Baily approached cautiously, prepared to jump back and make a dash for the back door.

"Buds. Word is Deputy Samantha Goodlocke called here last night and talked to Luther Hamby, said recently departed lowlife being a regular customer in this consummate shit-hole."

"Where you hear that, Mr. Rainwalker?"

"Some cowardly asshole whispered it in my daddy's ear. A protected confidential informant. Said you answered the phone, Buds. Said you told ol' Luther, 'Some bitch is on the phone for you,' then you had a good laugh."

"Didn't know who it was. Honest. I thought it was one'a his

women wanting drugs, maybe one'a her johns acting up or in-law trouble needing him to bail her outa something."

Cody impaled the tavern owner with a hard stare.

Baily felt honesty would be the best route here. "I reckon it was Deputy Goodlocke, rest her soul, but it didn't sound like her to me. Sorry-ass Luther talked to her for less than a minute, come back to the bar, and told me she said come see her, she had something to tell him that'd clear him of any wrong."

"He leave right away?" Cody asked.

"Naw. Hung around for another half hour or so, drunk a couple beers, like he's getting hisself worked up to something; then he lit out."

"Anybody go with him?"

"Naw—went by hisself."

"Anybody seem interested in what he's up to?"

"Ever'body's doing their thing."

"Which is getting shit-faced, preparing to go out and drive drunk, run into trees and light poles, maybe over innocent citizens."

"Mr. Rainwalker—I just serve this shit."

Cody took a long pull on the bottle of vodka, then threw it across the bar to crash into a liquor rack and a long mirror that appeared never to have seen a cleaning cloth. Broken glass fell to the floor.

Lifting the gas can with the back of his forearm, Cody brought it to his lips, drank a long draft, and swallowed hard. "Fucking gasoline tastes better than the rot-gut you serve. Gimme a bottle of scotch."

Baily brought the bottle, cracked the seal, and handed it over. "Don't get too much call for scotch whiskey."

Cody took a swig of scotch, then lifted the gas can again and took a drink. He took another and spit it over the bar. "Got a light?"

"Please, Mr. Rainwalker! Don't burn the place down. Nobody will sell me any fire insurance."

"Got a light?" Cody put his hand on the butt of the sawed-off.

Baily took a lighter from his pocket and tossed it onto the bar.

"A Zippo," Cody said. "You know, Buds. This place is a fucking eyesore. I bet if this rat's nest burned to the ground, Highwater Town would get a City Beautiful Commendation." He started flicking the lighter just enough to bring a few sparks.

Rooster had pulled his pickup to within inches of the block wall of the HillTop Tavern. He stood in the bed, nose pressed to a small, grimy window, peering in at Cody and Baily and the drama unfolding at the bar. "Cody's gettin' ready to light 'er up." Rooster looked thoughtful for a few seconds, then hopped down and ran around to jump in his truck and drive it out of harm's way.

The crowd, pressed around the town crier, fell back a few paces, prepared for the excitement. "Haven't had a good fire in town since Carl got herself thrown offa the fire department," a man said to the crowd in general.

Cody turned to look over his shoulder as the front door opened and Bubba and Jolinda strode in, side by side.

Baily was cheered and slightly emboldened, though still aware Cody was drunk and well armed. "Deputy. I'm sure glad you're here. This drunk is threatening to burn me out."

Cody's head whipped around. "Minute ago you was calling me Mr. Rainwalker. Now you're calling me a drunk? Jolinda, Bubba. Like you to meet Buds."

"Hello, Buds," Jolinda said. "Place smells like somebody's been pissing on the floor—for about a year."

"Hello, Buds," Bubba said. "Lady's right. Smell in here would knock a buzzard off a gut wagon. Health department been in lately?"

"Health department?" Baily was irate. "This drunk is carrying firearms, which is against the state law."

"Notice he's drinking scotch," Bubba said.

"That's what he ordered," Baily said defensively.

"You served a man whiskey you say's drunk and carrying firearms? Gonna have to place you under arrest and shut you down."

"What about Cody Rainwalker?" Baily said.

"Cody Rainwalker was sent in here as a private citizen to check this place out, see if he could get served illegally."

"I don't believe it."

"It's true," Cody said. "Sorry Buds."

The ambulances had come and gone. The paramedics had hauled the injured men out one by one.

A hush fell over the crowd surrounding the parking lot when first Jolinda, who went to open the door of her truck, then Cody, swinging his gas can in one hand, exited the front door of the HillTop. Next came Baily, hands cuffed behind him, followed by Bubba, who closed the door and hung a closed by order of the sheriff's department sign on the knob.

Cody was beginning to feel the booze; the crowd looked blurred. He staggered toward Jolinda's pickup only semi-aware of his surroundings.

Bobby Joe broke away from the crowd, ambling along like he was leaving the scene now the excitement was over, and stepped up behind Cody. He still wore a cast on his arm. The cut on his nose had not yet healed completely, still had a tint of blue surrounding it and a midnight-black middle. Coming close to Cody's back, he brought back the hand with the cast, prepared to hit the staggering man a heavy blow to the head.

Jolinda stepped up and, taking a full swing, hit Bobby Joe in the face with the aluminum Little League bat she carried in her truck. The crowd said, "Ooh."

Bobby Joe fell to the gravel, brought both hands to his bloody face, writhed in pain.

Bubba stepped over and looked down at the would-be attacker. "Bobby Joe. My advice to you is get some fucking hospitalization insurance."

In Jolinda's pickup, Cody laid his head against the headrest. He felt he was going to be sick. "Where you going, honey?"

"Taking you to the hospital."

"What for?"

"What for. Drinking goddamn gasoline's what for."

"Honey, I may be drunk, but I ain't stupid. What I been drinking is spring water outa a newly bought gas can. Stop along the road and let me throw up. And I'm gonna have that dooms-day feeling again. I know it. Happens with all my vodka hang-overs."

Back home, Jolinda brought him another cup of hot coffee, black. "Here, drink this. How you feel?" She sat down across the little camper table from him, rested both elbows on the surface, her face cupped in her hands as she gazed at him with big-eyed love and concern.

Cody had an awful taste in his mouth. "Like I run outa gas."

Eyes narrowing angrily, she straightened, head snapping up. "Now aren't you a real homemade riot, Cody Rainwalker, walk-ing around drunk in a place like that. Bobby Joe coulda hurt you bad."

"Not with Mama Jolinda on guard."

"And now Uncle Ogden's saying it again."

"Saying what?"

"He heard what happened. He's saying you and me, we're a matched pair. That's what he's saying, and you're saying Luther put something in Samantha's drink and somehow Randy found out and broke up with her?"

"Don't know if he found out about the spiked drink. Samantha never told. Too proud, or ashamed, I guess. Could be Luther went to Randy and bragged he'd bedded his girlfriend. Luther is—was—that kinda lowlife."

"You think Randy killed them?" Jolinda asked. "I wish Luther was still alive so's I could kill him. I'd wear that aluminum bat out on his ass."

Cody took another sip of coffee. It was steaming hot. He blew on it, held it in both hands, felt the heat through the heavy cup. "Don't know who killed them. Guess Daddy will be check-ing it out, the alibis and all. Right now he's letting the rumors run they killed each other in some kinda showdown. So with Baily in the slam, nobody knows I'm deputized, and I wanta keep it like that as long as I can." He didn't want to burden her with the knowledge that a witness had seen a woman fleeing the scene and that a good footprint had been found.

"Was she tore up bad?" Jolinda asked.

"Real bad. Don't want to see anything like it again. First Luther messes up her life, then . . ."

"It's so sad," Jolinda said. "People like Luther want what they want and don't care who they hurt."

"Luther's house was wired for sound like Samantha's, and far as I can tell, the spare wiretap runs all way back to the phone company. Daddy's checking on it. I'm getting paranoid myself. Even paranoics have people plotting behind their backs. First thing in the morning, I'm checking out the trailer and the house for bugs."

Jolinda looked startled. "Why would anyone want to bug Uncle Ogden and me?"

"Don't have a clue. But I'll check it out just the same."

Twenty-four

After a thorough search, Cody found no eavesdropping devices at the house or in the trailer. So he set off to see Barry. He'd awakened as he predicted he would, with that doomsday feeling. Long ago he'd found that vodka brought on this reaction. Which was why he'd switched to beer or bourbon or rum or tequila—anything but vodka unless he wanted to get real mean drunk. Vodka always worked when he wanted it to.

As a younger man he'd one day made the connection to vodka and all the blue flashing lights and roaring down highways at killing speed and waking up with mysterious scrapes and bruises and that Sunday-morning-sidewalk feeling where you'd be a happy camper if you could slit your own throat.

What he needed was to sweat it out, but he felt too unsteady to go running; he'd likely blunder into a barbed-wire fence. Had that happened once or was that while he was drinking? Anyway, he'd learned his lesson.

His mood was right for Barry, the way he wanted to face him—furious over Samantha's death, not sure if Barry was playing him for a sucker. Had Barry killed Samantha, Luther, and the others for some as yet crazy unknown reason? If he had . . .

He'd just not bring that up in a conversation. Then folks wouldn't wonder later about Barry's caving accident and all those rocks falling on his head. That's what he always strived for, a detached attitude while running an investigation.

Barry was waiting at his house. The hounds from hell bayed for Cody's hangover, then, duty fulfilled, headed back to lie under the sweet gum. Maybe they smelled his breath. He grappled with a wisp of thought, but it eluded him.

He'd phoned ahead.

"What's up?" Barry asked.

"Little chitchat."

"Come up on the porch. Sit a spell."

"Let's walk. I'm all twitchy, can't sit still." He had cobwebs in his brain and cotton in his mouth.

"Hear you got drunk at the HillTop and closed it down."

"Needed closing."

"Bobby Joe's in the hospital. Jolinda musta got a good swing on him." Barry said it quietly, just making talk. He kicked at the dirt as he walked along. He wondered what Cody had for him. Nothing good, he bet.

"Good place for him. Keep him outa trouble till I leave town."

"You think he'll make trouble for Jolinda?" Barry asked.

"Even Bobby Joe's not that dumb."

They ambled back to the fields, kept to the road that led by the tenant houses. A mockingbird kept pace, flitted from tree to tree voicing a strident concern over its territory. "Tell me something," Cody said. "You got all this land here, good farmland plus the land the trailer park's on and some I don't even know about. Why do you want more?"

"Well, uh, man needs property. Needs to provide for his family and all. You know that."

"But what are you gonna do with it all? Raw land's never been a good investment in Mountain County, and most of it's vertical anyhow. It's not like folks're lined up looking to buy land to build houses or factories on. What about it? You gonna farm the land or build on it?"

Barry put his hands deep in his pockets and swiveled his head back and forth, looked at the trees and the mountains, then looked over at Cody and quickly looked away. "Uh, we, er, I was going to hold the land to sell and maybe sell trees off some of it, let somebody log it."

"Impressive. You're so rich, you're gonna give Uncle Ogden two hundred fifty thousand—quarter of a mil—for his farm, then sit on it and have a few logs hauled off. Didn't realize you were all that wealthy. Knew your family had money. And then you're interested in my measly hundred acres and a broken-down cabin,

I heard. No hickory or oak or walnut up that high."

"Land's important to our family. You know how it is." Barry stubbed his toe on a rock embedded in the roadway and almost fell. He took two quick steps to recover his balance.

"Cut the bullshit," Cody said. "First you tell me you're too preoccupied with business to kill your wife. Then you expect me to believe land that's been sitting two hundred years is suddenly going away if you don't run out and buy it. What's going on?"

Cody stepped out and turned to block Barry's path. He could see sweat on the other man's forehead.

Barry worked his face through a set of emotions: first anger, then frustration, then a grim firmness he reinforced by setting his mouth with a somber tightness. "I'm sorry, Cody, but I just can't tell you. It's a business deal that involves others, and if the word got out, it would change the outcome. Ruin the whole thing."

"How much you planning on giving me for my place?"

Barry was caught completely off guard. "What, about two hundred? Cash."

"Two hundred thousand for rocks and ravines and land you need a helicopter or ATV to get to in winter?"

"Sometimes hunters or fishermen or, you know, outdoorsmen will buy land if it's been split up into small lots."

"That what you plan on doing?"

Barry hung his head. "Sorry, Cody. Just can't tell you." He was aware of the angry look and braced posture of the detective.

"Other night I witnessed something that'll give me nightmares for years to come. Wanta hear about it? Samantha lying there all chewed up, her blood soaking into the carpet, all her hopes and dreams gone up in pain and out the window with the terror she died with. Don't want me to find out later your land deals had something to do with her dying. You really don't. I'm in what some folks might call a bad fucking mood."

Cody turned on his radio as he drove out of the driveway. He'd set the frequencies in advance. Barry didn't disappoint him.

"Highwater Town Foundry," the female voice answered on the first ring.

"This is Barry. Let me talk to Victor." The line rang forward immediately.

"Victor Willingham." The voice was high-pitched and country, cracked at the end.

"Vic, Barry. Cody Rainwalker was just over here and he's hot, wanting to know about what we got going."

"What does he know? He know about the man from Las Vegas?"

"He could've seen him with Michelle, checked him out somehow. All Cody lets on is he knows we offered to buy Ogden Two Bears's place. He thinks the killings are tied in with what we got going. He'll be checking around, you can count on it."

"Tell him anything?"

"That the deal was confidential and to say anything would ruin it," Barry said.

"When you and Michelle first came to me, I thought it was a mistake. I'm shooting myself in the foot. Salaries in the county will go sky high. Folks that work for me will either quit or want a raise. Want benefits, insurance, retirement, vacations, sick days, be no end to it."

"You're shortsighted; you'll make ten or twenty times more money in a year than you'll make in a lifetime of running your foundry."

"So you and Michelle say. Horace Hornsby's already getting jumpy, saying we're asking too much of him. Mountain County Savings and Loan ain't a big enough operation to finance all the front money we need. We need to go out of town for higher stakes, and the more people you ask, the more explaining you do. And the more explaining you do, the more people know."

Barry's voice raised a notch. "Goddamn Hornsby. All for it in the beginning. Now he's saying he may have trouble with auditors or bank examiners."

"You know I don't hold with cussing, and I'd appreciate it if you wouldn't cuss in my phone," Vic said.

"You'll be cussing if this falls through. Especially if word gets out and land prices skyrocket overnight."

"I'll see Michelle later today," Victor said. "We need to set up a meeting, talk this out, get Stan Bodine's input. If necessary Michelle'll have to fire Cody."

"Oh, that'd be great. Then folks'll say he was getting too close to the real killer and she fired him to protect me. Damn town'll lynch me," Barry said.

"Serve you right for cussing in my phone." Victor broke the connection.

Cody looked at the small receiver on the seat next to him. Handy little gadget. Why hadn't he thought of it earlier?

The Highwater Town Foundry was an ugly, square, three-story building that had been around since before the turn of the century. The dark red brick that made up its rough walls was uneven, not as smooth as modern-day building material. Original window panes were still in place, distorted and thick with grime. At the entrance, Cody noticed a twenty-seven-year-old Chevy pickup parked by the door in the slot marked "Mr. Victor Willingham." Standing on the concrete porch and looking down into the pickup's window, he saw it had a column stick shift and torn green plaid seat covers. The body had once been green but was now the blighted color of dying blackberry leaves.

"Who should I tell Mr. Willingham is here?" said the receptionist inside.

Cody recognized her voice from the overheard phone conversation. "Cody Rainwalker. Did Mr. Willingham's car break down this morning and he have to drive the old truck?"

"That truck is the only vehicle Mr. Willingham ever drives."

Cody nodded as Victor Willingham entered the room from a back office.

"Hello, Cody. Good to see you. Your uncle's told me all about you." Victor was tall and thin. His hair was on a trip from brown to gray. Gray eyes peeked from under bushy eyebrows. He wore dress pants, a light blue shirt with a faded ink stain on the pocket, and a frayed navy-blue tie. His shoes were laced black with pointed toes. To Cody they looked like they had been purchased from a 1920 Sears catalog.

Back in the shop area Cody could hear someone beating on a piece of metal with a large hammer. "Howdy, Victor. Uncle

Ogden's told me all about you also."

Victor narrowed his eyes, waiting for the rest, but that was all Cody had to say.

"Come in my office?"

"Be fine."

The furniture was from the same catalog as the shoes. A single bulb with a green metal shade hung from the ceiling. All other light was furnished by the barely transparent office window. "Did you know Tom Yount well? The guy ate by the rottweiler?" Cody said.

"Thought I did. Should have checked his references closer. Claimed he was retired from the marines, a major with administrative experience. Told the partial truth. He had been a major and had administrative experience, but he'd also been court-martialed, reduced in rank, and given a dishonorable discharge for theft and drunkenness.

"Started him here as an office manager, but he didn't work out. Moved him to the production floor, but he was too weak to pick up anything. He begged, so instead of letting him go altogether, I made use of him at my trailer sales lot."

"Ever see him with any of the murder victims—Taggart, Sharpless, or Justine?"

"No. Never."

"Witnesses say the dog pissed on his head after he killed him," Cody said. "Seems the pooch was a better judge of character than your personnel department. He have any knowledge of this top-secret business deal you and Barry and Michelle are cooking? Or didn't he have a Q clearance?"

Victor started to rise from his chair behind the ancient desk, settled back into the cracked, dried-out leather. "Now see here, Cody. Our business is confidential and has nothing to do with the murders. Michelle could find a reason not to use your services."

Cody stood and walked out into the hall.

Victor followed.

"I'm on the way over to present her with my final bill, then I'll be heading back to Nashville," Cody said. "Made it out first thing this morning. If a client's not honest with me, I can't help them to the best of my ability, and that's the only way I do business."

"Wait a minute. You quit now, entire county will believe you found something against my brother and was bought off."

"Folks are gonna think what they're gonna think. I have no control over that." They had walked down the hall to the lobby and were standing facing one another.

"Your uncle has a good job here. Jobs aren't all that easy to come by in Mountain County," Victor said.

Cody looked at the floors, the wall, the ceiling. "This place ever started burning, ten fire departments couldn't put it out." He walked toward the door, leaving Victor staring. He'd let 'em stew for a while. He had no intention of presenting Michelle with a bill. He'd see it through on his own after what had happened to Samantha.

"Telephone company says no law enforcement agency has shown up with a court order to plant a tap on Samantha's or Luther's phones," the sheriff said.

"Thought as much," Cody said. "The company have a tech check the frames?"

"Got on it right away. Called in an engineer from his home. They're real upset. Said a lot of weird things have been going on lately they can't get a handle on: equipment failures, customers losing service, bills being lost. Not daily, just ever' once in a while, maybe once ever' coupla months or so."

"You know a Stan Bodine?"

"Think I've heard of a realtor by that name. Seen For Sale signs with his name on them. He's not from the county. Has an office down in Tellico Plains, I think. What about him?"

"Just heard his name mentioned. What about somebody from Vegas being in town?"

"Vegas? Las Vegas? Hadn't heard that one."

"Any talk about starting up gambling casinos in Mountain County?" Cody asked.

"Gambling? In Mountain County? No way. All kind of state laws against it; plus the churches would go on a rampage. Be a war. Where you hearing this talk?"

"Folks speculating," Cody said. "What about Victor Willingham? He seems to be kinda tight—drives a dilapidated old truck when you know he can do better."

"You must be in asking mode instead of answering mode today, son."

Cody waited.

"I heard last Christmas," the sheriff said, "when the school was collecting donations and giving out food baskets to the needy, Effie Sue, Vic's daughter, called up and requested she be sent one. That's how tight that sucker is. Lotta folks that work for him are on food stamps, like Tom Yount. Vic bought the house he's living in thirty years ago and has the same furniture in it he had when he bought it. And most of it was already second-hand."

"He married? Don't look like a wife would put up with that."

The sheriff removed his hat, laid it on the desk in front of him, then wiped his forehead with a handkerchief. "When Victor married Shirley, his first wife, he had to convert to Seventh Day Adventist. Big family row over it, Willinghams being Episcopalian and all. Only way Shirley would have it, though. Victor gave in and then, some say, worked poor Shirley to death using her as a secretary and bookkeeper. She died about three years back."

"He remarry?" said Cody.

"Year later—married this woman from Knoxville. I'd guess Victor is about fifty-eight. New wife is about thirty-five, maybe even younger. Real good-looking woman. Goes to the gym, keeps herself in shape."

"New wife accept the Spartan lifestyle?"

"Ramona drives a new Cadillac, dresses real nice, but she still lives in their musty house over on Cherokee Ridge Road. They travel some, her and Victor—take trips out of the country. Don't think Vic had ever been out of Mountain County much before that."

Cody smiled to himself as he imagined Victor in London, Frankfurt, or Bombay with his pointy-toed shoes and narrow frayed tie, staying in third-class hotels with his young, pretty wife.

Twenty-five

The sun had plunged behind the distant mountains a half hour earlier, but darkness hadn't yet arrived. From his seat on the top of the bleachers Cody gazed across the deep grass of the pasture, down the gentle slope to a line of cottonwood and hackberry trees lining the banks of the Highwater River almost a mile away. It had rained earlier in the day; the sun had then come out for a few hours, long enough to create the mists that now clung to the ground like wood smoke on a rainy day.

The fog rolled along the river and swirled a hundred feet in the air. Looking over and beyond the thick mists, Cody eyed the forest ascending to the soaring red cliffs and hogback ridges of Turkey Mountain.

The pasture fence bordered the mowed sidelines of the grid-iron. A dozen cows in various shades of black and brown stood, ears alert, necks against the top strand of wire, watching the two teams warm up for the game. It was the first Mountain County High School game of the season, and the stands were full of cheering fans. Both schools' cheerleaders were taking their positions, and Mountain County's Marching Band quick-stepped onto the field to the clicking cadence of drummers tapping on the rims of their instruments.

The overhead stadium floods came on. Let the games begin, Cody thought, saw Bubba Whittlemore lounging near the concession stand drinking out of a paper cup. He'd drawn tonight's security detail. There were also patrols of the school area by deputies in cruisers.

Jolinda took her place on the sidelines as the first cheerleader to Cody's right. Robin Kingsly, tall and dark with long black hair, stood next to her. She looked enough like Jolinda to be her sister; there was definitely a family resemblance, although the relationship was not close. Second cousins.

She was slightly taller than Jolinda—"more voluptuous" was the phrase Cody searched for. He suddenly remembered the private mail clerk—Simcox?— and his description of "young, tall, long black hair, tits from here to yonder." How many fit that description in a fifty-mile radius? Robin sure did.

The band played the national anthem, the cows rolled their eyes and fled at the first clash of cymbals. The game started and Cody watched Jolinda as she jumped and yelled and clapped her hands, her eyes often cutting to him. Mountain County lost by a wide margin to their chief rivals, Polk County.

To Cody, after years of watching college and pro-ball on TV, high school games seemed like so much disorganized grab-ass, what with all the fumbles, miscues, and intercepted passes. He guessed if he'd stayed in the county he would feel differently. Alumni in the crowd, in their forties, were still wearing their black-and-gold school colors and knew every member of the team, their vital statistics, and the positions they played.

After the game he walked through the night's chill to the parking lot with an excited Jolinda, pumped from all the jumping and screaming. "Aren't you disappointed you all lost the game?" he said.

"We lose 'most all the games. I'd be unhappy clear to Thanksgiving if I let it bother me. After all, we are the smallest Tennessee county in population and the largest in area since about a third of the county is unpopulated national forest land. So we get less of a pool of guys to pick our players from."

In the pickup, she rolled down the windows and hollered and waved to her friends. "You're going to take me to get an ice cream, aren't you? Bubba and Robin are gonna be there. We can double date."

The Cove Road Cafe & Ice Cream Parlor was riotous—standing-room only. A country song on the jukebox could barely be heard over the din. Looking around at all the young, bubbly sweet things and their equally young, school-jacketed dates, Cody felt ancient in his RedHead logging boots, stone-washed jeans, plaid shirt, and black leather jacket. Biba was standing at the soda counter with three other girls her age. She waved. He smiled and waved back. Just like old home week.

When did the Bubba and Biba duet break up?

"Robin and Bubba've saved us a place in the back," Jolinda said. She grabbed his hand and pulled him through the crowd. Two girls eyed him, he eyed them back; they giggled, he didn't.

"Hi, Bubba. Hi, Robin. Robin, this is my fiancé, Cody." Jolinda winked at the seated couple.

Bubba was still in his deputy's duds. He gave Cody a smile and a slight nod. They were a little closer since the HillTop Tavern incident.

Cody smiled hugely. "Last time I saw you, Robin, was at a family picnic. You was eleven years old, and you sat on my lap and ate a hot dog. Got mustard on my pants."

Robin smiled and her eyes glistened at the remembrance. "Don't expect me to do it again. Jolinda might get jealous like she did back then. She pulled my hair and made me cry. You really engaged to Jolinda?"

"I was until this afternoon. Then I stopped by the courthouse and checked the records, and I'm afraid we're too closely related. She's my niece, you know. We get married, it'd be incest, and we could both do long prison terms."

Jolinda kicked him under the table. "You know that's a lie. We're no blood kin at all. I want a big dish of vanilla, three scoops, and chocolate syrup."

Cody saw Biba and her friends looking back toward the booth where he sat. He couldn't tell who they were looking at, but the girls huddled and whispered, then giggled. Lot of giggling going on tonight.

Each booth had its own private selector for the jukebox. He noticed "Big Bad John" was one of the selections. Would they have "Sixteen Tons" and "Teen Angel"?

"Jolinda," Robin said. "Aren't you scared with the killer loose in the county and all?"

"Not as long as Cody's here."

"Cody's not with you twenty-four hours a day. No telling who the killer's gonna kill next. My mother and I are taking turns sleeping at night, even though we got the dog. Zippy'll bark if anybody comes around, give us a warning at least. Won't bite nobody."

Jolinda's mood changed; she became quieter. "Lot of the girls are scared. Some of the guys too. He's killed more men than he has women. So far. Three to two."

Glancing up at a movement in front of him, Cody saw Randy Gateline approaching the table. A wave of half swoons rippled through the teenage girls. Randy was yuppied-out in blue slacks, a white shirt, and a Snoopy tie. "Howdy, Cody," Randy said. "Glad you could stop in."

Cody was confused. "You the official town greeter?"

"Evening, ladies," Randy said. "Bubba. How're you tonight? What it is, Cody, I bought the place out about a month back, me and the bank. Still letting Harold run it. He's getting ready to retire in a year or two."

"Damn, Randy," Bubba said. "Pretty soon you're gonna own the whole town."

Randy laughed, showed perfect white teeth all the way back to the molars. "Wish that were true. This is it for me. Can't clone myself. I'll change the place some, maybe start serving submarine sandwiches, add items to the menu as I go along. I just drop by every once in a while to see how things are going."

Robin had been watching and listening, eating her ice cream. "What do you think about this crazy murderer?"

A somber expression replaced the smile on Randy's face. "What scares me is he's probably someone we all know."

"You believe it's a man, then, and not a woman?" Jolinda said.

Randy looked surprised. "A woman? Hadn't heard that one. Can't imagine a woman killing folks like that."

He smiled again. "Gotta run. Hope you all enjoy the old-time tunes I put on the box."

After Randy had glad-handed himself around the crowd, the two couples continued their discussion.

"You think it's a little soon for Biba to be out having a big time?" Cody asked. "Hasn't been too long since her mother was killed."

Robin had finished her ice cream, scooted the dish back on the table, and placed her spoon beside it. "I was talking to her at school the other day. She sounded so sad. Says her Aunt Michelle is sending her to a therapist—a grief counselor, Biba called her."

"Randy's a hustler, ain't he," Bubba said.

Cody and Jolinda left the other couple talking in quiet tones. As they walked across the parking lot, Cody glanced at the drive-in window and saw Randy leaning with both hands on a light blue Cadillac convertible with a white top. His head was down near the driver's window. He straightened up and waved. The car drove off.

"Victor Willingham's wife," Jolinda said.

Cody thought about the picture in Biba's room. "Just out of curiosity, whatever broke up Bubba and Biba?" he asked.

"Bubba and Biba?" Jolinda looked startled. "You're all mixed up. Bubba hardly knows Biba. I don't think he's ever talked to her."

"Oh? I must be confused."

Twenty-six

Under the steep pitch of the overhanging roof, the porch offered a good dry place to sit out the weather. The rain had diminished somewhat but would come again intermittently, vary its volume from a downpour to a light sprinkle then back again to a deluge. The temperature had dropped ten degrees in the last few hours.

Cody breathed it in great draughts as he sat alone in the cane-back rocker. Jolinda had yawned off to bed. Ogden had already retired for the night when they returned.

"You stop by the store, pick up the hamburger?" the voice said in Cody's ear. "Yeah. Be home in five minutes. 'Bye."

He'd taken the radio out of his truck, had it operating on internal batteries. Using a small ear clip, he kept the volume turned down for private listening.

It seemed like the more questions he asked the more mysteries he encountered. Common sense told him if he kept asking around, someone would say something that would lead him somewhere to ask the right question.

Problem was everyone in town knew him and knew about the case he was working on. He wondered if that would help, perhaps cause someone to make that all-important phone call, give him a clue. Or would it make everyone keep their distance?

As Ray Blizzard liked to joke, "Door-to-door salesman in Highwater Town only works two weeks outa the year." The town was that small and its size was working against him.

"You scope the HAR?" a male voice on the phone said.

"Head-address register? Didn't scope it, but I stored eight bits to HAR memory, then read the register on the front panel lights. They're what they should be, an octal three two. Then I ran the CRC and LRC check."

"What you got, then, sounds like a problem accessing the data on the disk. Cables good and snug?"

"Yeah. We've had more problems with this phone system than with any in the company. Got lightning in the area right now, but it's the same in clear weather."

"I'm FedEx-ing a crash-kit. Got all the circuit boards in it you'll need and some ROM chips already burned in. They'll be there in the morning."

"Thanks. Had enough of this. I'm off to the hotel."

Cody knew what he heard wasn't two interplanetary beings talking, just two techs working on the phone system. Even the phones were spooky in Mountain County—as were the electric company and the water company.

"Seen the man?" Another cellular call had been placed.

"Man's laying low since all the action hit town and his pard got whacked."

"Yeah, got zero protection. Don't want us around."

"Score tonight?"

"Had to drive to Maryville."

"Can we meet?"

"Usual place?"

"Half hour."

"See ya there."

That conversation sounded interesting, Cody thought. Who was the man?

There was a dial tone, then the rapid keying of a telephone speed-dialing.

"Welcome to the voice mailbox," a pleasant, recorded voice said. "Please enter your access code." Six musical tones.

"Welcome to the voice mailbox of Marilyn Murphy. You have one new mail message. To retrieve your messages, please press three; to change your message, please press four. To erase your messages, please press six."

The caller obviously pressed three. "Marilyn, this is Jeff. If you need to call me I'll be at Kelly's until twelve." The caller pressed another tone.

"Message erased," announced the recording. The line disconnected.

There was silence for the next few minutes. Cody continued to rock, stopped, thought about all he'd read about electronic harassment and digital sabotage. If he was an evil person, or even an aggravating type, he could've recorded the incident, deciphered the touch-tone code to get the numbers, and caused poor Marilyn Murphy, whoever she was, an awful lot of grief by breaking into her voice mail and erasing messages. Could someone be getting into the phone company computers, causing problems and shutdowns? And the electric company? He remembered that Elton's electricity was about to get cut off that first day he was in town.

A computer hacker? Or a phone phreak? Could be—but what the hell would that have to do with some nut running around killing people?

Here he was walking around in full view trying to find a solution. There had to be a better way.

Later Cody thought of one.

* * *

Scanner waited impatiently for the lights in the camper trailer to come on. Cody had to be settled in for the night before he moved. Cody'd brought Jolinda home from the game; of that he was sure. Scanner wondered if Cody was in Jolinda's bedroom right now, pumping her like he had Samantha. That Cody—never turn your back on him, always up to something. Scanner just didn't trust him. If Cody was flat on his back, dead in his casket, Scanner knew he'd reach down and check his pulse, then check for a secret door. He thought Cody restless and unpredictable and dangerous. Scanner loved the dangerous part of him, and the unpredictability, too, if the truth was known, which it never would be because he would never tell it. So now Cody had set the stage for Jolinda's reward.

He would take her before he did Cody to pay Cody back for sticking his nose where it didn't belong. But it must be that both of them were taken. Even if Scanner stopped after accomplishing all of his goals, if Cody was alive he'd track Scanner forever, which sounded exciting except that Cody would of course catch him if he lived long enough, so what should he do?

Scanner realized that his thinking was so fast that sometimes he had to zip back and trap a thought or it would escape him forever.

Would Cody fuck her all night and leave in the morning or merely fuck her until she couldn't walk and then go to his camper? God, what a decision.

Scanner's thoughts were interrupted by the headlights of Cody's truck turning onto the road out of the farm's dirt driveway. He hadn't noticed before because of the screening foliage and his own runaway mind. Starting his vehicle immediately, he roared away.

* * *

The flare of brake lights in the distance caught Cody's attention. He could tell they were near the curve, over half a mile away. Somebody parked down there. Then it hit him. Was Scanner stalking him?

The headlights of the distant vehicle swept the trees. Cody stomped the gas. The truck leaped ahead. He lost the lights in front of him, thought the driver had turned them off.

Cody made a quick decision. One he had hoped to avoid. Rolling down the driver's-side window, he placed the magnetic blue dome light he'd requested from the sheriff's department on top of the truck and plugged it into the lighter socket. Bright blue flashes strobed the thick fog, creating an azure halo.

Undercover no more, he thumbed his walkie. "Mountain County, this is unit X-ray."

"Go ahead, X-ray," Wanda June said.

"X-ray is in pursuit of an unknown vehicle at high rate of speed on Stecoah Road, three miles south of the Cataloochie Road turn-off. Put out a BOLO."

Wanda June didn't hesitate. "Attention all units, be on alert for an unknown vehicle in high-speed pursuit by Unit X-ray on Stecoah Road coming up on Cataloochie Road Junction."

"Seven, going."

"Twenty-two, going." Three other cruisers called in they were on the way.

* * *

Scanner heard the calls on the police band. "Oh shit, oh shit," he said out loud in excitement and fear. Was his career to be ended so soon? Shouldn't have trusted that sneak Cody. Made him think he's in the house screwing Jolinda and he's onto him all the time, lurking on his back trail. And him taking money to fight for the other side. A conflict of interest. Cody was an asshole. So what would he do? Confront him? Call him a rotten detective? Scanner pressed the gas to the floorboards but ran into a heavy rain and was forced to slow. He needed to keep off the brakes or Cody would spot the lights, making it easier for the detective to track him. He didn't want to do a three-sixty either and roll the mother. Scanner almost lost it when a limb blew across the road. He swerved, barely recovered. The engine roared through the blackness.

* * *

Cody drove into the rain shower. Driving under water on a winding mountain road. Fun city. He couldn't tell if he was gaining. The wind accompanying the sudden rain rocked the camper shell and high cab of the truck. He needed both hands on the wheel to keep it in the road.

"Okay, Unit X-ray?" Wanda June hadn't heard from him since the chase began. He picked up the walkie to call in, changed his mind. Scanner was monitoring the airways.

"Unit X-ray? What's your twenty?" Bubba Whittlemore called from his cruiser.

Cody kept both hands on the wheel, barreled ahead through the rain maintaining radio silence.

* * *

Scanner knew what Cody was up to by not answering. Wanted him to think he'd run in a ditch. At least he had a worthy opponent.

* * *

With the window down, the roar of the big, all-terrain tires was deafening. A cold spray whipped the left side of Cody's face; he blinked the rain from his eyes. Should be near the junction by now. The rain and fog hid familiar landmarks, and he had forgotten the road's many twists and turns, sudden dips and rises. He passed several driveways in a row, tried to orient himself, couldn't identify them. Suddenly his radar detector warbled.

As he rounded a sweeping curve, he almost broadsided the cruiser blocking the road. He jumped on the brakes, wrestled the wheel, headed for the ditch. The pickup nosed down into the muddy, weed-choked gully. Cody banged his head against the sun visor when the truck came to an abrupt halt. Had the cruiser's emergency lights not been flashing, he would have hit it for sure.

Two other cruisers screamed in, sirens blaring and lights strobing as Cody climbed out of the truck and pulled himself up the embankment.

"Okay, Cody?" Bubba yelled.

"Yeah. Nobody in front of me? No car came by?" Cody walked to the cruiser. It had stopped raining. He looked back down the way he came. Nothing but fog.

"You're the first guy down the road. Shit! Thought you was gonna hit me for sure. My law enforcement career would've been over. And me so young."

"Guy must've pulled into a side road. I missed him in the rain."

A tall, lanky deputy ran up to the cruiser.

"Turner," Bubba said, "take your unit up the road. Stop anybody you see."

"And don't use the radio if you don't see him. Hump has a police band," Cody yelled at the deputy's retreating back.

Cody and Bubba waited at the junction while other deputies fanned out to widen the search. "Kinda tough not having a vehicle description," Bubba said. "Where'd you get the blue dome light?"

"Stole it during the confusion at a sale at Kmart." Cody was getting wet but he didn't care. He was excited, pumped from the chase. "We get a few license numbers, it'll be a lot more than we got now, which so far in this entire case is squat."

They gave it a few more hours.

While Bubba stayed put, Cody dropped his truck into four-wheel-low, walked it out of the ditch. Then he drove to make the phone call he'd been heading to make when he spotted the mysterious vehicle. A pay phone. Just to play it safe. When he came back through the junction, Bubba was still on duty, pulled to the side of the road, sitting in the darkened cruiser.

"Anything?" Cody said.

"Silent night," Bubba said. "You get the walkie at the same Kmart?"

Cody looked at him and grinned.

Twenty-seven

"Sawed-off twelve gauge?" Jolinda asked Cody over the breakfast table.

"You won't need marksmanship training." It was Cody's third cup of coffee. He was trying to wake up.

"You think the murderer was sitting down the road watching the house?" Ogden asked. "Maybe I should take off work."

"What I think's going on is this Scanner is watching me for some reason. Like you know, everyone thinks I'm the expert brought in from out of town. In Nashville I work a case and I'm anonymous. Here you can see me coming a mile off and folks know what I'm up to."

Jolinda wiped her milk mustache away with a napkin. "He's watching the camper, and when the light's off then it's safe for him to go kill somebody. Spooky to know he's been sitting out there all this time, maybe thinking about coming in here." She shivered in her chair.

"Don't ever want Jolinda here alone," Cody said. "She can stop by the foundry or the S.O., read a book or watch TV until one of us is here."

Ogden grunted and nodded.

"You think he's after me?" Jolinda said.

Cody narrowed his eyes and thought it over. "He may be after me or he may try to use you to get to me. Cops learn to protect their families from retribution. Learn it early on."

"One reason you don't hold a sawed-off to your shoulder is that burnt powder can blow back in your face," Cody said to Jolinda later. "Press it in the crook of your arm and grip it real tight." He was having her dry-fire the weapon—no ammo yet, just a click. She had fired rifles, pistols, and regular shotguns, but never the sawed-off that Ogden called his house dog.

They were between the trailer and the barn. He'd set up two bales of hay as a target and stepped off ten yards. "Will it hurt me?" Jolinda asked.

"Not near as much as the other guy. Loads are double-aught buck." Cody had shown her the safety in the trigger guard, how to click it off with the back of a knuckle. Had had her break the weapon open, load and unload, safety on, safety off. He stood behind her and had her dry-fire again and again until he saw the relaxed positioning of her shoulders.

"Let me see it a minute," he said.

"You gonna load it now?" Jolinda's expression was fearful.

"Not yet," he said, breaking the weapon open. "Look at the middle of the top bale. I want you to dry-fire the gun again. Try to aim it at the middle of the bale. A man's standing there, and you'll shoot him in the chest." He handed her the sawed-off. "Hold it tight, like you would if it was loaded."

Jolinda took the weapon and turned to the bale, clicked off the safety, aimed, and pulled the trigger. There was a terrific explosion and she was thrown back against Cody, who was braced to catch her. The shotgun landed four feet away.

Cody had wisely loaded only one shell.

"Ow!" she said. "Goddammit, Cody! You tricked me and that hurt!" She pulled away and rubbed her right biceps.

"Look at the bale."

She turned to look. "It's gone!" Hay was strewn all over the yard.

"Gone is what the sonofabitch you just shot would be. You are now officially qualified with a twelve-gauge sawed-off."

Titus Cornstubble squinted into the early morning sun and shook his head. "Naw, Cody. Haven't heard the howler lately. Last time it sounded like it was on that hillside." He pointed an arthritic finger up the slope from where they stood.

"Thanks, Titus. Bubba here will run you home. You hear the howler again, you let the sheriff's office know right away. There'll be a reward."

Cody climbed the hill and scouted around. He didn't know what he was looking for or if he'd recognize it when he found it. The area had been logged several years ago and was making a comeback. Walnut and maple saplings grew from high stumps they used as mother trees. Sumac grew in thick clumps and had budded the fruit that provided deer and other wildlife their change-up diet from acorns, beechnuts, and dogwood pods. Cody remembered as a boy he'd used sumac to make his bows because the wood was so resilient. When the wood dried out completely, the bow would break and he'd find another sapling of the right size and make another.

Nothing there, Cody decided after spending thirty minutes wandering the hill. Then he thought of another hill—Luther camped on it above Sanford Sharpless's cabin, smoking a cigarette. He headed to town, recalling training he'd received in army intelligence school. Hiding and Finding, the instructing major had called the minicourse. What had they called the fashioned hiding place? He remembered: a slick.

The threat of Scanner staking out the house, of being a perceived if not real threat to Jolinda, had energized Cody's brain. Last night's chase made him determined not only to clear Barry—if Barry was clearable—but to go after the killer with a fervor he reserved for personal conflict, which it was turning out to be.

The crime scene tape was still in place in Luther's front yard. Cody ducked under it and mounted the wooden steps to the front porch of the white frame house. The residence needed painting, he noted. He wondered if Luther had kin who would eventually get the house. He faintly remembered hearing about a sister who lived out of town.

Across and down the street, an elderly lady peered at Cody through the lace curtains of her living room window. She ducked back quickly when his glance came her way.

Inside the house, Cody tossed it. The living room first—turned chairs upside down, looking for documents taped to the bottoms, upset the couch, removed the cushions, tapped the walls. Down on his hands and knees, he removed throw rugs and tapped the floors.

Crawling into the kitchen he removed all the pots and pans from the shelves and searched. He checked the pantry behind the canned goods, ironing board, and iron. Nothing.

He moved to the bathroom.

His head was stuck into the shelves under the sink, so he didn't hear the front door open. He peered under the claw-legged bathtub. Went to the linen closet and tossed out towels and washcloths.

"We looked already," the sheriff said from the bathroom doorway.

Cody jerked backward and hit his head on the linen closet shelf. "Figured you did," he said, massaging the back of his head. "Just wanted to make sure you didn't miss anything."

"Neighbor called in."

Cody walked to the bedroom. Started his procedure all over again. "Luther was a sneaky bastard. Stands to reason he'd have a stash somewhere, and the easier he could guard it, the better."

In the bedroom closet he removed all the clothes from the pipe rack, threw them on the bed, went through all the uniform and jacket and pants pockets.

"Did that too," said his dad. "Only we were neater."

Cody was on his hands and knees again, dragging out shoes and boots, old boxes.

The sheriff put his hands in his pockets and stood there, waiting patiently.

Cody finally gave up. "Goddammit. There's got to be some leads in this case. Somebody had to leave something somewhere." He turned to leave, then glanced at the bed.

"We did it," the sheriff said.

"Turned over the mattress and box spring?"

"Yep."

Cody headed out of the room.

"Aren't you gonna hang the clothes back up? Luther's sister may be coming down to inventory the property."

Cody returned to the bed, grabbed several uniforms on hangers, headed for the closet, then stopped and looked inside.

"We tapped all the walls in there too."

"Look in the pipe?" Cody said.

"Huh?"

"The pipe—the clothes rack. Awful big pipe to hang this few clothes on." Cody went to the kitchen, came back with a heavy knife to pry up the bar's hold-down nails.

Papers and glossy color prints slid to the floor as soon as he brought the pipe out and shook it down. From the way they came only half open, Cody assumed they had been rolled up for a long time. The two men took everything to the bed and flattened them out on the spread.

In one print Luther was leaned back against the pillows of the bed Cody and the sheriff now sat on. He reclined nude with a broad grin of contentment on his face. His head was back. His eyes stared straight up at the ceiling.

Justine leaned over him from opposite the camera, facing whoever the photographer was. Her eyes were bright, almost feral, in the flash. She was also nude, with half of Luther's erect penis in her mouth.

There were three more photos of Justine and Luther in various poses of intercourse. Farther down in the stack were two of Carl Taggart orally copulating Sanford Sharpless, same bed, same room. There was another of Carl performing the same act on Luther.

Cody noticed the grim look on his father's face. "Those folks sure got around," he said.

"But what does it prove?"

"Of course the pictures will have to be blown up, examined in a lab," Cody said. "Let's see that first one again."

He rolled it out, took it over to a small bedside lamp. "Look over at the dresser, in the corner of the mirror."

From where the picture had been taken the dresser was to the right of the foot of the bed. The flash had made a slight flare, but next to the flare was the ghostly, hidden shape of a face. It looked female. Her hair looked a reddish blonde, but it was hard to tell. They looked at the other photos. The figure was not present.

"Any idea who that might be?" Cody said.

"Not a clue," the sheriff said. "I'll have it enhanced."

"Eerie, isn't it," Cody said, "looking at pictures of dead people fucking."

They turned to the rest of the papers. The first rolled up document was the copy of a loan application from the Mountain County Savings and Loan, filled out and signed by Carl Taggart. The amount requested was three hundred thousand dollars. It was stamped "Approved by Horace Hornsby, Pres."

"Wonder what Carl was gonna do with that kind of money?" the sheriff said.

"Who knows, maybe buy some property through real estate mogul Stan Bodine," Cody answered. "What all the movers and shakers in backward, unhip Mountain County are up to these days."

The other documents were from the bank as well. Copies of approved loan aps for Victor Willingham for seven hundred thousand dollars; Michelle Willingham, seven hundred thousand dollars; Barry Willingham, three hundred thousand dollars.

"Poor Barry," Cody said. "Must be awful being the low man on the totem pole."

"I'm gonna take a ride over to see Horace Hornsby," the sheriff said. "He should've come to me about Carl Taggart's loan. According to the date, it was approved a week before he was murdered."

Cody thumbed through the pictures again. "I'll ride with you."

"Lawyer sprung Baily," the sheriff added in exasperation, "so the HillTop mess will start up again. Had to stop on the way over and order some reporters off my tail. They got the office staked out, and most of 'em have police-band radios. We'll need to take evasive action."

Picking up the clothes-hanger pipe, Cody started to replace it, paused with a thoughtful look on his face, then banged it hard on the floor instead. A roll of bills fell from the end. He took a closer look. The bills were all hundreds.

He looked at his dad. "Ever think about Costa Rica?"

"Don't even joke about it."

They counted out over twelve thousand dollars.

"After we see Hornsby, what say we take a ride by the Taggart house. I remember Carl had a pipe like this in his closet," the sheriff said.

"Let's don't tell anyone we found these pictures or documents or the money either," Cody said.

The sheriff was surprised. "I'm not talking to the media. You know I don't crave newspaper attention."

"Not what I mean. Let's don't tell anybody. Especially not Bubba Whittlemore."

"Bubba! What the hell you mean by that?"

"Last night when I chased whoever it was that parked down the road from Ogden's, maybe they didn't turn off. Bubba was sitting at the junction and nobody went past him, he says. Coulda been him parked down the road."

"Can't be true. You don't know him like I do. Bubba comes highly recommended. The result of my efforts to recruit college graduates. He knows about computers, gonna help automate the paperwork functions at the S.O."

"Biba has a signed picture of Bubba in her bedroom at her Aunt Michelle's house, says 'Love, Bubba.' In an expensive silver frame. Bubba goes with Robin Kingsly. Jolinda says Bubba doesn't know Biba," said Cody.

"You're a detective all right," the sheriff said. "Observing and remembering, what it takes. Feel like I've let the county down, missing all the things I've missed on this case. But you're wrong about Bubba."

"I'm trying to put it together. It's there but I don't know where it all fits. You had Luther, man leading the investigation, misleading you from the git-go," Cody said with a shake of his head.

"You really believe Barry's innocent?"

"My way of thinking, he's still a suspect. Too-busy-to-kill-my-wife bullshit don't cut it. Sometimes I'm too busy to clean my office—so I hire it done.

"Whoever it is, though, is boring the shit outa me," Cody said. "Especially when he parks down the way from where Jolinda's sleeping. I'll not have that threat hanging over her head. Gonna put him down."

"Fine with me," the sheriff said. "Long as you know it's the right person and it's legal and clean."

Cody sighted through the pipe rack like it was a telescope then stuck it back in the closet, hung clothes back on it, and scooted boxes back in place. "You come up with anything about the woman your witness says she saw running from Samantha's house? Or the leather scrapings?"

"Like everything else about this case, we've run into a brick wall. Canvassed the neighborhood; and these are folks that'll come forward if they have information. Nobody else saw the running woman. Wondering if it was a man with long hair."

From the look on his face when they walked in the front door of the Mountain County Savings and Loan, it was obvious Horace Hornsby didn't look forward to their visit. "Afternoon, Sheriff."

"This here's my son, Cody."

"I remember Cody."

"What say we go in your office, close the door, and have a quiet talk."

Hornsby was wearing a red, white, and blue striped tie with his white shirt and gray slacks. His hair was short and light blond, his eyes a pale blue. His face was florid. He was chubby and perspiring, and the sweat made his skin splotchy. When he turned to enter his office they noticed damp spots on the back of his shirt.

The office was cool. Hornsby didn't seem to notice. He stepped to the rear of his desk then removed a handkerchief from his hip pocket and wiped his face. "What can I do for you gentlemen?" He motioned for them to take a seat.

They did, kept hard eyes on the banker, expressions somber.

Hornsby took his seat, fidgeted with a pen on his desk, opened his middle drawer, closed it without removing anything. Crossed his legs. Uncrossed them. Leaned back in his chair.

The two men waited.

Visions of slamming steel doors danced in Hornsby's head, although he couldn't imagine for the life of him what crime he had committed. He saw the vertical metal bars in their eyes, long-term confinement in their morose expressions.

Eventually the sheriff broke the silence. "You wanta tell us about it, Horace?" His voice was quiet, compassionate.

The even pace of it, the lack of inflection, increased Hornsby's fear inordinately, his face flushed even more. "Just, just what is it you want to know, Sheriff?"

"I want to know it all."

Cody had to grit his teeth. Didn't know the old man was this good, he thought.

"Oh. Well, it was like this. The Willinghams said I should give Carl Taggart the loan, and I shouldn't tell anybody about it—that they would guarantee repayment on their word but didn't want to sign anything because the word would get out if even one of the bank clerks knew about it and folks would wonder why." Hornsby stopped for breath.

The sheriff and Cody sat stone-faced.

Hornsby wiped his face again, looked at his handkerchief, and hung it on the arm of his chair to dry. "Wouldn't tell me why. Asked all three of them one at a time and all they'd say was there was going to be a big development in the county soon and the price of property would skyrocket. Said the town would double or triple in size in five years and there'd be hotels and stores and maybe we'd get a Wal-Mart and a Cracker Barrel in town. That's all I know. Honest."

"Why didn't you come to me when Carl was killed?"

"Wanted to, Sheriff. Victor called me and told me not to. Then Michelle called. Both of them said Carl got killed 'cause he was some kinda pervert; loan didn't have anything to do with it."

"Gonna tell me about Luther?"

"Oh, God! You know about Luther?"

"Horace, not much goes on in this town I don't know already or I don't hear about eventually. Want you to tell it to me though. In your own words."

"Don't know how Luther found out. The Willinghams sure wouldn't tell him. They hated him. Not enough to kill him, of course, but they hated the way he was, all sneaky and prowling around on the edge of things. I was afraid of him so I told him about the town maybe going into a high-growth pattern. He said

256

he already knew about that. He wanted details. Of course I didn't have any to give him."

"You give him the copies?" the sheriff asked.

"Copies? What copies?"

"Of the loan applications? Taggart's and the Willinghams'?"

"I wouldn't do that. Luther had copies?"

"Believe him?" Cody asked once they were outside in the sheriff's cruiser.

"What he's said already. Could still be holding back. Men'll go to the electric chair and keep some things to their self."

Keeping a lookout for reporters, they headed for the Taggart house. Becky Taggert let them in. "I thought you searched the house already."

Cody noticed she was a beautiful woman. Her brown eyes expressed intelligence, her long hair brown had a healthy shine, and her chin was firm; her posture was erect and she spoke with refinement. She was obviously well educated. Cody wondered what the hell she was doing with a perv-jerk like Carl.

"We did search, Becky," the sheriff said. "But we may have missed something important."

She showed them to the bedroom. Tears flooded her eyes. "It's too much for me. First Carl, then Samantha. I'm selling the house; I just can't live here any longer." She cried into her hands, then raised her head, wiped her eyes, and fled to the front of the house.

Cody and the sheriff laid the clothes from the closet on the bed, removed the pipe, found only one rolled-up sheet of paper.

"I got here first, assholes—Scanner." said the note. The words were made up from letters clipped from a newspaper.

The sheriff walked to the phone and called his office. "Send Thompson out to the Taggart house with his print kit. No radio traffic about it, and tell him to make sure he's not followed."

"Now the case's going somewhere," Cody said.

"Yeah," the sheriff said. "But I got a feeling the brick wall's right around the corner."

Twenty-eight

Monk was at Fuzzy's where Cody expected him to be. He didn't have much to say to the attorney, but wanted to feel the mood of the place, see if Monk had any comments on the case. He also wanted to take the pulse of the reporters who hung out there shopping for a story. He thought of feeding a reporter misinformation, perhaps saying they thought the killer might be a woman, but that kind of trick could result in a catastrophe if the killer reacted to it.

"Heard you were going over to tender your resignation," Monk whispered into Cody's ear, leaning against him, standing on tiptoe. He wore an evil grin.

"I just haven't had time to get there."

"It will be a new experience for Michelle. She usually gets what she wants."

"Not what she tells me," Cody said, tipping his beer for a long pull.

Monk's grin widened. Became more evil.

Cody saw there were four reporters at the bar. At least he thought they were reporters. The three men and the red-haired woman were strangers to him.

The short attorney was riding his shoulder in an obvious effort to keep their conversation confidential. "Heard our fine banker, one Horace Hornsby, was visited by seekers of truth. They find any?" he whispered.

"Not so's you'd notice," Cody said. He stared into the far dark corner of the bar, half expecting the shade of Luther to step out of the dimness and yell, "Surprise!"

"See someone you know?" Monk said.

"Shit. I hope not." The reporters had apparently given up on

258

Monk as a source of information. Cody noticed they were eyeing him closely, knew who he was from the town's gossip. None of them moved toward him, however. Probably were going to try to follow him when he left.

"Reporters were asking me earlier about a new deputy with a call designation of Unit X-ray," Monk said in a voice barely audible over the noise of the crowd.

"X-ray?" Cody said. "Must work for the hospital."

"Asked me about a high-speed chase out near your uncle's." Monk lurched suddenly and grabbed Cody's forearm for support.

Wasn't it time for Big 'Un to give Monk the heave-ho and drive him home? "Guess I slept right through it," Cody said. He looked up and saw the crowd part in ripples as the big bouncer approached. Big 'Un must've had that grin cast in bronze.

Cody caught Michelle arriving home. He held a sack of groceries and watched her disarm the security system via the keypad.

She opened the door and waved him in. The house smelled of cinnamon and of something baking. Housekeeper must do some of the cooking. He sniffed and decided it was apple cobbler.

In the kitchen he placed the groceries on the table.

Michelle was furious. "You here to quit?"

"No." He kept it laid-back.

"Then what the hell do you want?"

"To let you know that Diving Hawk Investigations just announced a twenty-five-percent rate increase."

She clunked down a gallon of skim milk in the big, double-door refrigerator and slammed it shut. "You're a bastard, Cody, you know that don't you? A fucking bastard."

"Works out fantastic when I've been hired by a family of assholes."

"A rate increase when you're also working for the sheriff's office trying to put my brother in jail with one hand and keep him out with the other? You jacking-off with the other hand?"

"On Thursday nights. Who said I'm working for the S.O.?"

"It's a small town. A very small town." Michelle stood in the middle of the kitchen and tried to stare a hole through him.

Cody's look was just as intense. "Who?"

"Oh, fuck. Who? It's all over the goddamn high school. Jolinda was bragging about it to Biba and Biba told me."

"If there's ever a conflict of interest on my part, I'll let you know. Now for you, and your high-faluting family, what about trying on obstruction of justice, telling Horace Hornsby not to tell about Carl Taggart getting a loan at the bank?"

Michelle picked up a box of crackers off the table and threw it at him. A halfhearted toss he ducked easily. "Like you said, Michelle. A very small town. Only I hear you hope it won't stay that way."

"I don't know how Carl found out, that twisted scum. He went to Barry, wanted in on the game. Barry freaked, of course. He can't think on his feet. Matter of fact, he can't think sitting flat on his ass."

"And Luther?"

"All the lowlifes came crawling out of the weeds. I don't know who told Luther. Even Barry wouldn't be that stupid."

Cody bent over and picked up the box, bounced it in his hand once, then placed it on the table. "Strike you at all strange, everyone who found out about your little scheme woke up dead?"

She didn't answer, instead turned to stomp into the living room, elbows bent, arms pumping, eyes narrowed.

Cody took his time, followed her. He thought she was over-acting.

Michelle plopped on the couch, sulked against his lack of appreciation of her cause. "What us Willinghams are doing will strengthen the economy of this county for a hundred years. I am not doing anything illegal, and I resent your fucking attitude."

Michelle dug in her purse, took out a checkbook, and wrote out a check, angrily tearing it out of the book and thrusting it toward Cody.

He grabbed it and headed for the front door. "The rate increase is still in effect."

"Bastard!" Michelle yelled. She kicked her shoes off and straightened out her legs.

Cody paused, didn't turn. "Slut!"

"Come back later and I'll fix you dinner. Burn some poor animal's flesh. We can test-drive the double-wide bed."

"I'll take a rain check."

"Do that. Carving another Rainwalker notch on the bedpost would be a milestone for a simple country girl."

Cody made sure he had no company when he left the county. The pay phone he remembered was at a crossroads sporting two drive-in markets, a tavern, a beauty salon called Tawny Image, a washerteria, and a closed-for-the-night farm supply store. He went into the first drive-in, bought a diet soda, and got some change.

His first call went to Noel.

"Hello?" said Noel, his voice muddled with sleep.

"It's Cody. I checked with the answering service and they said you called."

"Damn Ray Blizzard. He's disappeared. I don't know if he's off on a drunk or just took off. Hasn't been in all day. I went down this morning to get a progress report on your case and discovered the office hasn't even been opened. I picked up your mail and put it on your desk. Then I found a note from him in my mailbox. Said he's gone to Libya to help out his dear friend Muammar. He's funny as a fucking heart attack."

Cody watched a rusty pickup pull into a drive-in parking slot. Four small children bounced and wrestled on a sofa in the flatbed that was backed up to the cab. Four massive bloodhounds wagged their tails and hung their large heads over the tailgate, barked at Cody, then pointed their snouts in the air and bayed. The driver's door was wired shut with a coat hanger. Two rifles and a shotgun hung in the rear-window gun rack. The man driving crawled over his bored, passive wife and climbed out the passenger side.

"I hear dogs barking. You out hunting?" Noel said.

"Matter of fact, I am. You see Ray, get him sobered up and back to work."

"You're sure you don't want me to handle a case here for you?"

"Thanks, Noel. Not tonight."

Cody waited for the pickup hauling the kids and dogs to leave before he made the next call. It was a toll-free. A recorded female voice asked for the access code of the Skypager. He punched it in.

At the triple beep he entered a PIN number, then the number of the pay phone, stood back, and waited.

A hulking mechanic in greasy overalls stumbled out of the store and headed for the phone.

"It's busy for a few minutes," Cody said.

"Don't look busy to me, dipwad," the man said. His dark hair hung in his face. His eyes were unfocused. A smudge of black motor oil made a slash across his forehead. One boot was untied with the top folded over, and the lace flopped around when he walked. Standing in place, he swayed and rocked back on his run-down heels, waited for Cody to beat a swift retreat.

"Wife is sick, and I paged the doctor to give me a call. Be a minute." Cody reached in his pocket and pulled out a ten. "Here, go buy yourself a new pickup or something."

The man took the money, stared at it, then lumbered back to the drive-in.

Rate increase might just come in handy, Cody thought. The phone rang.

"Cody."

"Agent Ray Blizzard checking in."

"What you up to, Agent Blizzard?"

"Just finished piggin' out at the Tellicafe. What's your twenty? If you'll excuse the cop jargon."

"Standing on a state highway out in the middle of nowhere. Went into a drive-in market to get change; the clerk's wearing bright red rouge, silver eye shadow, and glitter in her hair."

"Sounds familiar. Wanta go ask if she was ever in Jackson County, Alabama?"

"Six feet, looks about two-fifty, wearing vivid orange leotards. Obviously a UT fan."

"It's her. I knew I'd find her someday."

"Any Nevadians in sight, or is it Nevadans?"

"I'll call him a Vegan. From 'Lost Wages.' Tall, gray hair, tailored suit, expensive shoes, leather—good-looking guy."

"Oh? Are y'all having drinks together later?"

"The Vegan had in tow one real estate schmuck, name of Stan Bodine; said scumbag yackety-yacked all through dinner about how important him and all his thieving Washington buddies are.

Ask me, if bullshit was music, ol' Stan'd be a brass band. I checked around Tellico Plains; seems Stan's fairly new in town but doing better than most as his office is real expensive-looking: leather furniture, wall-to-wall flooring, a window to peek in, the works. Only he don't seem to have any customers."

"You have the Vegan's name and address, place of employment, S.S. number, shirt size, sexual preference, next of kin?"

"In the works."

"Good work, Agent Blizzard. I have another mission."

As Cody pulled away from the market the mechanic charged out the door and gave him a wave. His other arm was wrapped tightly around a bulky sack.

Heading back to Highwater Town, Cody watched two separate banks of clouds close in on each other, meet, and block off the moon. Going to rain again, he thought. Five minutes later it happened, first in huge, intermittent splatters that sounded like rocks hitting the windshield and hood, then a steady downpour that immediately flooded the road.

Cody slowed to wipe the condensation off the windshield and to navigate a rough railroad crossing. As he leaned back in his seat the radar detector hanging on his sun visor gave a double blip. After clearing the crossing he noticed the glow of mercury vapor lights on a slight rise to his left. They illuminated the parking lot of the nursing home he'd seen earlier. Once again his father's big Dodge 4x4 cruiser was parked in front of the entrance. Cody knew the transmitter in the vehicle, even when on idle, could activate the radar detector this close.

"Unit delta, unit zebra." They'd swapped around call signs to hopefully confuse the killer.

"Unit delta," Bubba Whittlemore answered over the radio after a short wait.

"Twenty?" Cody said.

"S.O. Need to signal eight?"

"Negative. It'll wait till morning."

"Good deal. I'm ready to go off shift."

So his dad was at the nursing home without Bubba. Always a mystery. What was it Churchill had said about Russia, or the

USSR? "A mystery wrapped in an enigma," was that how it went? He was never good at quotes. Fit Mountain County though.

Thunder rolled heavily in the distance. A forked streak of lightning illuminated the peak of Turkey Mountain. A rabbit ran across the road, followed seconds later by a gray fox. Cody tapped his brakes but the predator had already dashed into the roadside bushes. Wonder what ol' Scanner's up to, Cody thought. His kinda night.

"Mountain County S.O., unit thirty-seven," the male dispatcher said.

"Unit thirty-seven."

"Mountain County, ten-forty-three-P, disturbance in progress. Louise at the Dixie Freeze is on the line. Says a buncha male subjects in front of the HillTop are lightin' farts."

"Say again."

"Advises lightin' farts. Says one subject dropped his pants and blew a flame like a Fourth'a July rocket, and now his drawers are on fire. Other subjects are standing around laughing."

"Ten-four. Should I handle it as a ten-thirty-five or a ten-fifty-nine?" the deputy said. A mental case or indecent exposure.

"Think it qualifies as a ten-seventy-three," another unidentified deputy said. "Hazardous materials."

"Naw," another said. "Attempted suicide. Ten-sixty-three."

"All right, children," the sheriff drawled over his walkie.

The airwaves quieted.

Driving past the HillTop thirty minutes later, Cody eyed the scrubby-looking crowd of onlookers, spotted two overweight paramedics loading a man into the back of an ambulance. An old-fashioned brass fire extinguisher lay in the middle of the gravel parking lot like a fallen soldier.

Twenty-nine

The rain had let up by the time Cody reached Ogden's farm. While he was locking his truck the skies opened again. He made a run for the front porch and got soaked. Under the shelter of the roof he listened to the pelting rain, peered through the torrent and heavy mist to the road, then around the farm, looking for movement; he saw nothing but the brown mules up close to the fence, staring at him, ears semaphored, attracted across the field by his arrival.

The living room was pitch dark; Cody moved by feel and recall, stepped lightly around the coffee table and headed down the hall.

"She's still awake." Ogden's voice seemed to float out of the inky gloom.

"Who you hiding from?" Cody said.

"Guarding."

One hand against the coolness of the wall, Cody guided himself to the bedroom door, then knocked lightly.

"Come on in, Cody," Jolinda called, barely above a whisper.

Moving to her bed and sitting down on its edge he reached out and touched her face tenderly with the tips of his fingers. Her cheek was feverishly hot. "You're burning up, honey."

"'Cause you're on my bed."

"Really, I don't need to ask. But it's important. You tell anyone about me being deputized?"

Jolinda breathed out a long breath. "Like you say. You don't need to ask."

"Cody," she called to him as he reached the door.

"Yeah?"

"I saw this thing in a magazine at the sheriff's office, a

hunting magazine. Forget what it's called. Fits over your elbow and comes down to your hand. Got two hooks on it and a little trigger thing."

"Yeah?"

"Quick release," Jolinda said. "That's what it's called, a quick release."

"What's it do?"

"Help's you draw a real heavy traditional bow. With it, even a wimp can pull a fifty- or sixty-pound bow."

"Thanks," Cody said. "In our arrogance we'd eliminated all the little old ladies.

"Goodnight, honey. Yell out if you hear anything."

"Goodnight, Cody."

"You wanta get an alarm system put in?" Cody said. His mind was conjuring all sorts of calamitous scenarios.

Ogden remained on the couch in the dark. "Already called. There's a three-week backlog."

"I guess you could say Scanner's good for business. Helping a stagnant economy."

"Some folks' business. Wouldn't imagine there's folks reading about it in the papers planning to move here for the excitement."

"You got any ideas, Uncle Ogden?"

"I've laid here at night, racked my brain and I don't have a clue. And I know ever'body in the county, ever'body. So when they catch him I'll be surprised that whoever it is could do such a thing. Doesn't make sense."

"Things make sense only when they don't make sense if you're looking for a wacko," Cody said. "Can't decide for sure—sometimes I think we are, then I think money and revenge are the motives, or power."

Ogden moved to a more comfortable position on the couch. "Willinghams? You think it's them? Or one of them? I can't hardly believe it. They always want more but they've never broke any laws I've heard about."

"Don't know. I'm not an experienced homicide investigator by any stretch. But there's background and foreground. What we're seeing is the foreground, about twenty percent or less of what's really happening." Cody's voice hardened. "Now I'm gonna take a look at the background. All that movement I've been missing."

Ogden heard a chill in Cody's voice he'd only heard before when his adopted nephew talked about the death of his mother and brother. There was that same raging iciness held just below the surface that made Ogden worry for the Colemans and the Crabtrees of the world. And the Bobby Joes, should that young man one day catch Cody in a black mood and finish his life staring, dead-eyed, at the rear headliner of a hearse. He knew his adopted nephew's capacity for violence. "Sounds complicated."

"Got good motivation," Cody said. "He's hanging around Jolinda, so there'll be no mercy." Cody felt around with one foot until he found the rocking chair, then slowly lowered himself onto the cushion.

"With you and your daddy and the deputies looking, you'll get a break soon."

"Hope so. Daddy takes it as a personal insult, some hump committing murder in his county."

"I've told you how your dad comes out here sometimes, just sits and talks. He worries about lots of things. Says he goes to sheriff's and law enforcement conferences several times a year and he hears things he don't like. Whispers and rumors. Says there's something really wrong out there in the country. He'd like to build a wall around the county, like the wall in China."

"You realize that didn't work. Can't fence evil out. Trying to just fences it in."

"May be right. Your daddy says the law enforcement professionals don't trust Washington. Big-city chiefs, some of them think the so-called war on drugs is a fraud, just another agenda to hand out powerful jobs. Most think illegal drug profits are going into the campaign coffers of the politicians—reason it's allowed in the country. Says the DEA couldn't be as incompetent as they are by accident."

"Wouldn't surprise me," Cody said. "But I think it's bureaucratic bungling. Since the government got computerized, they can fuck things up faster than ever. And it takes a strange breed of duck to reach the top in the government. Somebody that can't think straight no matter how hard they try and whose reality exists on a numbered form. I'm apolitical, or apathetic; don't know which, sometimes. Couldn't care less which group of crooks are running the government. There's really not a dime's worth of difference. When you get all the smoke and mirrors cleared away, it's all about money anyway."

"You've become even more jaded than ever."

"Yeah. What I'm gonna do right now is slither around the farm. Check for midnight skulkers. I'm taking the sawed-off for companionship."

"We'll stay inside."

He was outside on the porch before he remembered he wanted to ask Jolinda about Bubba and Robin, and the picture Biba had in the silver frame. Could Bubba be Scanner and Robin the black-haired beauty with "tits from here to yonder" who tried to frame Barry Willingham by opening an elusive mail drop? It would hold till morning.

* * *

Thunder rumbled in the mountains. Boomed. Rumbled again. Scanner gave up on trying to count the seconds between the flash and the sound. Just too many of them. It didn't matter anyhow.

What a great night for a killing. Mist hanging in the fields and along the rivers. The wind blowing tree limbs, making shadows dance on bedroom windows. Some poor bastard's lying wide awake, scared shitless, hearing the rain on the roof and wishing it would stop because the racket could muffle the sound of someone breaking the glass on the kitchen door. They're imagining something's sneaking around their porch or heading up the path to their house. Like he was some kind of phantom who could walk through walls, rip out guts and eyes, and disappear into the night.

And they were right. He could and would.

In his memoirs he'd call tonight the Night of Tight Sphincters. What a great song that would make. Night of Tight Sphincters—how melodious. His preview, of course, had been the

Night of Screams. His apex, his apogee. He dreamed of the run down the road after her. Like a great cat stalking its prey.

Pucker away, sphincters.

The law would also think it was a great night for killing and would saturate the community with their presence. He would fool them all. He'd stay here and type his adventures into his word processor, then do a little Internet surfing, hang ten on the Web. Later he would try out his latest Web browser, zip into one of the powerful search engines to locate a Wildcat BBS. Then he'd use the list-server as a jumping-off spot to find an anarchist bulletin board, log on to it, and pick up some more tips on eavesdropping or how to make a silencer or his own homemade explosives or poison. There was always something out there for a creative mind.

The uninformed, unlucky civilians would lie there, wait for the bump in the night. The psychology of nothing happening could be as unnerving as a bloody corpse falling through the ceiling. Smiling, Scanner bade a friendly nighty-nite to all the butt-puckerers. Especially Horace Hornsby. Horace was becoming a drag on the economy.

Thirty

The dirt road wound crazily for three miles through piney hollows and rock-walled ravines. Then it paralleled the swift rapids of Rattlesnake Creek until it eventually jogged away from the turbulent waters. Ogden had provided careful directions. But when the road suddenly ended, it left Cody stunned by its abrupt demise and flabbergasted by the numbers of wrecked and abandoned cars and pickups in the large bowl-shaped clearing. Up the hill toward a stony ridge stood ten or more scrapped school buses. Several had red-leafed sumac growing in their windowless interiors and heavy green kudzu vines sheltering their sagging tops.

A zigzag path bordered by ironweed cut into a greasy, tumbled confusion of transmissions, rear-ends, steering columns, wheels, bumpers, hoods, engines, and stacked tires. He aimed his pickup through the squalor. Leaning forward, gripping the wheel, he feared he would topple a heap of metal and end up buried under its weight.

After passing through the junkyard Cody drove on through an open gate with a battered stock gap. Then he turned right up the hill. From there he could see a garage and beyond it a house. As he drew near, he spotted a pair of booted feet protruding from underneath a gray Datsun hatchback. When he climbed from the truck he noticed the legs didn't budge. A loud hammering sounded from under the car.

The dog came at him from behind.

Cody was ready.

Ogden gave good directions.

The dog was huge and red, had a head and neck the size of a watermelon. His ratty tail stuck straight out behind for max

270

velocity. The mutt ran in a crouch and shot for Cody straight as an arrow with no hesitation at all.

Cody waited until the last second, turned and side-stepped, grabbed the wide leather collar in one hand and a muscular rear leg in the other, and used the animal's momentum to arch it over his head and slam it into the hood of his truck.

It made a loud thunk. And one loud grunt like a pole-axed bull.

Cody wrapped his hands around the dog's rear feet, swung it around twice, head down, then slammed its head against the rear fender. It flopped, unconscious.

The encounter had lasted less than fifteen seconds.

At the dog's yelp, Gary Gallegher slid from under the vehicle and watched as Cody stepped toward the old Datsun. The mechanic was big and broad-shouldered, with unkempt blond hair that hung to his shoulders. He was spotted from head to foot with dirt and oil. He grinned at his high school friend and wiped his hands on a filthy rag. "You don't like dogs?" he said.

"Not particularly," Cody said.

"Buster's part pit-bull, part rottweiler. Weighs near a hundred. Had his mama and daddy here until they got in a squabble and killed each other." He looked over at the prostrate animal. "Never seen a man handle a dog like that."

"Took a special dog-handling course at a government school I attended."

Buster groaned and rolled over. He didn't appear ready to get up.

"Security dogs are usually trained to hold a man until the handler arrives," Cody said. "Buster looked as though he had something else in mind."

"Barry said you might be around, asking about us being down in Marion County the night his old lady got killed," said Gallegher.

He turned and walked to the house, waving Cody along with a hand out to his side. "Buster's a disadvantaged mutt. He's lived out here in the woods all his life, never been to town, never seen TV, no proper obedience school, didn't have one of them privileged upbringings you hear about these days. I reckon he's like

271

me—unreconstructed. His philosophy is kill 'em and bury 'em. May dig 'em up later and eat 'em after they tender out. Cuts way down on yokels coming out to steal auto parts."

The house was a surprise after the junkyard and garage. A neat log home, it had a rock garden out back and a pond with noisy geese. An arched wooden bridge spanned the water. Beyond the pond a small white gazebo rested on a flattened-out rise. Gallegher lowered himself to the front steps of the cabin with a tired sigh. "Working man's day is never done, and mine's just getting started. Sit. Patsy won't let me in the house until I shuck outa these overalls and get barefoot."

Cody squatted in the yard and plucked a stem of grass. "How the hell did you wind up here, Gary?"

Gallegher smiled a sideways smile that half closed one eye. He glanced up through the branches of a walnut tree into the morning sun. "Ain't it a rip? What? Our graduating class, all twenty of us, you, Michelle, me, few others still left in the county. It's like the ambitious ones grabbed the diploma, walked out the front door, ran for the bus outa town, and never looked back. Like some kinda redneck diaspora. Sometimes I see one of our old classmates rubber-necking around town. Usually don't stay long. They look all outa place."

"But you got the accounting degree at U.T. Was gonna live the good life in Knoxville," Cody said.

"After about five years, I decided K-Town was a zoo with an interstate running through it. A fucking busy interstate. Then the job got to be 'If income is not reported on Schedule A, include form 5649 Revision B. Multiply line 45 by ten percent. Add line 47 then subtract from line 53.' You ever hear of anything so insane or nonsensical in your life? Nit-wittery carried to the extreme, legislated by a goofy Congress we're supposed to look up to. Shit."

"Thought all the dropouts were in the sixties and seventies," Cody said. He'd take his time getting around to it. It was a cool, pleasant morning. Although Gallegher and he had never run together as teenagers, they'd also never had a beef.

"Didn't drop out. Dropped in to a better life. What I was doing was running as hard as I could to keep from going backward. Now I drive around the county, maybe go down to Monroe or Polk County, up to Loudon, never get too far. There's no need to. If I see a car I like, I make a cash offer. Then I fix it up and sell it for a modest profit. Don't need a big one. All cash. No checks accepted. Only form I fill out is a receipt and a transfer of title. No banks either. Datsun I'm working on, I paid three hundred for it. I'll put in some time and a hundred dollars' worth of parts and sell it for eight hundred."

Another reason for the mutt, having cash money around, Cody thought. "What about the house?"

"I bought the logs and lumber and doors and windows, window inserts and drywall and sinks, joists, everything—cash money. Me and my brother-in-law put it up, dug the basement, poured the foundation, drove all the nails. Didn't fill out a single form, no interest deducted, no income, government don't know I'm alive. It's the way a man's intended to live."

"What about Social Security?"

"My motto with the government, I fuck 'em where they breathe. Don't want 'em around. I hate the assholes. Except maybe the space folks. There's a bunch of folks around here feel the same way and more arriving from big cities that're just fed up. I've got a satellite dish, see shit going on in D.C.—District of Crooks—and New York City. It turns my stomach."

"I don't guess you worry about the killer out here."

"Not unless he wants Buster hanging on the cheeks of his ass."

"You was with Barry?"

"We hit town about five till eleven that night. I remember I wanted to get a six-pack at the Tank 'n' Tummy; that's a drive-in on the way back. They close at eleven. That night they closed early."

"Barry said you all didn't get back until around midnight."

"He's mistaken. Like I told Luther when he was investigating before he was killed. Five before eleven. On the button. Checked my watch 'cause I was pissed about the store closing early."

"What kind of mood was Barry in?"

"Good mood. We'd found a new opening to a cave we'd been in a dozen times. I was too big to get through, but Barry made it up to the surface and waited for us to come around."

"How long was he outa your sight? That's what a prosecutor's gonna ask."

"'Bout forty minutes. Not long enough to drive ninety-five miles back home, kill his wife and Sharpless, drive back and meet us."

"Five 'til eleven?"

"On the money."

On the way out, Buster had recovered enough to chase Cody's pickup, tried to grab a rear tire in his huge slavering mouth and render it dead. Cody liked dogs. He'd thought of getting Jolinda one for protection. That's why he hadn't killed Buster.

Damn, he thought, after he'd passed out of the junkyard and was once again motoring alongside Rattlesnake Creek. He had forgotten to ask Gallegher whether he was a liberal or conservative. Probably a Mountain County moderate.

Cody eventually tracked down all of Barry's caving companions. One drove a road grader for the county, another worked at the foundry, another worked for T.V.A. at the Ocoee River site—made the long drive down and back every day, he'd said.

To a man, they all said Barry got back to the county around midnight. Something didn't calculate. But did it really matter? Like Barry said. He'd been too busy to kill his wife.

"Any ideas on the woman's footprint?" Cody said to his dad that afternoon. He'd dropped by the S.O. because he couldn't think of what to do next. Maybe being near the center of the investigation would stimulate his sleuthing skills.

"Ladies size nine and a half by the measurement. Could be a nine or a ten depending on the style. Most likely a nine and a half. Now all we have to do is go through the county trying that size on all the ladies. Like a slough-footed Cinderella."

"What size did Samantha wear?"

"Eight."

"Think the track's an old one, someone visiting?"

"Could be from a two-peckered buzzard for all I know.

Which is what a defense attorney will say if we ever present the evidence against their client, whoever it turns out to be."

Cody figured his dad must really be frustrated, going on like that. The whole town was probably putting the pressure on. Or he was putting it on himself. Likely both. "Speaking of defense attorneys, think Monk's in any shape to defend Barry?"

"Guess he'd taper off some. His A.A. sponsor from over in Madisonville is ready to hang himself. He'll probably give up soon and hang out at Fuzzy's with Monk. He's been back at it almost a year now, blew away five years sober. At his age, he may not make it back."

"Why's he drink like that?" Cody said.

"I had to lock him up again on a DUI two months ago. He drove his car out into a muddy field in the river bottom. The deputy chasing him got stuck but Monk was going round and round, crisscrossing the damn floodplain. He passed out finally, and the damn wrecker got stuck trying to get out to him. We eventually snaked a cable along and dragged the car. Monk told me that night he's drinking to forget."

"Forget what?" Cody said.

"I asked him that. He said he didn't remember."

"Then it must be working. Reporters tried to talk to me on the way in," Cody added.

"I been thinking about giving them something."

"Like what?" Cody said.

"Anything I give, the killer may use as a challenge, so I'll have to be careful. Have to be vague. Say we found something in Luther's original investigative notes."

"Did you?"

"Well—no. I went over 'em again and again. But it could cause this Scanner to show his hand, trying to find out who knows what it is. We know it's somebody we all know anyhow."

Cody thought it over for a while. "Sounds as good as any tactic to me. I like it. If anything goes wrong we can blame it on Luther."

The sheriff bit his lower lip, put off by Cody's dry wit. "I'll be very vague with the reporters. Subtle."

"I may head to Fuzzy's," Cody said, consulting his watch.

"Let it drop over there. Not straight to tell a reporter. Just accidently be overheard telling Monk."

"I had a terrible thought earlier," the sheriff said.

"Yeah?"

"What if he just stops? Never kills again. And we never find him."

Thirty-one

The previous night, even with all the rain, thunder and lightning, and flash flooding, Fuzzy's broke the all-time record for gross receipts. Tonight, now the weather had cleared, the record would likely fall. As a reaction to the heaven-sent windfall, Fuzzy was relaxing the standards somewhat, permitted Big 'Un to loosen his criteria for forcible ejection.

Fuzzy had driven by the Riverside Motel and Restaurant earlier on an intelligence-gathering mission and discovered that Elton, out of rooms, was renting space in his parking lot and the vacant field next door to some resourceful members of the media who'd brought along their own RVs. Cables strung from the motel's outside wall outlets provided electricity. Green plastic garden hoses supplied water.

Unwilling to risk life, limb, health, and reputation at the HillTop, and after getting a good warning whiff of the interior, the media folks stood three deep at the bar at Fuzzy's place and paid call prices for bar whiskey. If they didn't catch the killer soon, he'd have to build an annex, Fuzzy thought, an avaricious gleam in his eyes. He'd taken away the free peanuts, added an extra pizza oven and a popcorn machine, and hired a part-timer to feed the raw materials. Like a license to print money.

Women were standing at the bar now. An unheard-of practice for the locals. When local ladies were served, they always remained seated and had drinks brought to their table.

Not these big-city women. Brazen and loud, elbowing their way to the bar, they showed not the least bit of shyness in calling out, "Scotch over ice."

Cody found Monk surrounded by this tumultuous assault on the senses, flanked on all sides by media types offering drinks and outright bribes in exchange for information, no matter how trivial. Did Monk know if Barry was ever unfaithful to his wife? Did he beat her? Were they sexually compatible? How did the Willingham family gain its original wealth? Were they guilty one hundred and sixty years ago of stealing the land from the Cherokees? What about slaves?

"To the best of my knowledge, Barry Willingham does not own slaves," Monk allowed.

"Where is his son?"

"Away at a private school, the whereabouts of which cannot be disclosed. Now if you ladies and gentlemen will excuse me, I just dropped in for a taste."

Monk turned his back to the crush and spotted Cody. "I didn't hear you come in," he called over.

Cody was forced to elbow his way over to get near the flustered attorney.

Monk gestured toward the reporters with a backward wave of his free hand. "These fine media people expect me to hand over information about our client. Then they'll depict him negatively in their sordid rags. Perhaps cast his son in the role of a modern-day Eugene Gant. Sell a few tabloids. Know what I mean?"

None of the reporters were standing close enough to overhear them, but a little conspiratorial whispering would correct that. "Believe it or not, Monk," Cody said in a low tone near the attorney's ear, "Tom C. Wolfe would sneak by late at night to the old shacky-looking house I lived in up on the hill, whisper his long phrases in my head." Some months back, Cody had dug out several snapshots of the old home place. It looked nowhere near as bad as his bleak memories of childhood poverty. He did at least have a big yard and a dog and books that kept him occupied on long winter nights.

"Old rascal," Monk said. "I admired him despite his proclivity for verbosity, which I in my own loquaciousness can identify with." Monk peeked over his half-moon glasses, craned his neck, and glanced around furtively to check if Big 'Un had by chance overheard his musings. "Never any doubt what old Tom had for supper—or breakfast or lunch for that matter."

Monk dropped out for a few moments. Lost in deep reverie,

no longer present in the vulgar rowdiness and crush, he dwelt momentarily with remembered wealth and joyful learning. Grand times and faithful true friends were his once more. For an instant he came close to facing the demon that pursued him. He sensed within himself a deep yearning, a better way to avoid the life pain, the Weltsmertz.

With a floating lightheadedness he peered into the beautiful brown eyes of the woman he loved and twirled her around the dance floor. She was slender and graceful and she . . . In mid-thought Monk flicked back to the present; the suddenness of it rocked his upper body and caused him to stagger. He recoiled from Cody as if he'd been standing alone and the crowd had materialized out of nowhere. In confusion, he tried to refocus on his companion.

"Anything new in the investigation?" he said, looking dazed at his surroundings.

A heavy man with short, red hair edged closer. Cody looked away, gave the eavesdropper time to zoom in. He pretended to search the crowd for a familiar face, waited a long count before he spoke. "Everyone wants the killer brought to justice. That's for sure."

Monk took a knock of sour mash and smacked his lips. "Justice. That rarest of all elements. So elusive in this day and time."

"You're not going to go all melancholy on me now, are you?"

"No, brave Cody, homme de lettres. I will be blunt, as you are. Anything new?"

"Not really new. There's something old we've come across. But it's hot. Shouldn't even tell you, but you are my client's attorney, and the Willinghams are paying the toll."

Monk leaned closer and leered. "And a rather steep toll I'm told. Something old, you say?"

The red-haired man searched for misplaced keys in his pocket. He moved a little closer to Cody and Monk.

"Keep this to yourself, Monk. Luther may have been onto something and that's why he was killed. We found several over-looked clues in his investigative notes. Sheriff may have been a little hasty. It's amazing—explosive, really—the way it all comes together. I couldn't believe it. We can't put it out in the news though. It might send the killer on the run."

The attorney gripped his glass in tight anticipation. "Really?"

"Shh," Cody said.

"Oh, yeah. Sorry. Any idea who it is?"

"Could be."

"Who?"

"Now, Monk—that'd be telling."

"Yeah. It would be, wouldn't it."

Cody talked a little more small talk with Monk, then left. Outside in his truck he reached under the seat and touched the envelope that had been left there for him. He would read it back at the trailer.

The red-haired man hurried by, climbed into a muddy rental and sped away.

Cody hoped he hadn't laid it on too thick.

Elwood Crabtree's house was dark and quiet. Set back a ways from the road, it was beyond the protective circle of the nearest street light. Two giant hackberry trees in the front yard towered over the front porch and cast the dwelling into an even-deeper gloom.

Elwood went to bed early, with the chickens, his wife complained. Which was one reason that ten years earlier she had moved into the spare bedroom, with all of her belongings and a color TV. Another reason was his nonstop smoking. She'd once stocked the living room, bedroom, and kitchen with pamphlets and brochures on second-hand smoke. They spoke of how the spouse of a person who smokes was more likely to get lung cancer than the spouse of a nonsmoker, but it was all to no avail.

She made her irrevocable decision one cold, argumentative night when Elwood, out of matches, used one of the brochures to tag a light from a fireplace log. He scorched his fingers, dropped the tract, and came very close to setting the house on fire. There was still a singed spot on the carpet where his wife had thrown the dishwater.

She'd taken her clothes along to protect them not only from Elwood's tendencies toward pyromania but to remove them from the stench they'd hung in for years. It still took a tall can of Lysol a week to disperse the smell, but she thought the results worth the expense.

Elwood was pleased as well. He bragged to his brother Elton, "Old bitch snores like a power saw and would gripe if she was hung with a new rope. Now I can fart and pick my nose without her getting that disgusted look on her face. She's just not harmonious."

That night, Elwood didn't know what woke him. An out-of-place night movement, a breeze from an open window or door, or a light pressure on the mattress near his head. He only realized that one moment he was sound asleep and the next wide awake, sensing something was terribly wrong in the room. He lay there under the covering of only a light sheet. The house was warm from his wife cranking up the heat. He stared toward a ceiling invisible in the blackness of the room, his heart pounding in his chest. He was afraid to turn his head left or right, to breathe in or out.

He heard no unusual sound. From the kitchen came the light hum of the refrigerator. A car went by on the distant street. Through the closed door of his wife's room, he heard the motor rattle of her night breathing, a stop and start on each intake and exhale.

It's nothing. Just woke up from a dream. Killer being loose is giving ever'body the willies. I'll just lay here and go back to sleep.

But he couldn't. Somebody was in the room. He could sense it.

He finally gained courage. "I—is somebody there?"

"Just me." The whisper was inches from his ear.

"YA!—" Elwood's scream was cut off by a powerful hand over his mouth.

"Be still," the voice hissed.

Elwood couldn't breathe. He tried to sit up.

"Be still or I'll suffocate you," the voice whispered. "They'll find you in your bed in the morning. Say you had a heart attack."

The grip loosened slightly, and Elwood drew in a quick gasping breath. All he was allowed. The rough hand clamped down again.

"I'll let you breathe if you be quiet and be still. Okay?"

Elwood's eyes were bulging, he was losing consciousness. He gave a series of rapid nods.

The grip relaxed, but the hand didn't move far. He felt the heat of it against his lips. If he tried to scream, he knew he would die.

"Who are you," he mumbled into the palm.

"Why it's me, Elwood. Your old friend, Cody."

"Oh, God, Cody. Don't kill me. Please don't kill me. I didn't mean anything to happen to Simon. Honest. Your little brother was sick. I been to church and asked forgiveness if I did anything wrong. Prayed for him. You gonna kill me?"

"Not this trip, Elwood. I've got a full schedule. Something that always strikes me as odd, folks who're always talking about church and eternal life are the ones most afraid to die."

"Just please don't kill me."

"Won't if you answer a few questions. Truthfully. Most of them I'll already know the answer to. You lie, you die."

"Questions? What questions?"

"You may've heard talk around town. I'm conducting a murder investigation."

"Goddamn! Why didn't you ask me to come to the sheriff's office, 'stead of scaring the dog shit outa me."

"Yeah? Then I touch on something you don't wanna talk about, you start asking for a lawyer."

"I wouldn't do that, Cody. Honest."

Cody felt the vibration of the man's fear through the mattress. "This way you get to be more comfortable. You don't have to sit on one'a those hard, jailhouse chairs, inflame your 'rhoids."

"You wanna know something? Just ask."

"About you and Luther. All about you and Luther."

"Aw, now Cody. Why don't we let the dead rest in peace?"

"Gimme some quick answers or you're gonna be keeping Luther company."

"Me and Luther didn't do much business. Just a few downers ever' once in a while and the nitrous oxide. He couldn't get enough'a that laughing gas. That's it. Luther got most of his stuff somewheres else."

"Where? From who?"

"Sneaky bastard never told me. I'd name a price for something, he'd say he could get it cheaper from his main supplier."

"Was it Gateline's Pharmacy? He get stuff from Randy?" Cody asked.

"You kidding? Randy's a straight arrow. He don't bend the rules the least bit. Luther went after Randy a coupla years ago. Randy threatened to turn him in."

Cody put a little more pressure on Elwood's mouth. "I don't think you're telling me all you know."

"Wha—whatcha want? Ain't much more to tell. Go ask my brother. He rented rooms to Luther sometimes. He'd bring in young girls, get 'em flying on that laughing gas, and they'd talk outa their heads and fuck your brains out."

"I'll be asking around. You hold out on me, I'll be back. Next time, no more Mister Nice Guy."

Elwood's sheets were soaked from the sweat that still poured from his body. Even his hair was wet. He felt water trickle down his leg. That was sweat, wasn't it? "Told you ever'thing, Cody. Honest. Wouldn't lie to you. Last thing I'd ever do. Promise me you won't sneak up on me anymore, scare me to death. Just call me on the phone and I'll meet you anywhere. Just ask. Cody? Cody? Where are you?"

Elwood found himself talking to an empty room, ran into the bathroom, and vomited into the commode.

Thirty-two

If what Elwood said was true, Cody wouldn't waste Ray's time having him put a tail on Randy. Tracking Gateline was one of the missions he'd assigned. He let himself in the camper trailer and turned on a light. After getting a beer from the refrigerator he sat on the couch and opened the envelope Ray Blizzard had dead-dropped under the seat of his truck.

The first page was a fax cover sheet from an agency in Las Vegas. Ray had networked the firm to get info on Rick Staros, who was hanging with the real estate jerk.

"From auto tag info received via telephone, we furnish the following as per your request," read the fax.

Subject is Richard G. Staros, resident of Las Vegas, residing at 11930 Mockingbird Lane. Subject is a self-employed business counselor and investor in properties and represents "confidential interests." Calls to the subject's secretary resulted in investigator being informed Mr. Staros takes new clients by reference only.

No criminal history could be determined. A search of the newspaper morgue for past events in which subject's name was mentioned proved negative.

A low-profile interview was instigated with several of subject's neighbors, both business and residential. Subject is not believed to be married, although he has frequent overnight female guests. Subject does not associate with neighbors except to say hello. Some neighbors feel subject is "connected," because of the appearance of some clients who were seen arriving with bodyguards.

Home is an approximately four-thousand-square-foot brick home located in an upscale neighborhood. Security is expensive and sophisticated. A search of records at the county register's office reveals the home was purchased over five years previously. There is no mortgage holder.

A computer search of courthouse records, namely past and future dockets of Civil Court, indicates subject has not brought suit against anyone in the last three years nor had any been brought against him.

Page three of the fax was an invoice for $425.00. Page four was a handwritten note from Ray:

Robert "Bubba" Whittlemore, born Mountain County, moved to Sequatchie County age three. Mother, Ruby Whittlemore, now Bledsoe, remarried widow of Andrew Whittlemore who died three years prior to Bubba's birth. It appears young Bubba was a bush baby as Bledsoe came on the scene when Bubba was six or seven. One older sister, Glenda Whittlemore, née Roberson, five years older than subject.

Subject was graduated from Sequatchie County High School, was a good student and played on the football team. No hero. Just played. Local sheriff says subject gave no problems around town as a young man and was pleased Bubba may be chosen to attend the FBI academy, the bullshit I was handing out as my cover.

Subject graduated from M.T.S.U. in Murfreesboro, Tennessee, and one year later hired on with Mountain County S.O.

No negative info could be gained about subject, however it is noted the investigation was conducted in a rural community and these folks don't say squat to anybody they don't know real well.

Subject's mother, Ruby, had some strange kind of seizure four years ago and is on total disability, unable to walk or care for herself. What informants did talk indicated Bubba always blamed somebody or something for his mother's condition and seemed driven by either revenge or guilt.

Subject was married his last year in college. Union lasted only six months as subject came home early from a basketball game one night and caught his wife in the embrace of a local pharmaceutical executive, or in street terms, a drug dealer.

As for Randy Gateline, your local heartthrob and success story, this old boy's ass is dragging. I'll hang a tail on him sometime in the morning. If I get up.

Over and out.

Cody turned out the lights and waited in the darkened trailer for ten minutes, thinking, while his eyes adjusted to the dark. Should he go page Ray, cancel the tail on Randy, give him another task? Like a background on the Reverend Sonny Todd? No, he'd do that one himself. How did Mrs. Ruby Bledsoe fit into all this? Or did she?

Once he could make out the shape of the furniture in the trailer, he left the trailer, took a quick look around, then headed for the house to stand his tour of guard duty.

"It's just a simple mistake, Barry. Calm down," Michelle said into the phone.

"Goddamn Horace is what's wrong. Got my account all fucked up, and I think he done it on purpose. He's gonna chicken out on the whole deal now that the sheriff and Cody's been over to the bank questioning him."

"You're getting all your exercise by jumping to conclusions. One thing doesn't necessarily have anything to do with the other."

"You're not looking at the statement I'm looking at. It's got all these payouts that's impossible and none of the deposits. I got a good mind to go over to his house and kick his ass."

Michelle made a disgusted sigh into the phone. "What you need to do, Barry, is settle down. It's your ego. You wanta kick somebody's ass 'cause Cody hinted he'd kick yours. In the morning, all calm and collected, go over and see Horace and get it all straightened out."

"Okay, Michelle. If you say so. But he better act right. I can't believe you've hired a investigator that threatens me."

"Consider yourself lucky. He called me a slut."

Thirty-three

At breakfast the next morning Cody was muddled from his on-and-off sleep pattern and from his attempts at sleeping in the overstuffed chair in the living room. Jolinda kept feeding him coffee.

"I heard on the news where your daddy says Luther's old notes may lead to the killer," Ogden said as he poured hot maple syrup over his pancakes.

"That right?"

"Nashville station also says an unidentified source close to the investigation hints the sheriff's office may have the killer's identity. An arrest could be imminent."

"You feeding them that bull?" Jolinda said. "I know you, Cody Rainwalker. Sounds like something your devious mind would come up with."

"I haven't talked to the press. 'Course they're always eavesdropping on conversations."

Jolinda laughed, tossed her long black hair back over her shoulders. She wore an eagle feather over her ear and a light-weight red sweater against the early morning chill. "And you just happened to say something to somebody in the earshot of a reporter. You think that'll make the killer walk in and give himself up. I'm saying 'himself.' Could be 'herself.' Haven't all the male possibles been investigated?"

"Not all. Whereabouts have been checked by the deputies; fact, they're still on it, talking to neighbors, corroborating alibis. Speaking of which, where'd you get the eagle feather? You know going after eagles is illegal?"

Ogden looked from one to the other, continued eating. At times being around the pair was like being in a veritable combat zone. He'd witnessed these early morning spats for years. At least they weren't throwing things today.

"I'll have you know an eagle gave me this feather, Mister Smart Ass."

Cody stuffed a forkful of pancakes in his mouth, talked around them. "Knocks on the door, says, 'Here's your feather, Miss Risingwaters. Have a nice day.' Tell it to the wildlife folks on your way down to the state lockup."

"You're coal-bucket dumb. You know that? Along the road out front, there's this big raccoon been hit by a car. It wasn't dead, but it was hurt bad. A real young eagle tried to snatch him up and they had a tussle. Eagle flapped and strained but couldn't get the coon off the ground. He'd bit off more'n he could chew. Anyhow, he flew away and a big feather fell off him and landed on the hood of my truck."

Ogden stopped chewing and said, "Your grandma would say that's big medicine."

Cody was impressed. "Big medicine," he said.

"Maybe the feather will help me make an A on my math test today."

"How's Biba doin' in school?" Cody said. "Her aunt says she's smart. She a straight A student? Make the honor roll and all?"

"She was always the top student in class until around the middle of last year. Then her grades started to fall off. She even went up to a special school in Maryville two nights a week, took advanced classes in calculus and computer programming. Now she's dropped down to maybe a solid B plus."

"Understandable, her mama getting killed and her daddy being put in jail," Ogden said.

"Her grades started falling long before that, Uncle Ogden," Jolinda said. "Why're you checking on Biba?" she asked Cody suspiciously.

"I was out to Michelle's house when she first hired me. She showed me Biba's computer setup. There was a real macho picture of Bubba on her dresser. All outdoorsy. He had a hunting rifle."

Jolinda's mouth flew open. She dropped her fork to her plate.

It splattered syrup on the front of her sweater but she ignored it. "Was it in a silver frame?"

"Matter of fact it was."

"That picture was stolen from Robin's school locker. She's going to kill Biba. I wanta be there. She's been in a rage about the picture for a month. Accused me of hiding it to tease her."

Cody rested his chin in his hand, elbows on the table. "As a great big favor to me, don't say anything to Robin yet. Let's see how all this ties together, if it does. May not mean anything except Biba has a silent schoolgirl crush on Bubba."

Cody could tell from Jolinda's expression she couldn't wait to tell her friend. She was bouncing in her seat nervously, wanted to head off to school early.

"Please, Jolinda," Cody said.

"Oh, all right. But I can't wait until you nail the killer so I can tell Robin who stole her picture. You think there's fireworks now, just you wait."

"Thanks, honey," Ogden said.

"Biba can be strange sometimes," Jolinda said. "Then other times she's real sweet and caring. She comes to class sleepy a lot. Says she stays up late chatting on the Internet. It's addicting, she says."

"How do you mean, strange?" Cody said.

"At times, she's real quiet, like you, Cody. Contemplative, you call it. Like her brain flies away to some other planet. Other times, she'll laugh a lot, cut up and act silly, like she's laughing out of control, then she'll stop and look around to see if she's made a fool of herself. Other times she's spiteful and mean. The other day she was picking on this boy who doesn't have good clothes to wear to school. Hurt his feelings."

"Children can be cruel at times," Ogden said. "And a young girl growing to womanhood is driven and torn by all kinds of emotions. I know that by observing someone I know real well."

"Very funny," Jolinda said. "Like, I mean when she got her new car last June. Her Aunt Michelle bought her a white Dodge Stealth—expensive car, big engine, every option you can buy. They had to search all over before she found the exact one she wanted. Bought it off the floor in Morristown.

"The salesman told her 'break it in like you're going to drive it, young lady.' She said 'thanks' and laid rubber all the way across the showroom floor and was outa there. Disappeared for three days, then showed up like nothing happened. Kids say she went on a Mountain County honeymoon."

"What's that?" Cody said.

"She was shacked up somewhere."

Later that morning Cody checked in with Noel, who was still on a rampage about Ray. Cody always played his cards close to his chest and so did not enlighten the aggravated computer guru as to the Alabamian's whereabouts.

"Hear on the news your daddy is close to making an arrest."

"Don't believe everything you hear, Noel, and nothing you read about this case. Reporters are making shit up 'cause they're just like us. They don't know anything."

"I think Ray is in town, not coming in the office to make me think he's up to something. You know how he likes to get me stirred up. Makes his day."

"You see him, tell him to get his ass to work."

"Are you positive I can't help you out somehow?"

"Know anything about hackers?"

"Why do you think the banks and insurance companies pay me the big bucks?"

"What about telephone hackers? Phone phreaks?"

"Usually one and the same," Noel said. "Techno-nerds, some people call them, except they don't usually fit the out-of-shape-couch potato nerd pattern seen in movies and on TV. Some are techno-revolutionaries, anarchists, arsonists—usually teens and the like out to bring down the soulless corporations and their fat-cat lawyers. War against the breadheads, some call it. And they can be good at mechanical hacking, also, like picking locks, breaking into cars to steal cellular phones. Some of them are into carding—stealing credit card numbers and telephone card numbers, charging stuff so they can live free. Others pick up and leave menus on computer bulletin boards for explosives, flamethrowers, and sink-brewed napalm.

"Bank I contract to had a group of phreaks virtually seize a section of their voice-mail system. Held it hostage for days. Used it to leave messages, trading codes. One of the security types just happened on it. Heard all this phreak-chattering and hey-duding in their impenetrable hacker jargon. Kicked them out of the voice-mail system, and the bolder phreaks called bank officers at home demanding their section of the voice-mail back. Ballsy bastards."

"You ever hear of one getting into, say, a city or regional phone system?" Cody asked. "Rerouting calls, things like that?"

"Not my area of expertise. Diverters, they're called. I did hear of a big case like that. Don't recall all the particulars. I can check around. Phone company was embarrassed their security was so lax so they hushed it up. Or did they call in the Secret Service? People are surprised taking down hackers is one of their chores."

"Thanks, Noel. Appreciate the help."

"Scanner, the killer calls himself! You think he's a computer hacker, don't you?"

Cody could tell Noel was chomping at the bit again, wanted him calmed down. "Not that I can tell. So far, I believe he's using a police scanner to monitor telephone conversations."

"You hear about it?" the sheriff said.

"'Bout what?" Cody said. He'd stopped by the S.O. after lunch because he was all out of ideas and didn't know where to look next. He'd hit the brick wall his dad warned him about.

"Damn Barry had a spat with Horace. Went in the bank all red-faced and hollering. Something about his account being all messed up."

"News to me," Cody said. "Guess Barry's feeling the pressure of his deal going sour. Putting the big clamp on his pocketbook."

"Horace called an hour ago. Said the account statement was out of whack but he thinks Barry overreacted. Said Barry threatened to slap him shit-faced. I may drive by later, calm Barry down."

Cody plopped onto the beat-up desk, rapped a tattoo against the wood with his heels. "Our little subterfuge got quite a reaction in the tabloids."

"Started to believe it myself. Went back and read all the reports one more time. Thought back through where the bodies were found and on what day of the week, the weather, anything that could have a common thread we already don't know of besides the ribbons and the brutality of it."

"One thing you're leaving out," Cody said.

"What's that?"

"All the victims knew something about the covert deal the Willinghams are cooking. Everyone but Samantha. She may have known something, but not thought it important or relevant enough to pass along."

Anytime Samantha's death was mentioned the sheriff felt a restlessness come over him. He knew he'd have that feeling until he brought the killer in. He paced the narrow confines of his office, stopped and flipped up several wanted posters on the wall, then turned to face Cody. "What about Sharpless? We don't know that he knew anything about a real estate deal. He knew something but not everything."

"Remember the snapshots? I'd say him and Carl were kinda close."

"There is that," the sheriff said.

"I'd like to get out and turn over a few rocks. Just don't know which direction. It's not like we're running down a dealer or a prolific burglar, something where we can take our time and wait for the breaks."

"Something else strange happened," the sheriff said in a quiet voice. His demeanor suggested this last happening was totally beyond him.

"What's that?"

"Elwood Crabtree's in the hospital. Had some kinda fit last night. His wife called 911 and said he was hearing voices in the house but there was nobody there. He's sedated. Told Bubba you visited him in his room talking about Simon and the killer."

"Guilt and fear can do weird things to a man's mind," Cody said, shaking his head. "Seeing an apparition of me in the night . . ." His face was full of sadness. "What's the prognosis?"

"His old lady wants him locked away in a laughing academy for a few months. Saw Monk about filing papers on him. Said he's goofy as a hydrophoby rooster. He's so drugged up he may go along with it."

"Well, the doctors know best." With a shrug and a smile, Cody left the office. The sheriff watched him out the door before he finally gave it up and laughed.

Johnny Knight and Albert Feltus stuck their heads in the room to see what was going on. "Cody say something funny?" Albert asked.

"He sure the hell did, Albert. He sure the hell did."

Damn, that boy could lie.

Thirty-four

Gateline's Pharmacy was set back from the highway between a food market and a video rental store. Its single front window was crammed full of notebooks, crayons, cheap calculators, vitamins, Halloween decorations, an aluminum walker, a senior citizens discount placard, a three-day trial membership at Gateline's Health Club, and an ad for guaranteed two-day photo finishing.

Directly across the street, with a good view of the narrow driveway that wrapped behind the one-story concrete-block building, stood an ancient frame house with peeling paint that now served as the office of a we-tote-the-note used-car lot. A stupendous weeping willow tree stood in the front yard, trailing its flexible limbs all the way to the ground.

At the rear of the house a trampoline had been set up. A group of children took noisy turns at bouncing and squealing while a beagle hound stood by barking and wagging its white-tipped tail.

Ray Blizzard parked his old Chevy Nova down the street a hundred feet in front of a weed-choked abandoned lot that held the bombed-out remains of a service station. A signpost imbedded in the crumbling concrete held a wrecked sign that still carried the message "Reg: $1.49 gal."

No wonder the fuckers went outa business, Blizzard thought.

At first the car lot's owner eyed Ray dubiously, rocked his rocker on the uneven rotted wood of the shaky front porch, and considered strolling over and asking the loiterer what the hell it was he wanted. The battered Chevy carried an Alabama license plate. What did somebody from there want in Mountain County? He did approve of Ray's rear bumper sticker: "Don't blame me. I voted for Jefferson Davis." At least it wasn't a Yankee sneaking around up to no good.

Ray pranced around in full view, consulted his watch. Got in and out of the car and put on a good demonstration of someone waiting on somebody who hadn't arrived and was long overdue. He was dressed to blend into the environment with his faded jeans, a torn jersey, and a red billed cap with a feed-store logo stitched on the front. Eventually he became invisible, as he'd hoped to, appearing to give it up, left the driver's door open and snapped a newspaper in front of his face, pretending to read all about the killer that stalked the county.

Shortly past the lunch hour, Randy's truck hove into view from around the corner of the video store. Ray recognized it from the description Cody supplied and from the tennis ball riding the CB antenna just above rear-bumper level.

Hump was more'n likely going for lunch, which he wasn't gonna get any of, watching his ass.

Randy waited for a few cars to pass then hung a left onto the main drag and gunned it.

Ray gave him a few seconds, then followed, leaving the lot owner to relax completely now the threat of a potentially nefarious nogoodnik was obliterated from his mind.

A half mile later, tailer and tailee passed the sheriff's office. Ray spotted Cody's truck nosed into the wall of the building. Another half mile and they came to the Riverside Motel and Restaurant. Ray half expected Randy to pull in for a noonday bite, but he didn't. They continued on out of town with a line of other pickups, delivery trucks, and passenger cars completing the procession.

After climbing a steep grade Ray saw the dingy block building on the left. The sign read "HillTop Open," and Ray tried in vain to mentally will his quarry to drop in for a cool one. Another mile and they were on the open road of the highway.

Ray dropped back, held it on the double-nickel, which was what Randy was doing. Cars would come up behind them, tailgate until the yellow dashed line appeared, then careen around them, crazily heading for the next moving roadblock.

When Ray first moved to Nashville to work with Cody, he'd

told his boss, "This damn town. No matter where I drive, my bumper grows an asshole. Don't matter if I drive thirty or a hundred, there's always some asshole back there wanting to pass."

"Welcome to the fast lane," Cody had said.

After thirty miles Ray started wondering if maybe Randy was going to a pharmacist's convention in Kansas City. He dropped back a few hundred feet, let other drivers swing in and out. Another fifteen miles and they hit Interstate 75. Randy chose the northbound on-ramp.

Ray passed it up, crossed over the interstate bridge, hung a U-ie and came back across the bridge in the opposite direction. He hung a left onto the on-ramp and tromped it, saw Randy's truck top a hill a mile away. He caught up a little, then kept alert for turn-offs. Fuck, he thought. Guy was headed for Knoxville.

A semi almost made him miss Randy's exit. Ray had been hiding behind it and barely glimpsed the pickup turn right off the exit-ramp. He cut off a driver in a van and ignored the finger.

Randy pulled across the interstate bridge and straight into a motel entrance.

Ray slid the Nova into a restaurant parking lot across the street. He had an easy view of the yellow-and-white two-story motel building.

Hopping from the truck, Randy didn't bother with a check-in ritual at the white-curtained office beneath the wide, peaked portico. He climbed the outside concrete stairs, stepped hurriedly along the iron-railed walkway and disappeared into a room.

Bingo, Ray thought. An indisputable high-nooner.

She arrived twenty minutes later, driving a late-model powder-blue Caddy with a white rag top. And to Ray she looked worth the wait—tall, blonde, built, shades, tight red pants, and a skimpy halter.

He snapped off ten with his camera as she closed the car door and mounted the stairs, zoomed in on her wiggle. A light knock and she was inside. He coulda stood a few seconds more of the wiggle.

Ray focused the big lens, tagged the license number for

posterity, then relaxed for an expected long wait, trying unsuccessfully to keep images from his mind of what it would be like to strap the shapely woman on for an intense session of slap and tickle.

The blonde reappeared two hours later. Her hair was a little mussed, but to Ray she didn't look like she'd hurt anything.

The Caddy tooled off. Ray expected the pickup to follow, but Randy didn't appear.

After slightly more than an hour's wait a white Dodge Stealth appeared, prowled the lot, and parked three rooms down. A young girl with strawberry-blonde hair swung out and eyeballed the motel parking lot. She wore white canvas shoes, a short, tight skirt, and a clingy yellow-cotton sweater. She skipped up the stairs and pecked on the door.

There was a brief glimpse of Randy in his shorts as he let her in.

Ray was sure he'd made the shot. Subject in skivvies. Perfect timing, he thought, laying the camera back on the seat. The mark of a true pro.

Two hours later his stomach was growling. He hoped this mutt wasn't going for the triathlon. Cody said hang with him so he'd hang to the bitter end. Unless he had a brunette in for dessert. Then he'd pop into the grease-pit for a burger.

A blonde, now a strawberry-blonde. Ray wondered if Randy had some whipped topping. He had to keep his mind offa food. Shit. Guy didn't give it up soon he might have to bail out and meet Cody for the late night gig they'd planned. Getting on suppertime and the young stud still had the room rocking.

Finally, some action. Randy left first, headed for the interstate on-ramp and droned off. For some unknown reason, Ray held his position and was glad.

The young girl walked onto the balcony and scoped the parking lot, then scampered down the steps and slid into the Dodge. Ray snapped a high-powered zoom shot when she swung one leg inside. She'd forgotten her panties. If she'd worn any to start with. He'd been flashed.

She cruised the lot slowly, exited, headed down the road a quarter mile away from the interstate, whipped a screaming

U-turn, flew by with a throaty roar of the powerful engine winding out, popped fourth gear and got rubber, wound it on up,
and caught the on-ramp in a tight lean that threw gravel and
dust.

Ray had a feeling something weird would happen. She was
covering Randy's back trail. Paranoid little muff.

Driving aimlessly, Cody was brought out of his reveries by the
insistent beeping of his pager. He was out in the boonies so it
took him twenty minutes to track down a phone.

Ray caught it on the first ring. "Talladega Raceway."

"That bad, huh?"

"Whyn't you tell me this mutt's a preacher?"

"A who?"

"Preacher. Laid two women in one afternoon, so he must be
hung like a stud donkey, and I'm watching him right now eat his
way through his third helping of fried chicken. If that don't
qualify him as a preacher, then my ass is a rocket-sled—which it
would've had to be to catch little Miss No-Panties in the maxed-
out Dodge Stealth. She blew the fucking doors offa all the buildings on the side road where I was parked. I passed this eatery on
the way back and saw the right-reverend's truck parked outside.
Found the horny bastard inside sniffing around the waitresses."

"Don't go hyper on me, Ray. Let's take it a step at a time."

Ray told Cody about the blonde in the blue Caddy.

"Ramona Willingham. Why am I not surprised?"

"Know her, huh? How 'bout an intro? Wanta hear about this
blue-veiner she gave me?"

"Next."

He spilled the tale of the white Dodge Stealth.

"Biba Willingham. Surprised at last."

"You know where all the talent hangs out, so show me where
Randy gets his endurance training. After Biba whipped that
strawberry flash routine on me, I been driving around with a
hard-on a wildcat couldn't claw."

Cody hung up, then phoned his dad at the S.O. "Got two
possibles on the mysterious face in the mirror."

"Don't think I want to hear it."

Cody told him anyway.

"Both of them?"

"Greedy ain't he," Cody said. "Times add up. Vic Willingham brings home a new, young wife. She has time to get bored. Randy suddenly ends his romance with Samantha and starts squiring Ramona. Haven't figured the timeframe with Biba. Jolinda says about a year ago Biba became distracted from her studies."

"Think one knows about the other?"

"Doubt it. And I don't know whether or not it figures into the case. Could be all this investigating we're doing is digging up the county's nasty little secrets and allowing the killer's I.D. to stay buried deep."

"I drive around this county and have observed for years now," the sheriff said. "Got all these deputies reporting to me, and I think I know all the citizens and what they're up to. Then I learn something I never suspected. And I notice you've switched from asking to telling."

"Got a suspicion Scanner's got me in mind for somewhere down the road. If he succeeds, I want you to know what bases I've covered."

They met Ray Blizzard at a predetermined spot in Tellico Plains, at the burger place across Old Highway 68 from the Tellicafe. Cody left his pickup in the lot and he and Jolinda rode in the back seat of Ray's Nova. Cody'd brought her along after discovering Ogden had been asked to work late at the foundry.

"Don't have to baby-sit me, Cody," she'd said.

"Get'n the truck."

To make a lark of it, she wore a cowboy hat from her closet, a leather jacket, and a black, fake pistolero mustache as a disguise. She'd fished this item from Cody's box of odds and ends behind the seat. Cody took precautions against being followed.

"Almost time," Ray said. He turned in his seat to face Cody and Jolinda. He hadn't remarked about the hairy attachment to her face.

"Asked her to shave it off," Cody said. "But she says it took over a year to grow."

"Had this gal down in Cullman. She had a full beard and she would get down and—" Ray stopped talking when he heard the sound of footsteps and the scraping of chairs over the radio's speaker. "Showtime."

They'd parked on the main drag in front of a gigantic wooden building that had to be one of the original pioneer constructions in the town. It resembled a cross between a barn, a tobacco warehouse, and a train depot, and at some time in its existence may have served a stint as all three. Under the massive overhang of the front porch, crouched the entrance to a pizza shop. Earlier, Jolinda had popped inside, mustache and all, and returned with a large pepperoni and three cold drinks.

"You're sure we're gonna be able to hear the bug this far?" Cody said.

"Checked it out this morning. Planted the bug in the real estate office a couple of days ago and I've been taping the conversations. That's how I knew they'd be meeting tonight. Got a VOX so it's activated by sound. Batteries are fresh. We'd be able to hear it even farther off but after today I'm not ever getting over fifty feet from an eating place."

There was the sound of more sliding chairs over the speaker, then male voices.

"They're late," a voice said.

"It's a good drive down from Highwater Town, Mr. Staros," another said. "They'll be along soon. Michelle requested the meeting."

"She didn't say what the problem was?"

"Not in detail. Something about a problem with the bank."

"Wouldn't be surprised, this hick town savings and loan she's using."

"You're right, there. Does provide the best confidentiality though. Oh. Here they are now."

There was a rumble of footsteps and the sound of a door opening and closing.

"Good evening, Victor. Glad you could make it. Michelle, you're looking as lovely as ever."

"Hello, Stan. You can stop the bullshit. We're already committed."

"Where's Barry?"

"Hi, Rick. Barry couldn't make it. Got this volunteer fire department meeting tonight. Duty calls. Vic and I can speak for him anyhow. We're family."

"Of course," Rick's voice said. "Why couldn't you have just called me or stopped by the motel?"

"Victor's concerned about things, the way things are going in Highwater Town."

There were more scrapings and rumblings as everyone obviously took a seat.

"They got this long table in the corner there," Ray said. "Bug's in the ceiling above it."

"Isn't all this illegal?" Jolinda said.

"Shh."

"What seems to be the problem, Michelle?" Cody thought the voice belonged to Staros.

"You can't have kept from hearing about this kook we've got running around the county killing people," Victor said.

"Of course. It's all over the news. Could not possibly have come at a more inopportune time. Michelle and I have discussed it."

Victor's voice was agitated. "I agree wholeheartedly. The sheriff dropped around and asked our banker some questions. It seems one or two of the victims knew of our business. Not the whole thing. Just that we're buying up real estate."

"That's not illegal," Staros said.

"The whole county's in an uproar, as you might well imagine. The law's turning every stone. The sheriff has Horace scared there's a tie-in between the murders and our business. Before that even, Horace was worried he may be allowing too much capital out on land speculation and auditors may come crawling out of the woodwork. And I'm not at all sure we should continue with this partnership."

There was a long silence. For a moment Ray thought the bug was on the fritz.

Staros finally spoke. "And why is that, Mr. Willingham?" Cody heard a threat in the voice; it hinted of concrete overshoes and bodies in the trunks of old Buicks.

"You already know my concerns about inflation in Mountain County," Victor said. "Wages going sky-high and all. What worries me is I haven't read anything about this big government decision in the news, or heard about it on TV."

In the darkened Nova, Cody, Jolinda, and Ray stared at one another in confusion.

Stan Bodine piped up. "Thank God for that. If you had heard about it, we'd be a year too late to move on it. You know the old Wall Street adage: Buy on the rumor, sell on the news. The National Park Service is not about to start a land rush by prematurely announcing the relocation of the main entrance to the Great Smoky Mountains National Park. There would be an upheaval of major proportions. Entire restaurant and hotel chains would be bankrupt overnight.

"The economies of Gatlinburg and Pigeon Forge would be devastated," Bodine continued. "Highwater Town would be inundated by land speculators. You can't picture the calamity."

Victor wouldn't be assured so easily. "The government will have to announce it some day. And I can't see any difference between now and later."

"You're right, of course," Bodine continued. "However, when they do make the announcement, all of their political alternatives will be in place. The vice president's cronies will have moved to grab their share. Especially on the North Carolina side. Timber and other natural resources are being considered. Billions—not millions, billions—of dollars are at stake."

"There's another factor involved also," Michelle spoke up. "Something Stan may not be aware of. To clear my brother of the murders, I was forced to hire a private investigator. He's good. Much better than I thought."

In the Nova, Jolinda proudly patted Cody on the back.

"He found out we're buying these properties," Michelle went on. "He believes they're tied to the murders."

Staros jumped on it. "Well, my dear, you are his employer. Why not fire him?"

"That's a trap. He's the son of the sheriff, and he'll stay on the case as an undercover deputy. Plus he's squiring around this young snatch named Jolinda, screwing her while he makes like

303

he's staying in this tiny camper trailer. That will keep him here a while. And if I fire him my brother stands a good chance of being convicted."

Ray's eyes bugged. "Undercover deputy? Wow!"

"Young snatch?" Jolinda said from the back seat. "That decrepit, wrinkled old pussy."

"I can see your dilemma," Staros said.

"It'll all blow over when the killer's caught," Bodine jumped in. "I hear on the news the sheriff is close to an arrest. For our plan to succeed, we must be properly positioned when the announcement is made in Washington."

"None of our talk here will bring Mr. Hornsby around, which seems to be our major problem," Staros said. "We should terminate our relationship with your banker friend. I can arrange the needed financing through a group of close associates in Las Vegas. The, vig—uh, interest will be slightly higher, but not out of reach. After all, your profits will be enormous. That old dry goods building you Willinghams bought for a pittance is an ideal spot for a high-rise hotel or one of your Cracker Barrel restaurants. The land alone will be worth a million."

Playing the salesman, Bodine went straight to the advantages of the deal. "The National Park Service's fed up with Gatlinburg. Why, virtually every weekend of the year it's gridlocked with yokels in overheated cars. One damn road through it to the park and nobody moving. Pigeon Forge's just as bad, and you can't get to Gatlinburg without first going through Pigeon Forge."

"We're all sold on the project, Stan," Staros cut him off. "Let's not belabor the obvious. Michelle, Victor, I'll handle the bankers. They're all friends of mine and not subject to nosy bank auditors."

The trio of eavesdroppers waited it out but from that point on it was redundant. Michelle and Victor agreed to keep on keeping on. They spoke for Barry also.

"I can't believe it," Jolinda said. "Highwater Town is going to become another Gatlinburg! Amazing! They could build one of those Sky Lift cable car things up Wolf Mountain right to your cabin, Cody."

"Over my dead body, they can."

"Wait'll I tell the kids at school!"

"Um, Jolinda."

"Oh, shit. I know."

Thirty-five

They finished their pizza, talked a few minutes, then Ray gave them a lift back to their pickup at the hamburger joint. "You in the same motel?" Cody said.

"First one on the left after you come to the river," Ray said. He'd had a full day and was yawning.

"I'm going to the ladies' room," Jolinda said, "and I want another soda with some ice. My mouth's dry after all the pizza."

Cody walked inside and got in line. It was peak business hours so he stood and shuffled, stood and shuffled. Jolinda joined him. They shuffled together.

When they were third in line, Cody looked up and saw a woman headed from the counter carrying a tray loaded with food and drinks. It was Michelle.

She passed inches from him, finally saw him. "Yeeeh!" she yelled, dropping the tray and showering Cody with Coke, ice, and fries. "Jezzus, you scared the tee-total shit out of me," she said loudly as she shook the soft drink from her hands.

Customers gawked like she'd cracked or was drunk.

Cody spread his hands to plead innocent; he had to play it cool. "You've met my pard, Wyatt," he said gesturing to Jolinda with her pistolero mustache.

"Hi, Jolinda," Michelle said, still shaky from the shock. Good God! she thought. Talking about those two just a few minutes ago and here they were right in her face like she had called them by up using some freak mental power.

"Hello, Doctor Willingham." Inwardly Jolinda was cracking up. She thought of calling the older woman a dried-up old cunt.

An employee with a mop and broom scampered toward them through the crowd.

"You must be up to something sneaky, Michelle, jumping like that," Cody said. "Guilty conscience?"

She gave him a quick, direct look, then averted her eyes. "It's just I didn't expect to see you here."

"You're good at scaring the crap out of people," Jolinda said to Cody on the way back to Mountain County.

"Like I said—guilty conscience."

"Like Elwood's?"

"How you like being a detective?"

"It's exciting. But I felt guilty listening in on a conversation I wasn't supposed to hear."

"Not my idea of how to spend an evening," Cody said. "But if it eventually saves a life or stops a killer, it's time well spent."

"You think Michelle's jealous of me? Is that why she says you're in the house screwing me and not out in the camper?"

"Somebody's seen me in the house, or noticed I'm not in the camper while I pull the guard shift. Can't think of where she picked up that bit of info if it's not from somebody that's watching the house. I'm sure gonna find out."

The pager woke him at seven. Still paranoid about the phones, Cody dressed and drove several miles to a service station where he waited ten minutes to make his call. The room clerk rang Ray's room.

"I knitted some socks while I waited," Cody said to Ray's sleepy hello.

"You're the one played reveille."

"Fax on ol' Stan was waiting on me last night when I pulled into the motel. Wasn't anything that couldn't wait."

"So confirm my suspicions."

"Stan the man, only he's got five or six aliases. Stan's had an eventful life. Most notably he's taken three falls in as many states for real estate fraud. He also seems to have forgotten to obtain his Tennessee license."

"We can move on to more pressing matters now," Cody said. "Abandon Bodine and Staros to their individual fates."

"What grabs me as weird about this one is you could've

had Stan Bodine and pal Staros run on the NCIC computer hotline."

"There's a deputy in the department I'm not sure of," Cody said.

"So what's next?"

"A down-and-dirty, get-personal, hometown background check on Randy Gateline."

Ray laughed into the phone. "You got more moves than a rhino on roller skates."

"You're kinda tricky yourself."

Ending the call to Ray, Cody dialed the sheriff at home and filled him in on the real estate shenanigans and Stan Bodine's criminal past.

"You gonna tell Michelle?" he said. He didn't sound fully awake.

"What? And interfere with the flow of the Tao?"

"There's times I don't appreciate your humor. Particularly first thing in the morning."

"I figured I'd start getting on your nerves sooner than later," Cody said. "Next you'll catch the killer just so I'll go back to Nashville."

"We busted the Howler last night."

"Yeah?" Cody said.

"Titus called in. Couldn't get in touch with you. We had deputies in pickups with light bars, on ATVs. Some had their SWAT outfits; don't get much chance to wear 'em. We hit the fire trails, had 'em completely surrounded, one deputy with a night scope on a thirty-aught-six rifle."

"Catch anybody?" Cody humored the sheriff.

"Sure did. Had 'em in the lights. I yelled out over the bullhorn for them to lie facedown and not move. Just like in the movies."

"And?" Cody said. He knew his old man was dragging it out for effect.

"Captured two young boys with a varmint caller. This electronic box about eight inches square. Calling coyotes they said. After they cleaned out their pants we hustled 'em home. Titus was disappointed."

"I'll get him a reward. There's a line on my billing form for informants."

"There's two funerals in town today. Justine Willingham and Carl Taggart. Johnny Knight and Albert Feltus will be mingling. Sharpless's body's being shipped to his family in upstate New York. Bubba's working with a state tech. He'll be videotaping the crowds at the cemetery. Then we'll review the tape to see how different people in the crowd behaved."

"Good thinking."

Cody headed back to the farm for breakfast.

"You plan on telling Michelle this Stan Bodine's a crook?" Jolinda said when he got there.

"I'll let you be the judge. Would the Willinghams take the time to help you if they didn't benefit in some way?" Cody said. He was savoring the aroma of homemade sausage patties sizzling in a big iron skillet. Ogden would have them seasoned with plenty of sage and cayenne peppers.

"Biba would. If it didn't hurt her somehow."

"She'll outgrow it. You heard the discussion at the real estate office—fake real estate office. Anybody mention cutting Joe Sixpack in on the profits? Let the townsfolk in on the secret so everyone can benefit? Did Michelle or Vic bring up the salient point that Uncle Ogden should be offered a million for his property? Since Stan has them believing the land will be worth five mil later on?"

"So you're not going to tell her?" Jolinda said.

"I'm gonna give it some time. Right now I think the killer is killing for anticipated profit on a nonexistent real estate deal. Let him think the profit potential's still there."

"Or let her think," Jolinda said.

"Okay. Have it your way. Let her think." Cody grunted a short laugh.

Jolinda knew Cody was up to something else. He was too quiet. A good sign he was plotting somewhere way back in his head. The suspense was putting her on edge. "Where's Mister Surveillance? Off to Nashville?"

"Ray's off on a well-earned vacation in the North. He really likes it up there. You know the time of the funerals?"

"Justine's at eleven and Carl Taggart's at two. You going?"
"Can't make it. Got more investigating to do."

No cars in the driveway. Cody couldn't tell about the garage. He parked his pickup near the front door, walked up, and rang the doorbell. He was sure Michelle would be at the funeral.

He'd watched her punch in the security code when she was bringing in the groceries, memorized the sequence: seven-six-one-two-seven. Cody waited for an answer to his ring, rang again. Nobody home.

The security touch pad was mounted on the outside wall next to the door. Cody punched in the code. The armed light went out. Three minutes with a lockpick and he was inside.

He moved fast, going to Michelle's bedroom and opening her closet door. It was a large walk-in. He switched on the light. Pausing first, he memorized the layout, then started the search. Her shoes were to the right, all neat and proper on a wire shoe rack. He knew the pair he was looking for, the tan pumps with the low heel. He'd noticed them when they had their dinner meeting at the Tellicafe. They were right in the middle, heels and soles up, as were all the others.

He picked up both shoes and turned them over. Checked the size: nine and a half B.

A long rough scratch marred the left shoe, on the inside near where the ball of her foot would be. Removing a plastic baggie from his pocket, he scraped a few grains of leather from the scratch and let the particles fall into the bag, zipped it closed.

He noticed a bit of caked dirt where the heel meet the sole. He bagged it also. Then he tossed the rest of the closet slowly and carefully, putting everything back in its place.

He checked his watch. He'd been in the house fifteen minutes.

Cody repeated the performance upstairs in Biba's room. Found nothing of interest in the closet. Went to a chest of drawers and struck out. Same with the dresser. Checked his watch. Thirty-five minutes inside.

He looked over Biba's computer and printer. There was not enough time so he didn't turn them on. He checked the wastebasket by the printer stand—empty. Efficient maid.

He found her stash in the bathroom under the sink. A long black wig, a baggie of grass, some pills, and a trace of cocaine. He tossed the linen closet and found nothing else. He trimmed a few strands from the wig, bagged them, then put it back along with the drugs.

Downstairs in the living room he removed the wall plate from the telephone connector, used alligator clips to connect the telephone bug. He replaced the plate, lifted a nearby phone from its cradle, then turned on his portable. He heard the dial tone over the radio's tiny speaker.

Take that, he thought. Two could play that fucking game.

On the front porch he checked his watch again. Forty-seven minutes in and out. Not bad. He reset the alarm, strode to his pickup, got in and left.

Next.

To get to Bubba's house, Cody was forced to drive up a steep incline cut into the side of the mountain. It was rough, rutted, and slick with muddy spots. He remembered the trail from his childhood and recalled it was subject to landslides as the grade dropped away sharply on one side.

A clearing had been cut in the trees one-fourth of a mile from the road's entrance. A grader had leveled a lot large enough for the small frame house and a thirty-by-thirty front yard, plus room for a satellite dish and a driveway. All else was brush and trees.

Cody didn't expect an alarm but found one. He almost walked in and announced his arrival to the world. Luck made him glance at an elongated window by the door and spot the wire.

In the bed of his pickup, under the camper shell, he scrounged in his equipment box and found what he needed—a good-sized magnet.

He guessed the magnetic reed switch would be mounted opposite the bottom of the door. Normally when the door swung open the magnet attached to the door would release from the alarm switch and allow the current to close. The plasticized magnet he held would prevent that—he hoped.

Placing it carefully on the outside of the door facing, Cody squatted and snugged it in place with tape. Standing, he retrieved a sheet of heavy plastic shim stock from his pocket, slipped it in the door latch, and opened the door. The alarm didn't sound, but it might be silent and turn on a red light in the sheriff's office.

Quickly locating the alarm pad on the inside wall behind the door, he breathed a sigh of relief when he saw the alarm light was a solid red. If he'd activated it, it would be blinking.

Bubba's living room was small, with only a couch, a matching chair, and a good-sized Sony Trinitron TV with a stereo and speakers. A hefty barbell set had been rolled to the wall and a bench-press rack placed partially over the long bar.

The bedroom was just as small. The bed was unmade, with blankets, sheet, and pillows stacked in the middle; a pair of jeans and a red shirt lay tossed on the floor at the foot. The small window was filled with an air conditioner that blocked out light— excellent for a cop who sometimes slept in the daytime.

The chest of drawers revealed an assortment of underwear, socks, and belts, and in the back of one drawer, an opened box of personalized checks addressed to Robert Whittlemore. On the top of the chest stood an eight-by-ten picture in a thin wooden frame of a slender black-haired woman with an arm around the shoulders of a twelve-year-old Bubba. Both were smiling and looking directly into the camera. Standing next to it was a slightly smaller snapshot of Robin Kingsly.

Opening the bedroom closet door, Cody first noticed the transceiver on the top shelf. He recognized it as a ten-meter ham rig. Bubba must know something about electronics.

He checked out the closet carefully. Just as he had done at Michelle's, he didn't move anything from its place without returning it at once. The closet was tiny, mostly taken up with uniform shirts and pants.

Something bothered him about the place, but he couldn't nail it in his mind. The bathroom was loaded with shaving gear and cleaning supplies. The kitchen was a claustrophobe's nightmare. Bombed out here, he thought, ready to leave. Then it hit him.

Back in the bedroom closet he tapped on the walls, found the fake one. There were two small latches, one at the top, one at the bottom. It was a tight squeeze but a panel swung out to reveal a recess almost entirely filled by a steel gun safe loaded with pistols, rifles, and a pump shotgun. Nothing was strange about that in this neck of the woods.

He found the laptop computer down beside the gun safe. He picked it up and flipped it open, saw it had the latest high-speed chip and active color. There was also a plug for a telephone line and a built-in CD-ROM drive. So Bubba was into computers as well. Probably had a built-in modem for going on-line.

The photo album was in a plastic sack on top of the gunsafe. Cody hesitated to check it. Too personal. He changed his mind, noted its position, then lifted it carefully out of the bag. There was no dust on the shiny cover.

He propped it on the chest of drawers and opened it. The first shot he saw was a picture of Bubba and Biba. They were out in the country beside a road, sitting side by side on the hood of a cruiser. Biba's head was on Bubba's shoulder, his arm was around her waist. Bubba had on his deputy's uniform; Biba wore short-shorts and a skimpy halter. Her white Dodge Stealth was parked in the background. The snapshot was loose, unlike all the others in the album, which were neatly placed on the pages with corner tabs.

Damn incestuous county, Mountain County. Peyton Place on steroids.

He flipped the first page and saw a picture of his dad. He stood, a much younger man than now, between the woman in the picture on the chest of drawers and Bubba, aged twelve. One arm encircled the woman's waist, the other rested on young Bubba's shoulder, hugged him close. He was caught in the middle of a pleasurable laugh.

There were other pictures of the sheriff scattered throughout the album. One was of Bubba's high school graduation, another as he received his college diploma in cap and gown.

Cody replaced the album, accidently hitting something that made a rattling sound as it fell to the floor. He stooped and picked it up—a small, brown pill bottle with a twist-off cap.

When he looked inside, he saw a wide assortment of pills. He replaced the cap, noticed the lack of a label, and returned it to the shelf, replacing the panel and leaving the house quietly. At the last minute he remembered to remove the taped-on magnet.

Thirty-six

"You come to the county so seldom," the whisperer said. "I'm gonna find me somebody can give it to me just as good as you do, only twice as often."

"Goddamn, woman. I'm over there two, three times a week. What the hell you expect?"

"I just want what I need and I need what I want. That's what I expect. You been doing it with your old lady so much lately, you don't have any left over for me."

Scanner listened closely for the slightest clue. Don't I know you, bitch? Who are you?

"You do understand I have a job, don't you?"

"I understand I lie here in the bed thinking about it. I need it so bad I go crazy."

"You sure your old man can't hear you?"

"Just a minute. I'll go check," she whispered.

Fuck her, Scanner thought. He wasn't going to let her drive him berserk. He flipped the membrane switch to monitor another call.

* * *

"How was the flight?" Cody asked.

"When the plane lands here in Harrisburg, it flies right over Three Mile Island. My ass was biting button-holes in the seat covers. I'm staring down inside the hole of this nuclear cooling tower wondering how much radiation's hitting my gonads. Then the pilot brings it across the river and right when you think of grabbing the seat cushion as a flotation device, he touches down on the runway. Wore out three rosaries."

Cody knew Ray was brought up Baptist. "You locked onto a target yet?"

"You kidding me? Just found a room. I'll start the search tomorrow. The hump being born here and having a sister named Regina that's sick a lot is not what I would call a glut of info. So tomorrow I'll have to hit the bricks, check back issues of phone books at the libraries, make a nuisance of myself at the courthouse. Woe is me."

"'Woe is you's right, you don't dig up something."

"You think this mutt's the killer?" Ray said.

"Don't know. He's calm and collected. Ambitious. Don't think he would risk his future. He's involved with the Willinghams though. I wanta know how involved."

"If I had a late picture of him, I'd show it to all the blondes and redheads in town," Ray said. "Bet they'll know him. And I'll hit all the fried chicken joints."

Later that evening, Jolinda's mood was solemn, a result of attending two funerals in one day, Cody surmised. She ate little, talked less, and went to swing in the porch swing after supper.

He let her alone for a while, talked to Ogden about how they would handle household security that night. As usual for him, Cody kept his information to himself. Not that he thought Jolinda or Ogden might repeat it. It was ingrained habit, drilled into him at training sessions at intelligence school, carried over into police work, then naturally continued when he became a P.I.

The news carried coverage of the funerals, with reporters up in everyone's face wondering when the killer would be tracked down and apprehended. An anchorwoman with bright red hair spoke at length of the fear in Highwater Town and the surrounding county. Three locals, when interviewed, expressed anxiety over their own safety and apprehension for the welfare of loved ones.

"What it feels like," said one young woman with a microphone held under her nose, "is there's somebody always there, hiding and watching me. You know how it is when somebody keeps staring at you and you can feel it on the back of your neck?

That's how it is. We live along this lonely road and at night, I always feel like someone's behind me, and when I turn to look, they're somehow behind me in the other direction. And somebody's just on the other side of the door, crouching and listening, waiting to pounce."

There was a close-up shot of Barry at Justine's funeral. Stonefaced, eyes downcast, he walked away from the grave with Victor and refused to be interviewed. In the background Michelle supported a weeping Biba. Walking along behind all glum and downcast was the young son, Edmund, home temporarily from boarding school.

Barry looks guilty as hell, Cody thought. Realized a large percentage of the viewing audience who bothered to track the case would be thinking the same.

He joined Jolinda on the porch when the coverage became redundant.

She glanced up when Cody approached. Remained silent when he timed an outward swing and plopped down beside her.

"Kinda sad, huh?"

"Yeah," she said. "I watched Becky at the Taggart funeral. There she is with children to raise and her husband's gone."

Cody didn't answer for a while, kicked the swing a little higher, then coasted. "She's young. She may remarry. Find a good man to help her raise the kids."

"I was putting myself in her place," Jolinda said. "It'll be tough."

"How did Biba act at her mother's funeral?"

"Doctor Willingham must've had her on something. She was crying but she acted numb, like she couldn't focus on anything."

Cody waited a minute before he continued. He was deep in thought. "Michelle? How did she behave? She seem overcome by grief?"

"I don't think she liked Justine a whole lot. Some say she considered her trash. Doctor Willingham never socialized with Justine, mostly stayed away from her own brother's house after he married her except for the mandatory occasions like Thanksgiving and Christmas. At the funeral, Doctor Willingham was—I don't know how to put it exactly. Matter of fact? She

317

wasn't smiling, of course, but she didn't seem too sad either. You think Michelle's the killer?"

"Now wait a minute, honey. Michelle's paying the bills. Let's don't go accusing her of any crimes except greed."

"It wouldn't surprise me if she killed Justine. Maybe somebody else killed the others. Doctor Willingham could've killed Justine because of Biba."

Cody stopped the swing, leaned forward and stared at Jolinda. "Killed her because of Biba? Now why would she do that?"

"Biba's like a daughter to Doctor Willingham. And the doctor didn't approve of the way Justine was raising her. I've thought about it some. She could've just gotten rid of her, and Sanford Sharpless too."

"Why?"

"I remember last year, Biba was telling me Doctor Willingham was raising hell with her mother about something. I think she took Biba along a couple of times when she was seeing other men."

"I've wondered along that line also," Cody said. "You think she took Biba out to Sanford Sharpless's cabin?"

"I heard she'd been out there and that she'd been smoking some grass. And one of the kids said something about them sniffing gas. Not gasoline. You know, the gas they give you at a dentist."

"Nitrous oxide?" Cody said.

"That's it," Jolinda said. "They had it in balloons."

"Did Michelle find out about that?"

"I don't know. But I bet if she did and Justine had taken her out there, Doctor Willingham would've killed her if she got the chance."

Later, Cody took the sawed-off and checked the barn, walked the fence perimeter, and scoped out the fields. The mules were more familiar with him now and trotted along for a few hundred yards. After completing his walking rounds he climbed in his pickup and drove back and forth on Stecoah Road to cover both directions.

Thirty-seven

The fierce autumn storm lashed Wolf's Head Mountain with gale-force winds, a drenching rain, and heavy booms of thunder. Fingers of lightning snapped and bit at some of the taller firs, lighting them up like Christmas trees when high electrical currents danced along their branches. In the valley below, an ominous Stygian darkness kept the already overwrought inhabitants of Highwater Town looking over their shoulders in fear. It was as if a grim practical joker, aware of the terror the act would cause, had thrown a thick blanket over the town and sat back laughing at the results. In many houses all the lights were on, doors and windows were locked tight. Moisture hung so heavy in the air that the few streetlights in town were surrounded by glowing halos.

The savings and loan's silent alarm logged the incident at 8:40 P.M. An alert console operator called the Mountain County sheriff's night dispatcher with the proper codes. The radio signal went out. First, a warbling, five-second tone, then the announcement of the male dispatcher. "Mountain County to all units, code one thousand A, silent alarm at Mountain County Savings and Loan. Be advised front door sensor and inside motion detector show a ten-fifty-eight-P in progress, prowler on the premises."

"Unit delta, going. One minute away," Bubba Whittlemore responded.

"Ten-four, unit delta. All available units, signal six, assist unit delta at Mountain County Savings and Loan. Code one thousand P. Mountain County Sheriff's Office. K.I.A. eleven-forty-five, twenty-forty-two."

Bubba sped his cruiser down Cove Road at eighty-plus. He'd engaged the blue emergency lights and the module that alternated the right and left headlights. He kept his hand near the switch for the siren in case one of the residents pulled out of a driveway in front of him. Customers in the Cove Road Cafe & Ice Cream Parlor saw the combination of pulsating white and blue lights and ran out onto the sidewalk across from the savings and loan to gawk.

The deputy misjudged his speed as he skidded into the bank's parking lot, stood on the brakes in a smoking squall of locked-up tires. He had the cruiser in park and was on the pavement before it stopped rocking. The shrill rising and falling wail of sirens sounded in the distance as his backups zoned in.

Inside the bank, a man ran for the glass front door, silhouetted against the interior lights.

Bubba drew his weapon.

The ice cream parlor crowd "Ooohhed," and stepped back a few steps.

Barry Willingham threw the bank door open. Blood covered the front of his shirt. He stood there a few seconds, confused, a look of disbelief stamped on his face. Then he headed down the fifty feet of walkway that separated him from Bubba.

"Freeze!" Bubba said, going into a shooter's crouch. He turned the right side of his body toward Barry to present a more difficult target. He aimed his pistol at Barry's chest.

Barry slowed. "I'm in real trouble!" he sobbed. "Horace is dead." He took three more halting steps, then stopped and looked around him, spied the crowd across the street.

Straightening slightly, Bubba crouched forward. "I want you facedown on the sidewalk! Now! Hands out to the side. Now! Move!"

Casting a glance at the stunned spectators, Barry moved a few steps forward. Those people were his neighbors. "Let me explain!" he yelled.

"Barry, I don't want to hurt you. Get down on your knees first, then flat on your face. Do it, man, do it!"

Barry's hands went up to his tear-streaked cheeks, then he realized the reaction could be taken as a threatening motion. He stared at the blood on his hands, then went to his knees.

Two more cruisers arrived in a frenzy of sirens, flashing lights, and slamming doors.

"Let me—"

"I mean it, Barry. Facedown on the sidewalk." Bubba moved forward, lowered his pistol to cover Barry's chest.

Barry finally acquiesced, let go of his ruling-class image. Swallowing his pride, he rocked forward on his hands, lowered his chest to the hard concrete and ate dirt like common folk.

Bubba was on him in a flash, cuffed him. "Watch him for me, Buford," he yelled to an approaching deputy. Bubba made his way to the bank's front door. Knowing what waited for him inside, he opened it and went in.

Arms pulled high and clasped over his head as if to protect himself in death, pants and boxer shorts pulled to bent knees now locked to his chest, Horace Hornsby's body lay curled on its side in a fetal position. Blood spread out before him like a gruesome Rorschach. Red tributaries flowed under his desk.

Bubba squatted and leaned sideways to see the handle of the hunting knife protruding from the dead man's chest. He reached for his walkie. "Unit delta to Mountain County S.O."

"Go ahead."

"Mountain County, we have a ten-fifty-one victim deceased. You wanta notify Sheriff Rainwalker at his Station R. Suspect is in custody."

"Ten-four, unit delta. You have an I.D. on the suspect?"

"'At's ten-four. Suspect is Barry Willingham."

"This is unit one," the sheriff drawled over his walkie. "All units signal sixteen this incident."

The news spread like wildfire through the county. Customers at the Cove Road Cafe & Ice Cream Parlor called home. The killer had been caught. The media monitoring the police bands were ecstatic. They could write that long-awaited story and return to civilization. Half the town converged on the scene.

At the farm, Cody had been thumbing through one of Ogden's latest acquisitions, *The Audubon Society Field Guide to North American Trees, Eastern Region*. He'd placed his walkie on the coffee table in front of him and was studying the range of red spruce and the virgin spruce and fir forests still standing in the Great Smoky Mountains National Park. He realized with pride that these same great trees also found safe haven on his mountaintop.

He ignored the silent alarm call. Most were false anyway, an employee forgetting the alarm and opening a door. But when he heard Barry was in custody, he called to Ogden, who was in his bedroom thumbing through the *Farmer's Almanac,* and told him what happened.

"You going to the bank?" Ogden said.

"There'll be plenty of folks there. I'm thinking of running over to Michelle's, see if she's home, have a little chat. Funny thing about Bubba. Always first on the scene, just like at Samantha's."

Ogden studied him carefully. "You're thinking Michelle coulda done this, let Barry take the fall? And maybe she's somehow in cahoots with Bubba?"

"Don't know what to think. May be some sibling rivalry in the family. There was a witness report of a woman fleeing the scene at Samantha's. Either her or Bubba could easily get close to Hornsby. Do I stand relieved of guard duty?"

Ogden snapped to attention. "You are hereby relieved. I'll get the shotgun."

Turning off Cataloochie Road into Michelle's driveway, Cody was immediately confronted by a heavy patch of fog reflecting his headlights back in his eyes, cutting his vision to a few feet. Then he was through it and into a lighter mist. Moisture clung to the short needles of the hemlocks lining the drive. Droplets of water fell to his windshield like second-hand rain.

There was no one home. Biba's Stealth and the doctor's Blazer were nowhere in sight. He thought about letting himself inside again but reconsidered and drove back down the drive toward the road. He found a dirt road several hundred feet from the driveway entrance and backed in to wait.

An hour and fifteen minutes later Michelle droned by and turned into her drive.

He made note of the time but did not move. Five minutes later she was on the phone. He could hear the tones as she dialed.

"Hello?" Cody recognized Victor's voice.

"Message on my machine said urgent," Michelle said.

"It's happened again. Barry's been arrested."

"Oh, shit! What happened?"

Victor told her of the murder of Hornsby.

"Oh, God. What's next? I told Barry to stay away from Horace."

"I don't know all the details yet. Where've you been?"

"Looking for Biba. She's disappeared again. She gets upset and just takes off."

"You think she's up at Sonny Todd's?"

"Didn't think of that. I'll call and check, then I'll go down to the jail and see what's going on. I never thought a Willingham would have to go to the jail like common trash to see a locked-up relative. It's humiliating!"

"Call me when you find out something," Victor said.

Michelle's next call was apparently to the Reverend Sonny Todd. The phone rang twenty times before she gave it up.

She dialed another number right away. "Wilderness Gorge Motel and Resort. How may I direct your call?"

"Mister Richard Staros, please."

"Hello?" a male voice answered a moment later.

"Thank God you're there," Michelle said.

"What's going on?" She filled him in.

"What's happening in that one-horse town?" he asked. "Probably haven't had a murder in five or ten years; we try to do some business and it's genocide time. Only thing I know to do is keep our heads down."

"You're right, of course, but it's one hell of a distraction. When can I see you? I'm all tight and nervous."

"Why don't you drive on over now?" he said.

"You talked me into it. I was gonna go by the jail but there's probably wall-to-wall television crews out front just waiting for me to come lumbering down the sidewalk."

Cody watched Michelle pass him in the Blazer. He bided his time for another hour to see if Biba would show, then gave it up and left.

The Mountain Church of Jesus was only five miles away. He took a slow drive by the front of the place. It was dark and he

323

didn't see any cars. He passed it again, went down the road, and turned around in a dirt driveway. Back at the church he turned in the drive and drove up to a log barricade and stopped, getting out of his pickup.

As he walked up the drive to the mobile home he glanced into the woods on his left. He felt nervous without a flashlight. The area was as quiet as a graveyard and as black as the inside of a cave.

The shadow of the double-wide loomed over him. He felt for the door and knocked. Waited. Knocked again. There was no answer.

Around the back, he peeked into a window. The only light inside was from a computer monitor. The flickering screensaver gave off enough light to show him no one was at the keyboard.

He went to the front door again and knocked louder. There was still no answer.

He was backing away from the barricade to turn around in the church lot when he spotted headlights coming up the road. He switched off his lights, got out of his truck, and stepped around behind it.

The Jeep Cherokee pulled into the driveway and stopped. "Three-eighty. You wanta get some safety cones from the County Road Department. Put 'em around the front of the S.O. to keep the crowd back." Cody heard Wanda June's voice blasting from the police-band radio inside the Jeep.

"'At's ten-four."

Whoever was driving the Jeep hit the brights and illuminated Cody's truck. He stepped partially into view.

"Hello," called Sonny. "You're sure visiting late. To what do we owe the honor? You have a spiritual awakening?" He cut the headlights.

Cody had kept one eye closed when the headlights hit his face. He'd learned the trick in the service. When a flare turned night into day, it ruined your night vision. At least now he had night vision in one eye. He stepped toward the Jeep.

The interior lights came on as Sonny opened the driver's door. Cody saw Brandy on the passenger side.

"Whatcha got in your hand there, Sonny?"

"Pistol. Didn't know who was here."

"Wanta put it away?"

"Sure. Here. I'll toss it on the seat."

"Put it on the top of the car and step away."

"Huh?"

"Top of the car. Let me hear it."

"Oh, I get it," Sonny said. "Don't want me to toss it to Ma Barker. Have her come out with six guns blazing."

"Let me hear it."

"You got it, Cody." He clunked the pistol to the roof of the Jeep.

Cody walked to the driver's side and positioned himself where he could keep an eye on Brandy through the open door. "You hear about the killing?"

"Heard all the hullabaloo. Knew something was going on. We didn't know there had been another killing, though."

"Horace Hornsby was murdered."

"Oh no! Did they catch the killer?" Sonny said.

Brandy reached to the rear seat for a sack of groceries and slid out the passenger side, then walked around the front of the car to join them. She stopped beside Sonny.

Cody gave himself some room. Moved back two steps. "Caught Barry in the bank with blood all over him."

Sonny threw up his hands in exasperation. "Then you don't have the killer. Barry's not the type. I don't know him well, but Justine did. She told me there was no violence in Barry."

"You better get down to the S.O. and tell the media. They got him tried, convicted, and in the electric chair. Been grocery shopping?"

"That and grabbed a pizza and took in a movie over in Sweetwater. We've got a new database query program running a debug on the computer. Even at thirty-six K-baud, it'll take forever," Sonny said.

"You out here checking up on us?" Brandy said.

"Don't feel too honored," Cody said. "I've been checking a lot of folks tonight. See anybody you know over in Sweetwater?"

"We were talking about that earlier tonight," Brandy said. "It seems we never see anyone we know when we go out. Weird. We know a lot of people, members here at church, but we never see them around town."

"What Cody's getting at," Sonny said, "is can we prove where we were and when."

"Oh," Brandy said. "We can tell you the name of the movie, and I know the girl that waited on us at the pizza place. Don't know about the times, though. Do you, Sonny?"

"Not enough to swear to. Are you implying that we're suspects?"

"I'm just checking around right now. Seeing where folks were when the crime went down. Lot of people out and about tonight."

The media swarm around the sheriff's office forced Cody to park down the street. They spotted him headed up the walk and converged, shouted questions, blinded him with flashes and video-camera floods. "Is your client's brother guilty of murder, Mr. Rainwalker?" a reporter shouted.

"Of course not."

"Are you here to confer with the suspect?"

"Is he here?"

"Yes," a chorus answered him.

"Then I'll confer." A deputy stood back to allow him entrance, then quickly moved to block the reporters.

"You tell the press anything?" the sheriff asked Cody just inside the doorway. He looked harried. A folder was clutched in his hand. He used it to motion Cody to follow him into his office.

"Ever'thing I know," Cody said.

"Which is?"

"Not a damn thing."

"Least we got the same info."

"How's Barry holding up?" Cody asked. Once in the tiny office, Cody grabbed the wooden chair. With no conscious thought, he watched the closed-circuit TV monitor as it flitted from one jailhouse scene to another.

The sheriff leaned against the wall and beat his leg with the folder. "Blubbering. Says he didn't hurt nobody. Says it over and over. I'm letting him calm down then I'll go talk to him some more. Hopefully Monk can be sobered up enough to put in an appearance."

"Horace was stabbed, I heard. What else?"

After drawing a deep breath and letting it out slowly, the sheriff walked to his desk and perched on its edge. "Murderer used one of Barry's real expensive hunting knives, has this elk horn handle on it. A Bowie knife, really. A big one. Fourteen-inch blade."

"That's a machete."

"Probably cost Barry better'n five hundred dollars. Another expensive toy. Knife had a good slant on it when it entered the body or it woulda exited the back. Poor ol' Horace had his pants and drawers pulled down and was tagged on the pecker with a blue ribbon. Steel tag driven right through the head of it, gave me the shivers. Found the clamper under his desk. It's a tool farmers use to tag the ears of their livestock."

"The supposed theory that Barry's tagging the dicks of all the guys that humped his wife?"

"If it is, I hope he's got a big roll of ribbon." The sheriff looked sheepish. "Now, I shouldn't have said that."

"Anything else?"

"We've finally got us a crime scene. We're bound to have fibers, and hairs and prints, forensic science stuff just like the big-city boys. We've followed the book, minimized contamination of the evidence, just like Luther should've done—and we'd had our killer if he had. Too bad we can't prosecute him. We may even have a witness if we get lucky."

"What does Barry say?" Cody said.

"Before he fell apart, he blurted out that Horace called him at home, asked him to come to his office. Said he'd found out what had happened to mess up Barry's account and he saw a way to advance more money for the loans."

"I'll wait until in the morning to talk to him." Cody fumbled in his pocket and brought out an envelope. "You believe Barry?"

"Fella recently showed me a phone trick," the sheriff said. "I dialed my pager on the office extension. Then I had Bubba hit redial on Horace's phone. Low and behold, Barry's home number appeared on my pager."

"Neato. You think it's another setup? Or is Barry sharp enough to dial the number in case someone checked?"

"Bubba's leaning toward Barry being the killer. Still, I've got deputies going all over the bank, interviewing folks next door at the ice cream parlor, going from door to door in the area. Hopefully we'll come up with something."

Cody slapped the envelope against his hand, wanted to get up and pace, but the room was too small. "Did wily entrepreneur Randy Gateline happen to be next door at his newly acquired ice cream parlor?"

"Matter of fact, I heard he was. He was questioned and it'll be in a report. Don't know how wide the window of opportunity is here. If Barry's telling the truth, Horace could've been killed an hour or even two hours before he arrived. We'll have to get a good handle on time of death."

"Bubba was the first one on the scene," Cody said. "Mighty handy."

"Still beating that horse?"

"Making an observation. Oh yeah—I found Cinderella."

"Cind . . . Who?"

Cody took the clear baggie from the envelope and handed it to his dad. "Read it and weep. Leather particles from a size nine-and-a-half shoe with a nasty ol' scratch." He forked over the other baggie. "Dried dirt from same."

"Who?"

"Sure you wanta hear it?" Cody said.

"Michelle?"

"Glad to see you're still alert at this hour."

The sheriff stood and walked around his desk. He opened a drawer and brought out a roll of masking tape, tore off a strip, placed it on his desk and started to write on it.

"No," Cody said.

"I'm going to mark these as evidence."

"I broke into her house and put the snatch on it."

"Then they can't be used," the sheriff said.

"It's info, at least. And here's another mystery solved." Cody handed over the baggie with the black hair from the wig.

"What's this? Michelle dyeing her wuss?"

"You oughta know, saw your initials carved on her head-board," Cody snapped back. "What we have here is trimmings from the black wig Biba wore when she applied for the mail drop over in Madisonville. One used to pick up the bugs."

The sheriff considered his son. "I didn't take a vow of celibacy when I took office. Only that I'd uphold the law. Biba? Setting up her own father?"

"Don't know. The further I get into this shit the less I under-stand it. If I'd stop investigating now I bet I'd be money ahead."

The sheriff put the baggies in his desk drawer and closed it. "Any more gems of wisdom you wanna drop on me tonight, or you think I'm confused enough?"

"I heard the call come in, drove over to Michelle's, and sorta hid down the road. She didn't show until about two hours after the report of the alarm. Biba hadn't shown an hour later when I gave it up."

"Well goddamn. Maybe we should lock the whole family up. Then if the killings stop, we've got 'em."

Cody knew when the old man'd had enough. He stood and walked to the door. "I'll leave the case in your capable hands."

"You find some more confusion, don't hesitate to call."

"I'll do that. You got a back door I can use?" Cody asked.

"All smart-asses leave out the front."

Thirty-eight

"Look, Cody!" Jolinda called to him from the living room the next evening. "You're on the news."

He picked up his coffee and a country ham and biscuit from the kitchen table and joined her on the couch. The shot showed him arriving and refusing to speak to reporters. His departure was just as forthcoming.

"Why aren't you talking to the reporters?" Jolinda asked.

"A private detective's mode of operation is keeping out of the limelight. What chance do you have of following someone if they know who you are and what you're up to?"

"Ever'body in Mountain County knows you anyway."

"Well, ever'body in Nashville don't. And I want it to stay that way."

"If I had a business and I could get some free press, I'd take it in a heartbeat. You get well known you can hire the followers and all those nosy men to peep into folks' bedrooms. You're just dumb and you're not thinking ahead. When we get married, I'd rather have you at home looking at me than at some naked woman through a keyhole."

Cody squirmed on the couch. Jolinda was the only person who could talk to him like this. And he was beginning to wonder why he let her. "Honey, most of my cases are insurance cases. Seeing if the claimant is actually hurt or running some sort of scam."

"I remember you telling me insurance companies are a pack of assholes, and they'll pull any trick to keep from paying. You said they're in the business of collecting premiums, not paying claims."

"Sure some memory you've got," Cody said. "Bet you ace all your senior exams."

330

"Whata you think, I'm stupid? You have any real suspects in the killings?"

"Me? I'm just the guy brought in from outa town to help Barry."

"Well remind me not to hire you to help me," Jolinda said. "I don't want to end up in the slammer."

"You don't understand."

"I understand he's not home. And I don't believe he killed anybody."

"I don't either," Cody said. "Somebody's setting him up."

"You know who?"

"When I know who, I'll have the killer."

Sheriff Rainwalker's voice sounded from the television. It was from last night's interview in front of the bank. "Barry Willingham was captured at the scene. He is a suspect in the murder. Please note I did not say Barry Willingham is a murderer. He is a suspect and presumed innocent until proven guilty. Thank you, ladies and gentlemen. That's all I have. Goodnight."

"Your dad really handles the press. What're you gonna do today to earn your money?" Jolinda said.

"Not talk to the media, that's for certain. Think I'll go out to the pasture. See if I can still ride one of the mules."

"That sounds productive."

Back in Harrisburg, Ray Blizzard considered the two-story Victorian in front of him. It was right out of Vincent Price and badly in need of paint. What a gloomy-looking dump. Must film all the horror movies here. The house had once been a pale green; now it looked camouflaged. Vines growing up the front wall of the house were beginning to turn to their autumn colors. The walkway was cracked and crumbled. Grass grew unchecked in the wider gaps.

The heavy iron gate swung open easily on well-oiled hinges. He noticed the boards on the front steps were loose and rotted along the edges. The porch swing was rusted, and leaves had blown in piles next to the wall and railings. The screen door was unlocked. He swung it open and knocked on the glass oval in the heavy wooden door.

Earlier, in his hotel room, Ray had watched Cody on TV. Things were going from hot to scorching, and the client was back in jail. Ray had spent the previous day in the library and court-house looking up old addresses, deeds, death certificates, law-suits, and marriages—anything relating to the Gatelines.

He couldn't locate Regina Gateline. She'd not married there, bought a home there, signed up for electric there, or the best he could tell, ever had a phone in Harrisburg or the surrounding area.

He'd decided to go to the old neighborhood and ask around. Coldiron was the name of the family now residing in the old house, according to the name on the mailbox. Wallace Gateline had died when Randy was eighteen. Cody'd said Samantha'd told him the mother died a few years later. She may have moved, then died.

The first neighbor wasn't very helpful. She was aged and bent and wouldn't unlock the screen, remaining half hidden behind a green metal door. "Gateline? Never heard of them. Only lived here three years," she said, brushing back a thin wisp of gray hair. "Don't know the other neighbors either. Don't want to."

The neighborhood had the appearance of a once-elegant sub-urb gone to seed. Dilapidated old cars were parked along the curbs. People walking the streets looked beaten down, avoided direct looks. A result of high unemployment, Ray thought. But didn't we have low inflation? Cheer up, folks. Wall Street's doing great.

The next house he went to was better kept—a one-story brick with white painted shutters and a new roof. The grass was trimmed and the walk was swept clean of falling leaves. The lady who answered the door was obviously a holdover from the old neighborhood, with some of its lost refinement. Her voice was low, cultured. She left the screen locked, her hand on the main door, ready to slam it in his face.

"Yes? May I help you?" she asked.

Ray flashed an official-looking fake I.D. "Yes ma'am. Sorry to bother you. I'm conducting a background check on Randy Gateline. Do you know him?"

"Why yes, I remember Randy. He was a beautiful child and a

handsome young man. All the young girls liked him."

"Yes ma'am," Ray said. "That's the same Randy." He wondered if she'd know about the fried chicken.

"What's he done?"

"Nothing naughty, ma'am," Ray joked. "Randy's been nominated by the governor of Tennessee to take a seat on the state pharmaceutical board. All board members must pass a rigid background investigation. That's why I'm here."

"Now isn't that just grand. Randy was always a shy child. He never had any trouble at school that I heard of. He never created turmoil in the neighborhood. His sister, Regina—if one didn't know there was a year's difference in their ages, one would think them twins. The resemblance was simply amazing. You'd have to see it to believe it. Poor Regina. I hear she's ill."

Ray held his notebook across one wrist, writing notes. "Where does Regina live now?"

"I don't know. Randy and Regina left home at the same time as I recall. Shortly after their father died. He left a small estate, I understand. Enough for them both to attend good schools. That's so important, don't you think?"

"Oh, yes ma'am. Absolutely."

"They were strange, you know. Very eccentric."

"Randy and Regina?" Ray asked.

"The parents. Once I heard the mother sitting on the front porch having this animated discussion with another woman. When I passed the front of the house I discovered she was alone, carrying on both sides of the conversation."

Ray looked up to make sure she wasn't putting him on. He saw the sincere look, then wrote a few notes. "Fortunately, Randy's mother being kinda strange won't cancel his nomination."

"Well, I should hope not. Wallace was the father's name. He was strange also. A very strict disciplinarian, he was. Many times I overheard him dressing down those two children for their behavior. I think he believed in physical punishment to the extreme. Mr. Auretta conveyed to me on one occasion at least he had noticed bruises on both children."

"Mr. Auretta?" Ray asked.

"Yes. Michael Auretta. He was their history teacher at the high school. You may want to talk to him. He would know much more about Randy than I do. Randy was his student for a number of years. His name is in the local directory. He's retired now."

"Thank you. Can you think of anyone else who may have direct knowledge of Randy's character?"

"No. You've talked to his mother, of course."

"His mother? She's not deceased?"

"Oh, no. She married Mr. Coldiron shortly after the children left home. Then a year later, he had that horrible accident."

"Accident?"

"Yes. He fell from his bedroom window and impaled himself on a pointed rod of the iron fence that runs along the side of the house. Sharp as a lance. I heard his screams that night. It was horrible."

"I bet it was," Ray said.

Ray hoped the old broad wasn't home. He could visualize her crouched behind the door with a razor-sharp butcher knife, mumbling to herself. She opened the door so quickly after his knock it scared him.

"What you want?" Mrs. Coldiron demanded. She was tall and emaciated. Her cheeks were hollow, her chin long and pointed. A garish slash of lipstick was smeared across her mouth. The rouge highlighting her cheekbones was dark brown. Two ball-bearing eyes bore into Ray. She'd tried to dye her hair red and failed; it had ended up a yellowish orange.

"It's about your son, Randy," Ray said.

"What about the bastard? He die? Leave me some insurance to fix up this falling-down mausoleum?" She stayed halfway behind the door.

Ray was convinced she clutched at least a bayonet behind her back, maybe a grenade. "No ma'am." He went through the same spiel he had handed the neighbor.

"Bullshit. He sent you here to spy on me. Him and his sister, neither one of them were ever worth a shit. Don't know why I didn't abort both of them. Randy never had any respect for his father."

"No ma'am. This is an official investigation. Your son is being considered for an important job."

"Well, fuck him! And fuck you too, you dopey-looking little shit. Now get your ass offa my porch or I'm gonna turn the god-damn doberman loose on you."

Thirty-nine

There were still a few die-hards hanging on at the S.O. when Cody arrived the next morning. His shoulder was sore where the mule'd thrown him, but he felt better about the ordeal. His ego was more bruised than his body. He'd remounted Rosencranz, who stood stock still after bucking him off, and surprise of surprises, the animal'd made a few halfhearted attempts at sending him over the fence, hawing and kicking, then relented and gone galloping around the pasture with him on board. He'd felt like a teenager again.

He parked in between two cruisers and headed for the front door.

"Mr. Rainwalker," an attractive brunette called to him. A burly cameraman trailed her with his camera riding his shoulder. "You have avoided commenting on the case up until this point. Is there a reason for your silence or are you just bashful?"

Cody stopped and turned to face her, smiled directly into the video-cam aimed over her shoulder. "To tell the truth, ma'am . . ."

"Sandra."

"And call me Cody, please. To tell the truth, Sandra, I've been too busy tracking leads in this case to give interviews. Then, of course, I have the confidentiality of my client to consider."

"Do you feel at all odd about working at cross-purposes with your father on this case? After all, he's trying to convict Mr. Willingham and you are working to clear him."

Cody relaxed before he answered, considered carefully what he was going to say. "My father and I are working toward the same end—to catch the killer holding this county in a grip of terror. When that end is accomplished, my client's brother will be cleared of all charges."

"Are you following any new leads?"

"The sheriff has already announced he's uncovered interesting twists in Luther Hamby's investigative notes. Luther might have been close to an arrest before his murder. My father has shared that information with me, and I am working that particular lead at this time. I can tell you it concerns the veracity of a certain person's alibi. Now if you will excuse me, I need to confer inside." He went toward the front door.

"Glad to hear we're close to an arrest," the sheriff said. He'd opened the door and overheard the interview with Cody. "Let me know when it goes down."

"Barry in?"

"Check with his secretary." The sheriff jerked a thumb toward the cells.

"I'm really in some deep shit now," Barry said a few minutes later. His eyes were red from lack of sleep, and his hair needed a comb run through it.

"That's a slight understatement," Cody said. "You wanta fill me in?"

Barry's hangdog expression was back. He slouched on the jail bunk, a portrait of dismay. "Horace called me about eight. Said he'd found what was wrong with my account. I told him to get it corrected and started to hang up when he said I could have the loan."

"The loan?"

"Yeah. We had this big row earlier because he wouldn't approve any more borrowing on my property. So he said he was ready to approve the loan and for me to come on over."

"After hours?" Cody watched Barry's facial expression closely to pick up on any deception.

"Yeah. He said he was working late and he wanted to make it up to me about the mistakes. He sounded real nervous."

Cody visualized the knife held to Hornby's throat while he made the call. "So you showed up?"

"Horace said he'd leave the door unlocked. Said to come on in and he'd be in his office working," Barry said.

"And what did you find when you got there?"

"The lights were off, and I thought he'd gone home. So I pushed on the door and it opened. When I called out, there was no answer. There was light from the street so I walked on through the part where the teller windows are and went into his office. Then I reached inside and turned on the lights."

Cody had settled on the opposite end of the cot from Barry. He nodded, rocking his head and shoulders. He thought he understood the plan, and it was brilliant. Took a lot of guts to pull it off. "And you saw Horace."

"He was lying there, all curled up. I bent down and tried to turn him to check if he's alive, and I got blood all over my hands. I tried to wipe it off on my shirt. Then I saw my hunting knife sticking outa his chest, and I panicked. I wanted to get the hell outa there. When I ran out the door Bubba was standing there with a pistol pointed at me. And that's it. I had to get down on my face in front of ever'body."

"Did anybody else know you were going to the bank?"

Barry thought a minute. "No. I called Michelle. But she wasn't home."

"Did you pass a cruiser on the way over? See Bubba? Anything like that?"

"I could have but not that I really noticed."

"Anybody out on the sidewalk up or down the street when you came in?"

"I pulled the truck around to the side, so I didn't notice," Barry said.

"Why'd you pull around the side?"

"Horace said to. Said he didn't want anybody to think the bank was open. Said he was afraid he'd have people walking in and talking to him while he's trying to get caught up."

"See, Barry, you didn't tell me that before. Now think, man. Anything else you didn't tell me?"

"I'm scared. I can't think straight."

"You can relax," Cody said. "I don't think you killed Horace, and I don't think my daddy thinks it either."

"Then why am I here?"

"Probably the best place for your dumb ass right now," Cody

said. "Someone wants you for a fall guy. And you make a good one, blundering into shit. The county attorney is going to recommend no bail at your preliminary, and the judge will go with it. So you're here until the real killer is found."

"Well thanks a heap."

Cody stood up and stretched. "You're welcome, Barry. Won't even charge extra. Next time you're up on a murder charge, tell the truth to your attorney and anyone else trying to clear you."

Cody's harangue didn't cheer Barry up. "Any ideas on who it is?"

"Not any based on solid evidence or a real good guess, even. My bet is when we find him, it'll surprise us all. Be the last person we expected."

"Got any plans?" the sheriff said when Cody returned from his visit to Barry's cell.

"I'm running down to Tellico Plains to pick up something," he said.

"Wish I could get out of town for a couple of months," the sheriff said. "I'm busier than a one-armed paperhanger. You'd think all the common criminals would see how overwhelmed we are and take some time off. Tomorrow morning, barring some unplanned event, like another killing or three, I'll be heading over to Michelle's house. Gotta ask her to account for her time on the nights of the murders. Ask her if she has any tan shoes with a scratch on them, few timely questions. If she hands 'em over, then it'll be nice and legal."

"You gonna ask for permission to search?" Cody asked.

"I'll have deputies standing by in case she says yes. Which I think she will. No way I could get a judge to okay a search warrant. Not enough to go on. We could go for a conspiracy charge. Might work."

In Tellico Plains, Cody picked up the prints from the film Ray had dropped off. Then he swung by the vacation cabin to see if Staros was still in residence. The Mercedes was in its slot in front.

He stopped at the Tellicafe for a sandwich, then headed back to Highwater Town. Going to rain again, he thought, looking at the darkening sky.

Forty

The building had been here a while, Ray thought as he pulled into the lot of the restaurant where he would meet Michael Auretta. Inside, the entrance was dark after the bright, late-afternoon sun. He blinked, looked around at the ancient coat rack in the hallway, the dark wood, the heavy curtains on the window.

He sniffed the air, savored the spices, the distinct odor of oregano in the air. And garlic. He loved the smell. It reminded him of Europe, where he would be still if a pack of idiots hadn't decided to give peace a chance. Should've saved themselves the trouble. It'd never work.

The carpet was thick and he felt his heels sink as he walked to the hostess stand. No one was there. He waited.

The hostess showed up a few seconds later, all white teeth and blonde hair in a white blouse, a full multicolored skirt down to her ankles, and a bright apron embroidered with red roses and white daisies. "How many for dinner, sir?"

"I'm meeting someone—Mr. Michael Auretta."

"Yes, sir. Mike is expecting you. Follow me, please."

She led him to a table where two men waited, one middle-aged, the other years younger.

Ray had only expected one person to meet him. "Mr. Auretta?"

"Mr. Blizzard?" The older man stood as he spoke. "Mike Auretta. This is my son, Andy. He insisted on coming along. In fact, I don't think I could've come without him."

Ray shook hands with both men then took a chair. Mike was about Ray's height, only stockier. He wore a gray suit with a pale blue tie. His dark brown hair was short.

Andy was taller, thinner, his hair a lighter brown. He had on jeans and a red, white, and blue jacket with a Danforth anchor patch on the front and the outline of a yellow sailboat stitched on the sleeve.

"Andy and Regina were real close. Actually, they were engaged at one time. Andy thinks you may know where she is."

"I'm sorry to disappoint you, Andy. My background investigation concerns Randy Gateline, not Regina. I was going to interview her if she was handy, which I guess she's not."

Andy's face fell. His shoulders slumped. "The last word I had from her was over a year ago. She was up near Philly. A small town called Essington, near the airport and shipyards, I think."

"Sorry I can't help you," Ray said. "Mike, can you give me some insight into Randy's character? What I'm looking for, as I explained over the phone, is anything in his background that could come back to haunt a politician nominating Randy for an important post."

"Mr. Blizzard," Mike said. "Why don't we just cut the bull-shit."

Ray grinned. "Funny—that's the second time I've heard that during this investigation."

"Bet she threatened to put the dog on you."

"She did," Ray said.

"Dog was run over three years ago. Mrs. Coldiron still walks around the house whistling and calling for it. I haven't been a teacher all my life, Ray. In another life I was with O.N.I.—Office of Naval Intelligence."

"Yeah. I know. Five Thirty-Third Military Intelligence was my last service assignment," Ray said. "Europe."

"We're an up-to-date family, the Auretta's are. Got a color TV, take the newspapers. We even watch CNN. I know where Randy is living now—Highwater Town, Tennessee, where the serial killer has killed four or five people. Do you think Randy is involved?"

"If that was the case, you'd be talking to law enforcement, not private," Ray said.

"Come on, Ray," Mike Auretta said. "They have a guy in jail and the news says he has this P.I. looking to clear him. If you want me to be candid, you need to reciprocate."

"Okay. I work as an investigator for Cody Rainwalker; he's the P.I. you've heard about. Cody and I were together in M.I. when we were just starting out as kids. We're trying to uncover something, anything, and we don't have a clue, and I guess you heard there was another killing last night. Randy's just one avenue we're checking."

"Going to the expense of coming all the way to Harrisburg means your boss is more than slightly suspicious of Randy," Mike commented.

"We've checked out other subjects just as thoroughly. The family that hired us is wealthy. They want a complete background on even the most remote possibility."

"You're wasting your time investigating Randy," Andy piped up.

"You're probably right. But you see, once I do, it's one more person eliminated. My backup profession is electronics. I'd be working at it now if I spoke fluent Japanese. In troubleshooting a complex electronic problem or failure, you slowly, step by step, eliminate all the possibilities."

"I taught history for a number of years," Mike said. "Randy and Regina were students of mine. Both were brilliant, could read a page and come near to reciting it back to you. They were whizzes in math and chemistry also. Randy went to college and so did Regina. Then there were some financial difficulties. Randy went into the navy and let Regina graduate first. Then he got out and went back to school himself.

"They helped one another. Randy helps Regina today, I'm sure, wherever she is. He sent her money after she started having her, uh, difficulties."

A waitress came and took their orders. Ray ordered the veal, pasta, and a salad. He stuck with water; didn't want to get started too early. "Did Randy ever show any tendencies toward violence?"

"None at all. Just the opposite. He was an appeaser. He didn't like trouble in any form. Even though a lot of violence was done to him."

"In what way?" Ray asked.

"The father was very abusive, a strict disciplinarian, some call it. The old man owned his own architectural firm and was very proper in public, but he was a notorious alcoholic despite his success in business. In his home life, he'd go roaring through the house, punching his wife and children. I'm sure that's why the widow is the way she is, after all the years of abuse. She's survived several strokes."

"Sort of a house devil and a street angel," Ray said.

"Regina was abused also," Andy said. He was squirming in his chair, getting himself worked up. "We were in school together. We're the same age. She'd come to class with a big bruise on her leg or on her arm where that sonofabitch'd kicked her or grabbed her. It continued until she graduated from high school. Then Randy got her out of there. I've always been grateful to him for that."

"How'd Mr. Gateline die?" Ray said.

"Drunk in an automobile wreck. Fortunately, no one else was hurt," Mike said.

"Did the police investigate?" Ray asked.

"If you're asking if Randy killed him, staged the accident somehow, then no. Randy was upstate, in school. I called him myself less than an hour after the accident. There was no way he could've done it. Besides, he was scared to death of that old bastard—with good reason."

"You say Regina is having problems," Ray said. "What kind of problems?"

Mike's wine had arrived. He swirled the dark liquid around his glass and stared at the results, taking a sip before answering. "Regina received a degree in psychiatric nursing. Graduated with honors, as did her brother in his studies. Then she started out in the footsteps of the old man, on the sauce."

Andy didn't like the remark. When he spoke there was anger was in his voice. "Now, Dad. That's not fair. If I'd been abused and cast aside like Regina, I'd be living in a cardboard box clutching a bottle of gin. Regina's a good person. A beautiful person. I've got to find her."

He turned to Ray. "You've got to help me find her, Mr. Blizzard. I can't stand it anymore, wondering where she is, if she's alive, or in some nursing home somewhere with her brain destroyed." He buried his face in his hands.

"I need to interview Regina to complete my investigation, Andy. If I find her—and we're good at finding people, my boss and I—I'll tell her you want her to get in touch."

"Oh, God, that'd be fantastic," Andy said.

The food came and they ate in silence. Ray had a glass of wine afterward. He let Michelle Willingham pick up the tab.

Andy handed him a two-year-old wallet-size picture of Regina from his billfold. "I have others, but this is the best one for showing around, I think."

Damn. She was beautiful, Ray thought. He put the picture in his coat pocket for safekeeping.

They walked outside and shook hands. Ray gave them the name and number of the hotel where he was staying. "You think of anything, just give me a jingle."

"You know there is one thing that would make Randy mad," Andy said.

"Oh, that," Mike said.

"What?"

"Randy has always been very handsome," Andy said. "I've often wondered why he didn't take advantage of his good looks, you know—model for magazine ads or become an actor. Anyway, the kids at school got it in their heads that because of his looks, he was gay. He wasn't. He liked girls.

"Anyhow, the boys would pester him and call him names like sissy and queer. He'd just laugh at them, tell them to ask their girlfriends. That really angered them, and the taunting escalated; they started calling him Peggy Sue. I don't know why that name over another. One day after school, I saw him go into a rage over being called Peggy Sue. Beat the hell outa this guy, broke his nose. Nobody called him that again."

Ray drove back to the hotel, stopped in the lounge and had a few, then went to his room. He read over his notes—nothing significant to report—made some changes, then called it a night.

The phone woke him from a sound sleep. "Yeah?"

"Mr. Blizzard? This is Mike Auretta. I thought you'd want

to know. We were watching the news. It just happened a few minutes ago. Turn on your TV. Your boss, Cody Rainwalker—he's been shot!

Forty-one

Cody had rolled into Highwater Town just as it was getting dark. The rain had let up. A few stars twinkled boldly through the clouds.

He thought he'd earned a beer today, at least. Not much more but at least a beer. He had to push his way into the doorway at Fuzzy's. Once the crowd saw who it was they made a path for him.

"Hey! It's Cody. Let him through!" a stranger yelled.

Monk scowled alone at a corner table. Big 'Un stood guard over him.

"What gives?" Cody said, pulling up a chair.

Monk was morose. "Damn reporters won't leave me alone."

"And Fuzzy furnishes a guard, toll-free?"

"Figures I'm a big draw. If I leave, some of the heaviest drinkers may follow suit. That'd kill his ass."

"So why don't you leave?"

"Are you serious? And do what, pray tell? Attend a chamber music recital by a string quartet? Escort a lady to the ballet? The pressure of the chase must be altering your judgment."

Monk didn't seem to be his old garrulous self, Cody thought, yelling for a beer.

"I feel I have let my client down," Monk said. Sadness didn't become him.

So that's what was wrong, Cody thought. "Is Barry forthcoming to you about his real estate venture?"

"That's another thing. I feel the Willingham family has no trust in my discretion."

"Don't know why. I've never heard of you letting them down."

"If it wouldn't do so much damage to Barry, create such chaos and speculation in the tabloids, who are in a feeding frenzy on this case by the way, I would tender my resignation forthwith if not fucking immediately."

Monk was even more tipsy than usual. Under normal circumstances, Big 'Un would have already taken him to his apartment.

"'Scuse." Monk grabbed the edge of the table as a crutch, stood, and wobbled off to the men's room.

A reporter instantly took his place. It was the heavy redhead from the other night.

Cody considered feeding him another line of shit, but reconsidered. Something like that had a way of coming back and biting you in the ass.

"Mr. Rainwalker, my name is Steve Belton. Could I get a statement from you?"

"Concerning what?"

"The killer, of course."

"Okay. I think the sonofabitch is an asshole and deserves to be prosecuted to the full limits of the law. You can quote me."

"How humorous. What I had in mind is an exclusive. Just who do you think the killer is?"

"You really expect me to tell you? How much you had to drink?"

"Not near as much as your attorney friend. So you won't tell me?"

"Say I do know who the killer is. And say I do tell you. What's to prevent him from fleeing the country? If he thinks he's safe, he'll hang around. Make sense to you? Where the fuck you from anyhow, Steve? Up north?"

"I'm from Ohio—Toledo. There's no need to be rude."

"Whatta we playing here? Fucking lift-ass?" Monk had returned from the men's room and wanted his chair.

"Excuse me, but I was just asking Mr. Rainwalker a question."

"Well get the fuck away from me or I'll have my praetorian here break your goddamn back over his knee like a dry stick." Monk jerked his head toward the big bouncer, who stared straight ahead like he was deaf. "Then he'll kick your asshole up around your neck and strangle you to death with your own sphincter muscle. A gory end befitting someone who would steal my place."

The reporter scooted off.

Monk blinked after him, tried to sit, almost missed the chair. Cody guided him, then walked over to Big 'Un. "Tell Fuzzy if you don't take Monk home right away—this place'll be closed in five minutes."

The bouncer rumbled off like a charging bull, knocking reporters from his path.

Fuzzy bent his head over to hear Big 'Un's whisper, glanced into Cody's hard eyes for an instant, then nodded.

The crowd gave way this time, flinched to let him pass, then closed in behind him like water.

"Time to go home, Mr. Monk."

"It's about fucking time."

Cody lasted another fifteen minutes, ordered another beer, and tried to watch TV. It was too noisy and the crowd kept pressing in. Worse than some of the clubs on Second Avenue on Friday night, he thought. He drained his beer and headed for the door.

The red-haired reporter trailed twenty feet behind. He had hopes of approaching Cody in the parking lot now the drunken lawyer was out of the way. His editor was putting the pressure on—get the story or else. He hadn't said what the "or else" would be, but the reporter's imagination conjured himself standing in one of the long lines common all across the country now-adays, filled with middle-aged and older unemployed college grads.

The pace and the tension of the chase were starting to wear on Cody. He wanted to go to the farm, relax, get a good night's sleep. When he had arrived at Fuzzy's, he'd been forced to park out at the curb due to the full house. Now as he walked across the down-sloping gravel lot to his truck, he noticed a man angling toward him with a vigorous gait. Cody saw that he was big, didn't recognize him.

In the last few feet of his approach the stranger increased his pace, stepped quickly to block Cody's path. He was almost as broad as Big 'Un, though not nearly as tall. He had a big, square head and a leather-billed cap. The long leather coat he wore looked out of place and too heavy for the weather.

Cody slanted to go around him. "Sorry. No interviews."

"Your name Cody Rainwalker?" The man stepped to block him again.

"That's right. Like I said. No interviews."

"Got a message for you, Cody Rainwalker. Man says to go back to Nashville where you come from. Quit snooping in things that don't concern you."

Cody couldn't believe what he was hearing. "What's your problem, asshole? Somebody steal your fucking brain?" He started around the man again, not expecting the attack.

The man moved quickly for his size. He'd obviously planned the move beforehand and stepped in fast, swinging for the side of Cody's head. Cody was already moving away but the wooden club caught him behind the ear. The force of the blow sent him to the ground.

Kicking for the head, the attacker missed his target, punted again, and caught Cody in the stomach with a jolt powerful enough to lift him off the ground. The pain from the kick was terrible. Cody grunted when the heavy boot connected. Steel toes for maximum damage, he would remember later. Rolling down the hill, he tried to escape what he knew would follow. Heavy gravel bit into his side and back.

Seeing all this, the red-haired reporter scrambled back inside. "Somebody's attacking Cody!" he yelled, then ran back out to see the action.

The crowd followed him out, flooded the parking lot around the entrance. An alert reporter ran to his vehicle for his video-cam.

The assailant pursued Cody as he rolled over and over. Tried for another kick.

This time Cody was ready. Catching the man's ankle in his left hand, he raised himself on one knee and popped the mugger in the lower gut with his fist, then came all the way to his feet. Both fighters blinked in surprise at a bright light that came on and illuminated the parking area.

The attacker let out a moan of pain from the blow, swung hard, and caught Cody on the forehead with the bludgeon.

Cody staggered back, allowed the man to close with him, punched him in the sternum. The attacker fell back stunned as Cody caught him on the chin with the heel of his hand in an upward motion that snapped the assailant's head back and sent him backpedaling ten feet down the lot to the street, where he landed on his back.

"You motherfucker," the man said, climbing to his feet. His hand was quick, and when it came out of his coat pocket he held a pistol; he fired as he brought it level.

The flash of metal in the floodlight made Cody leap to the side and roll. Still, he felt the fire of the round as it raked his side. Behind him someone screamed. He rolled twice, reaching for his automatic with his right hand.

The shooter fired again.

Still on the move, Cody heard the ricochet. Saw the dust puff from the driveway. Then he was on his feet in a crouch.

"Put it down!" he yelled to his attacker.

The pistol moved to track him; the man's finger squeezed the trigger.

Cody fired his H&K three times. Two quick rounds struck the man in the chest. For a nanosecond Cody paused on the third round, knowing the man was already dead on his feet. But he was already committed, the action programmed into his brain, so he popped the attacker in the middle of the forehead from fifteen feet away, slammed him backward into the gravel.

Cody heard the arriving sirens as he passed out.

Pandemonium reigned. People screamed. Three men ran to Cody's side.

"Holy shit! Goddamn! I never seen nothing like it!" In their panic the reporters were running in circles, shouting incoherently to one another.

The cameraman couldn't believe what he'd seen through his viewfinder, what he'd captured on tape. He didn't know whether he should run for the satellite truck, beam what he had to the network, or stay until the deputies and the ambulance appeared. He stayed.

Reporters in other areas heard the call on their police bands and headed for the scene. "Mountain County S.O. to all units, ten-fifty-two-P in progress at Fuzzy's tavern. Multiple ten-eighty-three, shots fired. Officer down. Repeat—officer down. First unit on the scene, signal five."

"Goddamn. A killing a night. This burg's where the action is," one reporter said to his partner.

"Let's roll," the other answered, grabbing a camera.

"Guy over here's been shot," a reporter called. He was crouched by a moaning man who lay supine on the ground. It was the heavy, red-haired reporter. He'd screamed when he stopped the round that scraped Cody's side. "He's hit in the thigh! Lotsa blood here! Somebody call for another ambulance."

The round fuzzy blur grew minute by minute as it approached from a great distance, then at last came into focus. Jolinda's face. "Jolinda," Cody tried to say. It was more of a mumble. "Jolinda." He got it out that time.

"Lie still, Mister Rainwalker," a male voice said from beyond his line of vision. "You've been hurt. Don't try to move just yet."

"Hurts," Cody said. "Burns."

"Is he going to be okay, Doctor?" Jolinda asked.

"Would you step out of the treatment room, Miss Risingwaters? You're blocking our access to the patient."

Cody blacked out again.

Jolinda was there again. So was his father. "You okay, son?"

Cody blinked at the light, focusing slowly, felt Jolinda's hands on his hand. "You tell me. Didn't you talk to the doc?"

"Big gouge along the left side. The round hit a rib and scraped along your chest, then took out a bystander. They're working on his leg down the way."

"Head feels like a tree fell on it."

The sheriff pulled a chair near the bed and squatted on its edge. "Attacker—Ramon Leonard his I.D. says—had a short wooden club, actually a sawed-off nightstick. Caught you with it twice. You got stitches fore and aft."

"Who was this guy? Why'd he come after me?" The pain in Cody's head was arriving in throbs, one for every heartbeat. Jolinda placed her cool hand on his forehead. That helped.

"Another northerner," the sheriff said. "This one from up Chicago way. Had a slip of paper in his pocket that had your good buddy Stan Bodine's name and phone number on it."

"Hope the department didn't go charging over to arrest Mister Bodine," Cody said.

"What! Make a move without consulting you first? We're sitting on it."

"Good show. Maybe ol' Stan thinks I was about to blow the whistle on his scam. This case is getting more and more complicated."

"The attacker had the club as his primary weapon," the sheriff said. "What he came at you with first. Probably had instructions to scare you off."

"Yeah. Dumb me," Cody said weakly. "If I'd just let him beat the crap outa me, I wouldn't a had to shoot him. When will I ever learn?"

Jolinda spoke for the first time. "You almost get yourself killed, and you lie there and crack jokes. It scared me to death when I heard about it. Goddamn detectives on TV are always getting knocked in the head. No wonder they don't have any sense. You wanta end up like that?" She squeezed his hand and he squeezed back. She bent over and kissed him on the cheek. He felt the wetness of her tears.

"Hell. I thought he was some sorta aggressive reporter at first."

The sheriff stood, held his hat in both hands to cover his chest. "Got a deputy on your door all night. I've talked to the sheriff over at Monroe County, let him in on Mister Bodine's little game. He'll wait and watch. Federal boys may come into it eventually."

"Let's get our problem solved first," Cody said.

"My feeling too."

Ogden came in as the sheriff was leaving. He talked to Cody for a few minutes, saw Cody was tired, and left. A few minutes later Cody drifted off to sleep.

Jolinda pulled a chair over and placed her head on the bed near him. She stayed with him all night.

Forty-two

"Four hundred dollars for a leather coat! You keeping track of all the condoms and toilet paper you use on the job?" Michelle was red-faced with fury. She stormed around her living room, swinging her arms.

Cody was wary, half expected her to pick up something and throw it. He was ready to dodge but didn't want to move too quick. He thought of the three stitches behind his ear and the four on his forehead with a bandage to protect the cut. His head still ached and his ribcage was sore. All in all, he wasn't in a very good mood and surely didn't need any more pain.

"I'll start charging for 'em when the IRS makes me depreciate toilet paper over three years. If you'd been up front from the start, this shit wouldn't have happened. And I wouldn't have that man's death on my conscience."

"What did your attacker have to do with me? I'm sorry you were hurt. If I didn't need your help so bad I'd fire you."

"If I didn't need the money so bad, I'd quit. I think it has something to do with all this secret business you got going that you won't let your most trusted servant in on. And I'm afraid I've got some bad news for you." He held up an envelope.

"The good news, bad news routine?"

"Ain't no good news." He hoped he wasn't telling her too much—what if she was the killer after all? Nah.

She held out a hand. The action said: Hand it over, I can handle it.

He gave her the picture of Biba getting into her car.

"So Biba isn't wearing panties, you pervert."

"Here's where she left them." He showed her the picture of Biba with Randy standing in his underwear in the motel door.

355

"That sonofabitch!"

"And prior to this romantic episode . . ." He handed her the picture of Ramona. "Same day. Coupla hours earlier."

"Oh, goddamn. Now isn't this terrific. Victor is going to shit himself, and I want to be there to watch. I warned him about that bitch, but he was pussy crazy."

Cody walked over and plopped on the couch. The ordeal he'd dreaded for days was over. "This one time, I want to call the shots. Don't mention to Victor or to anybody what I've just shown you."

"What! I've got to tell him. And that goddamn Ramona—"

"It'll all hold for two or three days. Do what I ask. This will all be over soon." He hoped he wasn't whistling in the dark.

"Wait a minute. You don't suspect Randy of being the killer, do you?"

"I don't know who the killer is. But it's all tied in together somehow. You've hired me to help. So stand back and let me."

"How in the hell did you have time to do all the investigating you're doing and still find out about Randy, Biba, and Ramona?"

If she only knew, he thought. "Got a high-speed rear-end in my pickup. Like the business card says, I'm a detective." He wasn't about to let anyone know of Ray's role in the case yet.

"I do have more pleasant news," Cody said. He was observing Michelle closely now to test her reactions.

"I've got cancer? My home is about to be invaded by terrorists?"

"Better than that even. My dear old daddy is coming to talk to you." Cody tried a sweet smile for spite; he loved that leather coat. What came off was an evil grimace.

"Kurt is always welcome here."

"He's bringing some friends."

"Who?"

"A team of deputies to search your house, if you let him."

"What! Now you're being an asshole."

"Tell it to Papa. Seems like some loose ends are hanging out there, like a woman's size-nine-and-a-half footprint found at the scene of Samantha's and Luther's murders. An old shoe, scratched. The visit'll be real friendly and informal."

She bounded up like he'd goosed her. "You're really enjoying yourself, aren't you?"

Cody was not enjoying it, but he wanted to twist the knife a little more to get her reaction. He watched her eyes. "You know, I've thought of this and I'm sure Daddy has also. There could be two killers with a hidden agenda, or three. You could do one and Barry could do the next. Don't know about Vic. He's too tight to spend the gas to get him to the scene. How do you all decide? Draw straws?"

Her first reaction was a horse laugh. What'd that prove? That she's either innocent or very good.

"We're the Willingham family, not the Manson family."

"At the rate you're going you'll be even more deadly and famous."

"If I wasn't enjoying this so much, I'd throw you out of the house."

Cody stood slowly and headed for the door. "I was leaving anyhow. Think I hear Daddy and company arriving. You know, Michelle, doctor or no, sometimes I think you're as fucked up as I am."

"I admire a man who doesn't take himself so seriously. Any other man would be trying to convince me how macho he was, gunning down somebody in a showdown." Michelle moved toward him. "I think you will find out who the real killer is. You're just that goddamn mean."

"It's more important now than ever," Cody said. He paused at the door and turned back to her. Outside he heard car doors slamming.

Curious, Michelle moved even closer. "Why's that?"

"Either me or Jolinda is the next target."

From her hiding place at the head of the stairs, Biba watched Cody leave. Randy and Ramona? Tears streaming, she ran to her room to stand behind the curtain, gazed down from her window as Cody approached his dad and talked to him. Cody turned and gestured toward the house with a jerk of his thumb.

Biba was shaking. What did Cody know? Was the sheriff

going to arrest her aunt? Then her father and her aunt would both be in jail.

She was so confused. Maybe Bubba could help, or Sonny Todd. She went to her vanity and removed the pill bottle from the drawer, twisted the lid, and took out a white tab of methamphetamine hydrochloride, dry-popping it with a quick toss of her head. It would take a few minutes she knew; she hoped the headache she felt coming on would be intercepted by the upper. Ten minutes and she'd be able to think clearly.

She stuffed the plastic pill bottle into her pants pocket. Going to her closet, she grabbed a light jacket, then headed for the rear stairwell and the back door.

"Reckon you saw the news," said Cody into the pay phone.

The line was noisy. Ray sounded a long way off, which he was. "Amazing. Absolutely fantastic. Never saw anything like it," he said.

"Wasn't all that special," Cody said.

"Whatta you mean? I saw the headlines in the grocery checkout line. DC-3 lands thirty years after it was reported missing. Skeleton of the pilot and crew still on board. Saw something else should interest you."

"Yeah?" Cody said. "What's that?"

"An article on how to contact your guardian angel."

"Now you tell me. You dig anything up?"

"I found out our pronging champ, Randy, don't like to be called Peggy Sue," Ray said. "Sends him into a rage." He told Cody the story.

"You flew a thousand miles for that?"

"Let me tell you," Ray said. "I go into the lounge last night. This gal bartender asks what I want, so I order my usual, Jack Black and Seven. She brings the drink, and I slug it back, and it like to knock my dick in the dirt. Call her over and asked what the hell it was. 'Just what you ordered,' she says. 'Johnny Walker Black and Seagram's Seven.' I tell you, these Yankees don't understand English.

"And I may have a track on the sister. I'm going to Philly, area called Essington, later today. Regina may be up there."

"And you'll tell me she don't like to be called Ralph. Any negative info on Randy?" Cody said.

"Had two real charmers for parents." Ray filled him in on the elder Gatelines and the lack of negative information on Randy.

"Noel's about to go off the rails, wondering where you are."

"Yeah. I know," Ray said. "Ain't it fun?"

Cody hung up, then called Noel. The computer guru was hyper.

"You okay? You're on the news here every night. You and your murder case."

"Kinda sore," Cody said. "I'm gonna need a long rest after this is over. Anything worthwhile going on there?"

"Goddamn Ray called and left a message on my voice mail. Acted like he was gonna tell me where he was. Then he said, 'Uh-oh. Something just came up. Gotta go.' And he hung up. He's trying to drive me nuts."

"If you see him or talk to him, tell him I said get to work," Cody said.

"You're into the most exciting case I ever heard of for a P.I. Why can't I come over and give you a hand? Hell, I'll be your chauffeur if nothing else." Noel was talking like a speeded-up tape.

"Hopefully it'll all be over soon. Then we'll talk about you getting your license," Cody said. Noel was right. There was a use for computers in investigations—a lot of the crooks used them.

Jolinda was waiting at the S.O. "Why can't I go on home by myself and feed and water the mules? And I need to get supper ready."

"Just a little while longer," Cody said. "Don't want you out there on the farm by your lonesome. This killer was sitting down the road from the house for a purpose. Had it staked out. Could be stalking you or me or both of us."

"Are you still hurting?"

"Some. I won't be doing any running or weightlifting for a day or two, that's for sure. Tomorrow morning I'm going over to Spring City. There's a fellow over there, retired now, used to be Sonny Todd's supervisor when he worked at Watt's Bar. I need to interview him. I want you to go along with me. Keep me company."

"You're just afraid to leave me alone," Jolinda said. "Of course I'll ride with you. Leaves are turning and it's going to be a beautiful day."

Despair was the word that came to Ray's mind as he walked the grimy streets near the shipyard. The streets were in disrepair. Buildings still in use looked abandoned. The abandoned ones appeared balanced on the edge of doom, awaiting that final cataclysm that would send them tumbling into a heap.

The hotel he'd checked into last night in Essington resembled a fortress. He'd worried that if it caught fire he'd have to blast his way out. Even with the credit card to pay for the room, the night clerk needed two additional forms of I.D. Whatta place to live, he'd thought, comparing it to Sand Mountain in his home state of Alabama. He would be a lush if he hung around the neighborhood for a week, damn place would depress him so.

Ray really had no good leads. Just Regina's picture from Andy and the knowledge that she was alcoholic. Best place to look for an alcoholic is in a pub, he thought, so he went from bar to bar showing the picture. He'd thought it over carefully, how to go about it. Should he dress as a guy on the skids himself? He decided on the harried civil servant approach. His cover was he worked for disease control and Regina's brother had developed a rare, hereditary kidney disease. There was a good chance Regina could develop the disease, and she needed to be warned. As a kicker he told everyone he questioned that the disease was highly contagious.

There was no lack of places to look, with three bars on every block, most of them dives. The drinkers were mostly a rough-looking bunch, mostly out-of-work shipbuilders and dock workers.

He'd waited until noon to begin, bombed in one place after another as the day passed. He bet he'd hit better'n a hundred joints. A personal record.

By six his feet were killing him and he was irritated at the surly attitudes of most of the bartenders and patrons he approached with the tale. Worn out, he allowed himself two beers and a Reuben sandwich as he talked with a big shipworker, a welder who said he'd been out of work on and off for four years. "Only people with job security are the fucking politicians," he said. "We'll have to bomb them out of office. Then the country can get straight again."

"Damn good idea," Ray said as he sipped his beer. "When do we start?"

"Lemme see that picture again."

Ray handed it over.

"You say this girl's been hanging in joints around here? Looks too classy."

"She's got a bad drinking problem. More'n likely she don't look that good now," Ray said.

"Place called Wayne's down the block," the welder said. "Now I'm not saying this girl is one of 'em, but some of the girls get desperate and hook for drinks. You may wanta check in there."

Wayne's was worse than a dive. It was a crash landing. The floor hadn't been swept in at least a week, and the windows were so dirty you couldn't tell whether it was day or night. But if you were bottomed-out enough to drink in Wayne's, what difference did it make?

The bartender looked at the picture. Ray could tell by his eyes he knew her. "Never came in here," he said.

"This young lady is likely desperately ill by now," Ray said. "We need to find her before she spreads her infection to thousands of people."

"Like I said. She's never been in here."

Ray showed the picture to a customer at the bar. The man smelled so bad Ray held it out at arm's length.

The man smoked a cigarette without removing it from his mouth, let the ashes fall where they may, even on his filthy, torn coat. "Got a picture of the top of her head? Only view I ever get of the girls in here caging drinks."

"Let's hope you've never had sex with this girl," Ray said. "If so you'd need immediate hospitalization."

"Yeah? Well, I never seen her."

He was about to leave, call it a day, when a woman at the bar motioned to him. Wanted him to buy her a drink, he guessed.

Her hair was a mess. The jacket she wore had once graced an expensive store window but was now ready for the trash bin. Her blouse was torn near the collar and couldn't be properly buttoned, hung open to reveal a dirty brassiere. Her eyes were red, rheumy, windows with a direct view of her pain. "Can I see the picture?" she asked.

"Sure," Ray said and handed it over.

She looked at it, brought it close to her face. A slight smile came to her lips. It changed her face entirely. A younger woman showed there for a instant, then faded. "It's Reggie."

"You know her?"

"Why you looking for her?"

He told his story. He had it down good by now.

"Her brother, you say. What's his name?"

"Randy Gateline. He's a pharmacist down South."

"She's real proud of Randy. He's helped her. As much as he could."

"He wants us to find her now," Ray said. "This disease can be treated if caught in time."

"She's gone," the woman said.

"Gone?"

"Got where the bartender and the guy you were talking to at the bar were roughing her up. A girlfriend over in New Jersey—Hazlet, up by East Brunswick. She went to stay with her."

Finally, Ray thought. His feet were killing him. "You know the girlfriend's name?"

"Better'n that. Got her address in my purse."

"Would you give it to me, please? Regina and Randy will be eternally grateful."

"I don't know. You don't plan to do her no harm, do you?"

"Definitely not," Ray said. "Did she ever mention Andy?"

"You know Andy? She always talked about Andy and she'd cry, bawl like a baby."

"Andy wants to help her. Said when I found her he'd come to help. Even if it was to the end of the earth."

Ray left her two twenties.

On the way out of the bar the customer that had refused him any info called him over. "You say this girl is contagious?"

Ray eyed the man. "Highly contagious. If you've had any contact with her whatever, you're infected."

"Not that I have or anything, but what're the symptoms?"

"Very elusive symptoms, very elusive. And vague. First you would notice some redness in the eyes. Or is that last? I'm not a doctor. Every so often you'd experience slight diarrhea. Then you'd have intermittent spells of not being able to sleep at night, but once you fell asleep you'd sleep like a log and have trouble getting up in the morning. In the morning you'd crave liquids, have this awful taste in your mouth. And sometimes you wouldn't be able to remember what you'd done the night before."

"Wha-what if somebody has all this?"

"I'd advise them to get to a hospital right away. The truly terrible thing about this disease is there's not five doctors in the entire country that can diagnose it with any accuracy. Most will misdiagnose it as over-use of alcohol. You take care now. Gotta run."

Forty-three

Well before crossing the Tennessee River on Highway 68 headed toward Watts Bar Nuclear Plant, travelers spot the two gigantic, concrete cooling towers rising above the hills and forest. The dam itself, forming Watts Bar Lake, is ancient in comparison, a boater's and fisherman's paradise. Some retirees dock their houseboats at the large marina, live on the river full-time. There's an abundance of land available in the surrounding hills and mountains for getaway and retirement cabins.

Cody and Jolinda drove over the dam and took the sharp curves that led by the nuclear plant's entrance. Cody took it easy because of the deer-crossing signs. A few seconds later, Jolinda spotted a doe with two fawns feeding in high bushes on the side of the road. She saw plenty of deer around the farm but always became excited when she saw fawns. They were so beautiful to her. A symbol of true innocence.

"Feeding on sumac fruit," Cody said. "This time of year it's real plentiful."

"What's the point in driving all the way over here to see this man when you could've called him on the phone?" Jolinda wanted to know.

They could see the lofty ridges of the Walden's Ridge now as they headed toward Highway 27. Trees had changed color in the higher elevations. "I always like to look at the person I'm interviewing. If they're lying I can spot it sometimes. Then there's body language and facial expressions and just the feeling you get talking to them."

Jolinda scooted closer across the front seat; he could feel the length of her thigh pressed to his. "This man worked with Sonny Todd?" Jolinda asked.

"He was his supervisor for about four years. I talked to him on the phone a couple of days ago. Couldn't see him earlier because he went out of town to visit his son. Gist of the telephone conversation we had, him and Sonny didn't get along all that well."

For a few miles they were slowed by a truck hauling a half load of pine logs ahead of them. It turned off into a logging road and they speeded up. "Spring City's north on 27?" Jolinda asked.

"Yeah. We'll dead-end into 27, then hang a right. Couple of miles then take a dirt road up the mountain."

Cody followed his own directions, and they soon found themselves in front of a mailbox that read Jenkins. "Must be it," Cody said.

The house was a ranch that sprawled around the contours of a bluff overlooking the valley two thousand feet below. The driveway approached from the side and gave them a full view of the deck built on the solid rock of the overlook. The vista was outstanding.

"Oh, I love this," Jolinda said. "Let's build a house like this when we get married."

"Hope your dowry's at least three hundred thousand."

"Oh silly."

Jack Jenkins was tall and gaunt. His cheeks were sunken and his eyes protruded; his nose was long and straight. He walked slightly stooped and looked a little sick, Cody thought.

"Like to sit out on the balcony, enjoy the view while we talk? Another month it'll be too cold."

"I'd love that," Jolinda said.

Cody made the introductions.

"You wanta talk about Sonny Todd?" Jenkins said.

"That's right," said Cody. "What do you know about him?"

"That'll ruin my whole day. I can't think about him without getting mad."

There was a line of chairs near the railing. Jolinda slid onto one and hooked her ankles over the bottom rail. Cody turned so he could see the man he interviewed. "Why's that?" he asked. He watched the man closely.

"We just never got along. Sonny could never accept authority, and I had the misfortune to be that authority. And of course we worked for the federal government. So I couldn't fire him."

"What exactly would he do to upset you so much?" Cody asked.

"Wouldn't listen to a damn thing I said, to begin with. Then he'd argue with a fence post. He was the most inflexible, obdurate, unyielding, bullheaded, obstinate man I've ever met."

"Kinda stubborn, was he?"

"You could say that. Paid off when he was working on a problem; pursuing a software bug in one of the systems, he was absolutely tenacious. But he could be the same way over what to eat for lunch, for God's sake. I'm sorry. Just thinking of it upsets me. I haven't been well lately."

Cody gave the man a few seconds to regain his composure. "How did Sonny feel toward you?"

"Hated me. Despised me. He hated all authority. I never could prove it was him but . . . Say I would go out of my office for a few minutes. I'd come back and my coffee would be all over my desk. More than likely poured all over some important documents. Other times I'd log on to my computer and not be able to get into the system. He'd change my password—and me a manager in Information Services."

"Sir, I hate to make you discuss this. It's important, though," Cody said.

"You say you're with the Mountain County Sheriff's Office. I didn't ask for I.D. Guess I should, you know. And the young lady. Is she a deputy also?"

Flipping his wallet open, Cody showed Jenkins Samantha's badge. "Jolinda's my niece. She wanted to see how police work's conducted."

"That's fine, then. What happened to your head?"

"Had a little accident," Cody said.

"Oh, sorry. Anyway, Sonny would undermine me any way he could. Undermined the project also. He'd tell everyone who'd listen that if TVA was still building dams, he'd never live downriver from one, and did they realize TVA was now operating nuclear plants. Disloyal, that's what he was. And he was a snitch to the NRC. I could never prove it, but I swear he was the one leaking all that information on safety problems."

Guy's gonna go ballistic any minute now, Cody thought. "NRC?"

"Yes. The Nuclear Regulatory Commission. They had an office in the OP building at the plant. Sonny had a friend over there."

"He get along with everyone else?"

"Not anyone in authority. Higher-ups in I.S. were always waiting for him to make a mistake. Then they'd come down on him. He'd retaliate by messing up their projects on the system. Lot of stuff simply disappeared. He was a hacker, that's what I called him. He'd hack into systems, break the password code. Look into information he had no right looking into."

Cody thought it over a minute before he continued. "Say if there were some kind of big land management deal going on with the federal government. Like the park service or the Department of the Interior. Could he gain access to that information?"

"Oh, sure," Jenkins said. "Sonny was with the agency a long time and moved around a lot. He worked at Norris for a while. That's where they do the watershed studies—all the rivers and tributaries. They generate the maps there, in Chattanooga, too, on the CAD mapping system. That's Computer-Aided Design. He could find out anything you wanted to know about land use."

"Well, thanks for your time, Mister Jenkins. You've been a fount of information, and the sheriff's department appreciates it."

"Always a pleasure to help the law."

"Whatcha think?" Jolinda said once they were in the truck.

"Sonny probably aggravated this guy for the fun of it. The important thing is the info Sonny can check up on, say about the park service, if he wanted. He could know the land deals are a fraud if he took the time to find out. Then again, maybe he didn't and he doesn't really care. Why it would drive him to kill someone, I don't know."

Jolinda yawned and stretched, laid her head over on his shoulder. "You going to talk to Sonny?"

"First thing in the morning," Cody said.

"You see a restaurant, let's eat. I'm starving."

Cody's pager went off as they crossed I-75. Cody found a pay phone.

"You're working late," he told Ray.

"I've found some info on Regina. She's in Hazlet. About a three-hour drive from here."

"Hazlet. Sandy Hook. Right across from the big city. Nice place, really. You think it's worth the time?"

Ray didn't really know, but he wanted to find Regina for Andy. He was turning into a regular cupid. "I've come this far. Got an address. I can probably talk to her tomorrow afternoon."

"Hell, the Willinghams can afford it. They're even buying some nonexistent land so people can take nonexistent vacations," Cody said.

"Let's hope they don't pay you in nonexistent money," Ray said.

* * *

After an hour surfing the Internet, Scanner had come across info about yet another anarchist bulletin board. He jumped off the Net, fired up a com program, keyed the phone number into his computer, and tapped his foot as his modem dialed.

MANTRAP.ZIP urban and wilderness traps to make your victim's life miserable.

NEW ID.ZIP how to disappear forever with no trace.

DISGUISE.ZIP how to walk invisible in your own neighborhood.

CREDIT.ZIP how to hack the credit bureaus.

CLAY.ZIP build your own claymore mine. Impress your friends, and enemies.

FUND.ZIP how to hack electronic fund transfer systems.

STASH.ZIP how to hide anything from everyone.

HIDE.ZIP how to survive on the run.

PICK.ZIP pick any lock made.

SEMTEX.ZIP make your own plastic explosives.

DETONATE.ZIP make detonators from materials available at the hardware store.

He'd much rather be logged on to the anarchist BBS than scanning the radio frequencies. Certainly since that whispering bitch had taken over. It was getting impossible for him to turn the radio on and not hear her give-it-to-me-good chatter. Was she that big-assed Roberta over at the vinyl plant? Could it be her? If he knew for sure, he'd kill her in a New York second.

A few things in the bulletin board service directory might come in handy. Especially the disappearing act if someone got on his trail. Someone like Cody Rainwalker. If he lived.

Forty-four

After driving Jolinda to class the following morning, Cody headed to Mountain Chapel Road and an unannounced visit with Sonny and Brandy. The cool autumn air had dried the roadway surface. His truck kicked up a dust cloud that followed him down the single-lane winding road.

Brandy was dressed in jeans and a man's T-shirt, up on a short ladder painting the white trim over the church's front door. Cody spotted her before he turned into the church's driveway. When he pulled to the log barricade and stopped between the Cherokee and a Camero, she climbed down, placed the brush on a paint can, and walked toward him. It was obvious she wasn't wearing a bra.

"Hello, Cody. Heard about you getting hurt—sure glad you're okay. What brings you out on such a fine autumn morning?" she said.

"You're mighty chipper this morning," Cody observed with a wide grin on his face.

Brandy smiled and stretched her arms over her head, her breasts rising under the thin cotton of her T-shirt. "It's the mountain air. Mountain air and sea air. I love 'em both. If I had to live in a city, I'd get sick. You come to see Sonny?"

"Rather look at you, but it's Sonny I've got to see. He here?"

She tilted her head and smiled at him. Gave him plenty of time to look her over. "Up at the trailer. Logged on to somewhere, working."

"I'll walk on up then, if it's okay." He headed up the path.

"It's not bad news is it?" Brandy called in a concerned voice.

Cody looked over his shoulder. "I hope not."

Sonny opened the door after Cody's light knock. "Why, hello, Cody. Come on in. Happy to see you up and about. You had breakfast?"

"Jolinda cooked up a whopper this morning," Cody said.

"Jolinda's a fine young lady. She'll make a man a fine wife some day. Wish she'd come out and join the fold. We need thoughtful, intelligent members like her."

"Jolinda's like me. She's all Catholic-ed up. When you take it on young, it's hard to get over."

"As it should be," Sonny said. "How about some coffee?" He motioned Cody to a living room couch.

Cody took a seat. "Don't mind if I do. Black."

Sonny went to the kitchen, then came back with a saucer and a heavy brown mug full of steaming coffee. "You didn't come all the way out here to talk religion, did you?"

Funny how folks living in rural areas always said "all the way out here," Cody thought. It was like they wanted to exaggerate their isolation. "'Fraid not. What I want to talk about is hacking."

"Interesting subject," Sonny said. "Almost as interesting as religion."

"Can you tell me what you know about it?"

"Hope you can stay for supper."

"Gimme the short version," Cody said.

"Any particular area of hacking?"

"Why don't we start with banks."

"Of course banks are a sought-after target. Not by your ordinary hacker, though. Hackers are normally out to show the straight people how intelligent and creative they can be. It gives youngsters a feeling of technical superiority. Heady stuff for a teenager—a real power trip. Banks are normally targeted by adults, for money. Hackers reject the financial aspect unless it somehow helps them acquire additional computer equipment."

"Would a hacker get into a bank's computer and foul up someone's account?" Cody said.

Sonny smiled a knowing smile. "Is that what's been going on? We've heard of folks in town having trouble with their electric and their water bills. We thought it might be a hacker. Haven't heard about the bank angle.

"To answer your question: It's been known to happen, for revenge."

"You know of any hackers in town?"

"No, I don't. But computers are getting cheaper and the cheaper they get, the more kids have them. I don't have contact with many kids unless they're church members."

"What about Biba?"

"Biba's not a hacker. She has the ability but not the inclination. She'd rather be helpful than hurtful."

"Have you taught her how to log on to systems remotely?" Cody asked.

"Sure. I taught her about the Internet. With Telnet you can log on to a system in Russia if it's open to the Net."

Brandy came in to get a cup of coffee. "This a private conversation or can anybody eavesdrop?"

"We're discussing hackers," Sonny said.

"Oh? Somebody getting revenge?" Brandy said.

"We haven't discussed that angle," Cody said.

"When I think of hackers, I think revenge," Brandy said. "Like a kid having their parents' car repossessed because they won't let him drive it or teenagers going after a teacher they hate. We're sort of out of it here. The computer community, I mean. In Cocoa Beach there were the people from the space center, Cape Canaveral Air Force Station, and the Space Command and Joint Stars at Patrick Air Force Base. A real high-tech community. Not much of that around here."

"Can either of you break into systems, create havoc if you wanted to?" Cody said.

"How much are you paying?" Sonny joked. "Both of us have the expertise. It would depend on the level of paranoia of the system manager of the targeted system. A good manager can't sleep at night, lies awake thinking about how someone can break into his system. The Electric Co-op and local banks more than likely have little or no security to speak of because they don't have pro system managers."

"What about telephone hacking?" Cody said.

"Much more costly to businesses than computer hacking. A teenager will break into a computer and leave a message: 'Yah-yah-yah, I broke into your system, you dumb rodent, and you can't find me.' Telephone hackers make free long-distance and overseas calls by the thousands," Sonny said. "Steal cellular phones and phone codes. It's a regular industry; guy in Miami say will set up shop in a phone booth to let immigrants from South America call home for one-fourth the price."

Cody couldn't figure out how the telephone hacking info related to this situation. He wasn't about to give out any knowledge about electronic eavesdropping on telephone conversations. "Saw an old friend of yours yesterday—Jack Jenkins," he said instead.

"You must've attended a Nazi Party rally."

"Jack said you were a hacker when you worked for TVA."

"By his definition, I guess I was. By logging into different systems, I found a lot of problems with the plant the bosses were trying to cover up. I'm outa all that now, thank the Lord. Out of TVA. Out of NASA. Just sitting here on the side of this mountain breathing God's clean, fresh air."

"I guess you'd like to keep it that way?" Cody said.

"Well, of course I would. Why do you ask?" Sonny said, his brow furrowed.

"What if you heard Highwater Town was going to get a new tourist industry? Motels and crowds and traffic."

"You trying to make me sick to my stomach?" Sonny said.

"How would you react to that kind of news?"

"Justine was talking about something like that before she was killed. About the government doing something here. She didn't offer details. You talking about the same thing?"

"Could be," Cody said.

"If you go outside and look under this so-called mobile home, even though it's sixteen feet wide, you'll see a set of wheels. I would mobile this sucker somewhere over to North Carolina. That's the reason I moved up here in the first place, to remove myself from the path of progress."

"Goes double for me," Brandy said. "On clear nights we walk out on the mountain and look at the stars. That means more to me than a motel or people spending money."

"Yeah," Sonny said. "I walk out here, up that trail through the hemlocks and spruce. There's a clearing up there on the ridge. From it, I can see seven mountain ranges. Not seven mountains. Seven mountain ranges. Like Brandy says, the stars at night go on forever. I look up at them and I know without a doubt there is a God. In a city with the drugs and the crime and the politicians, I begin to doubt."

"Are the murders tied in with this business Justine was talking about?" Brandy said.

"Why do you ask that?" Cody said.

"Answering a question with a question," Brandy said. "You drive all the way out here to talk about hackers, and you've talked to Sonny's old boss. It doesn't take a rocket scientist to put it together. You suspect we have something to do with the murders."

"I'm questioning lots of folks. Also there's the tie-in of Samantha, Justine, and Carl all attending your church."

Cody leaned over and placed his empty cup on the glass-topped coffee table. "Either one of you know anything at all about the murders? Anything you can tell me, no matter how insignificant it may seem to you? Something you saw. Something you heard."

The couple looked at each other thoughtfully. Both gave a negative shake of their head. "Nothing I can think of," Brandy said.

"Me neither," Sonny said.

"Something I wonder about, Sonny," Cody said. "With all your expertise, having all the prestige that being a computer consultant with NASA would bring, why didn't you move into another high-paying job?"

Both Brandy and Sonny shut down. Sonny's face showed an intense anger. The two of them looked at each other like they were the only ones in the world who understood what was really going on. Sonny finally broke the silence. "I applied at one place after another. Prestige from working at NASA? You should see some of the pampered, snot-nosed managers who yawned their way through my interviews, then placed my resume on the bottom of the stack. Couldn't wait for it to end so they could rush out and hire a fellow snot-nose, fresh, know-nothing out of college that'd work for burger-flipping wages. Then they could sit around with their spoiled-rotten, pimply-faced friends and whine about how tough life is.

"It's age and money. My son in California is thirty-four years old and won't work for peanuts, so he's being discriminated against because of his age. Thirty-four! Can you imagine that? Years of experience, graduated from a good engineering college with honors, and sometimes he's had to cut grass for a living. I don't know what's going on out there in our country, perhaps a conspiracy of the mediocre and incompetent, but if it's called progress, I don't want any."

Later, Brandy walked with Cody a short way down the path toward his truck. Staring at the thick, black hair that hung slightly over his collar, she could sense the intense energy and danger he radiated as he picked his way down the steep hill. Not long ago, this attractive but chilling man had killed someone. She knew the feeling well.

Cody stopped and turned to look at her. His dark eyes seemed to lance her soul. She knew she must be careful; there was a limit to what he'd accept of her barbed comments and sharp attitude.

"Guess I hit on a sore point," he said.

"Yeah. Sonny won't buy a house or a new car or expensive clothes or a new TV. He built clone computers for us rather than buy a name brand from companies that're firing all their experienced workers. Says he won't contribute to an economy that's declared him expendable. He's extremely bitter. He gets on the Internet late at night and joins these discussion groups with other men and women his age and younger that feel the same way. They swap lists of companies that discriminate against anyone over twenty and simply don't trade with them, try to undermine them in any way they can."

Cody stroked his chin with the palm of his hand, then dropped his arm to his side. "Hope I didn't upset your day too much by coming around."

She gave him an understanding smile. "We understand and

accept what you have to do. And I hope you catch the killer. Whoever it is."

Cody turned to leave her, then looked up the hill at the stack of hay bales behind the double-wide. Someone had drawn a bull's-eye target on an old sheet and fastened it to the hay.

"Target practice?" Cody said.

"Huh? Oh, that." Brandy's smile evolved to a nervous frown. She averted her eyes, then realizing what she had done, looked straight at Cody.

"You or Sonny been shooting a pistol?"

"No. Uh—I have a bow. I used to shoot in competition. It relaxes me. I don't hunt or anything. I won't kill a deer or a bear or even a rabbit." Brandy wished Cody would go ahead and leave so she didn't have to explain. She should have listened to Sonny.

"What kind of bow?"

"It's an old Bear recurve. At one time I was expert. Now I shoot for fun," she said.

"Mind if I see it?"

"See it? Oh, the bow. Sure. Why not." Brandy led the way around to the back of the trailer. "There's a storage thing under here. Handy for when I want to come out and shoot." She indicated a small door at the mobile home's base, bent over, turned a latch that allowed a metal flap to drop down. Then she reached inside the recess and pulled out a bow and a quiver of arrows.

"You buy those arrows at the Stick and String?" Cody said as he pulled one of the arrows from the quiver and examined its aluminum shaft. Brandy knew it was similar to the one used to kill Sharpless. The color and brand were different, though, and a field point was screwed into the tip instead of a razor-sharp hunting head.

"Yeah. And the string and the wrist guard and the shooting glove. Only place around."

"What kind of draw that bow got on it?"

She showed him the numbers on the side of the bow. "Fifty pounds. Anything heavier and it'd wear my arm and shoulder out shooting at targets. You know, shooting fifty or a hundred times."

"Hefty pull for a slight young lady like you," he said. There was a smile on his face, but she could detect the edge in his voice.

Brandy's mouth and eyes were tight, grim. "If you know how to prepare with the proper exercises, there's no problem in using a heavy bow. My dad showed me how. I've got a fifty-five-pound dumbbell I use to perform archer's movements. Builds strength. Just bend over and place my hand on something solid and pull the dumbbell up like I'm drawing a bow. The movement puts muscle in my arms and shoulders and latissimus. And I do bench presses for my triceps."

"Reckon you can draw a seventy-five-pound bow?" Cody asked. He looked her dead in the eyes. She imagined him walking around back there in her head, peeking into old steamer trunks she thought she had locked, where her deepest thoughts hid.

Brandy smiled quickly, fleetingly, but the frown returned just as fast. She formed her mouth into a pout. "Why don't you just say 'like the bow used to kill Sanford Sharpless.' The talk was all over town. The type of arrow used, the draw weight on the bow. Yes, I can draw one. Not in target shooting, though. A bow like that isn't practical. I could draw one maybe five or six times, then my arm would give out. You've got to understand, though—I would never shoot at anybody," she said.

But she knew Cody would think that it only took one time to kill.

After watching Cody drive away, Brandy went back inside the trailer. Sonny had apparently been watching out the window.

"Thought I told you to leave the shooting alone for a while," Sonny said.

"I was bored and needed some exercise. Who would've thought he'd come up here and notice."

"What's done is done," Sonny said. "Let's just hope Cody and the sheriff don't do any more digging."

"Notice you didn't tell him we knew about the National Park Service planning a southern entrance to the Smokies."

"Well, you know how the law is; no sense inviting trouble," he said.

"Yeah. Trouble's the last thing we need right now," Brandy said, walking over and looking at the computer screen. "With luck, the Willinghams will get taken down."

"Come here close a minute," Sonny said. "I saw something interesting move under that paint-speckled T-shirt you got on. I think Cody was watching it too. Let me get under there and check it out real careful."

On his drive back to town Cody wondered if Sonny and Brandy hated progress enough that they would stand in the way of it by killing its promoters. The man seemed angry enough at society to harbor a grudge, want to withdraw from the mainstream. Anger like that was more prevalent now. People outraged at government and private institutions, planning strategies for fighting back. Could be a revolution brewing, but he didn't wanta get his hopes up. It would be good for the P.I. and security businesses.

The real question was: Did Sonny, acting alone or with the assistance of the well-endowed Brandy, try to take out all persons involved in the real estate deal? But why Samantha—and Luther? Did they just happen to uncover something or be in the right place at the wrong time?

Engrossed in his work, Randy Gateline hooked a finger in the black arm band he wore in memory of Samantha and slipped it higher on his arm. Then he began to count Mevacor tablets out of a large, plastic bottle into a dish. He upcapped a small prescription bottle and hit the key on the computer to print out the label. The dot-matrix print head wiped back and forth in two swift motions then spit out the paper. He tore it off, exposed the adhesive backing, and placed it on the bottle with a quick, practiced wrap, pouring in the thirty pills and dropping the prescription into a small sack. He turned to place the large bottle back on the shelf.

"Yaaah!" he screamed at the silent man standing two feet behind him. "The fuck did you get in here?"

"Sign on the front door said Open," Cody said. "Figured you were ready for business."

"Aaaah. We are. Open, I mean. I just didn't see you come in. How'd you get behind the counter?" Randy said. His hands were shaking.

Cody kept his expression bland, his voice calm, matter-of-fact. "Just reached over and undid that half door. You was busy. Didn't wanta disturb you. It's a downright pleasure seeing a man perform work he's so obviously good at."

"Scared the hell outa me. Killer loose in town and I turn around and see you standing there staring at me. Man—thought he had me for sure. Excuse me for yelling."

"I need to ask you some questions about the murders. When you sold those arrows to Barry, were there any others like them in the store?" Cody said.

"No. Luther was around asking that right after Justine and Sanford were killed. Al—Al Thomas—runs the Stick and String for me. He special-ordered those arrows for Barry. Real expensive, so we don't keep them in our inventory," Randy said. He had his composure back now. He was breathing normally and smiling. "I showed Luther the order forms."

"Ever order any of those same arrows for Brandy Brusseau?"

"Brandy? From up at the church? Not that I remember. You may wanta check with Al. He's open early now. We don't usually open the place until two, but Tennessee bow season just opened up for deer. It's our busy time."

"I'll do that. You ever sell any archery supplies to Brandy?" Cody said.

"Not me. I don't think Al has either. I would've seen it when I did the books, unless she paid cash."

"You got a computer to do all your books?"

"Couldn't do 'em without it. I have an accounting package that saves me time. Otherwise I'd never sleep," Randy said.

"Did Samantha call you on the night she was killed?"

The unexpected switch of subject made Randy hesitate before he answered. "Samantha? No, she didn't. Why do you ask that? Samantha and I broke up some time back." Randy gave Cody a curious look, like he should have known this already.

"Why?" Cody said.

"Why what? Why did we break up? I tried to explain it to her—it was her job. She just didn't understand. I worried all the time; I couldn't be married to someone who was constantly in danger. If she had only resigned. Now look what's happened to her, it's just terrible. Imagine how it would have hit me if she was my wife. It would have devastated me; I wouldn't be able to function. I'm very sensitive like that." It was obvious to Cody that Randy didn't like the direction the conversation was taking. Cody decided to push a bit more.

"How'd you feel when you first heard she'd been killed?" He was giving the young pharmacist his intense gaze now, staring into Randy's eyes like he was dipping into his soul.

"Sad. So sad. Even more than I was saddened to hear of the deaths of the others. In a small town like this, murder is not an impersonal thing like in a large city."

"You seeing anybody now? Engaged again or anything?" Cody said, his eyes still boring into Randy.

"Been too busy lately with taking on the ice cream place and everything," Randy said.

Heard that too-busy routine before, Cody thought. He wanted to grab Randy and shake him, tell him what an idiot he'd been to let Samantha go. Cody took a quick look around the rear of the prescription counter, then focused his attention back on Randy. Judging Randy's love life or how he treated his women wasn't why he was here. He needed to keep a professional, detached attitude. "Carl Taggart? He ever buy any archery equipment from you or come to the gym?"

"Carl? Be surprised if he ever exercised in his life or engaged in any sports—indoors or out."

"Horace Hornsby? You ever have any harsh words with him?"

"We got along great. He lent me the money to open the Cove Road Cafe & Ice Cream Parlor. Am I a suspect in all these killings? Anybody knows me can tell you I wouldn't harm any-body or anything."

"Well, thanks for the info," Cody concluded, purposely not answering to keep Randy off balance. "I'll let you get back to work. Just got all these loose ends I need to check."

"Good luck with the investigation," Randy said. "Sorry you got hurt."

After Cody left, Randy made his way to the front of the store. He looked around. The place was empty of customers this early in the morning. The cashier arranged packs of chewing gum in a display case. "Margaret, did that man who just left here ask for me when he came in? The man with the bandage on his head?"

She looked around the store in confusion. "What man?" she said.

Forty-five

Sheriff Rainwalker arrived at the S.O. earlier than usual that morning. He'd stayed up until midnight doodling at his kitchen table, obsessing on the murders, trying to grab that nebulous clue he felt lurked somewhere in his mind, to come up with something he'd missed. Had Samantha ever said anything that would clear up the mystery? Or Luther? Was there something in the hundreds of pages of documents, something an interviewer had missed, a fingerprint, a crime-scene photo or another piece of forensic evidence that would lead to another question asked that would lead in turn to the killer?

Fortunately there hadn't been any reporters out front when he arrived. He wasn't in the mood for them anyhow. He blew through the lobby without so much as a wave to the dispatcher, went directly to the file cabinet, and dug out the reports on witnesses Luther had interviewed. He was looking especially for witnesses who corroborated the claims of suspects whose alibis Luther had checked out. Like Barry and Sonny and Randy and now Michelle. Okay, I'll even backtrack Bubba in the logs, he thought guiltily. Shows I'm really desperate.

A vision of Luther popped up unbidden in his mind. What had Luther really been up to? Placing the large file under his arm, he poured a cup of coffee one-handed and went in his office to browse and brood.

At his desk he thought of a scenario that, if he let it, would send him off on another tangent altogether. What if the killer was not a local but someone from out of the county? A traveling salesman, say, who came and went with an unscheduled frequency? Or just someone from an adjacent county? If the man had been commuting or perhaps calling on his regular customers in town for years, he would know the town and the surrounding area like a native.

Really, there were hundreds of suspects and no real leads except the real estate scam. That was the only common factor, and even that didn't hold true in the killings of Samantha and Luther.

He spread the file before him and thumbed slowly through the pages. There just had to be something there.

Bobby Joe Jennerton cleaned the pistol one final time, applied a thin coat of oil to its Parkerized finish, then wrapped the weapon in a heavy cotton cloth. He jerked his leather jacket from the back of the kitchen chair and stuffed the .38 revolver into a side pocket. Cody had embarrassed him for the last time. The only way he could get his self-respect back was to put him down in front of the whole town.

He'd suffered the silent stares of his workout partners and casual acquaintances at the health club and those of his fellow workers at the limestone rock quarry. He knew what they said behind his back, what was behind their phony smiles and invites to play pool or drink a beer in their trucks at lunch. Thought he wasn't a man because he'd let somebody smaller whip him. He bet Cody couldn't do it again in a fair fight. He wouldn't fight fair, though—used all them quick moves that tricked you and throwed you off balance.

Then Jolinda had took him outa action with her baseball bat and ever'body seen that. Wouldn't do to go after her. Whole town'd be down on him if he did.

But now he had this little dog that barked here and bit way out yonder. Luther'd gave it to him that day Cody beat him up. See how Cody liked that. What he'd do was cruise on his bike, and when he saw Cody—he'd clean his clock for good.

Ray Blizzard also got an early morning start. He drove the rental across the Walt Whitman Bridge and headed for the New Jersey Turnpike, took it north to East Brunswick, and wound his way into Hazlet. When he arrived in town, he stopped at a service station and discovered he was only three blocks from Regina's girlfriend's apartment.

The house had a narrow street frontage and a nonexistent front yard that placed the front steps right at the sidewalk. The frame structure ran deep on the lot and had a driveway. There was just enough room for him to get off the street and touch the front bumper of his rental against the gate.

The apartment was on the third floor of what had once been a three-story, single-family dwelling. Regina's girlfriend's name was on the mailbox, scrawled on a card taped to the metal. "Doris Wisniewski," the label read, a ball-point-pen-drawn arrow indicating the driveway and a side staircase. The gate was unlocked, so he let himself inside and walked to the foot of the steps.

He'd thought long and hard on the cover he would use. He knew if he tried the wrong one, came on too strong, he could lose her for good. She'd simply disappear until he ran out of time.

Hell. He'd try honesty. That'd be different.

Doris had mousy brown hair, sad brown eyes behind horn-rimmed glasses with lenses thick enough to be bullet-proof. She wore an old house coat and fuzzy house slippers. Her thin body looked as if she'd been recently released from a concentration camp. "Yes?" she said, blinking up at him with an owlish stare.

"Doris Wisniewski?"

"That's right. Whatcha want?" she said. The tone of her voice said she considered him trouble.

"I'm looking for Regina Gateline. Friend of hers told me she lived here."

"Whatcha want with Regina? She's not here right now."

"It's about her brother and a friend of hers, Andy. You know where she is?"

"Went to the Rusty Anchor to get a drink or two. She'll be back later tonight."

Must be a real slow drinker. Ray checked his watch. It was twelve-thirty. "Where is this Rusty Anchor? I may join her."

"You a lush too?"

"I'm working on it. The Rusty Anchor?"

"Hell. What could it hurt? She's broke, so maybe you could pop for a bottle. Go down to the next street and take a right. It's in the middle of the block."

"Thank you very much, Miss Wisniewski. Could I bring you something back?"

"Yeah. A new fucking life."

Room after room lined both sides of the long, narrow hallway. There were two hospital-type beds in each room, an open door leading to a bath, a color TV in some, two flimsy wooden wardrobes, bedside tables holding pictures of long-absent family members, and grimy windows that couldn't be opened. Here and there an elderly person or two in bed or sitting in a wheelchair waited for the Grim Reaper to hit their room number on the lotto wheel. The entire building smelled of urine and disinfectant and worse.

The halls were like the spokes of a wheel. The hub was an octagonal nurses' station where TV monitors provided views of each hallway to help in intercepting escapees. In front of the counter an emaciated female patient, tied in a wheelchair with a thick canvas strap, pulled on the arm of a fat woman in a white uniform. The nurse was eating a handful of cookies and watching a soap on the portable TV on the counter.

"I gotta go to the bathroom," the sickly woman said.

The nurse ignored her.

"Can I help you?" a nurse behind the counter asked Cody.

A bent, elderly man was also restrained in a wheelchair in the middle of the hallway. One wheel of the chair was obviously locked. He turned the unlocked wheel desperately, succeeded only in propelling himself in a tight circle. Both employees disregarded his actions.

"Ruby Bledsoe's room number," Cody said.

"Miss Bledsoe? She's in seven fourteen. That's her in the rec room. By the door, reading the magazine."

"Please. I gotta go to the bathroom," the woman pleaded again.

Cookie Face ignored her, watched the two-dimensional drama on the screen.

"Mistreating the elderly is a crime in this state," Cody said to the nurse. He wore his executioner's face for effect.

"Don't mistreat no elderly here," Cookie Face informed him.

"State inspects here alla time. We always gets the high marks."

Cody showed her his badge and I.D. "I'm witnessing a crime, and it's my duty to make an arrest—or are you just hard of hearing?"

The nurse grunted and pushed herself from the cookies and TV. "Come on, Miz Wilson. We gone take you to the bathroom."

Badge comes in handy for something, Cody thought.

Cody stopped outside the glass door of the rec room before he entered. He didn't see much rec. Just a color TV out of vertical sync, with a rolling picture that these poor people just sat and stared at like they were watching an award-winning movie.

Ruby Bledsoe's legs and arms appeared normal, Cody thought when he saw her up close. It was her chest and shoulders and back that gave her the look of having survived a horrendous automobile crash. Her left shoulder jutted forward at a painful, impossible angle. Her spine at a point between her shoulder blades was curved so badly she was forced to hold her chin up in order to see at eye level.

But Ruby's face was still fairly young-looking. Her chin was firm, her blue eyes alive and alert. She'd applied lipstick this morning, just like always. Stiffly painted her nails and combed her hair. Combing her hair was the worst; lifting her arm sent shooting pains into her deformed back and shoulder. So many of the patients wouldn't comb their hair. Depression, a giving up. The first signal they'd rather die than contend with the boredom and loneliness, the surly and uncaring staff, the son who never came to visit, the daughter who didn't care.

Ruby was lucky in that respect, and even though her body was crippled, she never gave up. When ol' Death walked in here, she'd look him right in the eye and say, "Here I am, Death. Come on in. Been waiting on you, but you're gonna have a long, hard fight."

Cody opened the door and stepped inside the room.

Ruby looked up, placed her magazine open and facedown on her thigh.

"Mrs. Bledsoe?" Cody asked.

Her smile was welcoming. "You're Cody. I wondered when you'd be along."

"Yes ma'am. You know me?"

"I've seen pictures of you. Saw you on the TV. And Kurt talks about you all the time. He's so proud of you. I hurt for you, Cody, seeing that bandage on your forehead. Just happy you weren't hurt any worse.

"You want to roll me over to those chairs over there? We'll sit and talk," she said. "Then I won't be breaking my neck trying to look up at you."

He unlatched the brakes and pushed the chair across the room. One of the big side wheels had a flat spot that made the chair jolt slightly every few feet and the front wheels wobbled.

"Looks like I need a front-end alignment," she joked.

The chair Cody sat on gave him no confidence; one of the legs wanted to slide out to the side, and someone had tried to reinforce it with strips of white surgical tape. "You're Bubba's mama. What I don't know is how long you've known my daddy."

She raised her chin as far as she could and laughed heartily. "I don't know who came the closest in predicting when you'd show up, me or your daddy. He said you'd be here soon. I said sooner. I guess I came the closest."

"Why's that?"

"Kurt says you're a natural-born sleuth. Says you watch and listen and keep your mouth shut and maybe don't even think about all the information your eyes and ears are gathering. Then one day, what is it they say? Eureka. And you've either got the answer or you know where to go to get it."

"If I'm so smart, why don't I know what you're talking about?" Cody said.

"You're over halfway there or you wouldn't be here with me," Ruby said. Her eyes crinkled with humor. A glimmer of recognition crossed Cody's face. He sat back, thought for a moment, looked at Ruby.

"Say I do know what's going on. Why did I have to find it out on my own? Why didn't someone just tell me? Save my brain all the calculating time?"

"I guess we're cowards, Kurt and me. Innocent cowards. But cowards just the same. How it is—you sit around and talk and say you're going to do something that takes a lot of moral courage and you never get around to it," she said.

Cody looked steadily at her, nodded. "I reckon that sorta makes Bubba and me . . . half brothers."

"Do you find that distressing?" she said. She was serious now.

Cody shook his head. "Bubba seems like good folks. I'll just have to get used to the idea; nothing I can do to change it. Does he know?"

"He's known since he was twelve. He likes you, but he's been afraid you won't accept the situation with grace."

"Like I say, it'll take some getting used to. I've been running all the pieces through my mind—what I assumed were the facts, that is—but I didn't connect them all until now. What I don't know is what happened to you. Were you in an accident?"

Ruby's smile disappeared, replaced with a look of deep sadness that showed mostly around her eyes. She looked at her feet, then returned her gaze to him. "You mean being forty-five years old and having the honor of being the youngest patient in the nursing home? I worked as a checker in a grocery store and hurt my back lifting bags. Workman's comp doctor the store sent me to gave me some pain pills—Percodan. To make a long story short, I got hooked, tried everything in the world to get off 'em. Went to another doctor, and he prescribed something else, and pretty soon I was hooked on two pain pills."

Cody relaxed in his chair. He had places to go but knew he needed to hear this out. He'd heard many drug addicts were initially hooked by their doctors. Hadn't even the White House physician enabled Betty Ford's habit by prescribing sedatives? And later the same had happened to President Bush with the Halcion doses to help him sleep. Back then it had given him a warm fuzzy feeling at night to imagine the Russian premier stoned on Stoli and the American president zonked on a Valium derivative and Scotch, them sitting there pissed at each other with their fingers on the launch buttons.

"It went on for a couple of years," Ruby continued. "Right at the last, I was buying my pills on the street. Meet the drug man. God! What a time.

"I was determined to shake it; went cold turkey. When Bubba

388

and his sister found me and took me to the hospital, I was already into convulsions. I broke all these bones myself, my own muscles did it. Contracting to where they tore away from the bone.

"Here I am. The result of my own actions. My children took care of me for a while. But they got their own lives. Your daddy says to come live with him and he'd get me a nurse. I'm not gonna clutter up his life either for the time I have left."

"Wasn't Daddy around to help?" Cody said.

"Your daddy and I met right after your mama divorced him. He was at a real low point."

"Yeah," Cody said. "I remember. So was I." He recalled that when he was told of his parents' imminent separation, he'd hidden from the reality of it by taking his dog and going up on the mountain. He'd stayed gone for almost a week.

Ruby flinched with a quick intake of breath. Her pain was written in the way she narrowed her eyes to a squint. "I could tell you that story, but it's your daddy's place. Anyhow, I was only around for a short while, then I moved over to Pikeville. Neither one of us knowed then I was pregnant with Bubba." She paused and winced again. "Don't know whether I'm up to telling the whole story just now."

Cody stood. "I'll come back to see you again, if you don't mind. We can talk some more."

He reached down and took her hand, brought it to his lips, and kissed the back of it. "God bless you now, Miz Ruby. And you take care of yourself."

She had to turn her head to one side to see his face. "All this happening to me is the reason Bubba went into law enforcement. He's really down on drugs and drug dealers. He's obsessed. Hates 'em with a passion."

"So do I, ma'am," he said.

Tears streamed down her cheeks as she watched him walk away.

The front porch of the nursing home was long and deep. Rocking chairs were lined up in a straight row for the patients. The sheriff was in the first one by the door.

"Wondered how long it would take you to get here," he said as Cody exited the building.

"I'm in a visiting mood," Cody said.

"And an arresting mood, if the administrator's telling it right."

"I'm deputized and sworn to uphold the law," Cody said.

"You hire on full-time, we'll need a new wing on the jail. And the hospital."

"Don't forget the cemetery," Cody said. "Main reason I left the LAPD was they were too picky who they arrested. Didn't ever take down a businessman for screwing over his customers. But a customer screwing over a powerful businessman, it was life and three weeks. That's what I like about being private. I don't discriminate except for personal reasons. Right before I came over this time I was reading in the Nashville paper about this grand gentleman, a lawyer hired by the Coleman Law Firm. Gonna be a 'counselor,' they called it, to the nursing-home industry. What he's gonna be really, and the paper knows it, is the guy who funnels the bribes to the legislators to pass laws favorable to the nursing homes."

"Who am I to change the way things work all over this big, wide country?" the sheriff said. He paused. "So what do you think about this? I mean about Ruby?"

"It was all a long time ago," Cody said.

What Cody always said when anyone brought up a painful incident from the past, the sheriff remembered. "Son, your mama drove me away; I'd a never left on my own. She wouldn't let me come around the house without threatening to shoot me. All because I wouldn't kill Coleman for stealing the land. She signed it away. He tricked her, I agree. But you can't kill a man for that; least not and get away with it. God, I thought she knew better than to deal with any lawyer."

Seeing his father plead made Cody uncomfortable. He'd always carried a picture in his mind of the old man's unyielding strength. "I got to digest this a bite at a time.

"Went by to see the Reverend Todd and his main squeeze," he said to change the subject. "Dropped in on Randy. He seems a bit jumpy." He relayed what he'd learned from the visits.

"You are in a visiting mood," the sheriff said. "I was gonna go by the drugstore and talk to Randy later on. Just covering some ground already covered. Checking on times and witnesses. I'll stop in and visit with Ruby a few minutes first."

The Rusty Anchor was some improvement over Wayne's, but not much. At least they had their own parking lot. Ray wondered how they'd gotten the huge oxidized namesake to the roof and how securely it had been fastened. If it fell, it'd take out some customers, he thought, gazing up at its precarious perch.

Inside they had tried for a nautical look, but had accomplished a shipwreck. Portals and ropes and nets and a harpoon too close to the bar where a drunken patron could grab it to settle a score. One thing you could say for it, though, place sure smelled like fish.

Regina sat at the bar looking fifteen years older than the picture he carried. He watched her in the mirror. If she'd bothered to comb her jet-black hair this morning, she'd missed her head. The rims of her sunken eyes were red. The pouch-like bags beneath them dark, almost black. Her skin had a yellow cast; Ray looked at her eyes and saw they were yellowing too. He walked toward the other end of the bar to get a drink and maybe move in on her slowly.

She stared at the mirror and watched him watch her, swiveled on the barstool to follow his progress. "You know me?" she said.

"Beg pardon?"

"I saw you looking at me. You know me?" She wasn't unfriendly, just curious.

"Let's see if I can remember," Ray said. "Uh . . . is it Regina?" He pointed a finger at her as he said her name, like he'd shot her with an invisible pistol. For the bang, he levitated both eyebrows.

She took her drink off the bar and tossed what little liquid was left down her throat with a backward jerk of her head. "How'd you know my name? Have we talked before? I don't remember things as good as I used to."

Ray stood in place, rolled his eyes to the fishnets, rubbed his chin in concentration. "Let's see. Did I talk to you in here the other night—or was it four or five years ago?"

"See. You don't remember either. Did you buy me a drink?"

"Young lady, if I didn't, I will certainly make up for that over-sight. Bartender, bring the lady a drink, and I'll have a draft beer."

"You wanta sit here and keep me company?" she said.

"Why, ma'am, that's mighty kind of you. I'd be honored."

"You talk funny," she said through her laugh, a short, high tinkle.

"What my mama used to tell me," Ray said as he climbed on the stool. "Said I dressed funny too."

Forty-six

"Damn," Cody said as he walked into the Riverside Restaurant, "place's almost as crowded as Fuzzy's." He couldn't spot a vacant table and was prepared to leave when he glimpsed Bubba waving at him from a corner table.

He was far from desiring a heart-to-heart about being a newly discovered relative, but couldn't think of how he could ignore the friendly greeting. He walked over to the table, eyeing the noisy crowd on the way. At a table on the opposite side of the room, he spotted Monk sitting across from a gray-haired, skinny man with a dense circle of smoke around his head.

Elton was at his station in the back. The place was loaded with out-of-towners, mostly reporters and other newshounds, cameramen and technicians and whatever hangers-on were needed to operate all the high-tech satellite gear parked around the motel.

"Busy, ain't it?" Bubba said when Cody arrived at the table. A harried waitress was there with a cup and a plastic pot of coffee as soon as he took a chair.

"What you been up to this morning?" Bubba said. "How's your head feeling?"

Cody guessed he hadn't heard about the visit to the nursing home. "There's not much pain. I've been trying to gather up some loose ends. Went by and talked to Randy, drove up Mountain Chapel Road and saw Sonny and Brandy. Who's Monk talking to?"

"Don't know his name, but I heard from the sheriff he's Monk's AA sponsor, come over to gather the lost sheep back into the fold, or whatever it is those folks do. Monk's getting kinda bad, having trouble getting up in the morning, which I can understand. I drank like that, I couldn't get up, period." Bubba had his walkie on the table in front of him, volume on low as he listened to the buzz of calls.

"Monk's thinking the Willinghams're losing faith in him," Cody said. "Hate to think I had to depend on him to defend me, shape he's been in lately. Drunk or not, though, he's one'a the few lawyers I ever liked. Man's actually educated."

Elton appeared out of the crowd and stopped by the table. "You hear about ol' Elwood having nightmares about you?" he said to Cody.

"Seems like somebody said something," Cody said.

Elton shook his head sadly. "Put Elwood's brain in a hummin' bird, he'd fly backward and suck a mule's ass for a mornin' glory. I told the waitress to give you boys real good service. We really appreciate the law around here." He hurried off to stop and talk at another table.

"Nothing like family loyalty," Bubba said. "One'a the goals of my law enforcement career is to put Elton away for about two years."

"Yeah. He'd make the pope hire a hit man. You ever hear of anyone in town being referred to as 'the drug man'?" Cody asked.

Bubba smacked his cup onto the table and leaned forward. "I ever did, I'd track his ass down and put him out of business. Why you ask?"

"Something I overheard. You know, Randy—with the access he has to prescription drugs, he'd be a natural as a supplier around town." After talking to Ruby Bledsoe, Cody had also speculated drugs would be a heavy motivator for Bubba and could drive him to murder. Were the victims involved in dealing? Surely not Samantha.

"I haven't been here that long," Bubba said. "Going on seven months now. I did have a discussion with Luther once, asked him about Randy. He said he was clean. I don't know whether I believe anything Luther told me now or not. I asked Samantha also. She said Randy was straight. Said he'd never consider breaking the law."

Kennie Calhoun had noticed Cody's arrival at the Riverside. He was sitting with some of his coon-hunting cronies swapping lies about the fantastic tracking capabilities of their hunting dogs. "'Scuse me, fellers. Gotta make a quick phone call," he said.

He weaved his way through the crowd and went outside to use the pay phone mounted on the motel's wall.

"Yeah?" Bobby Joe answered on the first ring.

"Thought you said you's looking for Cody," Kennie said.

"Am."

"Well he ain't at your house where you're hiding out. He's eating lunch at the Riverside," Lonnie said.

"Well, goddammit! I'm on my way."

Sheriff Rainwalker recognized Randy's truck as it headed toward him around the curve. On his way back from the nursing home, he was headed for Gateline's Pharmacy to ask more questions about Randy's whereabouts on the nights of the killings. He flipped on his blues, rolled down his window, and flagged the druggist down.

Shook up after Cody's eerie arrival and departure, Randy had worked at getting caught up on his prescription filling and book work, then noticed the time. He had to run over and meet Ramona at the motel. And why hadn't Biba called?

He was on his way out of town when the sheriff flagged him down. Now what the hell did he want? He hoped it wouldn't take long. Ramona could get impatient when kept waiting. He pulled to the side of the road.

The sheriff made a U-turn, then pulled behind Randy's truck. Both men got out of their vehicles and met halfway between them. The road was narrow, so the sheriff motioned Randy to step to the edge of the grass. Behind them soared a steep embankment overgrown with kudzu vines and the red leaves of a sumac thicket. The road made a hairpin turn, then climbed steeply to pass over the gradient.

Neither man saw the figure who pulled to the side of the road and peered down at them.

The waitress brought Cody's food: country-fried steak, turnip greens, sweet potatoes, and a hefty slice of skillet-fried corn bread. He dug in.

"Elton's gonna miss all the business once the excitement's over," Bubba said. He'd finished eating and was sipping his coffee.

"'Bout like Fuzzy," Cody said. "Murder's been a windfall for him."

Bubba picked up his walkie and brought the speaker to his ear. He listened for several seconds, turned up the volume slightly, then placed it back on the table. "Sheriff just made a vehicle stop," he said. "Randy Gateline."

Cody continued eating. Nodded his head that he'd heard.

Mounted up and ready to ride, Bobby Joe fired up his motorcycle. He'd slipped on the black leather jacket with the pistol in the pocket, checked to see it was secure. The way he had it planned, he wouldn't need a quick draw. Just stand to one side of the door real close with the pistol held under his coat. He'd lean against the wall real cool-like, say hello to everyone that passed. When Cody walked out the door, he'd pop him in the side of the head. A real easy plan.

He moved his hand to his face and felt the tenderness there. There were bruises under his eyes and around his nose, a constant reminder of his humiliation. His chest and throat ached from time to time, made him carry visions of Cody around, rent-free, in his head. He envisioned himself a vengeful character from the past, a wronged cowboy riding to settle the score.

After today, he thought, the whole county would know what he was made of. He gave the bike some gas, let out on the clutch, and roared out of his driveway to meet his destiny.

"What's going on, Sheriff?" Randy asked.

Sheriff Rainwalker waited for a noisy truck to pass. "I was on my way over to your store to ask you some questions, saw you coming down the road, figured I'd save myself the trip."

"Cody dropped by earlier. Scared the hell outa me. I turned around and there he was like he'd walked outa the wall."

"Has a knack for that. He was a little boy, you'd think you's all by yourself, and there he'd be. Can be unsettling. What I wanted to see you about—"

The first shot missed the sheriff by a foot, ricocheted off the roadway near his foot. "What the hell?" he said. Drawing his revolver, he crouched and spun to look up the hill.

Randy ducked as well. "Up there," he yelled, pointing at the guardrail up the hill. Someone was hunkered behind it aiming a rifle down at them.

The second shot went wild. They heard the crack as it passed over their heads.

The sheriff brought up his pistol and got off two rounds. He was way out of range but the noise would keep the shooter's head down, he thought. He brought his walkie up. "Ten-eighty-three. Shots fired at—"

A terrible burning sensation cut through him as the round hammered him high in the chest. Then he was flat on his back, staring up through bright autumn leaves at the sky. His radio and pistol clattered to the road as he fell; he tried to raise his head but couldn't. He groped for the walkie.

Randy cringed on the road beside him. "Sheriff, you hurt bad?" He saw the blood splatter on the fallen man's chest.

"Radio," the sheriff managed to say before he blacked out.

The radio lay partially under the sheriff's leg. Keeping as low to the ground as possible, Randy reached for it. Two more shots rang out, twanged off the roadway.

"This is Randy Gateline," he said into the walkie. "Sheriff's been shot. Somebody's still shooting at us from high on the S-curve near the highway junction. We need help."

Wanda June was on it. "Mountain County to all units, we have a four thousand P, shooting in progress, officer down— sheriff's been shot, all units respond code six." She gave the location. "Stay on the air, Randy."

"They're still shooting! Get somebody over here fast!" Randy said.

"Wanda June, this is three-eighty. I'm on the way."

"Ten-four, Burton. All units signal ten."

The cruisers called in as they vectored to the location.

When Bubba heard the call on the walkie he was out of his chair in a flash.

Cody knocked his chair over and was hard on the deputy's heels. His ribs ached with each step.

Elton had been monitoring the police band. "Sheriff's just been shot," he yelled. Most of the crowd came to their feet and headed for the door.

Bubba was first out, Cody crowding behind him.

"This is three-eighty," the walkie squawked. "Got the four-thousand suspect in sight, headed east down Cove Road." The undulating wail of a siren was heard first over the radio, then in the distance as it approached the restaurant.

"It's a white sports car running flat out! I'm doing a hundred and it's walking away from me! Can't hold these curves with the cruiser!" Burton's voice was coming in jerks; he was breathing hard.

"Keep it calm now, Burton," Wanda June said. It was a part of her job to calm officers during a high-speed chase.

"I'm calm! I'm calm! Holy shit! He's running through town at over a hundred."

"Ten-four. There's a ten-forty-seven rolling. You still with us, Randy?"

"I'm here, Wanda June. Sheriff's unconscious. Blood all over his chest."

Bubba was in his cruiser by now, starting it. His emergency flashers were on.

Cody started to ride with Bubba, changed his mind, and ran to his truck. He grabbed the dome light from the floorboard and slammed it on the roof. The entire parking lot was filling with spectators; he waved them away. "Get the fuck back against the building," he yelled. He turned on his walkie to see how the chase was progressing.

The white Dodge Stealth flashed by running a hundred-plus. The deep roar of its mufflers followed it down the highway.

Oh shit, Cody thought. It's Biba. He had seen a flash of strawberry-blonde hair.

The cruiser screamed by, trailed by two others only seconds apart.

Cody and Bubba got on it at the same time, scratched gravel out of the parking lot.

A motorcycle was pulling in just as Cody hit the edge of the roadway; he almost hit it, swerved, and slid around, his rear wheels biting gravel. Straightening out, he completed the arc, his tires peeling out when they hit the hardtop road.

"Yeeeaaah!" Bobby Joe screamed. His world was the grill and front bumper of Cody's truck. He laid it down in the stones. Momentum zipped him across the lot. Fear kept his hand on the throttle. The bike made a quick circle, then ran away from him and headed for the field where the reporters had parked their trailers. Bobby Joe went solo, kept on trucking toward the restaurant's front entrance.

A great cloud of white powdery dust flew airborne in his wake. The gravel was eating him up. The building loomed closer, but he could do nothing to retard his progress. In his adrenaline-pumped mind it seemed to take forever, though not long enough. He tried spreading his arms and legs to slow himself down. It didn't seem to help.

Three reporters leaped into the air to allow Bobby Joe to pass under them. They hit the ground and swiveled their heads to witness his collision with the building.

He punched into the wall like a battering ram. Bounced back, rolled over twice, and lay still.

Tears flowed down Biba's cheeks. Escape was her only thought as she sped away from the sirens. She'd closed her eyes on the last few shots; she didn't know the results of her shooting.

The tailgate of a gravel truck loomed in front of her; she grabbed fourth gear and jumped around it. A car heading toward her took the ditch as she scraped along its front fender.

The truck's driver heard the sirens over the thunder of his exhaust. He'd seen the Stealth almost wreck as it careened around him. Hauling on the steering wheel and jumping on the brakes, he pulled to the roadside and let the cruisers pass. Four sped around him only seconds apart, followed by Cody in his truck.

What's that idiot in the pickup trying to do? the driver wondered.

Bubba was on his radio. "Mountain County this is Delta. Shooter's headed for Monroe County. Put it out."

Wanda June was on the Tennessee sheriff's net. "Monroe County Dispatch, this is Mountain County Dispatch."

"Go ahead Mountain County," a male dispatcher answered.

"We are in pursuit of a white Dodge Stealth, wanted for a ten-fifty-two shooting of an officer in this county, heading into your county on the North Highway."

"'At's ten-four, Mountain County. We'll set up a ten-seventy-three." The dispatcher called the code for a roadblock.

Wanda June came back on the air notifying the highway patrol.

Traffic was slowing Biba down. She couldn't get around all the cars. She darted out into the oncoming lane only to be forced back by a line of vehicles. There was a blare of noise as drivers laid on their horns. She looked around for an alternative—a business driveway, a gas station for a U-turn, anything. Deep ditches lined both sides of the two-lane road. There was nothing in sight that would help.

An orange sign flashed by on her right. "Bridge work ahead," it said. Traffic funneled to a single lane.

She popped out into the oncoming traffic, saw a sudden opening, and went for it, shot ahead for a few car lengths, then screamed around the right side of a car in her lane. Both right tires went off the shoulder. She tried to bring it back, saw she wasn't going to make it, then stood on the brakes and jerked the wheel to the left.

This brought her out of the ditch. Her right front quarter panel caught a concrete roadside marker and spun her even more to the left. The car flipped, slid on its top, then bounced back on all four wheels. It shot ahead out of control and hit the bridge's concrete railing with the passenger-side fender. Then it spun into a work truck, causing the sports car to whip around and slide backward down the single lane. It came to a sudden halt when the rear bumper impacted with a grader.

Astonished workers stood gaping as four cruisers arrived on the scene, sirens blaring, followed by a pickup truck with a flashing blue light. Five Monroe County cruisers roared in from the other direction. Deputies ran to the Stealth with guns drawn. Bubba ran with a fire extinguisher, sprayed the area around the gas tank.

"Get that ambulance in here," he yelled to Burton. The deputy sprinted for his cruiser.

Back at the S-turn, paramedics loaded the still-unconscious sheriff into the back of the ambulance. "What we'll do," one said, "is get to a clear spot. Got the life-flight chopper headed down from Maryville. Can't get in here."

Still in a daze, Randy sat in the back of a cruiser, gave the deputy his account of what happened. He felt lucky to be alive. "Bullets were whizzing all over the place," he said. "This county's getting downright dangerous. I'm afraid to go out anymore."

Forty-seven

The media invaded the hospital in Maryville. Satellite trucks parked in the emergency parking lot, in parking spaces reserved solely for doctors, all over the street in front and to the side. Excited reporters resorted to any and every pretext to gain entrance, one even claiming to be the sheriff's brother. So aggressive was their onslaught that some members of the media had to be forcibly removed by the Maryville P.D.

The conditions of all three emergency patients from Mountain County had been deemed serious enough to be taken to the more modern and better-equipped facility at Maryville. On his way, Cody stopped by the high school to pick up Jolinda. The two of them now waited in the emergency waiting room along with Bubba and several other deputies, watching it all on CNN.

"Sheriff Kurt Rainwalker is reported in guarded condition after being shot with a high-powered rifle," a female reporter was saying. "This comes on the heels of another shooting in Mountain County in which the sheriff's son, Cody, was wounded and his assailant killed.

"The suspect in the sheriff's shooting, Biba Willingham, is also in guarded condition. The teenager was captured after crashing her car following a high-speed chase in which she attempted to elude Mountain County sheriff's deputies. Speeds in excess of one hundred twenty miles per hour were reached during the chase. The sheriff's department spokesman, Deputy Robert Whittlemore, told this reporter that although Miss Willingham was not wearing a shoulder-harness seat belt, both airbags in the Dodge Stealth did deploy and prevented her from being killed outright in the crash.

"Bobby Joe Jennerton, a motorcyclist injured as a result of

accidentally becoming involved in the chase, is in serious condition after he lost control of his vehicle in a restaurant parking lot and crashed into a building. He has sustained head injuries, a broken clavicle, and severe cuts and bruises. Mr. Jennerton was arrested when deputies discovered he was armed and in possession of an undisclosed quantity of cocaine and marijuana.

"Deputy Whittlemore states he believes there is no connection between these incidents today and a rash of murders that have plagued Mountain County, although a motive in the shooting has not been determined. Stay tuned for a special report, 'County of Fear,' which airs tonight at nine."

Cody caught Bubba's eye, jerked his head for the deputy to follow him. Cody led the way to a quiet stairway.

"What's up?" Bubba said.

"Tell me about you and Biba," Cody said. He'd put his executioner's face back on. His ancestors had used it on other tribes who invaded the hunting grounds.

"Me and Biba? What about us?"

"Biba's got a picture of you at home, right by her computer, signed 'Love, Bubba.' And you got a picture of her in your album at home, her head resting lovingly on your manly shoulder. Yet you're not supposed to know her all that well."

Bubba was astonished. "So you're the one broke into my house. You sneaky asshole. You're gonna have to show me how you did it, bypassing the alarm and all. May come in handy someday. Thought things had been moved around some. Then I said, nah, my imagination. So, shit, you know it all and you ain't said squat. Daddy's right. You're closed-mouthed to the point of fucking lockjaw." Bubba's eyes were hard. He half expected Cody to come after him.

"Yeah. I know it all. Except for Biba."

"Robin snapped the picture of Biba and me," Bubba said. "Biba's been getting herself into trouble with drugs, uppers and downers. And her mama and daddy had been on the outs for years. That had her all messed up. We were trying to help her, Robin and I. Biba and Robin have been kinda close on and off for years. And we promised we would keep it confidential. Sonny Todd talked to her some. Biba said he told her some stories about how girls have really got themselves messed up with drugs. He showed her some things with computers, thought it would get her headed in another direction. She musta stole that picture of me. Robin said it was taken from her locker."

"And then she ends up shooting Daddy. What the hell for?"

Bubba shrugged his shoulders in exasperation. "I can't figure it either."

Wanda June was still on duty. Cody called her from a pay phone in the snack bar. "Sheriff's condition is stable," he told her. "Doctors will know more in the morning. What I need, on the quiet, is an NCIC check on Sonny Todd and Brandy Brusseau. I want it followed up on if there's negative info."

"Okay, Cody. I go off shift in an hour. Anything happens with the sheriff, call me at home. Mayor and the county commissioner were in an hour ago. They've appointed you sheriff until your daddy's better."

"Oh, great," he said. "Just what I needed. Wonder how all the deputies are gonna take that news?"

Cody was headed back up the hall when his pager went off. He returned to the pay phone.

The page was from Ray. "Sorry about your daddy. Just saw it on the news. Hope he makes it okay. This is a bad time, I know; wanted to let you know I got Regina Gateline in my hotel room."

Cody was not in the mood to continue the Gateline investigation, thought it a dead-end. "Well, good for you. Guess you're looking forward to a night of fun."

"You bet. She's already puked on me three times."

"Didn't realize you were into that, Ray. Whatever trips your trigger."

"I'm trying to get her sober enough to make sense," Ray said. "I've got Andy—he's an old flame—on the way down to help me. This girl belongs in a hospital."

"You and your old flame enjoy. I think it's a dead issue now. Randy Gateline is another wrong turn I took in the case."

Ray ignored Cody's sarcasm. "She says Randy can do no wrong, walks on water, able to leap tall buildings. Other things she tells me make me sick. Like her father sexually abused her."

"Lot of that shit going around," Cody said. "Stay with it, now that you've gone that far. But be ready to bail out and head back. May have some new suspects that need a close look."

"I'm withholding drinks from her. She says she wants to stop. But she goes into withdrawal and I give her a sip to stop the shakes."

"Well, hang in there. Let me know if something breaks."

"Yeah. Good luck to your dad."

Back in the waiting room, Cody headed for Jolinda.

"I just heard on the news they appointed you sheriff," she said.

He looked over at Bubba, who was leaning against the Coke machine. "Think you can handle that?"

"If you can," Bubba said. "Just glad they didn't throw it at me. Albert Feltus and Johnny Knight and the other deputies won't care. They're where they wanta be."

"This is gonna bring even more reporters into town, and the place's full now," Cody said. "Wonder if a sheriff can declare a state of emergency and run all the sonsabitches back home?"

"Better get off on the right foot with them," Jolinda said. "You don't find the murderer right away, they'll hang you out to dry in the press as incompetent."

"Now aren't you full of good news," Cody said.

An exhausted-looking doctor sought them out in the waiting room. He was tall and thin; his pink scalp shone through a few strands of hair. "Sheriff's going to make it. Recovery will take a while, and he'll never have full use of his right shoulder. He'll be able to move it, just not lift any weight to amount to anything."

"That's great, Doctor. Thanks," Cody said.

"What about Biba?" Bubba said.

"Oh, she'll pull through. You'll have to talk to Doctor Parsons. Miss Willingham has multiple fractures and head injuries, I hear. It'll be a long road to recovery."

It was almost midnight when Cody and Jolinda arrived back at the farm. Bubba had followed them as far as the S.O. He was taking the duty tonight.

Ogden was still awake. They filled him in on the details.

"I'll take the guard duty tonight," he said. I slept some earlier."

Cody went out to the trailer to spend a restless night before finally dropping off to sleep in the early hours of the morning.

* * *

"You was supposed to come over tonight," the whisperer said.

"Traffic's a mess, all the excitement in the county over the shootings and ever'thing," said the male voice on the cellular.

"Well, I still need it, excitement or not. I like the kind of excitement you give me," she whispered.

Scanner was recording the call. He would listen to it over and over later to try to identify the whisperer.

"Not tomorrow night, but the next. I can make it then."

"I don't know if I can wait or not. I just lay here and think about it, and I wanta just go out and look for somebody. Got somebody in mind, as a matter of fact."

"You trying to control me with threats? Sometimes I think you're nuts. You sure your old man can't hear you?"

"Just a minute, I'll check." There was a thunk as she put the phone down.

Scanner thought, Oh shit, not that again. He knew what was coming. She was back in a minute, breathless.

"He's watching the TV. I told you before, all he ever does is eat, sleep, watch TV, and fish for bluegill. He don't ever give it to me good like you do."

"Gotta go," the male caller disconnected.

Scanner forced himself to a partial calm. He swore he'd find the whisperer one day. Then he'd kill her. But Cody was the sheriff now. He'd lay low for a while.

* * *

The alarm jangled Sonny and Brandy awake. They had set it for five. Sonny turned to the young woman and kissed her lovingly on the lips. "You sure you wanta go through with this?" he asked.

"We talked it all through last night. I think we need to get away for a while. This place's no good for us right now."

Sonny sat up and swung his feet over the side of the bed. "We'll come back when it all quiets down. Don't you worry."

"I don't know," Brandy said. "I could hear the wheels turning in Cody's brain when he was here yesterday. He'll follow it through. Heard too much about him to believe anything else."

"Whatever you say. You may see it different later on. Let's load the Jeep and get an early start."

Cody was up early. He'd planned to meet Bubba for breakfast at the Riverside. "Robin's coming over this morning," Jolinda said. "Uncle Ogden's not going in to work. Says us girls need some looking after."

"Good of him to give up his time," Cody said. He'd suggested it to Ogden.

The Riverside crowd bordered on a riot. All the reporters were trying to talk at once. They yelled across the already noisy room to their friends and enemies in the business. When Cody walked in there was a sudden hush, then the noise started back up again.

Wasn't this where he came in?

Bubba was at the same table in the corner as yesterday. "Morning, Sheriff," he said.

"Don't rub it in," Cody said. "Hear anything about Daddy?"

"Called the hospital, said he was resting comfortably. But he's not ready for visitors. Biba's still in serious condition. Can't ask what her motive was yet. Her aunt thinks it's because the sheriff was over searching the house and Biba thinks he's gonna have her daddy and her aunt in jail."

"Whatever," Cody said. "She's in for it now. Willingham money won't keep her from doing time."

"Drugs. We should pass a law where we could kill all drug dealers on sight." Bubba wore a mask of anger. His voice was harder than Cody had ever heard it. "Somebody supplied Biba with drugs. And that somebody may go free. Just ain't right."

"Wouldn't have thought drugs were making an inroad here," Cody said.

"They're everywhere," Bubba said. "Robin says some of the

kids at school are discovering purple haze—the hallucinogen."

"Robin's gonna spend the day with Jolinda," Cody said.

"Yeah. She told me." There was a faraway look on Bubba's face.

"Mountain County, unit one," Wanda June called over the radio.

"That's you, now," Bubba said.

"Oh, yeah," Cody said. He picked up the walkie from the table. "Go ahead."

"Sheriff, you wanta signal six the S.O.?"

"Ten-four." He walked outside to the pay phone and called in.

"Whatcha got, Wanda June?"

"NCIC you wanted last night came back clear on Sonny Todd. Brandy Brusseau did time for killing her husband. And guess how she killed him?"

"Don't tell me—with a bow and arrow?"

"How'd you know that?" Wanda June said. "Sheriff over in Cherokee County, North Carolina, said her old man was always beating her up. Coming home drunk and all. She shot him with a pistol once but the husband wouldn't press charges. Sheriff's office took the gun away and he come home one night drunk, starts in beating on her, so she put an arrow all the way through him.

"She did eleven months, twenty-nine days on involuntary manslaughter; jury wouldn't convict her on anything else. Then she goes down to Florida, Cocoa Beach, where she has some drug problems, the Brevard County S.O. says. That's where she met Sonny Todd."

"You do good work, Wanda June. Remind me to tell my daddy you deserve a raise."

Same routine when Cody entered the Riverside Restaurant for the second time that morning: a three-second hush, then chaos. It was becoming routine. Back at the table he told Bubba about Wanda June's report. "Take a ride with me after I eat?"

"Sure thing."

His breakfast arrived and he talked his way through it. Several reporters stopped by. He told them there was no news.

"Mountain County, unit one." Cody caught it this time.

"Go ahead," he said into the walkie.

"Sheriff, man name of Ray Blizzard says he's been paging you all morning. Needs to talk to you right away." She gave him the number.

He looked down at his belt. "Damn. Left my pager at home," he told Bubba.

He called from the pay phone again.

"Where you been?" Ray wanted to know.

"Forgot my pager. You got anything?"

"Same old stuff," Ray said. "Getting ready to bail outa here. Wanted to let you know—Andy, the boyfriend, is here. Regina keeps going on about the old man and how Randy saved her. He's a saint. It's a dead end. I'll go back and talk to her again, tell them goodbye, then I'm outa here."

"Something else I'm looking at down here," Cody added. "Make plane reservations. Let me know what time you'll be getting into Knoxville."

"Anything?" Bubba asked after Cody returned to the table.

"Another dead end. My best suspect. Case is full of 'em. Brick walls, Daddy calls them. This Sonny Todd digging don't work out, I may wantta take a look at Johnny Knight. Time night Justine and Sharpless were killed, he was off duty. It's a long reach, but I wanta cover it. Even thinking maybe Barry did it. Gary Gallegher says there's time unaccounted for. I wanta follow that lead."

Bubba placed his coffee cup in the saucer. "Thinking over the other night when Barry come running outa the bank with blood all over him, what he looked like was scared and confused. Whatever or whoever our killer is, I don't think 'scared and confused' would describe him."

"You've got a valid point there. The videos you helped take at the funerals—anything likely on them?"

"We went over them until the wee hours," Bubba said, shaking his head. "Nothing. Took close-ups of ever'body we could think of."

"Maybe Sonny Todd and Brandy are in it together," Cody said. "Like she did the bow-and-arrow thing and he did some of the others. I didn't like some of the answers they gave, and they seemed to be holding something back. Or maybe you're the killer. Wanta confess?" Cody finished his coffee, waved at the waitress to bring the check.

Bubba stared at him. "You gonna start on me because . . ."

"You want to tell me about your divorce, about the drug dealer your wife had an affair with?"

Bubba slammed his cup on the table; his face grew red as he leaned toward Cody. "My divorce has nothing to do with this. I found out my wife was an addict; she'd do anything to get a fix. See why I hate fucking drug dealers? How did you find out? What am I now, a suspect?"

"Tell me about the bottle of assorted pills in your closet, on top of your gun safe. What are they—vitamins?"

"You done a real good job of searching my place. Biba handed 'em over to me. What you didn't find—"

"Mountain County, unit one," Wanda June said over the radio.

"Go ahead," Cody said.

"Blizzard guy is back on the phone. Says he needs to talk to you again."

"Ten-four."

Cody stood up and walked out the door, saw the pay phone was busy, walked back in, and headed toward Elton's perch. "Need to use your phone," he said to Elton. He turned to keep his eyes on Bubba.

"This here's a business phone," Elton said. "Public phone's outside."

"You sniveling little shit. You like me to take two wraps around your scrawny neck with the phone cord?" Cody said.

"Help yourself, Sheriff." Elton handed him the phone and put some distance between them.

Ray must have his flight info, Cody thought. He wouldn't have time to pick him up at the airport. Ray could rent a car and drive down from Knoxville. "What's up?" Cody said when Ray answered the phone.

"I'm going nuts up here. This father of theirs, Regina and Randy. Lowlife of all lowlifes."

"You told me," Cody said, watching Bubba, who had gotten a coffee refill and looked like he was calming down.

"You just wouldn't believe the old man, what he did. Regina says he would make them suck him, stand in front of him when they were young kids. It made me so sick, I started crying and Andy started crying."

"Is sick. But couldn't it wait?" Cody said, noticing Bubba had reached into his pocket and pulled out a small notebook, reading through the pages.

"You're not listening, goddammit!" Ray swore at Cody. "He'd be drunk, the old man, and when they did a good job on him, he'd give them an award, he called it."

"A what?"

"A fucking blue ribbon. Regina sobered up and says she called Randy about forty minutes ago. He hung up—"

Cody dropped the phone, ran to the table, and grabbed the walkie. "Wanda June, I want a stop-and-hold out on Randy Gateline." From the corner of his eye he saw Bubba's jaw drop.

Cody's heart was pumping hard. "Stop-and-hold," he continued. "Consider him armed and dangerous, approach with caution. Suspect is wanted for the murders of Justine Willingham and Sanford Sharpless and all the others. Notify Monroe and Polk Counties plus Cherokee and Graham Counties in North Carolina. Call Tennessee and North Carolina highway patrols, put out a descrip on his truck. I want this county locked down tight. Put it out!"

Cody ran for the door. Bubba was right behind him.

The Riverside went from chaos to bedlam in two seconds. "Randy Gateline! Killer's Randy Gateline!" Dishes clattered to the floor, chairs and tables were upset in the mad rush for the door. Elton was trampled when he tried to stop the reporters from leaving without paying their bills.

The warbling tone went out over the sheriff's net. "Attention all units. Mountain County Sheriff's Office is issuing a stop-and-hold on Randy Gateline. Suspect is to be considered armed and dangerous. Approach with caution. Wanted for the murders of Justine Willingham, Sanford Sharpless, Samantha Goodlocke, Luther Hamby, Horace Hornsby, and Carl Taggart. Authority

Mountain County Sheriff Cody Rainwalker, K.I.A. Eleven-forty-five, zero-seven-forty-five."

Cody jumped in his pickup. Reporters scrambled for their vehicles. "Mountain County, unit one."

"Go ahead," Cody said.

"Nine-one-one hang-up at Ogden Two Bears's place. No answer on call back."

"Put it out, Wanda June. I'm on my way there."

Forty-eight

Robin answered the knock at the front door. "Why, hello, Randy. What're you doing out here?"

He was surprised to see Robin. "Jolinda here?"

"In the kitchen. C'mon in."

"Driving by, had car trouble," Randy said. He stepped inside the door, saw Ogden on the couch. "Hello, Ogden. How're you this morning?" As he finished the sentence he pulled a .22 automatic out of his pocket and shot the seated man in the chest.

Robin grabbed Randy's arm, screaming, "What're you doing?"

He swung at her and missed, pivoted to get a better swing, slammed her in the face with the pistol.

Robin went down with a cut across her cheek.

Jolinda had heard the shot and came running, skillet in hand. Seeing the pistol, she threw herself at Randy. He turned to grab her. She popped him over the eye with the edge of the hot iron skillet.

He staggered back, put a hand to his forehead. It came away covered with blood.

Jolinda moved in on him ready for battle. When she swung again, he jumped back to avoid the skillet, then stepped forward, used the pistol to slug her a glancing punch under the jaw that stunned her. He quickly moved behind Jolinda and pressed the pistol to her temple. "Be still, you wild bitch. Drop the skillet or I'll put a bullet in your brain."

The skillet hit the floor with a loud thud. "You're him, aren't you? Scanner?"

"Right. I'm Scanner. And your fucking boyfriend tricked me. I was watching him, and he had one of his people chasing around behind me. Sneaky bastard talked to my sister in New Jersey."

Jolinda was afraid to struggle; she knew Randy must be nuts. "Ray Blizzard. He had Ray Blizzard on you. I should've guessed. And Cody'll be on you soon. He'll rip your head off and shit down your neck."

Randy didn't doubt it. Cody was more than likely on the way. "You two're just alike. Wild animals, always ready to fight and scratch. I'm getting you out of here. You're my ticket to any-where. Cody'll give up anything for you."

"If you've killed Uncle Ogden, Cody'll stick his huntin' knife up your ass and jerk it to your chin."

Busy with Jolinda, Randy forgot about Robin. Half con-scious, she had managed to crawl to the hallway phone, pick it up, and dial 911.

"Mountain County Sheriff's office," Wanda June answered.

Randy caught the movement in the corner of his eye. He dragged Jolinda over to the hall with him and clubbed Robin down with the pistol, hanging up the phone.

"After Cody gets through with you, Bubba will kill you," Jolinda said. "You don't have a prayer of getting outa this county."

Randy's forehead was swelling; his vision was blurring. "Help me get Robin on her feet and out to the truck or I put a bullet in the back of her head."

Jolinda with one arm, Randy with the other, they walked Robin between them. When Randy got near his truck, he heard Wanda June put out a call over the air. "All right, Jolinda, reach into my truck and bring out the portable scanner. A wrong move and Robin dies."

She retrieved the portable and started to hand it to him. "Hold on to it," he said. "We're taking your truck."

He put both girls in the cab. "Don't try to run. You won't make it," he said before walking around to the driver's side.

Inside, sweat soaked Ogden's body. His breath came in quick, jerky gasps. Somehow he'd managed to slide off the couch and crawl to the front door, leaving a trail of blood on the living room carpet. He dragged the sawed-off along, thumping it along each time he reached out with his right hand to pull himself a few inches forward. He had reached the porch when Randy stepped around the rear of the truck. He aimed low to keep from hitting the girls. Thirty feet, Ogden thought. Little far, but it's all I got. He fired one barrel, the weapon jumping from his weakened hand and tumbling down the steps.

"Aaaah!" Randy screamed. A single slug tore into his left thigh. "Oh shit, oh shit," he moaned as he hobbled to the driver's door. "This goddamn family is nuts."

The truck was a four-speed floor-shift. It was going to hurt like hell working the clutch. Randy started the truck and headed for the drive, turned right, away from town on Stecoah Road. He had to make it over the mountains. It was his only hope.

Two minutes away from the farm Randy heard over the radio that the first deputy had arrived at the farm. "Goddamn Ogden," he said to Jolinda.

"Just a taste of what's waiting for you," she said.

They listened to the calls coming over the radio.

"Mountain County, this is two-ninety-seven, get a forty-seven to the Two Bears's farm. Ogden's been shot. Bad."

"Ten-four."

"This is Buford again. Ogden says Gateline turned northeast on Stecoah Road driving Jolinda's truck. Has two hostages at gunpoint—Jolinda Risingwaters and Robin Kingsly."

"Ten-four, two-ninety-seven. All units, we have a ten-sixty-seven. Suspect has two females at gunpoint."

Cody rolled by the farm at a hundred per. He'd never driven the truck that hard before, didn't realize the pickup would run that fast. Bubba and three other cruisers trailed only car-lengths behind.

"Mountain County, two-ninety-seven. Ogden says he caught the suspect in the leg with a shotgun slug. Suspect is wounded."

Good ol' Ogden, Cody thought. He sent a silent message for him to hang on. The road started to climb. He knew it led to Bull's Head Gap and a passage through the mountains. He also knew it would be blocked by the North Carolina law.

The Jeep Cherokee was loaded with clothes and suitcases, some pots and pans. Sonny thought they'd stay a week or so until Brandy calmed down, then he could head back to his trailer and the peace and quiet he longed for. He hadn't wanted to ride through town and take a chance on Brandy being stopped and questioned by the sheriff's office so he'd put the vehicle in four-wheel drive and taken a shortcut on a fire trail. It would let him out on Stecoah Road near the North Carolina line. From there he would find somewhere to stop and let Brandy relax.

The fire road intersected with Stecoah Road at the point of a tight curve. Sonny pulled onto the blacktop directly in the path of Jolinda's truck.

Randy didn't have time to get on the brakes. He swerved, almost went over, then straightened it out. Sonny's Jeep caught him hard in the driver's door, knocking the truck off the road. Randy, heading for a huge hemlock, whipped the steering wheel again. This took him tearing through a tangle of scrub pines and into a break in the trees. There was no road, but Randy kept it moving, bumping, and rocking along. The truck climbed a sharp rise and the trees closed in. He'd run out of a place to go.

Jolinda began a low chant.

"The fuck's that for?" Scanner growled. He was pretty sure he would be killed on this mountain; his mind retreated into the Scanner persona.

"Your death song. This is the spot where you will die," she said. "Cody will come for you now."

"Shut up, you crazy bitch. You're scaring the shit outa me with that Indian stuff."

They could see the road through the trees, saw Sonny Todd get out of his Jeep and look at the damaged hood. Steam began to form a cloud around the vehicle. Sonny jumped back as Cody's pickup, then four cruisers, almost rammed the Jeep.

The sirens were switched off.

All was silent for Scanner now except for the wind in the pines above him.

Fear gripped him as he leaned forward in the driver's seat and watched the men below get out of their vehicles, form a tight circle, and confer. He could barely make out Bubba pulling a long sniper's rifle from the trunk of a cruiser. The other deputies grabbed their riot shotguns from dashboards. Three more cruisers arrived from Mountain County. A North Carolina highway patrol car wailed in from the opposite direction at high speed, blowing a huge cloud of dust in its wake.

Frantic, Scanner looked around for escape. His eye was almost swollen shut. His leg was throbbing and bleeding. Everything had been going according to plan—until Michelle Willingham hired Cody. Was Jolinda right? Would he die on this spot? Not if he didn't lose his head. He must remain calm. If calm was what he was. Scared shitless was a better description. But if he didn't panic, he could make it through. He had to stay near the hostages.

"Welcome to the big leagues," Jolinda said.

"I hear any more lip outa you and I'm gonna kill both of you," Scanner said.

"No, you're not," Jolinda said. "'Cause if you do, you're a dead man. And you know it. The only hope you have is to keep us alive."

More cars arrived below: reporters, satellite trucks, and an ambulance. "Your chariot has arrived," Jolinda said, pointing at the ambulance. "Coming for to carry you home."

"Goddammit, you don't shut up, I will kill you. I still got Robin." Scanner gestured toward the unconscious girl in the front seat.

A news helicopter arrived, hovered a hundred feet above Scanner and his hostages. The down-blast from the chopper's rotors created a turbulence of leaves, twigs, and pine needles.

"Tell 'em to get the chopper away from the hill," Cody yelled. "Could spook that crazy bastard."

Deputies tried to wave it off. The pilot ignored them.

Cody turned to Bubba. "Put a volley across their bow, Mister Whittlemore."

"Aye-aye, sir," Bubba said. He brought up the thirty-aught-six and put one close enough for the pilot to hear the crack. The chopper swung away.

"I'm going up there," Cody said. "It's what he wants." He handed the H&K to Bubba and began the long walk up the incline.

* * *

"Cody's reading my mind," Scanner said. "He's coming to me."

"Coming to kill you, Randy."

"I'm Scanner. Won't do anything as long as I have you."

It was a long walk up the hill. Cody turned to watch Bubba get into position with the sniper's rifle. Even with the powerful scope it was a five-hundred-yard uphill shot. Not easy. But Cody had decided that negotiations to release the girls would have to be done delicately—and unarmed. He turned again and continued climbing, using the scrub for cover.

Below, the media was dispersing, aiming and focusing the expensive, light-gathering lenses on their still and video cameras. Cody knew they really didn't care who died up here this morning. Just so it made the early and late editions. If not, then it wasn't reality anyway.

Cody crept from the pines lining the road and stopped when he was twenty feet from the driver's-side door. "Wanta come on out, Randy?"

"I am Scanner!" called the killer.

"Scanner, then," said Cody. "Save ever'body a bunch a trouble. Get you to a hospital. They can help you."

Scanner stuck his head out the window and yelled his answer, "By locking me away in a place for the criminally insane? Walk around on Thorazine all day, every day. Sound like fun to you?"

"More fun than sure death on a lonely mountainside. You've caused enough pain. Samantha, the woman who loved you, is dead. And Biba may be crippled for life."

"Fuck them. They were just like my mother. Pretended to love me. Then cursed me behind my back. My mother—once I was through here, I was going back to kill her. Come on closer," Scanner taunted. He wanted to shoot Cody in the head. A just punishment for upsetting all his careful plans.

Cody considered his options, took two steps closer.

"Closer."

Deliberately, Cody turned his back to the truck, took two backward steps toward it.

"Turn around," Scanner demanded, his voice rising.

"Get out of the truck. Then I'll turn," Cody said.

"I'll get out—but I'll keep you between me and snipers." Cody heard Scanner open the door.

"Bubba won't shoot. He's afraid he'll hit one of the girls," Cody said.

"I'm out," Scanner said. "Come on closer."

Cody backed up two more steps.

"Hand me your pistol," Scanner said. He moved a little to his left to keep Cody directly between him and the deputies.

"Sorry," Cody said without turning. "Left it down below."

"Turn around!" Scanner yelled it this time. Cody ignored him. "You know, don't you, you bastard? You know about face to face! You're sneaky."

Cody backed up two more steps. "Face to face is your signature, Scanner. Part of it, like the blue ribbons. I'll turn if you tell me why you're doing this. Why you started it in the first place."

"I thought you knew. You're not as smart as I thought."

"Why?" Cody waited, tense and alert.

"They were gonna make another fortune, the Willinghams were. Already rich. When Ramona and Justine told me about the real estate deal, I made my plans. I was already fucking Biba and Ramona by then, and Justine sometimes, when I wanted information. I decided I'd frame Barry for murder, then later frame or kill Michelle. Then I could choose either Biba or Ramona to marry. I'd have all the money. I would be in charge.

"Only when I killed Sanford and Justine, it changed, became less about the money and more about me. More about power."

"Good plan," Cody said. "With a little luck it would've worked. But you couldn't help using the blue ribbons, doing to others what was done to you. Don't you see—you caught yourself."

Scanner snarled. "I wouldn't have if you'd kept your nose out of it. If damn greedy Luther hadn't got wind of something and put the pressure on, told me he'd tell Barry and Victor and I'd be run outa town if I didn't get him drugs to sell and cut him in on the deal."

Scanner struggled for control. "Now turn around like you promised," he said, deadly quiet.

Cody backed up one more step.

"Turn around!" Scanner yelled.

Slowly, an inch at a time, Cody turned to face him. Scanner brought the gun up to Cody's head.

Cody saw it was a .22 auto. Very lethal if Scanner shot him in the head.

He took another step closer, kept his arms at his side. "Let the girls go, Randy. You have me. You'll never leave here alive either way."

"If I die, it will be after you," Scanner said. "Why'd you check on me to begin with? Why send someone to talk to my sister?"

"The dogs."

"Dogs? What're you talking about?"

Cody forced himself to take it slow and easy—one false step and he would die. "When I was at Barry's and you pulled up in your truck, his dogs didn't bark at you. Who else could come around and steal his bow, tiger claws, and knife? The dogs' silence made me curious enough to take a closer look."

Dogs. Brought down by fucking hounds? "I know a secret," Scanner said, "about you and Samantha. Should I tell Jolinda before I kill her?"

"Yes. If you let me tell my three secrets first," Cody said.

"What three secrets? How can you know any secrets?"

"I know three. And if you kill me before I tell them, you'll never know."

"What are they?" Scanner's eye was aching. His leg was shaking; it was about to give out. He'd have to pull the trigger soon.

Cody forced a big smile. "First one: The entire real estate deal is a scam. Bodine is a swindler. Served time for real estate fraud. There's not going to be a new south entrance to the Great Smoky Mountains National Park."

"What? You're lying!"

Cody kept his hands at his side, remained perfectly still. "It's true. You did it all for nothing. If you'd got away with the murders, you would've still had nothing. Monroe County Sheriff's Office is on the way to arrest Stan Bodine."

"Goddammit! I was tricked. Oh, shit. Since you got here, I haven't had anything but bad luck."

"You killed for nothing, Scanner. For nothing."

Scanner pushed the pistol into Cody's forehead. "Number two."

"Your real name is Peggy Sue," Cody whispered.

"What? How—"

Moving instantly, Cody swept the pistol away and down with his left hand. He flinched at the explosion of the weapon discharging, then jerked at the searing pain where the round had caught him in the hip. He felt a moment of lightheadedness as his vision swam in a sea of red. His leg began to collapse, and he almost went down. Gathering his strength, Cody swung his right fist but misjudged his target; his punch glanced off Scanner's cheek.

The pistol fired again. Cody felt a burning pain in his calf. Scanner followed up the shot with a blow to Cody's forehead with the butt of the weapon.

With a desperate lunge, Cody thrust the weapon away and delivered a powerful blow to Scanner's larynx.

Scanner grabbed his throat and fell to the ground, thrashing about. Cody collapsed on top of him.

"Can't breathe," Scanner rasped, clutching his throat.

Cody rose to his knees, tried to crawl away, and nearly fell on the supine man again. He heard Bubba and the others already on their way up the hill.

Jolinda jumped out of the truck and ran to him, tears running down her face.

"Stay back," Cody told her, weaving to his feet. "Get back in the truck and take care of Robin. Get medics up here!" he yelled down the hill.

"What's the thir . . ." Scanner hissed from behind Cody.

"What?" Cody asked, turning.

"The third secret?" Scanner whispered laboriously.

"The third secret," Cody said, looking down at the purple splotch forming on Scanner's swelling neck, "is I can kill you while you blink your fucking eyes."

The killer lay still for a few seconds, arched his back, sucked in air. He rolled his head toward Cody. "Gotta stop her," Scanner said.

Cody could barely hear him. He moved closer, went down on his knees. Blood from the cut on his forehead dripped onto the downed man.

"Whispers all night. Old man fishes. She's gotta be stopped. Her fault. 'Give it to me good' she says alla time. Whispers about me behind my back, whispers at night," Scanner croaked. Down below, two North Carolina highway patrol cars screamed in.

Cody had his head down to hear, but couldn't make out what Scanner was saying. "Did you say 'night whispers'?" He's insane, Cody thought.

Scanner was shaking his head. "I'm crazy," he rasped hoarsely, reading the look on Cody's face. "They'll try and try but they won't ever convict me. National attention. Some big-time lawyer will come in . . . work for nothing to get his name in the paper and on TV. Few years in a hospital."

"You're probably right," Cody said. "But we'll try to save you anyway."

The chopper was circling closer. The paramedics were a hundred yards away. Cody turned and waved them on.

"He can't breathe," he screamed over the noise of the chopper.

The paramedics went to their knees, placed a plastic bottle and mask over Scanner's face, and began pumping it, trying to breathe for him. Jolinda again ran to Cody. He put his arm around her shoulder and hugged her to him. "You're okay," he whispered. "Okay." Then he fell.

Later the medics tried to revive Cody. He came to for a few seconds. "What's going on?"

"Guy's dead," one of the paramedics said. "We couldn't save him. You did a real number on his throat."

There was commotion on the hill all around Cody. He heard the thumping of the chopper, sirens off in the distance, men yelling, then everything went black.

Forty-nine

On a cold, clear, October morning, Sonny Todd delivered the eulogy at the graveside service for Deputy Sheriff Samantha Goodlocke. Law enforcement from surrounding counties and from across the state were there in dress uniforms to pay their respects. Rifles fired over the flag-draped coffin, and the flag was folded and presented to Samantha's tearful and still-devastated parents. All three major networks and CNN covered the service.

Sheriff Kurt Rainwalker and his son Cody sat in wheelchairs in front-row seats. The sheriff still looked weak and drawn. Cody had a gimpy leg the doctors said he should stay off of for at least another week. As the crowds began to disperse, the sheriff looked over at his son. The tired smile on his face was forced. "Now aren't we a couple of bad asses?" he said.

For his part, Cody was still in a rage, but everyone to blame was dead. Really only two: Randy and Luther. There was no one else to vent his anger on, nothing to strike out at. Stan Bodine had somehow avoided the Monroe County Sheriff's Office and had vanished off the face of the earth. Cody wondered if the Nevada crowd had sent him on a long voyage. Rick Staros had scooted back to the secure, burglar-alarmed confines of his home in Vegas.

Out of the corner of his eye, Cody spotted the Willinghams as they stood to one side of the crowd, heads bowed. They couldn't be blamed either. There actions had been just greed as usual. Michelle had been the only one in the family with the guts to approach him after he was shot. She had visited him at the hospital twice. The second time she brought a nice check.

Brandy stood a short distance away. She caught Cody's eye several times, looked at him with dark, expressionless eyes, then smiled slightly and turned her gaze to the ground in front of her. Cody let his eyes linger on her as he thought of the past few days. There were still mysteries out there.

Ogden was still in the hospital. The doctors said he would make a slow but full recovery. Biba would have an even slower recovery. Maybe knowing she would stand trial for attempted murder inhibited her healing. The fact she'd felt jilted in love and was shooting at Randy, not the sheriff, wouldn't allow her to walk on the charge.

Randy had tricked her, had had her believing her father had killed her mother. He had kept her supplied with the drugs that fed her addiction and addled her thinking. Biba might get some sympathy from the jury on that.

Cody looked out over the mound of flowers surrounding the grave, out over the ancient and new tombstones of Owl Hollow Cemetery, out over the Highwater Valley to the craggy slopes of Wolf's Head Mountain, and remembered how Samantha in her loneliness had come looking for him there. The high peaks and ridges were covered with a blanket of fresh snow. He closed his eyes and pictured his cabin with its wintery coat. Samantha's face swam into view. There were tears in her eyes.

Cody blinked the vision away and watched the coffin being lowered into the earth. This was real. This was now. He could only store away yesterdays for an ever-fading memory to recall.

Two ravens flew in from the forest and called hoarsely. They circled the crowd at the gravesite and winged away.

For Cody, the last week had been a dreamy haze of doctors and nurses, needles and stitches, watching the news, and assuring Jolinda, who stayed at his bedside constantly, that he would live and be able to walk. Reporters had tried to gain entrance to his hospital room. They had been kept away at his insistence by hospital security and by the Blount County Sheriff's Office. He'd sent word he would grant a short interview the day after Samantha's funeral, but wondered now if that hadn't been a mistake. He really didn't feel up to it.

Looking over his shoulder, he could see Ray Blizzard and Noel Saylor standing with their heads bowed, hands folded in front of them. The press had been ordered to leave Ray in peace or leave, period. It was an unsteady truce. After all, he had been the detective who called in the clue that cracked the case. He had been trapped at the Newark airport by the media and almost missed his plane. Reporters were waiting when he landed in Knoxville, but the Knox County Sheriff's Office had whisked him out of their reach.

Cody knew the case would die a quick death in the public's eye. Next week something else would be on their minds.

Noel had been at the Jack of Eagles Club in Nashville that afternoon when the hundredth or so replay of Cody facing down Scanner had been aired on TV. He'd sat at the bar and beamed at the brunette in her cute playing-card outfit. "That's my friend Cody Rainwalker. His office is down the street in a building I own. I'm going to work for him as a P.I.," he'd told the waitress.

"Better find some bullet-proof underwear," she'd said as she stared at the set with her pretty blue eyes. "Sucker's been shot three times this week."

"You see how that guy tried to save the killer's life?" a customer said. "Even after the man shot him."

Later, Noel had been called in by the Mountain County Sheriff's Office to sort out Scanner's computer files. The killer had left behind a detailed scenario of all his crimes, although the files were encrypted and it had taken Noel several days to break the password code.

After doing so, he'd been immediately immersed in a maniac's nightmare. Noel had relived Scanner's stalking and killing of Justine and Sanford. He'd read how the killer had hidden remote tape recorders in the forest to confuse Sanford and make him think Barry was hunting him.

Noel had also uncovered Scanner's account of his abduction and murder of Carl Taggart. Carl had cried after his hands were tied and he finally realized the game he wanted to play was not the game his sometime lover had planned. He had run and cried and screamed. Scanner had laughed. "You can run faster than that, Carlene," he had called back to the cross-dresser from his pickup's open window as he bounced down the rough fireroad with the man in tow. He'd even wondered at the time if he should have put one of those redneck, cardboard signs in the rear window of his pickup: man in tow.

At the end of the run, when the victim could no longer stay on his feet and had been dragged behind the pickup, Scanner had stood in front of Carl as the victim coughed and wheezed, tried to get his breath. Then he'd plunged the sharpened file into the gasping man's chest and watched him fall to the ground. Scanner had felt elated, powerful, as Carl had died screaming at his feet. He'd felt so good he dragged the body another half mile.

Scanner had known Barry was planning to get new tires and had planned the killing to coincide with the purchase. He hadn't realized the body would be found so quickly. Luther had already planted the pictures when he'd searched Barry's truck earlier.

That was the biggest surprise for Noel—and everyone: that Luther had been a knowledgeable accomplice. Had in fact been promised an income and the sheriff's job as a reward for his complicity. Of course Luther's real reward had been having the top of his head blown off when Scanner thought Luther might break under the sheriff's questioning, confess, and implicate him.

Noel had cried when he read how Samantha had begged for her life. Samantha had asked Randy how he could think about killing her when she'd loved him so much. For an answer he'd forced her to call Luther at the HillTop. God, it had been hideous. Scanner had had Michelle's shoe with him, taken on a visit to her house. He'd worn Biba's wig in case someone spotted him leaving the house.

Scanner had also told poor, stupid, burned-out Tom Yount that Donna Sue was interested in him, that she would welcome his advances while her husband was out of town. Confusion in the minds of the investigators covering the case was his goal when Scanner had inadvertently sent the man to his death at the jaws of the ferocious rottweiler. Noel had yet to uncover a hint of remorse in the computerized notes.

Whichever woman—Biba or Ramona—Scanner would have chosen to marry should his plans have succeeded, would have lasted as his wife only long enough to ensure that their entire estate went to him. And to Regina, of course; Scanner would always take care of his sister, like a devoted big brother should.

By the time Noel finished reading the files, he was having second thoughts about the P.I. business. Cody had told him this was a once-in-a-lifetime thing, but once in this lifetime was enough for him.

Harder to decipher were Scanner's notes from the outlaw and anarchist computer bulletin boards. Eventually he found the places where the demented killer had educated himself on how to plant his electronic listening devices, as well as the sophisticated wire in Samantha's house. Scanner had downloaded all sorts of info and software on how to hack into the computers of the utility company and the telephone company. Confusion had been his motive. His long-term, grand plan, for whatever reason, had been to eventually eavesdrop on any phone call he chose.

Strangest of all had been Scanner's digital ravings about someone he had tagged "The Whisperer." There was a long list of women Scanner had suspected of being this "pure incarnation of the devil," as he called her in some of his rambling tomes, "the phone caller from hell" in others. There was another list of the numerous and simultaneous tortures he would visit upon her helpless body if he ever discovered her true identity.

"Yeah," Cody had said from his hospital bed where he lay in a fog of painkillers as Noel relayed the info. "He was sputtering something like that just before he died. Said she had to be stopped. Couldn't make heads or tails out of it. Said something about night whispers. Fucking loony tunes is what he was."

"Night whispers?" Noel echoed. "You think voices at night told him to kill? Poor devil."

Cody stayed at the grave to watch them shovel the dirt back into the hole. For the first few moments he cringed inwardly at the hollow clatter of the dirt striking the top of Samantha's coffin. A sound of finality he knew he needed to close this chapter of his life. When he felt his punishment was enough, he nodded his head at Jolinda, who stood behind him. She turned the wheelchair and rolled him across the grass.

"Howdy, Cody," a voice said from beyond Cody's vision.

Jolinda stopped and allowed Gary Gallegher to catch up. The man had shaved, but hadn't trimmed his long hair. He looked like a British rock star in his blue suit.

"Hello, Gary," Cody said.

"Central time," Gary said.

"Huh?"

"Central time. You know—the missing hour. What it is, I always set my watch back an hour when we go over to Savage Gulf. It's in the Central Time Zone. What happened, I forgot to set it forward when I came back to town. Reason I said we got back an hour before we did. It just came to me yesterday."

"Well, goddammit, Gary. Glad you finally came forward! We couldn't have solved all the murders without you." Cody finally had someone to vent his anger on.

"Well, shit, man," Gary said. He shrugged and held his hands out at his sides. "Turns out it didn't make any difference either way."

Cody's anger deflated just as quickly as it had risen. "Yeah. I guess you're right."

Jolinda rolled the wheelchair to her pickup. She helped Cody in the passenger side, then drove him to Maryville, where they visited Ogden Two Bears at the hospital.

One week later, Noel waited outside in his Mercedes while Cody made his way on crutches into the sheriff's office to say goodbye to his dad. Noel would drive Cody to Maryville to visit a greatly improved Ogden. Then they would go on to Nashville.

Cody felt somewhat closer to his father after all they'd been through during the past weeks, although he did not fully exculpate him for the pain of his youth. They'd had long talks, made plans to call one another, and Cody said he would be back for Thanksgiving and Christmas. Sheriff Rainwalker walked Cody back to the dispatcher's lobby. Wanda June was on duty and looking good.

"You and your husband oughta come over to Nashville one of these days, Wanda June," Cody said, "ride the General Jackson Riverboat, take in some shows, maybe go to the Opry."

"Just might take you up on that," Wanda June answered brightly. "Most likely I'll come by myself. My old man—all he ever does is eat, sleep, watch TV, and fish for bluegill."

The End

Acknowledgments

My heartfelt thanks to my loving and lovely wife, Judy, whose faith and support urged me on. Also thanks and appreciation to my three children, Debbie, Diana and Phillip, who believed in me and whose attitude was, "Go do it, Dad."

I was aided by Norma Jane Bumgarner (okiemom), whose lectures on passive voice and point of view were a great help, and I was encouraged by *St. Pete Times* investigative reporter Jean Heller, author of *Maximum Impact* and *Handyman*.

Thanks to Jerry, G. M. Ford of Seattle, author of the Leo Waterman Mystery Series, for introducing me to my agent, Alice.

A jaunty salute to Lani Kraus, Gruppenfuhrer of the wickedest and wildest writers' group on the Internet and to Tom Clancy, whose on-line advice was, "Just write the damn book."